TORRID

A SORDID NOVEL

NIKKI SLOANE

Text copyright © 2017 by Nikki Sloane

Cover photography © Tomasz Zienkiewicz

All rights reserved. Except as permitted under the U.S. Copyright Act of 1976, no part of this publication may be reproduced, distributed, or transmitted in any form or by any means, or stored in a database or retrieval system, without the prior written permission of the publisher.

The characters and events portrayed in this book are fictitious. Any similarity to real persons, living or dead, is coincidental and not intended by the author.

Aleksandar Edition

ISBN 978-0-9983151-6-4

This book is dedicated to all those who supported Sordid.

prologue

THREE YEARS AGO

My father's office made me uneasy. Today it was worse, because Ilia walked in as I was cleaning the desk. He was twice my age and married, but it did nothing to stop the way he looked at me. His blue eyes raked over my body and made my skin crawl.

He'd been warned not to touch me again.

The first time it happened, I didn't know what to do. He was my father's employee and had a temper. He'd kissed me with slimy lips, and when I pushed him away, he apologized.

The second time, he didn't. He grabbed me and pressed me against the hallway wall while my father was out, and the tongue shoved in my mouth was invasive. Ilia's hands pawing at me made me buck and squirm away.

I reminded him about his wife, but all he'd done was laugh and say it was my fault. I was too tempting to keep his hands off.

Somehow, no matter how hard I tried to avoid him, he found a way to get me alone, and his unwanted advances escalated. I stopped wearing skirts after he'd put his hand up one while my father and brother were meeting with the Italians one afternoon. Ilia was my father's right hand man, but the Italians were old fashioned and would meet with family only.

He threatened me, saying he'd tell my father I was trying to seduce him. Only a few people knew I wasn't actually a housekeeper, but Sergey Petrov's illegitimate daughter. My father hated me, and I wasn't going to let Ilia give him any more ammunition. I gathered my courage, marched into my father's den, and pleaded for help while my eyelashes were wet with tears.

He didn't believe me.

And it broke me almost as much as the day my mother died. I felt like there was nothing left of me.

It was a blessing in disguise, though. It focused my fear of Ilia, condensing and polishing it down until it was a sharp point of anger I could wield. I fought back against every unwanted stroke or caress, every time he put his mouth on mine, even as he became more aggressive and I knew my time was running out.

Soon, touching me wasn't going to be enough for him.

My half-brother Konstantine must have sensed something was wrong the day he'd come into my room, or maybe he'd seen Ilia go in there. I'd been changing and was down to my bra and underwear when the source of my constant torment slipped into my room and shut my door.

"Get out," I said, grabbing a blanket off my bed and using it to cover up.

Ilia gave me the sly smile he always did when he was going to ignore my protests and do whatever the fuck he wanted. He stalked to me, wrenched the blanket from my grip, and had his hands on me a second later. His disgusting lips flattened over mine, muffling my cry. His rough fingers wormed their way beneath the waistband of my panties.

"Stop," I said in a shaky voice.

My door burst open, and although Ilia moved fast, he was too late. My brother had seen everything, and his face turned to ice. Konstantine was barely twenty, and although he appeared skinny, he had a swimmer's build and was deceptively strong. It took him minimal effort to drag Ilia from the room and down to my father's office.

This time, when my father heard the story from Konstantine, he had no choice but to listen. My brother told my father to handle it, or he would. So Sergey gave Ilia a lecture, capped off with a throwaway threat not to touch me again, and Konstantine felt satisfied. My father's orders were supposed to be law.

It kept Ilia away... for a while.

Then, his desire-filled glances my direction were back. He stood too close whenever we were in a room together, and he lingered. He slid back into his behavior so slowly, I couldn't say anything about it. There was no specific moment when Ilia defied my father's order, but I felt it increasing every day.

Building toward something terrible.

I dreamed he died in a horrible, bloody way, and it wasn't a nightmare. It was a fantasy. I pictured different scenarios of his death in my head, and let them comfort me. Maybe I was naïve, but I believed bad people got what they had coming to them.

It was late morning when Ilia came into the office and I froze, the damp washcloth mid-wipe on the desktop. Alarm spiked and tensed my muscles. My father and Konstantine were out, and my stepmother and half-sister were in the garden in the back yard. It meant no one would hear me. I was alone, and the sly smile on Ilia's face told me he knew this.

"How are you today?" he asked casually, strolling toward me.

I stiffened and backed away, abandoning my task. "I'm fine. I've just finished."

When I tried to go around the far side of the desk and avoid him, he switched directions. "So, you have a few free minutes now?"

It hurt to breathe, and I sucked in shallow sips of air. "No, sorry."

"Come on. Don't be like that." He put his hands on my hips, one then the other, and pulled me up against him. I hated his touch so much, it burned. It scorched against my skin like a hot iron. His face was right in front of mine and his thick breath was stifling, using up all the air I wanted.

With his hands on me, I couldn't run. I had to fight instead, and my voice was full of warning. "Ilia, stop. You're not allowed to touch me."

There were weapons stashed all over the office. I'd cleaned this room every week for the last year, and knew the hiding places. There was a loaded gun Konstantine had showed me how to use hidden behind the books on the bottom shelf of the bookcase. A knife beneath the center couch cushion.

"I can't help myself," Ilia said. "I can't stay away."

He buried his face in the side of my neck. Shivers of disgust rolled down my spine as he sucked and licked. I put my hands on his chest and pushed as hard as I could, but he was so much bigger. I was a fly, barely of notice to a bear.

"No," I said, loud and angry. How many times had I said it to him before? How many more times would I have to say it, and would it ever mean anything to him? "My father gave you an order."

"He won't care. We both know he doesn't give a shit about you. Hell, if I asked, he'd probably give you to me."

Horror flooded along my skin. I knew in my heart what he was saying was true. "Konstantine—"

"You think I'm afraid of your brother? I'm your father's right hand. I can do whatever the fuck I want."

His hand snaked up my shirt, searching for my breast. *No more. This will stop.* I couldn't tolerate his touch another fucking second, and slapped him across the face so hard, my palm stung. He grinned his sick, cruel smile. He seemed to enjoy it when I fought back.

"You fucking bitch," he said, throwing me against the side of the desk. My knee cracked painfully against the solid wood. An angry sneer streaked across his face as he began to undo his belt buckle. "Now you're going to get it."

My knee ached, but I dashed around the desk, narrowly avoiding his grasp. I tore at the books on the bottom bookshelf, flinging them aside. My mind went blank with panic as I grabbed the gun. It was cold and dangerous in my hand. I wheeled around, aiming at his chest, and Ilia pulled to a stop.

He blinked, staring at the barrel. His reaction was pure disbelief. The corner of his mouth lifted hesitantly.

His lips tugged slowly upward into that same sickening smile. Was this how he'd look as he raped me? He'd never stop until he had.

The gun was heavy and rattled in my trembling grip. I could read his thoughts in his eyes. He didn't believe I'd use it on him. I was just a stupid girl, bluffing. Neither my threat or the chamber of the gun were empty.

"Oksana." He said my name in a demeaning tone and took a step toward me—

The kick on the gun was almost as surprising as the puff of red mist and fabric fibers exploding outward from his chest. He groaned a sharp sound, stumbled forward, and landed on his hands and knees. As blood began to drip from the hole I'd put in him, splattering onto the hardwood, I didn't feel horror or regret.

I felt absolutely nothing.

Empty.

The only thought running through my mind was I had just cleaned the floor this morning.

chapter ONE

NOW

Vasilije

Aleksandar bounced his knee as he stared out the rain-soaked window, and the noise got on my fucking nerves. Why was he so twitchy? This was the third meet and greet we'd done. I sat beside him in the back seat of a Lexus SUV and thought about making him stop by pressing the barrel of my Glock to his kneecap.

Not that I'd shoot him.

I mean, this Lexus just came into the dealership yesterday.

"Alek," I barked.

His knee stopped vibrating, his head swung to look at me, and I got a view of his stupid face. His forehead was too big and flat, and his eyes were small.

"What?" he asked. His leg went back at it, jackhammering his heel against the floorboard. Could he not hear how fucking irritating he was? I glared down at the offending leg, and it slowed to a stop. "Sorry. I had a Red Bull right after you called."

Great. He was jittery from too much sugar and caffeine, which meant he'd find some other way to annoy me in thirty seconds.

I couldn't stand unnecessary noise. Fingers drumming on a table made me clench my jaw until it ached. A pen clicking incessantly filled me with rage. And when Alek opened his dumb fucking mouth to say some dumb fucking thing, everything went red.

"How much further?" I raised my voice to John, my driver.

He glanced at the navigation system. "Five minutes."

Rain pelted the car, but otherwise the interior was quiet. The Lexus was a nice ride. Maybe I'd tell the dealership not to put it on the website for a few weeks. I was getting tired of the Porsche I'd loaned out to myself, and I needed to move it soon. Smart people didn't buy sports cars during the winter in Chicago, and smart people usually had money.

It was dark on the street. Either there weren't any streetlights, or they'd been disabled. Either way suited me. I didn't want anyone looking too closely at what was about to go down. I shouldn't even be here. This was beneath me, but my son of a bitch uncle had 'asked' me to oversee the Russian meet and greets, so I had no choice.

When Goran Markovic gave an order, it got followed.

I was going to change that someday, but for now I obeyed. I played my part.

John pulled up to a curb, put the car in park, and glanced out the passenger window. "You want me to leave it running?"

"No," I said, staring at the warehouse. I had a feeling this was going to take a while.

Alek got out on the sidewalk and looked up at the sky as if surprised it was raining on him. "Vasilije, you want me to get an umbrella?"

Even the way he said my name was irritating. He said it *Vah-seal-eh*, putting weird emphasis on the middle syllable, when everyone else said *Vah-sill-eh*. Because it was my fucking name.

I ignored him and got out of the car. It wasn't a downpour, but huge drops fell like they were being hurled at us from the moonless night sky. The warehouse had one yellowy light perched over the door, which barely lit the keypad beside the handle.

While Alek banged his fist on the door, I scanned the surroundings. No lights on the street, and no cameras, either. We were on the south side of the city, but it looked deserted and miles from any kind of life. Almost something out of a post-apocalyptic movie.

I'd bet my left nut most of the warehouse space on this block hadn't been leased in the last decade.

The door swung open and Filip, my uncle's head enforcer, stuck his head out.

"We're getting rained on," Alek whined.

Filip wiped the raindrops from his bald head, shoved his gun in the front of his pants, and pushed the door open further, moving out of the way. "You got here fast. Wasn't expecting you for another ten minutes."

I ducked out of the rain and stepped into a shitshow.

The first body was only a few feet inside. The guy was face-down with half his head splattered on the wall. "This one," Filip flicked a finger at the body, "tried to run." He spoke in Serbian. *"Little Russian pussy."*

Filip's men chuckled and murmured in agreement. There were at least seven of them I could see, and the other two were probably off herding the women. Including himself, Filip always ran a ten-man crew. He'd been working for my uncle for a long time and was sharp as a knife. I respected him, but had to be careful. Every action or phrase was reported back to Goran.

My uncle didn't trust anyone, including his own family.

Of course, there were a lot fewer of us these days. His son was four years into a twenty-year sentence at Wabash Valley Correctional. My father was dead, and my brother fled town. My aunt's husband wasn't blood, and he didn't have the stomach or the head for the business, anyway. I was a twenty-four-year-old college dropout and general fuck-up, and next in line, much to my uncle's displeasure.

If Goran had his way, he'd live forever as the reigning king of the Markovic empire.

Yeah, well, *fuck that.*

The only light on in the cavernous space was by the door, and it took my eyes a moment to adjust to the low visibility. There were two more dead Russians, laying in heaps on the bare concrete floor. Cleanup should be easy. It looked like tonight was the first time this place had seen any action in weeks. Brown beams stretched up as columns, supporting the roof.

"Did we know any of them?" I asked.

"No." Filip watched me carefully as I looked down at the body by my feet. "I don't recognize them."

"Where are the others?"

The talking between the crew stopped abruptly, and Filip's unease was visible. "That's it."

The rain must have soaked through my jacket and shirt, because I felt cold. "Just three? How many girls?"

"Fourteen."

I could hear them deeper in the warehouse, probably sitting on the floor in the darkness, quieting coughs and sniffles. I'd get to them in a minute. Right now, we had a serious issue. "Who the fuck sends three guys to handle all this?"

Filip reseated the gun in the waistband of his pants as if uncomfortable. "This was my concern as well."

I texted my driver to start the car. I wasn't taking any chances. My father had taught me if you got a hint of a setup, it was probably already too late for you. "Fuck this shit. Let's bail."

We were potentially walking away from a lot of money, but at least we were walking away. Filip nodded in total agreement with me and told his guys to roll out.

Alek looked surprised. "What about the girls?"

He wasn't asking about their well-being; he wanted some pussy. I glared at him. *"Glup ko kurac."* It was Serbian for *stupid as a cock.* "Grab one and let's get the fuck out of here."

He didn't need to be told more than once. What Alek lacked in brains, he more than made up for with loyalty and obedience, and I wanted to keep it that way. So I went with him, in case the girl put up a fight. We'd move quicker that way.

The women were huddled together, some clutching suitcases and bags like everything they owned was inside. Which was probably true. They were nearing the end of their trek from Moscow, or Saint Petersburg, or who the fuck knew what Russian city. Most of them had been traveling for days, and they sure as hell smelled like it.

Glassy, fear-filled eyes peered up at me and Alek, and two of the girls skittered backward on their hands and knees, wrapping their arms around each other. Sisters, no doubt. Every time we struck the Russians' fresh shipment of girls, I swore it'd be the last time I'd do it. These girls left their shitty lives behind for the false promise of America. Some even thought they were coming here to become models.

Too bad most of them were too skinny to have tits. Or hadn't ever seen a dentist.

Watching their dreams crumble into dust was a drag.

I also didn't like dealing with the girls because I never knew what level of quality we were going to get. Drugs and cars were products where I could rely on consistency. But I got why Goran was in the business of girls. Besides the money, there was a poetic justice to having the Russians do all the leg work to bring the women to America, and then we swooped in and reaped the profit of selling their whores.

I despised the way the girls looked at me, like I was their savior. They'd watched the Russian men they thought were helping them turn into their captors. When all hope seemed lost, the Serbians showed up and slaughtered the men. The girls thought we'd come to liberate them.

Wrong. They'd just traded one set of evil men for another.

Although, today actually was their lucky day. They'd have to figure out where to go from here, but at least it wasn't straight into the sex trade.

This crop of girls was just like all the others, maybe even uglier.

Pasty, bland faces over cheap clothes and unattractive bodies. Some weren't a total loss. With a shower and some makeup, they might even make money. I didn't look long because we needed to hurry the fuck up. Their hopeful stares were eating at me, so I withdrew my Glock and let the gun hang at my side.

There were gasps, and every gaze dropped to the floor in terror. I'd taken my gun out not just to keep the girls quiet and pliant, but to motivate Alek. "Pick one or I pick for you."

He frowned as if facing an impossible decision. Shit, it wasn't that hard. He wasn't going to marry the girl, he was just looking for a warm body to stick his dick in. Fine, I'd select a girl for him and we could—

I locked gazes with one of them.

All the others cowered in fear, but her? She didn't seem scared, she just looked tired. The gun in my hand was unremarkable to her. The other girls had vacant stares, but the blonde's eyes were full of fire and life. Heat licked across my skin, sizzling like a jolt of electricity.

She wasn't the hottest thing I'd ever seen. In another room, she'd probably look better than average. An eight at most. But among this crowd of ugly-assed bitches? The blonde was a ten. And she wouldn't fucking stop staring at me. It made my skin itch.

She looked too young to buy a drink, but old enough to get into trouble. Her thick hair was the color of wheat and hung halfway down her arm in waves. It was pretty.

Wait, what? Fucking... *pretty*? I tore my gaze away.

It was like Alek knew and latched onto it. "That blonde is fucking hot."

"She's all right. Hurry up."

Alek waded into the group of women. My interest sparked as he bent down and grabbed the blonde's arm. She looked alarmed, but didn't say a word as he hauled her up to her feet. None of the other women came to her defense. They were all in survivor mode, figuring as long as we were interested in the blonde, we'd leave them alone.

The girl was stiff as he tugged her along, and I clenched my teeth at Alek's tight grip on her arm. I didn't like his hand on her, which made no sense. Why did I care how he handled the Russian whore? I tried and failed to avoid her gaze and holstered my gun. The words came out before I had time to think about it. "I've changed my mind. Get a girl for you, I want this one."

He hesitated and asked it more surprised than annoyed. "Really?"

I'd never taken one for myself, but the girl stared at me like I was a puzzle she wanted to figure out. It could be fun watching her try.

Alek didn't act disappointed at losing his top choice. It was almost like he'd expected it.

Whatever. He understood who his boss was. He glanced around the group, then shook his head. "No, let's go. The rest of them are ugly."

Filip and his men had already gone out the back by the time we stepped out the front, and I held my hand up, shielding my eyes from the falling rain. None of this sat right with me. Goran was going to be pissed, and I'd likely be the one he'd take it out on. It'd been my call to bail, but at least Filip would back me up.

I yanked open the backseat door and stared at the girl, wordlessly commanding she get in. Her big, doe-like eyes blinked at the car, then her gaze shifted to me. My expression set. *You'll get in if you know what's good for you.*

She had a bag slung crosswise over her body, and she lifted the strap over her head to take it off as she stepped forward and climbed inside. My gun hadn't fazed her, which meant she didn't have a healthy fear of them, and it might make her more difficult to control.

I ducked into the back seat beside her and pulled the door closed with a solid thump. Her guarded expression and rigid posture showed just how uncomfortable she was. Her bag was in her lap, and she squeezed the strap with both hands so tightly, I could see the fatigued shake of her arms.

"You speak any English?" I demanded of her as Alek got into the passenger seat.

Her voice was soft and feminine. "Yes."

I didn't know how to feel about that. Sometimes it was easier when they didn't understand, so you could talk freely. Alek wasn't raised in a bilingual household like I was, and had trouble holding full conversations in Serbian.

"Home, John," I said. The car eased away from the curb. I yanked my phone from my pocket and thumbed out a text to Goran.

> **Me: Meet and greet fell through. Might want to check with whoever scheduled it.**

His text came through almost instantly.

> **Goran: Filip's on it.**

"I knew it," Alek said, his tone amused.

"What's that?" I peeled off my wet jacket, dumped it on the floor, and cranked up the heat on the rear console. It was forty degrees outside, which was average for November, but the rain had my skin chilled.

He turned around in his seat, staring at her while speaking to me. "That you'd go for her, Vasilije, if I wanted her first."

"Shut the fuck up." I turned my attention to her. "What's your name?"

She stared back at the warehouse and looked worried. "What's going to happen to those women?"

Not only did she speak English, she spoke it with *barely an accent.*

Breath gurgled in her throat as I wrapped my fingers around her neck and shoved her against the door. Her head cracked against the glass, and she winced. I focused in on the startled girl I had in my grip. Her pulse raced beneath my fingertips. Her eyes were wide and fixed on me. I'd slid across the seats and had my knee pressed against her thigh, and I was so close I could feel the heat rolling off her body. I felt her tremble.

In the darkened back seat, it was like we were closed in together. Just us.

Her throat bobbed as she swallowed hard. I abruptly had the image of my cock buried between her lips and halfway down her throat. Would she stare at me the way she did now? I scowled and pushed the thought away. So not the time.

"How come you speak English so well?" I said, hissing in her face.

Her voice was weak and tight, but my grip probably had a lot to do with it. "I watch a lot of American movies."

She gasped for breath as I released her, and I shifted back into my seat on the other side of the car.

"Your name," I spat out. "I already asked you once." If she didn't answer me a second time, I'd take her name away. I'd change it to 'whore' like my brother Luka had done to our stepmother years ago.

The girl hesitated, but then smartened up. "Oksana."

Her gaze drifted down and traced each strap of the under-arm holster I wore, and then lingered on my gun. Was she thinking about making a play for it? That wouldn't end well for her—or the resale value of the Lexus.

"Where'd you come from?" I asked.

"The airport."

Smart-ass bitch. I had my hand wrapped around her throat again, and this time I leaned into her so my lips were right by her ear. "People don't talk to me like that, especially not whores."

Oksana shivered and closed her eyes. Her sweater was thin and wet from the rain, and she was obviously cold. Her nipples stood out beneath the fabric. But I pretended her reaction was from the power I was exerting over her, or my proximity. I was a good-looking guy, and girls lost their shit when I paid attention to them. She gasped for breath against the squeeze of my fingers on her windpipe. I was certainly paying attention to her now, wasn't I?

"Kazan," she choked out. "I am from Kazan."

Her eyes fluttered open as I released the tension from my grip, but I kept my hand in place, making sure she understood who was in charge. She seemed to get it. Her heartbeat hammered away under my touch.

"Okay, Oksana from Kazan who likes American movies," I slid my palm down her throat until it rested threateningly at the base, "tell me how old you are."

Her bottom lip quivered. "Twenty."

The SUV went around a curve to merge onto the highway, and it forced my weight into her. She wasn't as bony as most girls, and I used the opportunity to get closer. I put my left hand up on the window behind her, trapping her in.

I'd thought she was mildly attractive back at the warehouse, but now I was seeing her up close and saw how wrong I'd been. Her skin was pale and smooth. Her dusty pink lips were lush and sexy, even as she parted them and took in a stuttering, nervous breath. Icy blue eyes were surrounded by long, thick lashes.

In another setting, after a shower and better clothes, she might even be a knockout.

Oksana was so far out of Alek's league, it was a good idea I'd taken her away from him. He'd come to expect this caliber of girl, and . . . forget it. It was just dumb luck a girl this attractive was in the batch tonight. It wouldn't happen again.

Her chest rose and fell with her hurried breath, and I slipped my hand further down until my palm was pressed in the center of her chest. She turned to look at me, wide-eyed, and her breath hitched. My fingers were dangerously close to her breasts, and I tugged on a smile.

She wasn't afraid of my gun, but my touch? It looked like it scared the hell out of her.

chapter
TWO

OKSANA'S CRYSTAL-CLEAR EYES studied me with fascinated horror. The girl needed to relax; I was barely touching her. Although, I was curious how she'd react if I actually did. If I slid my hand down another few inches and gripped her, if I pinched her nipple that was poking through her shirt, what would she do?

Would she fight?

Would she submit?

I didn't want an audience when I found out and eased away, giving her space. She shuddered with what I assumed was relief, and I grinned. Anticipation tightened inside me. I'd never broken in one of the girls before. Never had a desire to put my favorite thing—my cock—anywhere near the whores, but Oksana looked clean, and the idea of her on her knees before me was really fucking appealing.

"Open your bag," I said. "Dump it out. I want to see everything you've got inside."

She bit down on her bottom lip and reluctantly moved to do as ordered. She flipped open the canvas bag and turned it upside down, dropping clothes and books on the seat between us. I rifled through the ugly, cheap clothes and unsexy underwear, and shook out the three paperback books she had. There were ticket stubs from her flights, her visa paperwork, and sixty-two US dollars in cash. I pocketed it and her Russian passport, and her expression crumbled.

"What are you going to do with me?" she asked, barely louder than a whisper.

"It's all right," I said in an overly sweet tone. "We're going to be friends."

Highway lights streaked by, throwing a traveling beam of light over her face. She wasn't fooled. She must have a smart brain to go along with her smart mouth.

There was a composition notebook among her things, and when I picked it up, she inhaled sharply.

Her reaction announced this item was the most important to her, and I flipped it open, expecting to find pictures of family and friends. *What the fuck?* I yanked out my phone and turned on the light so I could make out what I was looking at.

Music.

Handwritten, messy sheet music. I paged through the notebook, intrigued. It was a third of the way full of pencil scrawled across the pages of repeating five blue lines. Notes were scribbled in the margins. I didn't read music, but I recognized the two different clefs. Piano music? *This* was her prized possession?

I turned back to the first few pages and studied the pattern of notes climbing up and down the lines. Oksana's expression was like she was standing naked in front of me.

I closed the notebook in my lap. "Where are the pictures of your family?"

"What?"

I narrowed my eyes. "Your parents. You left them behind and didn't even bring a picture?"

Her expression would have been heartbreaking, if I had a heart. Her tone was flat. "My parents are dead."

It was clear she wasn't talking figuratively. Pain lurked in her eyes, and . . . it fucking got to me. Orphan was a word my brother refused to use to describe us, but he was older. Luka was twenty-seven and going on fifty. He'd always been independent. But even at twenty-four, there were plenty of days where I felt parentless and alone. I didn't blame Luka for leaving, but it was surprising how much I missed him. He was the only family left I could trust.

So, Oksana was an orphan, just like me. Although, I highly doubted her situation was the same, unless her parents had been murdered by her own family, too.

"Put your shit away," I said.

She gathered her things and jammed them back into the bag, but kept stealing glances at the notebook I was holding on to. She wanted it, but was too scared to ask, and I enjoyed watching her squirm. Anytime I could be in a position of power, I'd take it, even if it was just over a Russian girl who meant absolutely nothing.

"I'm hanging on to this," I said, holding up the notebook.

I pictured the evil look on my face as I smiled. I was glad to have an extra piece to leverage. If she gave me a hard time tonight, I'd threaten to trash the book. That would motivate her.

She looked resigned and her shoulders sagged. "What will I have to do, Vasilije, to earn it back?"

My name on her tongue was strangely exciting.

She'd most likely picked it up when Alek had used it, but she'd avoided his annoying emphasis and pronounced it properly. Oh, she was smart, all right. With so few words, she understood her role, which was good. If you gave a woman an inch, she'd not only take a mile, she'd slide a knife in your back when she was finished. And probably smile at you while she watched you twist with pain.

There was only one way this was going to work. I'd establish my dominance over Oksana, fuck her until I had my fill, and then send her on to Mira, one of my uncle's associates who ran the whorehouses.

Her icy gaze didn't waver from mine. She watched me like a zebra drinking beside a lion at a watering hole. I stroked my fingers over the cover of her notebook, and she twitched as if I'd run my hand between her legs. Did I look scary to her in the darkened back seat, giving her a grin that was full of teeth?

My phone buzzed with a text message from Filip.

Filip: Meeting tomorrow 9am in your office.

It wasn't a question, but I'd treat it that way.

Me: Okay.

Obviously, we had shit to sort out.

The rest of the drive was silent. The girl stared out the window, looking at nothing because it was dark and rainy outside, and my house wasn't near anything else except for a golf course. I wouldn't say she'd relaxed on the drive, but when the SUV turned up the driveway and my home came into view, she tensed.

Did it look like a palace to her? It was illuminated with nightscape lighting, making the eight-bedroom home and attached six-car garage look grand and sprawling. It wasn't that big when there'd been a Markovic family living there, but now it was just me and felt cavernous.

Luka urged me to sell it. The taxes were outrageous, but fuck him. I could afford it and wasn't ready to let the house go. Was it guilt? I hadn't been in the basement since Luka and his girlfriend left.

John pulled into the garage. I grabbed my coat off the floor and flung my door open, climbing out with Oksana's notebook tucked under my arm. Alek was out of the passenger seat, and the strange expression on his face caught me off guard.

"What?" I asked.

His voice went low. "Vasilije, be careful. She makes me uneasy."

"You're worried about the girl?" Was he serious? He was acting weird, and I didn't like it.

"I should've picked an ugly one," he said.

He was getting on my damn nerves. "Aleksandar. What the fuck are you talking about?"

It was like he was suddenly aware of his surroundings, and his face went blank. "Nothing."

I moved so I was within striking distance, and squared my shoulders to him in a threatening stance. "You've got something to say, so say it."

He took a step back and put his hands up in a nonthreatening manner. He was reluctant to talk, but far more reluctant to fight. "You . . . always want what other people have."

My immediate reaction was to curl my hands into fists. I was a big guy, who liked to use my home gym. Alek was taller than I was, but he was soft. He was allergic to all exertion except for fucking. Shit, he got out of breath just going up the stairs. I could drop him with one punch.

But he wasn't wrong.

I did want what other people had. I wanted the respect our father had handed easily to my brother and not me. The loyalty Luka's girlfriend had given him. And most of all, I wanted my uncle's position at the head of the family business.

I peered at Oksana through the tinted window of the car. Yeah, I wanted her, too.

I wanted *everything*.

Tension released and I uncurled my fists as the backup plan formed. "I'll text Mira you're coming, and tell her I'm good for the money. Whatever you want."

My peace offering should have been more than enough. Alek was getting the better end of this deal, or so I'd heard, since I'd never paid for sex. He could have one or two girls tonight who were pros, rather than the shy Russian girl who might be a terrible lay.

He stared through the window for a long moment, watching her. I lifted my eyebrow into a sharp upside-down V. Did he want me to rescind my offer and end up with no pussy at all?

"Okay," he said finally.

"Good." I forced a smile. I treated Alek well, and he had spread the word to the other underlings who worked for the Markovic family. I'd been weakening my uncle's support system, rotting it from the inside.

Alek's expression turned serious and he spoke quietly. "You really think tonight was a setup?"

I shrugged like it wasn't a big deal, although it was. "We'd hit them enough times before. My uncle will see what shakes out tomorrow." I glanced over at Alek's car parked beside the Porsche in my garage. "Mira might tell you her girls are clean, but make sure you wrap your shit up tonight, or your dick's gonna fall off."

He gave a nervous laugh, and his eyes flicked once again to the girl waiting inside the SUV. "Same to you."

As Alek dug out his keys and moved to his car, I yanked open the back door and looked at her. "Out."

She hesitantly climbed out, and studied Alek as she did it. Her expression was emotionless, but I could see the panic in her eyes she was trying to mask. She wasn't that great of an actress, and watched him go like her last life raft was sailing away.

I told John to drive whichever car he wanted home for the week, and I'd text if I needed him. He took the Lexus.

I gestured to the door leading into the house, and my tone was clipped. "After you."

She pushed the door open, moving like it led toward her doom. I flipped the hallway light on, disabled the security system, and put my hand on her shoulder, halting her from going any further. She jolted under my touch and turned to face me.

"Hang this up." I shoved my damp jacket into her arms, took her bag from her, and dumped it onto the floor in the mud room to our right. She wouldn't be needing clothes, and the ones in her bag were hideous anyway. As she snatched down a hanger and followed my order, her silence bothered me. "Why the fuck are you so quiet? Don't you want to know what's going on?"

She slowed her movements, thinking about her answer carefully. "I have an idea of what you want, and it's probably better if I don't think about it."

"Why's that?"

"Because," she turned to face me, and her icy blue eyes cut me to shreds, "I'm sure nothing I say will stop it from happening."

Her judgement was bullshit. I hadn't even done anything to her yet, other than put my hand on her throat in the car, and her accusing glare made fire burn inside my head. First off, it was just sex. If she was willing, I'd do my best to make sure she enjoyed it. Second, I wasn't interested in trying to fuck a weeping girl while she begged me to stop. My dick threatened to crawl inside my body at the thought.

"Don't flatter yourself," I snarled. "I could text a girl right now and have her here sucking my cock in under twenty minutes."

She didn't flinch at the vulgarity. Oksana lifted her chin. "Then, why don't you?"

Instead of rising to her challenge, I grinned and filled my voice with mock excitement. "Oh, you wanna watch, huh? Maybe you want to take turns sharing my dick?"

Her face somehow went paler.

Since she was basically my captive, I could do whatever, including being honest. "What I want to do to you isn't about sex." I stepped close so we were chest to chest, and I watched alarm flare in her eyes. My tone was absolute. "It's about power."

chapter THREE

Oksana

I stared up into Vasilije's black eyes and shuddered. Was he saying he wasn't going to fuck me? I scrambled to find a new angle. No matter how much planning I'd done, so much of tonight had been unknown, and I hadn't expected to end up here, even though Aleksandar had assured me I would. Vasilije was greedy. He'd go for me as soon as someone else showed interest.

He looked different in person. The angles of his face were sharper, his shoulders broader, and his eyes deeper. I'd studied pictures of him, but in real life he was so much... *more*. More attractive, more imposing, and way more dangerous. I'd barely been able to breathe during the car ride here, and it had little to do with his hand clenched on my throat.

Once he'd staked his claim on me, my panic became less fake.

"Power?" I repeated breathlessly.

His irises were made of the blackest ice possible, and although he smiled and flashed his dimples, the warmth didn't reach his eyes. His hand gripped my waist, and when I instinctively tried to retreat, his fingers dug in.

"I don't like to be touched," I said and shut my eyes tightly. I hadn't wanted to reveal it, at least not yet, but there was no avoiding it now. I'd wanted to hold onto my cards for as long as possible. If he hadn't picked me tonight, I was to play the role of Aleksandar's girlfriend, but my ridiculous plan had worked.

What the hell was I going to do now? My next step was to get close to Vasilije Markovic, and I hadn't the faintest clue how. Despite what I'd told my father, seduction wasn't something I believed I could do.

My anxiety was crippling, and his icy cold hand on my waist was debilitating. I drew in a stuttering breath and forced my eyes open. He studied me like I was both grotesque and fascinating in the same instant.

I'd told Vasilije I didn't like to be touched, so his evil smile widened and his hand slid upward, his palm stopping on my ribcage. His thumb brushed the underside of my breast through my thin sweater and bra, and my skin felt too tight. It was stretched and pulled in a million directions.

"You don't like to be touched?" His deep voice was throaty. "Why?"

I couldn't tell him I'd murdered the last man to put his hands on me. "I like my own space," I said, rushing the words out.

If the devil took human form, he'd look exactly like Vasilije did now. Violently sexual and dangerously persuasive.

"Yeah? Get over it." He glanced around before settling back on me. "All of this *space* is mine."

The cold hand drew away, and my body felt hot in the aftermath.

He toed off his boots and carried my composition notebook under his arm as he went down the hall. He expected me to follow, so I did. It was getting hard to think about anything other than his plans for me, but I forced myself to focus. All of my work was laid down on those pages. They might as well have been written in my blood.

I'd been told Vasilije was nothing more than a good-looking thug. Dimitrije Markovic had two sons, and Luka was the smart one. But my information had been wrong, or at least incomplete. Vasilije might have flunked out of college, but I shouldn't underestimate him. He'd figured out the drop-off tonight was a setup, he didn't trust me, and worst of all, he knew the notebook was of value to me.

He was far from the dumb mobster-wannabe I'd hoped for.

God, I should have sucked it up and left my notebook behind, rather than just a copy. I didn't know how long it was going to take to do what I needed to do, and how could I be without my music for that long? I needed it to give me strength.

He led me into a darkened chef's kitchen, not bothering with the lights. When he opened the fridge, it cast a harsh glow across his body. I begrudgingly admitted the "good looking" label assigned to him was correct. He wore a dark, long-sleeved shirt over jeans and the fabric hugged the lines of his muscular frame. He pushed the sleeves up to bunch at his elbows then pulled a bottle of beer from the fridge, setting it on the counter.

His eyes and hair were both dark, and a day's worth of scruff shadowed across his jaw. He had 'resting-asshole face,' which made a promise he had no problem fulfilling. Hot and smug son-of-a-bitch. It was a look my half-sister Tatiana would chase after, if it wasn't attached to Goran Markovic's nephew and second in line to the Serbian crime family.

A bottle opener was dug out of a drawer and the cap popped, dropping noisily to the granite countertop, and I tried not to watch his hands or the way the tendons in his strong forearms moved beneath his skin. *Think about what those hands are going to do to you, Oksana.*

They might kill me. They certainly would if he found out the truth.

He leveled a gaze in my direction, and my anxiety increased tenfold. His stare was carnal and indecent. I should have been happy, but it was terrifying. It drifted slowly down my body, lingering first at my breasts, and then down to my hips. I already felt naked and exposed, which was sure to come soon.

The beer was Osterhägen, which was ironic. It was my father's favorite brand.

Vasilije drank a long sip, and then motioned to the hallway, carrying his beer and my notebook with him as he went. The Markovic house was elegant and classically decorated. It wasn't gaudy. The luxury was refined and understated. Another unexpected thing from him. I'd heard the Serbians loved to show off. They flaunted their mafia money, most of it made off the backs of my people.

We reached the entryway that led to several parts of the house. There was a home office to my left, a large dining room to my right, and a living room before us, with a staircase leading upward. My body seized as I noticed the black beauty sitting beneath a picture window. In the moonlight, the Steinway grand piano was utterly breathtaking.

Sheet music rested on the rack, and my heart thudded faster. "Do you play?"

Could I find common ground with him?

Vasilije turned to stone. "Fuck, no. That thing hasn't been touched in years." My hope deflated, but his reaction was . . . strange. He acted like the piano wasn't anything of importance, but it was just that.

An *act*.

When he guided me to the bottom of a staircase, my heart plummeted all the way to my toes.

Fear grew in me with every carpeted step I climbed beside him. My stomach churned with bile. If I threw up, he'd cast me out, and months of planning would be gone. I couldn't fail at this. I pressed my lips together and fought against my nerves. It was just sex. There were worse men I could fuck than Vasilije Markovic, I told myself.

We reached the landing at the top of the stairs, and he took my elbow, turning me to my right. His cold, dominating grip forced me down the hall and to the doorway at the end of it, where he pushed a door open and flipped on the lights.

The back wall was gray stone. An unmade platform bed was

centered beneath it. The room was stylish, matching the rest of the house, and not what I'd expected of a twenty-four-year-old boy. He closed the door behind us, pulled out his phone, and set it on a charging dock on a nearby dresser. Then he yanked open a drawer and dropped my notebook inside.

Off came the holster. He made a show of removing the magazine from his gun and emptying the round from the chamber. Was I supposed to be impressed? Konstantine had shown me how to do that, and faster, too. The Glock was put on top of my notebook and the drawer was shut, but I didn't feel safer. He was stronger and faster, and I assumed he could kill me without a weapon if he wanted.

"The bathroom is through there." He flung a hand to the doorway to my left. "Go take a shower."

Like I was unclean.

I scurried through the doorway and shut the bathroom door behind me, gripping the doorknob and leaning against the frame for support. I was so fucking stupid. I'd volunteered for this. I'd *asked* for it. But now that the moment was here, and I wasn't ready.

The bathroom looked like it had been lifted from the pages of a magazine. It was all soothing colors and sophisticated fixtures. The large glass shower had a seat in it, and I started the water, stalling for time so I could regroup.

I kept an elastic band on my wrist since I knew the day was going to be long, and drew my hair back, twisting it into a bun. I wasn't about to get my hair wet. It'd take hours to dry without a hairdryer, but I needed to get under the water to keep up my lie.

My traveling hadn't started in Kazan, Russia; it'd started in an affluent south side suburb this morning. I'd hung out in baggage claim at O'Hare for hours, inserting myself with the other girls who'd come in.

Shit, Oksana. Pull yourself together.

One spoiled little rich boy I could handle. That was what I'd told my father, and I would make myself believe it. Our families had been battling for control of Chicago for years, and getting inside a Markovic house was a huge advantage to Sergey Petrov.

Too bad for him my real goal didn't align with his.

I stripped and got under the shower, letting the scorching water beat down on me and steam the glass. My body was a tool. I'd use it to bring the Serbian mafia prince in the next room to his knees.

The pep talk I was giving myself died when the bathroom door swung open and a dark figure appeared beyond the fogged glass. What the hell was he doing? It was unlikely he could see me, but I covered my nakedness with my hands and moved to the corner of the shower.

The figure stooped for a moment, then disappeared, pulling the door closed behind him. Dread lined my stomach, making me feel heavy. When I shut off the shower and pushed the door open, it confirmed my suspicions.

Vasilije had taken my clothes.

chapter FOUR

Vasilije

I tossed Oksana's damp clothes in a laundry basket at the back of my walk-in closet, when I should have trashed them, but I was feeling lazy. No, not lazy. Too impatient to go downstairs and throw her shit in the garbage. If she took too long, I'd go in there and get her.

Had she noticed me when I ducked in the bathroom? I hadn't seen her, but I also hadn't been looking. I was saving that moment for later, and I was curious how she was going to react. Would she try to stay in the shower all night, or wrap one of the short towels around her body? Or would she come out stark fucking naked?

I lit up a joint and drew the smoke into my lungs. If Luka saw me smoking weed in the house, he'd lose his goddamn mind, but he wasn't here anymore, was he? I could drop ash everywhere and stink up the master bedroom. I didn't, though. I grabbed the bowl I used as an ashtray and went to the window, cracking it open a few inches.

Cold seeped in as I stared at the bed.

My father had fucked his whore on this very bed, which led to my mother's death. The mattress was new, but otherwise it was the same. Was I sick for moving in here? It hadn't bothered Luka when he'd done it. It was the biggest, nicest room in the house.

I only toked a few puffs and stubbed the joint out. I could get high as fuck some other time. Tonight, I just wanted to feel different. Better. I blew the air clean from my lungs out the window, and then slid it shut, quieting the sound of the rain.

The shower stopped, and I heard the glass door swing open. A smile burned across my lips. What was the Russian girl thinking about right now? Was she panicking? Was she going to look for a weapon to defend herself with? She could go ahead. She wouldn't need it. My attack on her wouldn't be physical.

There were a few quiet sounds, but nothing to give me a clue what she was doing.

The bathroom door opened.

Fuck. Me. Sideways.

I'd hoped she'd come out with a towel tucked under her arms, barely covering her pussy and ass, but instead she was wrapped up in a plush black robe. *My* robe. I never wore it and forgot it was hanging on the back of the door.

It was way too big on her. She had one hand clenched on the front, holding the robe closed in addition to the belt knotted around her hips. Her other arm hung at her side, and the sleeve of the robe went past her fingertips. She stood in the semi-hallway between the bathroom and the closet and peered at me, trying to hide any trace of fear from her expression.

She failed.

I wasn't ready for the sight of her wearing my robe, but strangled back the knee-jerk reaction of demanding she take it off. Drawing this out would be fun, and I couldn't deny there was something interesting about seeing her like this.

"That's mine," I said casually. "I didn't say you could wear it."

Her hand clenched tighter and she took a step back. Her voice was whisper-quiet. "You took my clothes."

"Yeah. So, you're naked under there?"

For a micro-second, she looked at me like I was a fucking idiot, and then it disappeared. Her expression went blank.

No answer was all the answer I needed. "How does it feel?" I asked. "You like my robe wrapped around your body? Hanging on your tits? Clinging to your ass?" Every step of my approach made her eyes twice as wide. "You like having my smell all over you?"

Her breath hitched.

I seized the knot of the belt, wrapping my fist around it and jerking her up against me. She stumbled into my chest and flung a hand out, but I didn't release my grip. Instead, I ran a hand over the part of the robe that covered her thighs, moving up until I was massaging her pussy through the fabric.

"It's so soft," I said. "Feels so good against your skin, doesn't it?"

"*B'layd!*" She spat the foreign word at me with horror. "Don't touch me."

I stroked her, pressing my hand deep between her legs, and got her to moan. I couldn't tell if it was all shock, or if there was pleasure mixed in, too. "I'm just touching what's mine," I said. "If you don't like it, take off the robe."

Oksana wasn't looking at me. Her gaze was focused on my brow, only giving the illusion of attention. She blinked furiously as I continued to slide my fingers over the robe. If she let me keep going, I'd have my hand inside soon. I'd already worked it beneath one side, bringing my touch closer.

She shuddered and her breath went ragged. Her chest heaved, struggling to process the air.

Her warm hand closed on top of mine on the knot, and I paused. "I'll give you what you want." She swallowed a breath, gathering strength. "Will you do the same? Please, Vasilije?"

Her tone was soft, but the words had meaning. Why did she hate being touched so much? She eased my hand away, and I allowed it. Relief visibly poured through her. The space was good for me, too. Blood was already pumping straight to my dick, and I didn't fucking like that at all. She was Russian.

Pussy is pussy, my dick fired back at me.

I turned and went into the bedroom, taking a seat on the edge of the bed, and leaned back, propped up on my arms. I wanted to take the robe off her. Slide my hands inside and peel it down slowly one side at a time, torturing her as I revealed every naked inch of her body. But making her do it under my command was better. I wanted her overwhelmed and buckling beneath my control.

She padded cautiously out into the light of the bedroom and stood before the bed, her gaze zeroed in on my chest. She said she'd give me what I wanted, but she hadn't a fucking clue what that was.

"Off."

The single word from me charged the air. It crackled with intensity as her trembling hands fell to the belt. Electricity sparked across my skin as she slowly worked the knot free. I'd given my staff orders, and I constantly told Alek what to do, but this . . . this felt different. My pulse kicked. Satisfaction flowed in my veins, stronger than the buzz from my joint.

"Look at me," I ordered. I wanted to see everything in her eyes as she became vulnerable.

But she kept her gaze on my chest and shook her head, sucking down a huge breath. "I can't."

Oksana moved fast, like she'd gotten a burst of courage. She shrugged out of the thick black fabric, and it dropped as a curtain to the floor. I—

Tits.

Her creamy skin and pink nipples were so fucking sexy, I forgot how to breathe. I liked the way her natural breasts sat like teardrops instead of the round globes of fake tits. I wanted to run my tongue down the curve of her flat belly, journeying on to the thin patch of groomed stubble covering her pussy.

My cock snapped to attention, jerking in my pants. She was too skinny. I could see the lines of her ribs, but otherwise she was flawless. Her waist was tiny, but her hips curved, and she had legs for fucking days.

"*Sranje,*" I swore under my breath. I dragged my gaze up to her eyes, but she refused to look at me. Her face was flushed red.

Her shyness annoyed me. Guys had to be telling her all the time how hot she was. I'd fucked plenty of girls who weren't as good looking, and when we'd gotten down to business, they'd raced to strip and show off their goods. They'd been proud, and it was sexy. So, this bashful routine was stupid and disingenuous.

I wanted her gaze on mine. The need was... surprising.

"Oksana."

Her blue eyes finally settled on me. Jesus fuck, what had my joint been laced with? Her haunting eyes made me want to stand up. They whispered to walk the five or six steps to her, grab the messy knot of hair on the back of her head, and slam my mouth over hers. I wanted to fuck her mouth, not with my cock... *but with my tongue.*

I was messed up.

She was trembling so hard, she mimicked a skyscraper the moment after the demolition charges on the supports had been blown. Barely held together and about to collapse. I sat up straighter so I could move fast if she did.

The longer I stared at her, the more I believed her shyness wasn't an act. She was legitimately terrified. So, why didn't she run? Why'd she take the robe off without a fight? I had to adjust my game to keep up.

I lifted my hands in a fake surrender. "I'm not touching you right now." I swept my gaze down her amazing body. "Even though I *really* fucking want to." It wasn't a lie. In fact... "I can't wait to slide my hands all over you. *Inside* you. Make you wet. Have you moaning for me to get you off."

She tore her gaze away and didn't know what to do with her hands. They moved nervously from her sides, to her hips, until she crossed her arms over her chest. Her anxiety was so strong, the taste of it was thick and intoxicating in the air.

I stood from the bed. "You don't like sex?"

Her bottom lip quivered. It took forever for her to answer me, and her voice faltered. "I... wouldn't know."

What the fuck did she mean? I laughed, but it died in my throat. *You've got to be fucking with me.*

"You're a virgin." I didn't ask it as a question, but my tone was skeptical.

She pressed her lips together in a thin line and nodded.

Was it true? The Russian whore was actually a virgin? She didn't like to be touched, and maybe she was religious enough to want to save herself for marriage. Her freaking out at being naked made more sense now.

My cock grew harder against the fly of my jeans. I'd never had a virgin before. When I was fifteen, one of my stepmother's friends popped my cherry while her husband played golf with my dad. All the girls I'd dated after that affair had already jumped on a cock by the time I got to them.

I was happy with my new toy, but to find out she was *brand new*? That I was going to be the one to tear open the plastic wrap and take her out of the box? I had to rein in my excitement. No one had touched her the way I was going to, and I'd *always* be the first.

Her expression was desperate. "Can we do this?" She shivered. "I want to get it over with."

I strolled close and dropped my voice low. "No."

Fuck, no. My laugh was evil. I wasn't going to give her exactly what she wanted, and besides, this was something to be enjoyed. *Savored.* All my plans for her shifted for the hundredth time tonight.

"You anxious to have me punch your V card?" I asked. "You get that I have to touch you to fuck you, right?" To reinforce it, I ran my fingertip down her arm, and grinned as she flinched away. I liked how skittish she was.

"I know how it works." Her shoulders were tight, but she didn't turn away or bend down to put the robe back on. Her body was saying no, but her words were telling me yes. It fucked with my head, when I wanted to do that to hers.

"Do you, now, virgin?" This time I trailed all of my fingertips down her chest, sweeping them over her erect nipple, and watched goosebumps lift on her skin. "You know what it's gonna be like when I push my cock inside and tear up your innocent little pussy?"

She gasped, choking on air.

The decision was made instantly. No fucking her tonight. Leaving her suspended in anticipation got me so hard, my dick ached. It came with its own pleasure, and I'd get my satisfaction from her in another way. Until I was ready, I'd keep pushing. I'd goad her to tell me to stop.

She blinked and tried to pull herself back together. Her hands shot out and latched onto my belt, and I stood there like an idiot, stunned. My cock was thrilled, but the rest of me was pissed. I was the one in control, not her. This was going to happen on my terms.

I grabbed her wrists and pulled them behind her back, forcing her to arch her breasts into me. The heat of them soaked through the cotton of my shirt as she pressed against my chest, and her chin tipped up. I stared down into her startled eyes. I wasn't the kind of guy to pay attention to eye color. I focused on the parts that interested me, the tits and ass. Yet I looked at every variation of blue in her irises.

"You're beautiful."

I froze. *What the fuck, mouth?* I tightened my grip on her wrists, wrenching her hands further behind her back, like I was punishing her for causing my stupid comment. The muscle along her jaw tightened, announcing she was clenching her teeth tightly.

She was naked in my arms, and our faces were only a breath away. Every second of silence that ticked by was heavier than the last. Her lush lips were right there if I wanted to take them. She didn't squirm in my hold or ask me to stop touching her. She just stood there, peering up at me. Waiting for me to do something.

So, fuck it.

I dipped my head down and pressed my mouth to hers.

chapter
FIVE

OKSANA INHALED SHARPLY through her nose when the kiss started. Her lips were soft and warm. I shifted the angle, finding a position that was more comfortable, since she hadn't moved. She didn't break the kiss, but she didn't put forth any effort, either.

Why should she? This was the dumbest fucking idea ever. What the hell was I thinking, kissing her? How virginal was the virgin?

Shit. What if this was her first kiss? It was awkward enough to be one. I felt like I was back in high school, fumbling around with a girl, not knowing what my next move should be. I hated the feeling almost as much as I hated how I couldn't peel my lips away from this epic fail of a kiss.

Her lips parted, probably to say something, but I didn't allow it. Instead, I shoved my way inside her mouth and felt the jolt go through her. The slide of my tongue over hers was a fucking activation switch, because she softened. Her tongue hesitantly sought mine. Her lips opened more and finally answered me back, making her a willing participant in the kiss.

My heart beat faster, and without thinking, my hands coursed up her arms, over her shoulders, and into her hair. I tugged her head back and forced my tongue deeper in her mouth. I took. I claimed. I owned her with my kiss, which was growing more intense every second. It was wild and verged on out of control.

Her hands tugged again at my belt, and I let her jerk the end of it free and undo my buckle. I was too focused on the way her lips moved against mine to stop her. She tore at the snap with shaky hands and dropped my zipper, brushing over my hard-on. I groaned against her mouth, but shoved her back, breaking the connection. Her eyes were full of chaos and confusion.

My undone jeans were caught on my hips, and my erection strained against the cotton of my boxer briefs, reaching for her through the undone sides of my zipper. Lust throbbed through my entire body. I felt it in every goddamn inch, and cursed in my head. Her lips were swollen from my kiss, and she panted like I'd been chasing her for hours.

Wasn't the weed supposed to make me mellow? All I felt was pulsing need and aggression.

I came back to her, fisting my hand on the knot of hair, and jerked her head back so hard, she let out a whimper. I crushed my palm to her breast, lifting and squeezing while my teeth scraped over the side of her neck. She smelled like my soap. I sucked on the spot where her pulse throbbed.

A trembling moan came from Oksana. It could have been panic, or surprise, or pleasure. I didn't know her noises, and fuck me, I wanted to learn them all. I pinched and twisted her nipple, going until she gave me another noise. It was a sharp hiss.

That was pain.

I let go and slid my hand straight down the slope of her body so I could press my fingers in the warm crevice between her legs. She gasped and tried to pull away.

That was shock.

My hold on her hair made it so she couldn't run from me, and as she bucked, I released my grip so I could band my arm behind her back and hold her tighter. Would I be able to find the sound she made for pleasure? My fingers searched over her damp skin.

I was too close and my hand was in the way, so she couldn't complete her task of getting my pants down. Her palms were on my shoulders, clawing and scratching at my shirt, trying to push me back. Or maybe hold on. My fingertips found her clit and stirred, causing her body to lock up.

As I swirled my fingers, her hands clenched and fisted my shirt. She grew wet.

"You don't seem to mind me touching you now," I said.

Her head tipped forward, and her forehead thumped into my chest. It felt like a surrender, and my chest grew five inches. I got drunk off the control, and twitched my fingers faster. A faint moan was muted against my skin.

That was pleasure.

Reluctant pleasure, but it'd do . . . for now.

"Has anyone touched you like this before?" My voice was uneven, surprising me.

Her forehead slid slowly up and down against the center of my chest in a nod. I stared down at the top of her head. Once again, she couldn't bring herself to look at me. I withdrew my hand from between her thighs and curled it around her neck, forcing her to stretch up and look at me with half-lidded eyes. I dragged my thumb over her lush, parted lips.

"What about this mouth? Anyone fucked you here yet?"

She didn't blink, and I was happy about it. Our connection was unbroken, even as she slowly shook her head no. Desire whipped at me, roaring into a frenzy. I used my hand on her throat to force her down. She buckled, folding her legs beneath her as I positioned her to kneel on the carpet. Her blue eyes peered up at me, nervous.

I'd never seen anything sexier than Oksana naked on her knees before me with her virgin mouth gaping. I pushed at the sides of my jeans and let them slide down my legs. My dick was so hard, it hurt when I tugged my underwear down, unleashing it. It bobbed in freedom before settling at full mast, angling toward its destination.

Her worried expression shifted to all-out fear when she was face-to-face with my cock. I had good equipment, and I was a fucking expert at using it.

NIKKI SLOANE

I spread my feet as far apart as the jeans down around my calves would allow, and put a hand on top of her head. I ringed my other hand around the base of my dick, holding it steady. "Open wide, baby."

She grunted in displeasure and glared up at me, opening her mouth to say something, but I just smiled and cut her off by shoving the head of my cock between her lips. Wet heat closed all around, and fire seared up my spine. Her tongue was soft against the sensitive underside of my tip, and I stroked against it as I pressed further inside.

Her hands flew up and she braced herself against my thighs, but I continued to advance and held her head steady, pushing in as deep as I could get. When I hit the back of her throat, she coughed and retreated, pulling away. She sat back on her haunches and pressed her fingertips to her lips, and fire burned in her watering eyes.

I smirked. "Too much for you? Imagine what it's going to feel like when all that's in your pussy."

I pushed her to the edge of disgust, but still, she said nothing. There was no attempt to stand or scramble away. She remained on her knees, obedient. Even when I pushed her head toward my crotch and traced the tip of my dick across her lips. I slid my damp, meaty flesh back and forth, searching for entrance.

"Open your goddamn mouth."

She followed my command. What would the virgin do if I slapped her with my dick? How much further would she let me push?

"There you go," I said, easing between her lips. "That's a good girl."

I'd been in her mouth all of three seconds, and I was worried I was going to lose control. She wasn't even doing anything yet. I held her head firm as I began to saw my cock in and out in long, slow strokes. Blood whooshed in my ears, competing with the wet sounds of my movement.

"Suck." My voice was breathless. "Move your tongue."

Shit. Why the hell did I tell her to do that? Pleasure pooled low in my stomach, snaking outward as suction tightened and focused the sensation. I couldn't stop the shudder when her tongue flicked over me.

"Fuck, yeah, just like that."

I worked my thick dick in and out of her mouth until it was glossy with saliva and I'd built to a steady rhythm. I'd never had to train a girl to suck me off before, and I enjoyed the role with her as my student. I plunged deep to the back, forcing my head into the tightness in her throat, and when she gagged loudly, dark satisfaction swept through me.

Was there any better sound than listening to a girl choke on your dick? If there was, I hadn't heard it.

Oksana's palms shoved at my thighs, and I stumbled back a half step, falling out of her mouth, letting her draw air into her sputtering lungs. I stroked a hand along my wet shaft, twisting my grip as she recovered. I wasn't going to last much longer inside her hot mouth. Should I come on her tits, marking her?

No. A better, more evil idea twisted in my mind.

"Has anyone licked your pussy?" My tone was sinister. If she'd never blown a guy, it seemed unlikely, but I wanted to be the only one.

Her face was already pink from when I'd made her gag, but it flushed brighter at my question. I was going to taste her no matter how she answered. Going down on a girl was almost as much fun as fucking them. It was when they were the most vulnerable, and my power over them was the greatest.

I could get a girl to agree to almost anything when my tongue was working her over. It was how I convinced the last one I was with to try anal. Too bad she'd given up after the first ten seconds, the quitter.

The girl in front of me wasn't a quitter. I'd been an asshole, and she took it. Her submission was insane. I could do damn near anything. All the sick desires. I'd never needed anything more than I did right now, not even the revenge I had planned for my uncle. As I demanded her loyalty and obedience, she gave it.

"Answer me," I ordered. "Has anyone gone down on you?"

"No," she whispered.

I shut my eyes against the satisfaction that flowed through my system. How the fuck had she stayed so innocent? I'd figure it out later. Right now, I wanted to dirty her up and make her mine. Get her addicted to my brand.

Her mouth was even hotter when I slid in this time. She didn't need any guidance. Her tongue tumbled over my dick, and the sound of the seal of suction breaking rang out when she let me pump faster. My hips thrust into her, fucking her face, and I latched a hand on the back of her head so I could keep my driving tempo.

"I'm gonna come in your mouth," I said, my words tight with pleasure. "You're gonna hold my cum in there until I tell you to swallow. Got it?" Heat blasted along my legs. Shivers worked their way up. "Not a drop until I say so."

Her fingers curled on my legs and her nails scratched at my skin. Her teeth scraped over the length of me, but it felt good. Since she couldn't take all of me in her mouth, I jerked off, sliding the vise of my fingers at the base of my dick in time with her lips.

I felt heavy. Like everything was hurtling inward, compacting under the crushing need to get off. I was so fucking close.

"Look at me." My voice was dark and loud, and almost a yell. Her gaze snapped up to mine, and I was done for. "Fuck, fuck, *fuck!*"

My release burst one fiery rush at a time, wracking me with acute pleasure on every spurt. She flinched as I came on her tongue, but I cased both hands on her head and held her still as I filled her mouth. My legs shook under the onslaught of my climax, and I wondered if I was holding her there or using her for support.

I slowed my thrusts to a stop, and drained every drop into her as the overwhelming feeling in my system began to subside. Holy shit, it felt amazing, and it seemed like she'd obeyed me. I didn't feel her throat bob with a swallow.

I pulled out slowly, not wanting any of my cum to leak out of those pink lips. She sat back, her hands on her knees and her lips pressed together, waiting for my command. I pulled up my pants and did up the fly, then bent and traced a fingertip down her cheek. "You like my flavor rolling around in your mouth?"

It was doubtful she'd answer, but couldn't anyway. Her cum-drenched tongue couldn't move under the gag I'd placed on her. I held absolute control.

chapter SIX

OKSANA

VASILIJE'S EYES GLITTERED WITH EVIL as he stood before me, wearing a smirk and all his damn clothes. I'd yo-yoed between outrage and humiliation during the blowjob, but there was another feeling off in the distance I tried to ignore. Did some sick part of me not mind this so much?

Since Ilia, no one would touch me.

At first, I preferred it that way, but time dragged on and it'd been three long years. I'd sat by, listening to stories from my friends about how they fooled around and lost their virginity, and curiosity ate at me. I craved to be like them and know what it'd feel like. Despite what I'd told Vasilije, I wanted hands on my body that weren't my own. He'd given it to me, hadn't he?

If I could speak, my answer would have been no. No, I didn't like his 'flavor.' It was salty and weirdly numbing, and saliva rushed to pool in my mouth to counteract it. The urge to swallow was immediate. I waited impatiently for him to tell me I could.

He grabbed the hem of his shirt and stretched it up over his head, casting it aside. The need to swallow now was shockingly urgent. His bare, toned chest made me hate him all over again. Why the hell did he have to be so good looking? And worse, why did he have to know it? I wasn't sure what kind of expression I had on my face, but it earned a smug, arrogant look from him.

Muscles curved under smooth skin, and my gaze wandered over his appealing and dangerous form. He was powerful in every sense of the word.

Vasilije tugged at my hair tie. "Down." He wanted my hair loose? I yanked the knot free, and then he flung a finger to the bed. "Get on your back."

My heart seized in my chest. I'd foolishly thought since he'd come that I was off the hook, but apparently sex was still in his plans. I should have been grateful. I was doing a terrible job of seducing him, but it was working anyway. I climbed onto my feet. Would he notice if I swallowed? Could I fake it that I hadn't? I had no idea what he'd do if I disobeyed, making it too risky. I fought the urge to choke and gag.

I'd only put one knee on the bed before his hands were there, shoving me down and pushing me to roll onto my back. A panicked hum came out, but I kept my lips glued together. I was right at the edge of the mattress, my feet flat on the floor, as he stepped between my knees and dropped down.

I lifted my head and stared at him over my nakedness. He wasn't looking at my eyes for once. His gaze was focused between my legs, and the cold pads of his fingers eased my thighs further apart. *Oh my God.* My heart beat loud in my ears, drumming out sound.

His black eyes peered up at me, and his smile was nasty. "When you start to come," his hot breath washed over my trembling skin, "then you can swallow."

I moaned my anxiety through pressed lips, and struggled to take in air through my nose. I was breathing so hard, I grew dizzy and my head weighed a million pounds. Vasilije Markovic was *right there.* He stared at my pussy like I was a decadent dessert he couldn't wait to eat.

The world slowed as he lowered his lips to me, and then time raced forward from a slingshot as his wet, soft tongue brushed against my skin. It was impossible to keep quiet, or stop my body from recoiling from the sudden sensation. My brain splintered under the stress of it. Did I *like* what he'd just done?

He did it again, and I jerked. It felt... nice.

Everything was buzzing as his strong hands smoothed up my thighs and he used his thumbs to peel me open to his invasive mouth. I clamped my hands down on the sheets beneath them, and bucked against the heat of each stroke he delivered. The sensation was intense, and erotic, and distracted me from the liquid I held in my mouth that I'd been desperate to swallow down seconds ago.

"Mmmm," he murmured. "You taste sweet."

I groaned and threw my arm up over my face, shielding my eyes from him. He settled in, and his tongue fluttered over my clit, drawing moan after reluctant moan from me. It felt good. What he was doing to me felt really, really good.

It was getting hard to breathe. I writhed on the mattress, sweating and flinching with contractions of pleasure as his mouth sucked on me. I'd spent the last month wondering if I could get Vasilije Markovic to want to fuck me. It'd seemed ridiculous, the idea he'd have any interest in me.

It seemed less ridiculous now.

His tongue dipped inside my body, spreading more wetness around. My arousal, really. Because what he was doing turned me on, and if I was honest with myself... maybe his complete control had, too. In my father's house, I'd played the role of obedient daughter for the last five years. I'd been trained to respond to strong men, which hadn't helped with the Ilia situation.

I arched up, biting on the insides of my cheeks, forcing myself to keep my mouth shut. His cum was thick around my teeth, serving as a muzzle. A gag.

He was doing something else now, and I had no choice but to lift my heavy head and peer down. He was alternating between his tongue and two fingers swiping furiously over the nub of flesh at the center of my legs. I was beyond conflicted. Letting him bring me to orgasm was a terrible idea. It'd give him more control, and he already had way too much. But if I came, I could swallow and regain the ability to speak. He'd reward me with both pleasure and freedom.

My hands ached from where I'd balled my fists in his unmade bed, thrashing against the burning heat and bliss pooling low in my center. His mouth was on me, and I watched his glistening tongue lick through my slit. Just the image was too much to bear, but then he opened his eyes and looked up at me. They were full of sin and darkness, and I was sucked into them.

Doomed.

Shudders moved in waves along my skin as I came. The detonation inside was catastrophic, and I went boneless, giving in to the orgasm. It felt like power flowed out of me and right into him. I swallowed an enormous, thick gulp, and gasped loudly as air poured back into my throat. It was followed by whimpers, because the sensations were still going. Heat blasted up my back and down my legs.

Vasilije didn't stop. His mouth continued to tease, and I was so overly sensitive, I reached down and shoved his head away. "Oh, God, stop."

His chuckle was pure evil.

As the orgasm faded, he stood, towering over me as he wiped his lips, and revealed the devious smile beneath. His hands rested on his belt, showing off his sinewy frame, and he stared at me, watching as I struggled to recover. His evaluating gaze was unnerving, and yet I wondered how I'd done.

Had I pleased him? Everything depended on it. Not just my goal, but my life.

I waited dutifully for him to give me my next instruction, but he viewed me like a man trying to figure out how he felt about an abstract painting. The room had been on fire a minute ago, but now it was freezing, and I shivered. I wrapped my arms around myself and tried to hold the heat in.

"Get under the covers," he said, sounding bored.

My head was a mess. The release he'd given me had a calming effect, and I worried he'd catch me off guard. The last thing I needed to be with him was relaxed. I moved up on the bed, yanking the fluffy comforter up around me, and sighed with relief on the inside. He'd seen every inch of me, but having coverage gave me a tiny kernel of strength back.

Trepidation crept in as Vasilije moved his hands to his pants and undid them. His jeans dropped to the floor and he stepped out of them, so he was only clad in a dark gray pair of boxer briefs with a white waistband. I didn't recognize the name brand printed across it, but chances were his underwear was expensive. My father was incredibly wealthy, and the Markovics surpassed him.

Vasilije never knew hunger or struggle. I was sure he'd lived a life where he got everything he wanted, and that included designer clothes.

My guarded gaze tracked him as he flipped on a bedside lamp, walked to the door, and shut off the overhead bedroom light. His back was broad and contoured with muscle. His ass was firm and tight, filling out his underwear, and I felt dizzy assessing him like this. I shouldn't appreciate how he looked, but he was the devil and, therefore, undeniably attractive.

Perhaps not mentally, or personality-wise, but physically? Oh, yes. There were absolutely worse men I could fuck than Vasilije Markovic. My mouth miraculously went dry as he turned and headed toward the bed, the very one I was sitting on.

His lips turned up in a cruel smile. "We need to get something straight. In the morning, you can leave if you want to."

Ice chiseled away at my spine. He was throwing me out? I'd come way too far to not—

"You won't, though," he added, climbing into the bed beside me.

I steeled my voice. "Why not?"

"Your people won't help you. You were the only girl we took, and there's no way they're going to believe I let you go. They'll think you're spying for me and probably kill you. If not, they'll pump you full of drugs and put you to work with the other girls." He pulled the covers up to his waist, like he was discussing something trivial. "At least you know how to suck cock now."

He said that kind of shit to get a rise out of me, but I refused to play into his hands. "I don't have to go to them."

"Oh, you got better options?" He looked impossibly arrogant. "The fuck you do. I looked through your shit. There's no phone numbers, names, or addresses. The group that picked you up outside the international terminal was your only contact."

"Maybe I have it memorized," I said, which was true. Of course I knew my own address.

"Yeah? What is it, then?" He smirked as he dished out the challenge. I wasn't about to tell him, and he took my silence as a victory. He thought he'd called my bluff.

"I could go to the police."

His laugh was cruel. "And tell them what? I rescued you from becoming a sex slave? Yeah, I'm a monster." He was both sarcastic and not. "You think my family doesn't own the police? So, you'll stay here until I'm tired of you, or realize what a stupid idea this is."

"Stay here?" An invisible hand squeezed my entire body. "In your house? With you?"

He turned off the lamp and flopped his head down on the pillow. "I always wanted a pet."

My mouth fell open. Anxiety was tempered by success, and I chewed back the need to tell the stupid boy I wasn't his dog.

"Lie down," he ordered. I couldn't see because the room was dark, but I could hear the smile in his voice, and rage turned everything red for a long moment.

I took a breath. *Get over this and play your part.* When it was done, if Vasilije was still standing, I'd make him heel like my fucking dog. The thought was enough to keep me quiet. I mashed the pillow and set my head on it, rolling away from him.

"Don't get any ideas about killing me." The mattress rocked gently as he shifted closer. "If you do, my family will make you beg for death, and then keep you alive for weeks while you do it."

"Lovely," I bit out.

He gave a humorless laugh. "You think I'm fucking with you? I'm not."

"I don't want to kill you, Vasilije." He was no good to me dead. How could I use him to kill my father then?

"Good. Don't bite the hand that feeds you, either."

I gritted my teeth and choked on the desire to tell him to go fuck himself. I jammed my eyes shut and focused on the pattern of the rain hitting the window. The rhythm was its own kind of music. I wished I had my notebook so I could jot down the percussion line. It was only across the room.

Fingers made of ice traced a line down my spine, and I flinched away.

"Tell me why you don't like being touched."

I scooted to the edge of the bed, as far away from him as I could get, but it made no difference. A hand locked on my hip, and the cool skin of his chest pressed against my back. He was freezing, which shouldn't have been surprising. I'd been told he was cold blooded.

"I just don't." My voice was small.

His hand tightened, driving his fingers into my skin like blunt icicles stabbing at me. "Why don't you like being touched? You're not going to want me to ask a third time."

Should I reveal the truth? I didn't know how he'd react. "When I was seventeen, a man . . . touched me when I didn't want him to."

Vasilije's hand was gone instantly, like I was damaged goods. *Shit.* The silence between us hung heavy, and only the rain tapping at the window let me know we weren't frozen forever in this painful moment.

His tone was strained. "Who was he?"

"Just some guy who worked for my father."

A lie. Ilia had been a rising star, poised to become one of the main figures in our business. He was young, but his family had vouched for him, and my father had welcomed him into the inner circle. Ilia had something I never would—my father's respect.

"What happened?" Vasilije's tone was sharp, as if angry, yet I had the strange feeling he wasn't upset with me.

"I told my father, and he had the guy ... sent away. Please don't make me talk about it."

He exhaled, as if reluctant. "Tell me how your parents died."

Wow. He switched from one awful memory to another. "My mother was killed in a plane crash when I was fifteen. It was a regional flight between Kazan and Kirov." This was true. I'd been instructed to stay as close to my real story as possible, to avoid crafting a web of lies I couldn't keep up with. "It made it very hard to want to get on a plane."

Also true, except my flight to the United States had come only a few months after she'd died. I'd been heavily sedated most of the journey, scared of falling out of the sky, and terrified of meeting the man who was my father if we didn't happen to crash.

"My parents weren't together. After she passed, I went to live with my father. Last year, one of his *business deals*," I weighted the word so Vasilije would know what I was alluding to, "ended badly, and my father was shot."

There'd been a delicate truce between us and the Serbians for several months last year, and when it fell apart, everything went to shit and my father took a bullet in his right arm. He lost some mobility permanently, but he'd survived. I'd let Vasilije believe otherwise.

"You live in this big house by yourself?" I asked, hoping to switch subjects.

"My parents are dead." His tone was cold. "My brother lives in Baltimore." The sheets rustled as he moved further away from me. "Go to sleep."

I was stunned, and rolled over to see if he was joking. "We're not going to . . . ?"

"Fuck? Not tonight." A lazy smile smeared on his lips. "Try not to look so disappointed. You'll have to wait a little longer, virgin."

chapter SEVEN

Vasilije

It was awkward as hell trying to fall asleep beside the naked girl in my bed. I rarely brought my hookups home, and if I did, we partied in one of the guest bedrooms. That way, I could bail afterward and escape down the hall. I didn't share my bed.

But I enjoyed how uncomfortable I made Oksana and didn't want to let up. She needed to stay on edge and always aware of me.

Her quiet breathing didn't bother me because it had purpose, but she silently tapped her fingers against the sheet, drumming out a pattern of some kind. I could feel the vibrations through the mattress. I shot my hand out and covered hers. "Stop."

Her warm fingers stilled beneath mine.

Well, fuck me, I was basically holding her hand. It felt weird and wrong, but I left my palm on top of hers because I always did the wrong thing. My hold of her made the tension between us skyrocket. After the blowjob, I'd been tired, yet now my dick was twitching, waking up and greedy for more. The plan was to draw it out, but maybe I'd fuck her tomorrow. I couldn't wait to watch her face as I buried my cock in her sweet pussy for the first time.

I drifted off into an uneasy sleep, keeping my hand latched onto hers.

♪

My eyelids popped open. It was still dark outside. I glanced at the clock—it was two in the morning. I was a light sleeper, but the rain had stopped, so that hadn't been what woke me up. I homed in on the sounds around, just as I remembered how I'd fallen asleep with a girl in my bed. A *Russian* one.

The sheets beside me were empty.

I jolted up, wheeling around. Oksana had put on my black robe, and she stood at my dresser with her back to me. It sounded like she was cautiously opening the top drawer.

Shit! I was off the bed and flew at her, slamming into her body with enough force to knock the gun from her grip. Down we went, her screaming in fear, and between the tangle of black fabric and her hands, I couldn't see my gun.

Instead of a safety snapping off or a magazine being jammed in place, there was a sound of . . . paper ripping? I fell on top of her and fought for her wrists, strangling each one above her head and pinning them to the carpet. Her wild eyes stared up at me as I straddled her hips.

She'd been trying to kill me, even after I'd made it clear what would happen if she was successful. Was she that fucking stupid? Where was the gun she'd gone for in the drawer? I scanned around, and when I saw the notebook laying awkwardly on the carpet, my rage evaporated. *Oh.*

I slid my hands away slowly, releasing her.

Oksana's head turned and she stared at the tented notebook surrounded with torn pages.

Her face crumbled and turned into a pure nightmare. Tears welled in her eyes. After everything she'd been through tonight, witnessing murder and then all I'd done . . . *this* was what made her cry? A few torn pages? I didn't know what to do. I didn't have sisters or a mother, and the only time women cried around me was when I was dumping their ass, and neither one of us wanted me to stick around.

I climbed off her, grabbed the lapels of the robe, and hauled her to sit up. "It's okay," I heard myself saying. "I've got tape. We can fix it."

She shrank away from me, wrapping the plush fabric tighter around her body, and wiped the tears away from beneath her eyes. Whatever sadness she had disappeared pretty damn quick, and was replaced with a guarded expression. Like she was embarrassed and ready to defend herself if I made a comment about her crying.

"I wasn't going for your gun," she said.

"I get that now." I picked up the notebook and the torn pages, and I could feel her searing gaze on me as I closed the pages inside and stood. She acted like I had no right to touch her stupid book. "What the fuck is this?"

"Music," she said. "My songs."

I must not have been fully awake as I held out the book to her. "Fine. You'll go downstairs and play one for me."

She looked at me like I'd just asked her to kill the Pope. "Now?"

Why the hell not? I'd had a surge of adrenaline when I thought she was going for my gun, and the effect hadn't worn off yet. I was jittery. She acted like this music was priceless. I was curious if I'd see value in it like she did.

Her expression was pure disbelief, and I hardened mine in response. "Let's go."

Oksana snatched the book from me, grateful to have it back, and she climbed to her feet. I followed behind her when she trudged to the door.

The rain had ceased, but the clouds blotted out the moonlight, and we could barely see the shape of the black grand piano sitting beneath the window. I flipped on the entryway light when we reached the bottom of the stairs and blinked against the chandelier's glow.

I gestured to the office. "There's tape on the desk."

She went in and I stood at the doorway, watching her bend over the desk and repair the pages. Her blonde hair looked white in contrast to my dark robe, and the sliver of skin between the lapels of the robe teased me. I could order her to take it off, but it was more fun if she accidentally flashed me.

When Oksana seemed satisfied with her work, she straightened from the desk and set her gaze on me. Her expression was hard to read. Was it fear? Excitement? Was she wanting an asshole as the audience for her music?

I glanced at the piano. The last person to play it had been my mother, who I had hardly any memories of. What would she think about this Russian girl laying her Russian fingers on the ivory keys?

I pushed the thought away. My mother had been dead for twenty years, and Oksana playing on it wasn't going to change that, or my memory of Luka sitting on my mother's lap while she played. She'd let him hit some of the keys while I'd pushed the pedals at her feet, demanding to be included in the song.

We went to the piano. I stood beside it, and Oksana's voice was soft and warm as she pulled out the bench. "I hope it sounds as beautiful as it looks."

She folded the music on the shelf like it was delicate. It was unnecessary. The piano was nothing more than a museum piece. My father tried to sell it once. I'd told him not to, but he hadn't given in to my demand until Luka sided with me. I'd thought the piano made my father sad, not recognizing at the time it was more likely guilt. Every time he looked at it, was he reminded of how he'd had my mother killed?

Oksana set her open notebook on the piano and sat on the bench with her back stiff and straight. Below the belt, the robe fell open and exposed one of her long legs clear up to the thigh, like she was wearing a dress with a slit up the side.

Her fingers were set on the keys. She drew in a deep breath—

"What's it called?" I interrupted before she could even start.

"Temperance."

What the fuck? I already hated it, but then she began to play and confirmed my judgement. The melody was obnoxious. It was up tempo and . . . fuck, I couldn't think of the right word. Jaunty? Yeah. It was *jaunty* as fuck, and I added it to my list of unnecessary noises. "Stop."

Her hands froze and the room went silent.

She turned slowly to look at me, gauging my reaction, and her lips twisted down in a frown. "When was the last time this was tuned?"

"Don't blame the piano. Play something else, Oksana. Something better."

She was more offended I hadn't liked her shitty song than when I'd shoved my dick in her mouth. This girl was something else entirely. She turned the pages and settled on a new song. Her fingers moved over the keys, sharp and attacking.

"Wow," I said flatly. "What's this awful one called? Let me guess. Abstinence?"

She inhaled so sharply, it was like I'd slapped her. Her fingers retreated from the keys, my words visibly stinging. A lesser guy would have been cut down by her vicious glare, but the blow glanced off me. When she tried to stand, I put a hand on her shoulder and shoved her back down to sit, and her ass thumped on the bench.

"Don't play happy music in my house," I threatened. "It doesn't belong here, and certainly not coming from my mother's piano."

Oksana stared at the book before her, considering what to do. Finally, she paged through it and selected a song in the middle of her scribblings. Her shoulders lifted as she took a breath and she pushed back the oversized sleeves of the robe. Her fingers crept back to the keys.

The song was quiet, slow, and eerie. My gaze followed every gentle movement of her hands as they worked up and down the piano, producing the hypnotic rhythm. I didn't listen to classical music. My phone was full of rock and rap music. I liked driving bass, hooks, and aggressive lyrics. Yet, this song, I didn't hate. Maybe she was right and the piano was out of tune, but its discord added to the unsettling music.

The chilling song seeped into the dark space around us. I hadn't turned on the light in the room, and it had to be hard for her to read her notes, but she probably knew it well enough, and I was glad I hadn't bothered with a lamp. This music wasn't made for the light.

Her brow furrowed as she peered at the book, and her chest rose and fell like she was out of breath. Why did it look like playing this song was draining her? It was fucking beautiful. My heart thudded a little faster, even as I stood like a statue beside the piano.

She flipped the page and kept playing.

Who knew black and white keys could make something so evil and perfect? I pulled my mouth into a twisted smile. The song was so different from the other shit she'd tried to play. The piano chords were still vibrating with the last note of the song when I spoke. Curiosity overrode my intent to be patronizing. "What's that one called?"

Oksana had gone back to not looking at me. She stared vacantly at her hands still resting on the keys, acting like she was recovering from trauma. "It doesn't have a name."

"You should call it, like, The Villain or something." Shit, was I high? How good was the weed in that joint I'd smoked hours ago? "It sounds like a bad motherfucker's theme song."

She winced as if she'd swallowed broken glass.

"What?" I demanded.

She opened her mouth to say something, but words failed her for several heartbeats. "I've never played it for anyone."

Dark satisfaction bubbled in my veins. Another first I'd taken from her. Maybe it could be my theme song. "Play it again."

"You liked it?" Her voice was coated in horror.

I paced behind her and gathered her long hair in my hands, coiling it into a rope, and leaned down so my lips were beside the shell of her ear. "Again."

She shivered and reached forward, turning back to the previous page in the book.

When she started over, I trailed the tip of my nose up the long slope of her neck, following it with the edge of my tongue. She sipped air through her parted lips, and swallowed thickly. Was it hard for her to keep playing as I sucked on her neck? Her hands didn't falter when I sat beside her on the bench, facing the other direction. She'd focus on the music, while I focused on her.

"Don't stop," I said, placing a hand on the exposed skin of her heaving chest, and slipped my fingers beneath the edge of the robe. I explored further, watching her as my fingertips found and circled the hard knot of her nipple.

The song was darker this time. Unapologetic. Was it the practice or my distraction? I pushed the side of the robe open, baring her naked breast. The sight of me pinching her pink nipple and rolling it between my fingers gave me a surge of lust.

I wanted to fuck her. No, I *needed* to.

Right here on this bench.

chapter
EIGHT

WAIT, THE PRACTICAL SIDE OF ME FIRED BACK. Not yet. I'd been with Oksana five hours and already felt a strange pull. What if I got inside her, body and head, and didn't want to leave? I'd never let a girl have that kind of power.

She was panting for breath when I slid my hand up her inner thigh. Her frantic gaze darted to mine, just for a moment, before returning to the notes that climbed all over the lines in her book.

"Open your legs," I said over the music.

She whimpered as her perfect posture cracked. Her knees eased apart. I pressed my fingers against her pussy, feeling like I'd been doused with gasoline and set on fire.

"Fuck," I said, thrilled. "You're wet."

She murmured something in Russian, and I had no idea if she was cursing me or begging me to keep going. My fingertips grazed over her clit, but she kept on playing. Sheer concentration pushed her forward, and for someone who cared so much about her book, she carelessly turned the page now. Like the taped-together paper was indestructible.

Her moan mingled with the sinister melody, and I burned so fucking hot, I was feverish. Half out of my mind with delusions. Touching her this way wasn't enough, and as much as I liked her villainous song, I wanted to disrupt and control. When my hand was on her, she should be thinking about me and nothing else. Not even her music.

I jerked the other side of the robe open so I could see both of her sexy tits, and leaned over to kiss her shoulder. I moved my mouth across her collarbone, working lower while trying not to bump her arms. When she stopped playing, I wanted it to be her choice.

I locked my lips around her breast and pulled the nipple into my mouth, sucking hard. She sighed loudly. What kind of frustration was it? Annoyance as she tried to play? Or was she aching for more? I flicked my tongue over the velvety-soft skin, teasing the nub.

She made it so close to the end of her song, but I pressed my middle finger deep inside her, and Oksana seized up. Her music cut off abruptly.

"Oh my God," she groaned, her hands clenched in fists and balancing at the edge of the keys. Her gasp echoed in the vaulted ceiling of the room.

"Look at me," I growled. When she didn't instantly comply, I slammed my finger violently in and out where she grew wetter with each deep thrust. She choked on air as her body tensed from the intrusion, but it didn't slow me down. I hadn't heard any protest from her, either.

Her head was tipped down, but it swung my direction, and I could feel her gaze moving up my body like hands across my skin. Desire screwed tighter inside me as her gaze rose over my chest. It lingered on my lips before she finally gave up and looked at me.

I wanted control, but the second that happened, someone else took over. My lips slammed against hers. Was she as hungry as I was? It fucking seemed like it. Her mouth moved against mine. The slide of her tongue past my lips was cautious and curious, and I liked the sensation. She could practice on me. Use my body as her personal fuck playground while I did the same to her.

I withdrew my finger and clamped both hands on her waist, right where the belt barely kept the robe closed. I lifted, urging her to stand, and it broke the kiss before she seemed ready. I gestured for her to come around the bench to where I was sitting.

"Get in my lap."

I tugged the belt open, revealing her naked body beneath the robe that hung on her shoulders, and used the two ends to pull her close. She put one knee on the bench beside me, which was exactly how I wanted her, so I yanked down, causing her to straddle my leg. She gave out a yelp of surprise, and her wet pussy slammed against my bare skin. The contact made my dick twitch.

It was warm inside the robe as I slipped one hand onto her hip. I crushed the other onto her breast, and dragged my mouth up her neck. My breath bounced off her skin and warmed me, almost as much as the body wrapped around my leg, draped in my own robe.

I pushed and pulled her hip, back and forth, urging her to grind on me while I claimed her mouth in something that was too brutal to call a kiss. My tongue slashed at her, and I bit her lip, hard enough for her to moan with a hint of pain. But her hips moved, and as soon as her painful moan was done echoing in the room, it was followed by one of quiet enjoyment.

She rocked on my thigh, riding me slowly at first. One of her hands was on my shoulder to brace herself, and the other cuffed my wrist by her hip. Her expression was confusion. She hadn't expected rubbing on me to feel good, but it obviously did.

"Faster," I commanded with a dark tone. I watched her pussy lips glide over my skin, and flexed the muscles in my jaw. I wanted to film this. She looked like a porn star as she ground her clit against my leg, and pleasure burned in her eyes. Her undulating body beneath the open robe was insane.

"You're making a mess on my leg." I could hear the smile in my words. "Your pussy's soaking."

My dirty words made her shy. Her gaze dropped, and something in me snapped. I dug my fingers into her hip, pushing and pulling her at a vicious pace. My other hand wrapped around her throat. Not to strangle her, but I was sick of her breaking the connection. I wanted her full attention. "You look at me when I'm talking to you."

She couldn't hide from me, and the sooner she learned that, the better.

Oksana kept up with the furious pace I demanded, and rode my thigh, all while her crystal blue eyes stared back. Her breathing had gone ragged, probably as much from the friction against her clit as the exertion. Her pulse roared beneath my hand.

"That's it, virgin," I said. "You fuck my leg until you get yourself off."

Heat flashed in her eyes. She didn't want my command to turn her on, but it did, and she did a shitty job of disguising it. Her mouth was slack, and breathy moans escaped before she could stop them. The girl thrashed against me, wild and desperate. Had she crossed the point of no return? If I took my hand off her hip, would she keep riding me until she came?

"Oh," she moaned. "Oh my God."

"Yeah. Fuck, yeah."

It was crazy how much this turned me on. Not just hearing her, but watching the way she fought to find her release. I hadn't done humping bullshit in years. Once I started getting sex whenever I wanted, what was the point? If a girl didn't want to fuck, no big deal. I'd go find one who did.

I currently wasn't fucking Oksana with my cock. But I had my hand on her throat, making her fuck me, with her gaze locked on mine, and this shit was . . . *intense*. Her warm body smeared her desire all over my leg, and her sexy whimpers swelled. Her expression begged for more, although she probably didn't even know more of what.

When her eyes began to drift closed, I readjusted my grip on her throat. "No. Eyes on me when you come."

There was a tight sound of frustration, but then it was too late. I watched the surrender shudder through her body, and felt her legs tense and strain as the orgasm hit her. Her eyes barely stayed open as she tipped her head back and she cried out, but she looked at me through slitted eyelids as she convulsed with pleasure.

Next to my cock, making a woman come was my favorite thing. I dove my hands beneath the robe and around her back, pressing Oksana's warm skin against me as the ecstasy continued to make her shake. Her arms were draped over my shoulders, hanging on, and, fuck me, I liked the feeling. She was falling apart, and I was holding her together.

Her head lolled forward and suddenly she brought her lips to mine.

She was kissing *me*, not the other way around. I'd been the one to initiate every time before, and I didn't like her taking the lead.

She was Russian, and I didn't want her getting all attached. I also didn't know why I'd fucking kissed her so much tonight, but this shit stopped right now. I rose from the bench so fast, it sent her tumbling to the floor with a shriek.

My dick ached. It tented my underwear, straining against the cotton, and the air was cold on the damp spot on my leg. Oksana gawked up at me. Should I shove my dick in her open mouth and make her take care of it?

No. I knew exactly where it would lead.

"I'm going to bed," I announced. I needed to get the fuck away from her. I wanted her so badly and was so goddamn hard, if I stayed, I'd end up fucking her right on the Persian rug beside the piano. I could take care of myself and be asleep in the next five minutes, which was the better option. I had a ton of shit to do tomorrow, on top of my meeting in the morning with my uncle.

"Stay down here, or sleep in one of the guest rooms." My tone was cold and impersonal, like she hadn't just been trembling in my embrace thirty seconds ago. "And give me back my robe."

Her reaction was . . . unexpected.

Shock faded faster than a gunshot. The look she had said I was safe from her ever kissing me again. I didn't offer a hand to help her up, and I was sure she wouldn't have taken it if I had. She rose on her own. She was supposed to be nervous or bashful as she stripped, but those emotions were gone.

She held the robe out by the collar to me, and as I reached for it, she let go. It dropped to the floor like a waterfall of fabric and left me grasping for air. I flashed my annoyance at her, but her gaze lingered on my throbbing erection. She looked at it, and Jesus, she was smug. Like she'd somehow won a fucking battle. Had she? She'd gotten her rocks off, and I hadn't.

"Good night," she said. She grabbed her book from the piano and floated away up the stairs. I stared at her as she turned left at the top, heading the opposite direction from my room.

What the fuck just happened?

♪

My uncle rarely came into my dealership. He managed the larger one that was right off the freeway. It was newer, better, and legit. All of the drugs and guns ran through the luxury used vehicle dealership my father had managed until I inherited it. It was only thirty miles to Indiana, where most of the guns came from, and the back roads leading to it didn't have cameras like the freeway exits.

Goran Markovic was smart, and because the FBI was always up our ass, he liked to keep his distance from the more lucrative business he ran. He sat in one of the chairs opposite my desk, and Filip took the other.

"How are things?" My uncle's tone was generic, and he looked at the screen of his phone as he asked it.

"I finally sold that Bentley," I said. It'd been in inventory for months.

"To that guy who test drove it six fucking times?"

"No, some older guy who lives in Iowa. Him and the wife drove in to get it." I watched Eric at the back of my office as he swept the portable reader over the picture frames on the wall. "That local guy was an asshole when he came in and discovered it was gone. He said I should have called him to tell him I was about to sell it."

Goran raised his eyebrow up into a sharp point. "What does he think we do here?"

I nodded in agreement. The son of a bitch thought he had, like, dibs on the car just because he'd test driven it a bunch of times. It was fucking ridiculous. "He only liked the idea of buying it. He was never going to commit."

Eric finished his sweep of the wall and moved on to the vents. It was pointless because I could see the dust still in the slats, meaning it hadn't been touched, but maybe the FBI had stepped up their game. Security was the top priority at Markovic Motors after a listening bug had been discovered in the break room of the main dealership two years ago.

We'd never learned if it was the Russians or the Feds who'd planted it. My suspicion was the government, since my cousin had been busted right before that.

Eric climbed down from the chair and turned the scanner off. "You're good," he said.

"Thank you." Goran dismissed him.

The satisfied look evaporated from my uncle's face as soon as the door shut. "The meet and greet was a setup in the texts we've been following."

So, that confirmed it. The Russians had planned an ambush. "You sure?"

Filip nodded. "They haven't used those cellphone numbers since."

"Jesus." Last night could have been a huge mess. I glared at my uncle. "What the fuck would have happened if we'd showed up ten minutes later?"

He stared at me the same he would an insect he'd squashed with his shoe. "Lucky for us, your father taught you some sense, and you and Filip were smart enough to see what was at play."

I stared at him critically, and he returned the look. Neither of us liked the other, but you couldn't pick your family, and we were stuck with each other. For now. My uncle smoothed a hand down his tie, and he looked around the office like he owned every inch. It was fine, I told myself. Let him think he owned me, in addition to this dealership. He'd never see my knife when it finally came for him.

Would I look like my uncle when I got older? Goran was fifty-six, but he'd aged well and stayed in good shape. He got plenty of cardio in, judging by the steady stream of whores in rotation. Pancreatic cancer had taken my aunt from him ten years ago, and he'd never remarried. Her death had given my uncle some gray hair and lines around his eyes, but if anything, it made him more intimidating, because it was proof the monster was real.

His eyes were as black as the barrel of my Glock, and men withered under his glare the same as my gun.

My uncle was right. I was smart enough to see what was coming. Did he?

"Without any new shipments to take from," he said, "it's going to squeeze that side of the business for the next few months."

It was out before I thought better of it. "Fine with me. I hate running the girls."

The Markovic hereditary trait was our pointed eyebrow. It arrowed up whenever someone pissed us off. My uncle's rose now. "Do you, Vasilije? And here I was, thinking you liked making money." He leaned forward and his dark eyes drilled into me. "You hate them so much, then why'd you bring one home?"

I faked indifference. "It was nothing. I promised a girl to Alek."

Shit. There was a flicker in his eyes. *Gotcha*, it said. Fuck, I'd stepped into a trap. My uncle was like fucking God sometimes. All seeing, all powerful. There was a possessive tug in my chest over Oksana. I didn't want her on his radar.

"What'd he do with her, then?" he demanded. "Mira said Aleksandar came by her place last night." His expression was hard as stone. "I don't like loose ends."

"No loose ends. I have the girl." I held up my phone. "Don't worry. If she so much as fucking sneezes, I'll hear about it."

His dark eyes went wide with outrage. "You *have* the girl? What the fuck? Get rid of her."

"I'll send her on to Mira when I'm done with—"

"*Get rid of her.*"

His words stopped me cold. This was an order, and disobeying it would be really fucking stupid. It was the right thing to do.

I leveled my cool gaze at him. "All right."

chapter
NINE

Oksana

It should have been hard to sleep in a strange bed under a Markovic roof, but staying alert around Vasilije was exhausting. I'd picked a luxurious looking guest bedroom with green-striped wallpaper, burrowed under the covers of the bed, and when I blinked, morning sunlight streamed from the window.

The house was quiet.

I grabbed a towel from the attached bathroom, wrapped it around my bare body, and made my way down the stairs. Vasilije had dropped my overnight bag in the closet by the garage when we came in last night, and I hoped it was still there.

I let out a deep sigh of relief when I spotted it, and gripped the strap with eager hands. I'd take every tiny victory I could, since I suspected my time with him would only get more difficult as it went on. *If* it went on. I ducked into the hallway bathroom and dressed as quickly as possible.

Even though the clothes weren't actually mine, the off-brand pair of jeans and thin camel-colored sweater made me feel like myself. The woman I'd been while wearing Vasilije's robe last night scared the hell out of me. I could tell myself I was only playing a role, but if that were true, why the fuck had any part of me . . . enjoyed it?

There was a simple note left on the table in the kitchen, scrawled in messy male handwriting, telling me to shower, eat breakfast, and be dressed to leave by noon. He wasn't kicking me out. He had other plans for me, and I wasn't sure whether to feel relief or trepidation.

NIKKI SLOANE

Not that I had time for either. It was already after nine, according to the clock on the security system display. There seemed to be one in every room of the house.

I rummaged through the pantry for something quick, and was surprised to find he had actual food in his house. He was twenty-four. I'd expected frozen dinners and beer to be the only staples he lived on. But he had fresh fruit. Bread. Even eggs and milk. I stared at the stocked fridge and tried to picture the mobster making out his grocery shopping list.

My stomach gurgled. I was starving. I had barely eaten yesterday, and wasn't sure when my next meal would come, so I cooked up a few eggs and scarfed them down. I drank a huge glass of orange juice and ate two slices of toast while I stood by the sink, gazing out the window at the golf course.

I kept my mind empty.

Thinking about what I needed to do not only brought anxiety, but analysis of what had happened at the piano, and I wasn't ready to go there. *Do whatever you need to do, to get the job done, Oksana. Sacrifices will have to be made.*

I scrubbed the dishes clean and put everything back just as I'd found it, then hurried upstairs to the green wallpapered room. There was generic shampoo and conditioner already in the shower there, which didn't have a masculine fragrance like the stuff in Vasilije's, as well as a hairdryer beneath the sink.

When I was showered and dressed, it left me ninety minutes to investigate and try to get to know him better. Less time, really. He was unpredictable and could show up without warning. I swallowed a breath as I stared at the door to his room, and scowled when I went inside and took in the unmade bed. A flash of dark, unwanted pleasure coasted through my body. He'd brought me to orgasm on that mattress with his head between my legs.

His gun and holster were gone. Did he always wear it, even at the dealership? How many used car salesmen were packing there?

The drawers contained clothes and nothing else. I surveyed the closet next, but there were only suits hanging on one side and casual clothes on the other. No safe. No backup guns. Nothing of interest, so my focus shifted to the office downstairs.

I had to be careful while digging around, though. The security system was sophisticated, and I couldn't tell if it had surveillance cameras attached to it. I plopped down on the chair behind the desk and moved the mouse, waking the computer up. A login screen appeared, giving me the out I needed to search the drawers. If there was footage, it'd look as if I were searching for a password.

I knew I'd never find one. Vasilije wasn't dumb enough to leave it around, but maybe there'd be something of interest in the desk—

There was a Smith and Wesson 9mm in the bottom drawer.

My gaze etched over every inch of the black metal. Should I swipe it and tuck the gun somewhere else? Not to use it on Vasilije, but to buy me time if he ever went for it to use it on me? I was usually so decisive, but my muscles locked up with indecision. What would happen if he checked on the gun and discovered it missing? He clearly thought I'd use a gun on him last night.

There was a quiet mechanical hum on the other side of the house—the garage door going up— which made the decision for me. I slammed the drawer shut and bolted for the piano out in the living room. I plunked my fingers on the keys and tinkered out an old recital piece I'd practiced so many times I was sure I'd forget my name before I forgot how to play it.

There was the sound of hard soles meeting wood as his footsteps approached. I couldn't see him, even in my peripheral vision, but I tensed under Vasilije's scrutiny. I shivered as he came close, and the temperature in the room plummeted.

"Time to go," he said.

My mouth went dry when I turned and set my attention on

him. The devil wore a navy suit, a white dress shirt, and a burgundy tie with the knot loosened at his neck. His dark eyes studied me like I was dangerous. Wasn't he the one who was armed? The tailored jacket hung beautifully, and I couldn't see the outline of his gun beneath his arm, but I felt its presence regardless.

"Hello," I said, steeling my voice as I rose from the piano. When he didn't offer any greeting, I was forced to continue. "Where are we going?"

His eyes swept over my body, and he didn't hide his disdain. "Shopping. You need clothes."

I wanted to point out I was wearing clothes, but then he might demand I take them off, so, as I'd done last night, I bit the inside of my cheek and stayed silent.

We didn't speak to each other as I put my shoes on and followed him into the garage. There was a white Porsche parked close, and he made it clear this was the car we were taking when he opened the driver's door.

I sat in the passenger seat, buckled myself in, and the air went thin as Vasilije started the car. It purred to life. Even though it wasn't warm, I set my sweaty palms on my thighs and tried to act unaffected. The interior of the sports car was dark, the space compact, and it felt like I was intimately trapped with him. He seemed oblivious to the tension between us that was stretched as taut as piano wire.

I should have gazed at my surroundings and pretended to be fascinated with the new-to-me American landscape as he drove, but instead I studied him. He hung the palm of his left hand casually on the top of the steering wheel while his right hand gripped the gear shift. The car was an automatic, but the relaxed posture made me think he'd be comfortable driving a manual. He probably had to be, given his job.

"Where did you go this morning?" I asked. "Work?"

He made a grunt of confirmation. I wasn't worth the effort to actually speak to today.

"What do you do?"

"I own a car dealership."

His fingers moved to the radio controls on the steering wheel and the rap song grew loud. Too loud to hold a conversation. It was fine with me. I'd rather listen to music anyway, even if it was a repetitive loop of a simple melody, more computer than voice or instrument.

The song ended and another replaced it. I deconstructed the tracks in my head, picking out what worked and what didn't. On and on the songs went as we drove on the expressway, flying through the I-PASS toll. The longer we drove, the more worried I became. He wasn't talking. Yesterday he'd been demanding and curious, but today he seemed to have zero interest in me.

My heart picked up and anxiety spiked in my bloodstream. Had he gotten bored with me already? Was he going to send me on my way . . . or worse? I curled my fingers inward, digging my nails into my thighs. I had to do something. I couldn't let him cast me aside, and I definitely wasn't going to let him drive me somewhere secluded so he could put a bullet in my head and dump my body.

"What the fuck are you doing?" Vasilije's harsh voice was loud over the angry rap spewing from the speakers.

I'd put my hand on his leg, high up on his thigh and an inch from his crotch. My lungs squeezed tight, making it impossible to breathe. "I don't know," I answered. Truer words had never been uttered. Sex was the only weapon I had access to right now. Too bad I wasn't sure exactly how to wield it.

The radio turned down to almost nothing. His voice was patronizing. "The little virgin got a taste of my cock and now she wants more?"

I swallowed a thick lump in my throat.

He took his eyes off the road for a moment to glance at me, and took in the hesitant look on my face. I'd been trying to be bold, but all my courage vanished. He flashed a knowing smile. "I'll let you blow me later. Just not when I'm driving a car I need to sell for seventy grand."

He put his cold hand on mine and pushed it away. I felt flushed. Shouldn't I have been relieved he'd rejected my poor attempt at seduction?

Faire Avenue was a high-end department store attached to one of end of a sprawling mall. Vasilije parked in the garage and said nothing as he got out of the car. He expected me to follow him like a servant, and I had no choice but to do it.

We had to be an odd match as we walked through the set of double doors. I wore clothes purchased from Goodwill, which probably hadn't cost much when they'd been new. He was wearing his suit with fancy shoes and accessorized with an expensive watch. It was basically male jewelry, because as we entered the store, he pulled his phone out and checked the screen.

"Are we on a schedule?" My voice was devoid of any emotion.

"We have an appointment." He pointed two fingers down the aisle, gesturing to the escalator up.

Overloaded Christmas trees decorated the intersections of the main flow areas, and glistening snowflakes hung from the ceiling. The holiday shopping season was already in full swing since Thanksgiving was later this week. The opulent displays made it easy for me to exaggerate my gawking at American culture.

When I stepped onto the escalator, Vasilije moved right behind me and climbed up onto my step, invading my space. A shudder thundered through me as he placed his hand in the small of my back. It wasn't a sweet gesture. This was about control.

He pressed me forward to the counter where two women were working. They both looked up at us at the same moment, and the conversation between them halted.

"We have an appointment with Daphne," he announced.

The younger of the two women, who was probably in her thirties, nodded her head of corkscrew tight curls and gave him a bright smile. "That's me. Mr. Markovic?" She stepped around the counter. "It's nice to meet you." They shook hands, and then she turned toward me, her hand offered. "I'm Daphne."

I acted on pure habit. "Oksana."

"Oksana," she repeated, and her eyes lit up. "That's so pretty."

Her gaze evaluated me from top to bottom, probably for sizing, and then it floated to him, evaluating for budget. If she was concerned about how young he looked, it didn't show. The ease in which he wore his tailored suit wasn't lost on her. He reeked of money and oozed confidence.

Daphne motioned toward the back of the store. "The fitting rooms are this way. I pulled a few pieces we can start with, and build from there." She talked as we moved. "Your boyfriend tells me you need to expand your wardrobe. Are there any pieces you'd like to see, or colors I should steer clear off?"

My *what*? I fired a stunned look at Vasilije, but he was tapping something out on his phone, texting while he walked and ignoring everything around him. I knew she was waiting on an answer, but my brain struggled to find one. "Uh . . . I don't look good in yellow."

Or as Vasilije Markovic's girlfriend.

When we reached the antechamber of the fitting rooms, he plopped down on the couch beside the three-panel full length mirror, never looking up from his screen.

Daphne grabbed a rolling rack with one manicured hand and pulled it toward the first dressing room, then unlocked the door and ushered me inside. She pulled several hangers down and hung them on the hook closest to the door. "Let's start with a few staple pieces."

She searched through the pairs of black pants until she found the size she was looking for and took them off the hanger, passing them to me.

"Try these, and pick one of the tops you like from the collection." She motioned to the other hooks around the room. "Anything you don't like goes here. Pieces that make the cut go here. If you need different sizes or styles, let me know and I'll be happy to pull them for you."

She flashed me a final smile, one that said I was a lucky bitch, right before she pulled the door closed behind her. I stared down at the pants I was clutching. The price tag said they were almost two hundred dollars.

As I changed, I could hear Daphne making small talk with Vasilije, and a sinking feeling came over me. There wasn't a mirror in this dressing room, and they were both waiting for me to come out and stand before them. Of course he'd want to inspect his purchases.

I hadn't fucked him yet, and already I was his whore.

chapter
TEN

THE NEXT HOUR OF TRYING ON CLOTHES reduced me to a doll for Daphne to dress up, and I was paraded in front of Vasilije as he scrutinized not just the clothes, but the way they looked on my body. Every time I came out of the dressing room, his gaze grew heavier, weighing me down until it was hard to move.

At one point, he sent Daphne off in search of a dress. "Something she can wear to meet my family," he said. It sent an icy chill crawling along my skin. The only family he had around to meet was Goran Markovic.

As soon as she was out of earshot, I turned away from the mirror and focused on him. "Why are you doing this?"

His dark eyes tightened on me, although he faked confusion. "Doing what?"

"Buying clothes for me. Saying you're going to introduce me to your family."

His smile peeled back and his dimple came out in full effect. "Because my uncle gave me an order this morning to get rid of you, and it'll piss him off."

Oh, shit. My mouth went slack, but Vasilije just laughed and waved my terror away, like it was no big deal the head of the Serbian mafia in south Chicago had ordered my death.

"I'm going to have fun fucking you, Oksana." His tone was low, but turned smug as he kept talking. "And probably a lot of fun fucking with him."

I turned away to hide my eyes, but it was pointless. Vasilije could see all three angles of my nervous expression in the mirror. I was a pawn in the game he was playing. Easy to move and sacrifice. Goran might be pissed at Vasilije, but who would be the most likely target of his uncle's anger?

I searched deep inside myself for the revenge that burned and fanned the flames. I wasn't a pawn. I was a motherfucking queen, the most powerful player on the board. Vasilije would be my pawn. A piece I'd move to get exactly what I wanted.

My nerves drained away. "If you're so eager to fuck me, why haven't you?"

He didn't look like a pawn when he grinned at me through the mirror. He looked like the devil again. "I like watching you squirm." The matter-of-fact tone dug in. He came off the couch and his hands slithered around my waist, pulling me back against him. Our gazes were locked on each other through the glass. "I'm enjoying taking you apart."

"You're not."

He pushed a lock of my hair out of his way and brushed the tip of his nose against the edge of my ear. "I'm not?"

"You can do whatever you want. It's just sex. It doesn't mean anything or give you power over me."

A thrilled smile spread on his lips like fingers sliding across piano keys in a glissando. "Spoken like a true virgin. Sex is all about power. And . . . whatever I want?"

That was what he'd focused on, and his words made my stomach bottom out. I clawed mentally to regain the ground I'd just given up. "It won't make a difference. I don't care."

He snorted. "Bullshit."

I watched his lips part, and the tip of his tongue peeked out, tracing a line on the curve of my neck. I shivered against his mouth. "I don't have feelings."

The body fitted against mine . . . had he just flinched? It was so subtle, I wasn't sure if I'd imagined it. "Right. Those weren't tears last night when pages got torn in your precious book."

I'd been overwhelmed physically, that was all. "I was exhausted. It wasn't an emotional thing, because it couldn't be. I don't have emotions."

There was no question of his pause this time, but he recovered quickly. "Nice try. I don't believe you for one fucking second. You're afraid of me."

"I feel fear," I amended. "I can get angry. But guilt? Shame? Empathy? No. I don't see the point."

"You don't see the point?" He looked amused. "What about happiness?" He threw the question in my face as a challenge. "What about *love*?"

"Love is for people with hearts. It's a weakness I, thankfully, do not have."

Who would have thought Oksana Kuznetsov could shock the devil? His mouth hung open, and the hands on my hips turned to stone. It was then Daphne reappeared with a fitted, black and white print dress. She lingered at the doorway with a slight smile. She thought she'd caught us in a quiet lovers' moment.

I strangled back a bitter laugh at the idea of us as lovers.

Vasilije separated from me and returned to his spot on the couch, his tone authoritarian as she handed me the hanger. "Oksana needs some things to go under that dress."

Daphne didn't bat an eye at his request for lingerie. "Absolutely. Would you like to help me select those pieces?"

"No, you know what you're doing. I want something white, though." His gaze slid from her to me, and it heated me to my core even when I didn't want it to. "Virginal, but sexy."

He was testing me.

He expected my face to turn bright red. He watched for me to display some sign of embarrassment, but I wouldn't. Yes, I was curious about sex and ready to experience it, but being a virgin wasn't a stigma. I broke his gaze and turned to her, delivering my comment flatly. "Like something for a wedding night."

Out of the corner of my eye, I saw Vasilije straighten, and I bit down on my cheek this time to stop my victorious smile. He didn't care for my analogy.

Daphne's perfect saleswoman persona cracked and an odd look flickered through her, then was gone. She nodded slowly. "I'll be right back."

I changed, letting the silky lining on the inside of the dress glide over my skin, and I zipped up. I stepped into the pair of black heels that once I'd determined were the right size, Vasilije had added to the list of things we'd purchase. The dress clung to my body, and even without a mirror, I knew I'd like the way it looked on.

Vasilije's eyes grew darker and hungrier as I stepped out of the room. His expression was raw and sexual, and every nerve ending in my body sounded an alarm. *This is what you want*, I reminded myself. I forced myself to keep my chin up as I strode to the mirror.

It was a simple thing, but cut just so. The black and white pattern gave me a figure. Somehow, I had curves in this dress, which fit like a glove. It ended just above my knees, which was the only disappointment. I wished it could block his view of how they were trembling.

Vasilije rose from his seat, and his expression screamed of desire and lust.

"Daphne's good," I whispered.

It got to be too much and I couldn't hold his intense gaze in the mirror. I stared at my feet, clad in the black pumps, as he approached. He swept my hair over my shoulder, and then grasped the back of the dress. I sucked in a breath.

He zipped me the rest of the way up.

I hadn't realized I'd stopped before the zipper reached the top. This man made me feel vulnerable and undressed, yet I wasn't sure how much I actually disliked that. His cold fingers did the catch at the top of the zipper. His accidental touch licked against my skin, and I jumped as if he'd burned me.

"I'm going to keep touching you," he threatened on a whisper, "until you get used to it."

What if that never happened? Was he sentencing me to a lifetime of his hands on my body? The thought was scalding, melting me from the inside.

Daphne appeared with several bras and panties attached to hangers, but she pulled to a stop as she saw me. "I'd swear that dress was made for you."

"Yeah," he said. "It's perfect."

The selection of lingerie was deposited in my fitting room, but as I moved to the door, his hand on my shoulder stopped me. "I'll come in and help you with that zipper."

His low words were meant only for me, and the air shifted, swirling around us. It charged the space with tension. Daphne exited the fitting room and looked surprised to find him standing beside me, right outside the doorway.

"Could you start ringing us up?" His voice was warm and persuasive. "There's nineteen hundred dollars' worth of clothes here, so it'll take a while." He gave her a pointed look. "I was thinking at least twenty minutes."

Her eyes widened and she glanced around, nervous. But Vasilije's carefully worded statement made it impossible for her to refuse him. She obviously worked on commission, and it was probably more than she'd ever made off a single client. She wanted to give her customer anything, even if that meant fucking around in a dressing room.

"Of course." She choked as if realizing how strange it sounded only as she was saying it, "Take all the time you need."

The fitting room was spacious until he stepped in behind me

and shut the door, closing us in together. There was the sound of Daphne collecting the clothes, and her footsteps faded away. I splayed my hands on the skirt of my dress and watched him with cautious eyes. What was he planning? Would he take my virginity right here in a Faire Avenue fitting room?

No. He was cruel, but this wasn't his style. And why would he buy me *virginal* lingerie if I wasn't going to be a virgin anymore?

With a rough hand, I was turned away from him and the zipper was drawn down to the base of my spine. We moved like a trained team, working toward a mutual goal. I slipped out of the dress and handed it to him to hang up, then went to the hangers of white mesh and lace. When I focused on the task of picking the right size, it allowed me to pretend this was fine.

I kept my back to him as I undid my cotton bra and put on the one that revealed more than it concealed. The cups were cut low, and carefully placed lace over the see-through mesh just covered my nipples.

"I don't need to try on the underwear," I said, when he pulled a pair from the hanger clips. "I'm sure it fits."

"Great." He seemed unable to look away from my breasts packaged in the flimsy, sexy bra, but his hand darted inside his interior suitcoat pocket. A small knife was retrieved, the blade flipped out, and he cut the price tags free. As soon as the knife was put away, the underwear was shoved at me. "Put it on."

I turned away from him once more, and was grateful there wasn't a mirror. The simple gray cotton underwear I had on was tugged down and kicked off. I stepped into the white lace, being careful of the heels I was still wearing, and pulled the fabric up onto my hips.

Like the bra, the bikini panties only had lace where it hid the naughtiest part, teasing elsewhere with the nearly translucent mesh. I shuffled on my feet, turning to face him.

"*Puši kurac,*" he uttered under his breath.

I had no idea what his Serbian meant, but the delivery sounded appreciative, and his eyes hooded. He advanced on me, his cold fingers sliding onto the bands of fabric at my hips, and he walked us backward until my back collided with the corner of the dressing room in a hollow thud.

Blood rushed in my ears and my nipples tightened. I was cold, that was all. They weren't tingling, or aching for attention against the cups of the bra. Because they couldn't be. I certainly didn't crave this boy's icy touch, or his angry, punishing kiss on my lips.

But when he gave me both, relief stormed through me, and invited crushing need to come along and play. Vasilije's kiss forced my lips open and he pushed his tongue inside my mouth, claiming ownership. Like my mouth was his fucking mouth and he'd stay as long as he goddamn pleased.

His fingers trailed over the lace on the bra. His fingernails raked over my distended nipple, and I shuddered with a sensation that was too close to pleasure to label as anything else. Unfamiliar lust pooled in my body, flowing to the center of my legs.

His touch was gone, as were his lips. He worked to undo his belt and his pants, and hurried to get his dick out. My pulse thundered along as he stroked his fist down his rapidly hardening length.

"Lick your hands," he said.

Watching him move on himself was hypnotizing, and I blinked through my haze. "What?"

"Or spit on them, I don't care." His expression was intense. "Get them wet and jerk me off."

His hands came off his dick, and he placed them on the wall on either side, trapping me in the corner as he pushed his hips forward. His underwear was pushed down so it cut across his thighs, and his hard, long cock jutted out.

His tone was sinister. "This is what you wanted when we were in the Porsche."

His dark eyes pinned mine in a challenge. I held his gaze as I opened my mouth and dragged one palm slowly down the length of my tongue. His eyes and nostrils flared when I gripped him with the wet hand, and repeated the same action with my other, slicking my palm over my tongue.

He was hard steel and soft skin. I barely had my other hand wrapped around him before he began to rock against my grip. He pumped and pushed the thick head of his cock through my clenched fists, and I watched with fascination as the pleasure rolled through him.

Vasilije had me literally cornered, but his hands weren't on me. His eyes drifted shut and his face twisted with enjoyment, so the only place we were connected was where I was touching him. Had he done it on purpose? I had hardly any clothes on, but with his pants down and his dick in my hands, he was more vulnerable than I was.

My hands began to dry, so I pulled one off and repeated the lick, rewetting my palm. He groaned in satisfaction and his eyes snapped open. He hinted at a smile as he watched me do the other. He more than approved.

I had no idea what I was doing, but *wanted* to. The better I was, the more likely he'd be to keep me around. So instead of holding still and letting him fuck my hands, I began to move on him. I stroked my hands together, sliding from tip to base and back again. Faster. Harder. I listened to how his breathing picked up and watched the muscles flex over his jawline as I worked him.

Once I'd crossed the border out of my comfort zone, I was in a lawless, wild place. I could do whatever I wanted. Totally free of judgement, rules, or consequences.

Vasilije's left hand came swiftly off the wall and he hooked a finger on my bra strap, tugging it down my shoulder until my breast was free. He captured my nipple between his thumb and forefinger, and clamped down. It grew hot and achy. The pinch was biting, and sharp pain shot up from his twisting grip, so intense it stole my breath.

"That hurts," I hissed, and tried to get away, but he had me wedged in the corner.

"Get used to the pain, baby. It's going to hurt when I fuck you."

I let go of him and slapped my palms against the walls, wanting to push off, but he didn't relent. The pain was acute. I was about to cry out when his grip abruptly shifted, releasing my nipple so he could cup my breast.

The sudden absence of pain was . . . interesting. The lingering sting on my skin was almost enjoyable. I sucked in air through my clenched teeth and stared back at Vasilije's bottomless eyes. I'd been watching his response when my hands were on him, and now he did the same to me.

"Pull the front of your panties down," he ordered. "Show me your pussy."

I leaned against the wall for support, hooked my fingers in the front of my brand new forty dollar panties, and stretched the elastic down. Although, they were his, weren't they?

"Oh, Oksana," he groaned. "So fucking wet. Your pussy's weeping for me." His right hand squealed as he slid it down the wall, and then he shoved it right between my legs. He ran his fingers through my arousal, and my knees went weak. I couldn't help the quiet moan he pulled from me.

His touch was *shocking*.

It felt good. It burned in all sorts of wrong and amazing ways. Another moan bubbled up and was about to break free when he withdrew and pumped his fist, wet from my desire, on his dick.

"Stay like that," he said in a rush.

His grip on my breast tightened, and his thumb brushed over

my traumatized nipple, bringing on a fresh wave of sensation. I was a deviant, braced against the wall in heels and expensive lingerie, one side of my bra off and holding my panties down while he jerked off furiously.

The tempo of his breathing changed abruptly, and he leaned in so the tip of his dick brushed against my clit. I gasped at the jolt of pleasure, but it was covered by his louder rasps for breath. His fist sliding along him was erratic and desperate, and suddenly he was coming. Warm, thick liquid struck me, spurt after spurt as his shoulders shook violently. His cum coated my slit and dripped onto the crotch of my panties.

I trembled so hard, I was vibrating against the walls.

Both of our gazes were pointed down, watching as his fist slowed to a stop, and the last jet of cum was squeezed out onto the fabric meant to cover the most intimate part of me. It was dirty. So erotic, I stared in disbelief at what he'd done. What *we'd* done.

Shouldn't I have felt something like revulsion? Disgust that he was degrading me?

I didn't. I only felt dizzy and out of breath. There was a throbbing in my body, clambering for a release of tension.

Vasilije straightened, and his cold hands clasped on mine, pulling them away from the waist of my panties. They snapped into place and clung to where he'd painted me. I gasped, but he threaded his fingers through mine and pinned the backs of my hands to the walls.

He gazed at me with pure arrogance lighting his eyes. He surveyed me like land he'd just conquered, and he claimed my mouth as his reward. His kiss was just like him. Aggressive. Dominating.

He pulled back so he was only a breath away, and his eyes were unfocused before he blinked the haze away. Had kissing me been the cause? His expression turned sly. "Get dressed, but those cum-filled panties stay where they are."

A new shudder rocked my body, laced with unexpected

satisfaction. I had the terrible feeling he was right. Sex was all about power, and if it wasn't already, soon it'd all be his.

chapter
ELEVEN

Vasilije

I ordered Oksana to stand still while I cut the tag off the back of the bra, and then watched her get dressed in the shitty clothes she'd been wearing when I'd picked her up from the house. She moved gingerly, and I liked it. I loved the idea of her pussy sticky with my cum, reminding her every time she moved who she belonged to.

Shit, I couldn't wait to fuck her, but lording the upcoming event over her was satisfying. I'd gotten her all keyed up, shot a load in her panties, and left her hanging. If she was a good girl, tonight I'd give her an orgasm or two, but that all depended on her.

I didn't owe her shit. I was about to drop two grand, so she could suck my cock for a month and we still wouldn't be square. Although, she hadn't asked for the clothes. She hadn't really asked for anything.

We got the last of the clothes together and I added to the pile Daphne was scanning at the register. I tossed down the two price tags from the bra and underwear on the counter. "She's wearing them," I announced.

And they're drenched with my cum, I wanted to add, but Daphne didn't strike me as the type who'd appreciate the detail. I'd thought about flirting with her for a half-second to see what kind of response Oksana had, but decided it was a bad idea. The saleswoman seemed too professional.

The Russian girl said she had no emotions, other than fear and anger. What about jealousy? Seemed to be the only emotion I felt these days.

I swiped my credit card and signed the electronic tablet, and glanced at Oksana while Daphne finished bagging everything up. My 'girlfriend' stared at the counter, looking shell-shocked. Or maybe she was just starving and tired. It was after two o'clock, and I had no idea if she'd acclimated to the time-change.

"Can you hang onto those for us while we grab lunch?" I asked Daphne, although I didn't use a questioning tone. With the money I'd just spent, anything other than a 'yes, sir' would be unacceptable.

"Absolutely. I'll put your bags in my manager's office. If I'm not available, just let anyone know and we'll get them for you right away."

"Great, thanks." I turned on my heel and headed for the escalator. Without a word, Oksana followed. She was so obedient, it was unreal. I didn't ask her where she wanted to eat lunch, or if she even wanted food. I was hungry, so we'd eat.

I thought this was awesome. There was no guesswork involved, and all decisions were mine. If I wanted to drag her ass into the disgusting Hooters at the other end of the mall, I could, and I bet she wouldn't say a goddamn word.

Instead I chose a burger joint nearby, where the walls dripped with obnoxious fifties diner décor, and when we were tucked into a booth, she stared at the menu like it was written in a foreign language. *Oh, shit.* Maybe it was for her. I'd left that note for her this morning, but she might not have been able to read it.

"Can you read English?"

Her blue eyes snapped to mine. "Yes. There are . . . a lot of options."

"Yeah, welcome to America. That's how we do it here." I set my phone down on the table so I'd see any notifications if they rolled through. "Get the Bacon Bleu Burger. It's good."

My casual comment hung awkwardly.

Okay. I hadn't thought this through. Sitting casually across from her at the restaurant felt suddenly like a date, and the odd look on her face made me wonder if she had the same thought. I needed to establish my dominance since we were in a new environment.

I dropped my menu and leaned over the table, keeping my voice quiet. "Tell me. Are those cum-soaked panties sticking to your pussy right now?"

Oksana blinked slowly. "Yes," she said, her tone plain. Maybe she'd been telling the truth about not feeling shame. The idea of it excited me.

After I'd ordered our lunch and the server disappeared in the back, I narrowed my gaze on Oksana's shoulders. She was stiff. Was her perfect posture from years of playing piano, or her unease around me? We needed to fill the silence with conversation because there was a kid a few tables over who was banging his fork on the tabletop, and if he didn't stop soon I was going to rip it out of his hands and stab his mother in the eye with it. "How long have you been playing piano?"

The question caught her off guard. "Since I was eight."

The *tap-tap-tap* of the fork grew louder. "And writing songs? When did you start doing that?"

"A few years ago."

I gnashed my teeth. Couldn't she help me out and give me an answer longer than four fucking words?

She drew in a hesitant breath. More was coming, but she wasn't sure if she should reveal it. "I studied to be a composer."

I couldn't wrap my head around it. "Like, Beethoven and shit?"

"Yeah."

Fuck me, the kid discovered the sound his fork made against his mother's water glass and began to beat the shit out of it. Beneath the table, I balled my hands into fists. "Tell me about the song last night."

Oksana could not only feel fear, she could experience panic. I already knew this, but I watched her eyes grow wide and color drain from her face. "I'd rather not."

"Why?" I demanded.

"Because it's private," she snapped.

"Wrong fucking answer, because now I want to know everything," I fired back. "And do I look like a guy who always gets what he wants?"

Her eyes went to slits. "Yes."

Smart girl. "I'll get it out of you one way or another, so do yourself a favor and tell me now." I leaned back in my seat and crossed my arms, barely noticing the kid anymore. "Or don't. That makes it more fun for me."

Oksana's gaze fell. "Usually when I compose, it's structured. I have a formula I follow and things I want to say with each bar I plot out. My decisions are—" she searched for the right words, "—carefully considered."

"Manufactured," I corrected. It explained why I hated the first two songs she'd attempted.

"The one last night, when I wrote it, it poured out of me. I heard the whole thing in my head before I put it on paper."

"Why was that one different?"

She knew the answer and didn't like it. She definitely didn't want to say it out loud. Her gaze darted from side to side, checking to see if anyone was listening. "Because I did something awful, and at the time, that song was my way of coping with it."

I sat upright. "Wait a minute. The song . . . is about you?" The bad motherfucker's theme was Oksana's? I couldn't believe it. "What did you do that was so awful? Kick a puppy?"

She leveled a gaze at me. "I killed someone."

The kid could have been banging a million forks against glass and I wouldn't have heard a single tap. The conviction in her was absolute. I'd had a guy brag to me once about a kill he couldn't take credit for, and knew instantly he was lying. There's a look you get when you've ended someone else's life, and it's a hard fucking one to fake.

She'd *really* done it.

Christ, Oksana was becoming more like me with every breath she took.

"Who?" I asked, interested. "How?"

She threaded her fingers through her long blonde hair, considering if she should answer. "The man who touched me when I didn't want him to." Her perfect posture wasn't quite so perfect now. "With my father's gun."

I don't know why I cared, but I did. Satisfaction rolled through me to know the guy who'd laid hands on her was no longer in this world. That she'd been the one to send him off? Even better. My chest expanded as I took a breath. "Gotta say, you are full of surprises."

She looked pensive as she reached for her glass of water. I'd press for details later, where conversations about murder wouldn't be considered inappropriate. She drank, and as I watched the delicate bob of her throat, all I could think about was last night when I'd had my cock shoved halfway down it. It was miracle she was still a virgin. I couldn't go two minutes with her and not think about sex.

We lapsed into silence, and our food came shortly after.

She picked up her steak knife, and as she cut the burger in half, I made a mental note to check the knives in the kitchen when I got home. I didn't believe she'd try to kill me, but better safe than sorry, and she'd confessed she'd done it before. The first one was the hardest. I found it much easier to kill after that.

"You don't seem like you're in a rush to get back to work," she said.

"I work half-days on Mondays."

She looked less than thrilled when she realized I'd be around the rest of the day, but had no comment.

She had eaten barely half of her burger when I'd finished mine.

I watched her push her plate away, signaling she was finished, and my eyebrow arrowed up. "You didn't like it?"

She startled at my tone. "No, it was good."

"Then, are you a fucking bird?" It would explain why she was so skinny.

"No, I'm not a *fucking bird*, I'm just full. This is too much food." The second the words were out, she looked like she wanted them back.

My annoyance dissipated somewhat. It probably was too much for her, since I had no idea what her life had been like in Russia. Could have been the *Hunger Games,* for all I knew. The burger I'd eaten was as big as my hand, and the dinner plate was overloaded with fries. It was almost too much food for me, and I was big guy.

"How bad was it in Russia?" I asked. "I mean, I figure it had to be pretty fucking bad for you to come here. You aren't stupid. It seemed like you knew what they were going to make you do once you got here."

She sucked in a breath. "I hoped for something else, but, yes. I told myself if it happened, I might get lucky and end up sold to some guy who was good to me. Maybe I'd even learn to like him after a while."

Like, not love, because like me, the girl 'didn't see the point' in love. I skewed my face with skepticism. "A girl as hot as you? Not a chance. You'd make a helluva lot more in a brothel than as a wife."

My compliment sat uneasy on her and was pushed away. "It doesn't bother you, selling women into slavery?"

Now it was my turn to glance around and make sure no one had heard her accusation. "Yeah, it fucking bothers me, but right now it isn't my call." Besides my weird moral objection, running the girls was the riskiest aspect of our business. The FBI had stepped up their investigation of sex trafficking in the last few years, and getting caught would mean your life was over.

I happened to like my life very much.

"What do you mean," she asked, "it isn't your call *right now*?"

I'd do away with running girls as my first order of business when I was in charge of the Markovic empire, but I wasn't about to announce it. "Forget about that. You didn't answer my question."

"Which was?"

"What your life was like. You know, before I swooped in and saved you from spending the rest of it making money on your back."

Her gaze narrowed. "Is that what you did?" Her patronizing tone was sharp. "Are you the guy I hoped I'd end up with?"

I smirked. "Fuck, no. I'm not going to be good to you. I think you know I plan on being very, *very* bad."

Something flashed in her eyes, but it wasn't panic. If anything, it looked dangerously close to excitement. It was gone faster than a muzzle flash, and her face turned blank. "We didn't have money. My mother was an opera singer, but she was an understudy, so she worked a second job when she could, so we could get by."

"Your father?"

Her expression soured. "He didn't know I existed until my mother died. She'd kept us a secret from each other."

"Why?"

"Protection. After I went to live with him, it didn't take long to realize he was not a good man."

"Because he was connected," I said.

Everything about her, from her expression to her rigid posture screamed she was holding back. "Yes. After he was shot, things became ... unstable, and I chose to come here."

She'd fled Russia, probably worried her father's associates would come after her, too. Parts of the Russian Bratva were ruthless, even more than us Serbs. One bad decision by their own soldier and they'd take out his entire family. And I knew those fuckers had no problem burning down a house with an innocent family trapped inside if it would give them an advantage.

Just ask Luka's girlfriend.

Thinking about Addison led me down a dark path and I didn't want to go there today. I'd like to dig into Oksana's backstory more, but it would have to wait until later, when we could be alone and it was safe to talk openly.

"Don't think this conversation is over," I said, tossing some cash down on the bill, "but we need to get going."

She had an appointment to keep.

chapter
TWELVE

DURING THE DRIVE BACK TO THE HOUSE, Oksana asked me if I liked my job. She was trying to make small talk, but traffic was fucking awful and I told her to be quiet so I could focus. Alek's car was parked out front in the circle drive. I already knew he'd accessed the house—an alert had chimed on my phone five minutes before. I steered the Porsche into the garage. "We'll put these bags in whatever room you slept in last night. That's your room now." I pushed open the car door and got out. "Take a shower and get cleaned up."

We lugged the bags into the house, but she froze in the hallway leading to the stairs, and I slammed into her, nearly knocking her over.

"What the fuck?" I demanded.

Her gaze was fixated on Alek. She was probably wondering what the hell he was doing here, and I should have given her a heads-up.

"Ignore him and keep moving," I said. "This shit is heavy." Alek eyed the bags in our arms with interest, and then looked at me like I might be an imposter. I sighed. "You're early. Is he here?"

Alek nodded, but his gaze went back to her. "Yeah, in the living room."

"Okay," I said. "Tell him I'll be there in a minute." I used the bags in my hands to push her forward and up the stairs. We went down the hall into the green wallpapered guest room. I dropped them with a thud in front of the closet, turned to face her, and put my hands on my hips.

She stared back, and anxiety grew large in her eyes. "What?"

"Don't bother getting dressed after the shower. I'll bring you my robe." I left her standing in the room with a resigned look, went to grab my robe, and she hadn't moved a muscle when I came back. I tossed it onto the gold brocade love seat. "I know how you girls can be. Don't take forever."

"Why would I?" she shot back. "It's only my third shower in less than twenty-four hours."

I ignored her quip and left her to it. I went downstairs and found Amit sitting on the couch, scrolling through his phone and a drink in his hand. *Good.* Alek was taking care of him. Amit was particular. If he wasn't treated right, he'd go straight to my uncle.

I explained what I was looking for, and then we made small talk until I heard the pipes overhead go quiet. Her shower was over. I motioned to the stairs. "Sounds like she's ready."

I pushed the bedroom door open without a knock, because it was my house and I owned everything in it, and she turned to face us. Like last night, her hair had been twisted back in a messy bun and wasn't wet. And once again, I admired the way she looked wrapped up in my robe, but I didn't get to focus on it for long. Her face was coated in fear at the short Indian man at my side, who was at least thirty years old than either of us.

"Oksana, this is Amit. He's a doctor."

She backpedaled until she reached the bedpost. It was mostly hidden by the sides of the robe, but she wrapped a hand around it and clutched it for support. Her chaotic eyes darted from him to me. "I'm not sick."

"Great," I said. "That means it'll be a short visit."

Amit carried his leather bag into the room and set it on the bed, but Oksana skittered away. There was nowhere for her to go, because I stood in the doorway and blocked her in.

"Relax," I ordered. "Amit examines every girl who . . . gets involved in the business."

"All of your whores," she said.

I shrugged, because what was there to say? She watched as he pulled a blood pressure cuff out of the bag, followed by a stethoscope, but it did nothing to soothe her nerves. Anxiety rolled off her in waves.

"It's all right, miss," Amit said softly. "I'm only going to make sure you are healthy. It will just take a few minutes."

Or a lot longer if she fought me on this. I was really hoping to avoid calling Alek up here to help me hold her still. That'd make everything more difficult, and I didn't want him to see her when she was fucking naked. Amit I could tolerate. He was a doctor.

"Oksana." She'd been obedient up until now, but I sensed this was her breaking point. "He's not going to hurt you." I weighted my voice, even though she was smart and had no reason to trust me. "You have my word."

Her shoulders were so tense, they were practically up to her ears. Her expression was both icy cold and fiery rage, and I watched her hands curl into tight, white-knuckled balls. A deep breath was drawn in, and blown out slowly as her eyes closed. "If I do this, I want something in return."

I raised an eyebrow. "Like, two grand worth of clothes?"

Her eyes popped open and zeroed in on me. "Hire someone to tune the piano."

A half of a laugh erupted from me, but she didn't smile, and I sobered. "Oh, shit, you're serious? No."

"Why not?"

Because bringing strangers into my house was dangerous. I could literally be inviting the FBI inside and offering them a million places to stick a surveillance device. This was my safe haven. The only place I could truly be me.

Amit chose that very fucking moment to pull the rest of his shit out of the bag and lay it on the bed. Latex gloves, an alcohol swab packet, a packaged syringe... and an ampule. Oksana gasped like I'd slammed my fist into her stomach and her accusatory glare cut right through me.

She thought I was going to drug her.

"That's not what you think," I said quickly. "It's so I don't knock you up."

Her blue eyes looked at me like I was a piece of shit, and I didn't blame her for the reaction. I'd told her if she left me and went to the Russians, they'd pump her full of drugs. To her, it sure as shit looked like that was what I planned to do.

I grimaced. "Okay, fine. I'll get someone to fix the fucking piano. All right?"

It was ridiculous I was negotiating with her. The girls at Mira's didn't have a problem with Amit. Actually, they loved the guy and teased him ruthlessly.

Oksana glared at him, still clearly full of suspicion. "That's birth control you're planning on injecting me with?"

He nodded. "If you are healthy and have good blood pressure, then yes, miss."

A reluctant decision was made, and her shoulders slumped. "Fine. Let's get it over with."

I grasped the doorknob and began to back out of the room—

"*Vasilije*," she cried.

The sharp way she said my name made me freeze. I stared at her with concern. "What?"

"You're going to leave me? With this strange man, who's..." Her eyes accused me of betrayal. The fight in her was gone, and her voice was broken. "Who's... going to touch me?"

Oh, *fuck*.

I hadn't even thought about it. An invisible hand wrapped around me and squeezed, sending all the pressure to my head. I stepped into the room, closed the door, and moved toward her. My voice was uneven. "I thought you'd want privacy."

It was a bullshit excuse. I hadn't been trying to leave to make her comfortable, I'd been doing it to avoid it being awkward for me. A strange sensation twisted inside my gut. What the fuck was it? *Guilt?*

And why did she want me to stick around? The idea she was more comfortable with me inside the room instead of outside it, made everything upside-down. Even more bizarre, I sort of liked how she wanted me near.

The relief that swept through her caused a pinch in my chest, making it hard to talk. Which was fine. I had no idea what to say. I stood beside the bed as she sat down on the edge of it and pushed up the sleeve of the robe, bunching it at her shoulder.

Amit donned his stethoscope, wrapped the pressure cuff tightly around her bicep, and began to take her vitals.

"Are you on any medication?" he asked, squeezing the balloon, and the needle on the gauge leapt upward.

"No."

"Do you smoke?"

"No."

"When was your last period? Are you regular?"

Oksana's gaze was fixed forward, staring at nothing. "A week ago, and yes."

Well, *fuck.* Here was another thing I hadn't thought about, because I didn't have a mother, or sisters, or even a serious girlfriend. Women had periods, and they needed stuff for that. Maybe Addison had left some girl shit in the house after she and Luka moved out. I made a mental note to handle that situation later.

Amit watched the needle fall slowly on the gauge and then pulled the cuff off with a loud, scratching rip of Velcro. "Excellent. Any medical history for you or your family I should know about?

Blood clots? Strokes?"

"No."

"Good." He dipped the head of the stethoscope between the V at the top of the robe and listened to her heart. "Deep breath." He moved the stethoscope to a new spot. "Again."

After a pause, he seemed satisfied.

Amit straightened, pulled the stethoscope from his ears, and slung it around his neck. It was a gesture he'd been doing for thirty years, and the last twenty of it for my family. Was Addison, studying at Johns Hopkins, doing this same thing right now? It was good she and Luka got out when they did. My uncle would have forced her to work for him. He'd love to have another doctor in the organization to make late-night house calls. One who would treat gunshot wounds without filing a state-required police report.

"Very good," Amit said. He gave Oksana a pleasant smile as he picked up the latex gloves and began to put them on. "Now, miss, I need you to move back, lie down, and open your robe."

Her breath left her in a sharp burst. She shot her hand out and latched it onto my wrist, where her grip was ferocious. Her gaze stayed forward, not looking at anything as she lowered down, and it exaggerated how rapidly she was breathing. How violently she was trembling. I had the ridiculous idea she clung to my arm, as if holding onto me might make another man's touch bearable.

Something inside me cracked.

When Amit's hands reached for the knot of her robe, her grip tightened and it squeezed the word from me. "Stop."

He froze at my command.

My mouth was dry and my tongue felt too big, but I got the sentence out. "We'll skip this part."

The doctor blinked with confusion. "But downstairs, you said you wanted—"

"I changed my mind," I snarled. *Goddamn it.* I scooped my free hand under her and lifted until she stood in my arms. I had to wrap both around her because she was too startled to stand on her own. Her chaotic blue eyes reeled around and found mine. I had no idea what expression was on my face, but hers softened. She was wordlessly thanking me for saving her.

I was a prick.

I tore my gaze away and stared at Amit's forehead and receding hairline. "Are you finished? Can she get the shot and be done?"

I was all fucked up. A brat who wanted to make sure his new toy was legitimately new, and not just advertising it. Even after Amit had warned me it might be impossible to tell, I'd demanded he check her virginity. He'd lectured me about the misconception of hymens and how often they broke or wore away, sometimes years before sex, but I still insisted. I wanted proof. I wanted to know if I was going to claim her virginity like a sick trophy.

The worst part was I knew she wasn't lying. The girl was so clearly a virgin from the way she thought sex wasn't about power to how she recoiled from a simple touch. She'd been on the verge of a nervous breakdown ten seconds ago when Amit reached for her.

As he tore open the plastic and paper around the syringe and prepared the shot, I shifted her in my embrace. Her eyes were vibrant blue, like Lake Michigan on a summer day. She drew in a deep breath through her nose as I felt the bottom of the robe moving. Her hands settled on my chest, softly clutching at my dress shirt.

"Vasilije, can you hold this?" Amit asked, pressing the bunched fabric in my hand that was at the small of her back. He needed me to hold it out of his way so he could slide his needle into the muscle of one of her cheeks. My gaze didn't waver from hers as I gripped the plush fabric. I could see every action in her expressive eyes. The smell of alcohol filled the room as he wiped the swab over her skin and she flinched, probably at the cold.

"Small pinch," he said.

Her pupils widened as the needle went in, but the Russian girl was deadly silent.

Plastic snapped, covering the needle, and then a Band-Aid was put in place. "All done."

I let go of the robe, dropping it to cover her exposed skin. She'd been leaning into me for support, but as she solidified, she didn't move away. I didn't either.

When Amit had everything packed up in his bag, he looked at me, expecting me to usher him downstairs so he could get paid. I hesitated. "I'll be down in a minute."

He nodded, and left us alone. The second the door clicked shut, the tension between Oksana and me spiked so intensely, I couldn't move. What was happening? How the hell did this girl have such an effect on me? I stood paralyzed as she inched closer, rising onto her toes. She was so close, I could smell the faint hint of the soap she'd used in the shower. Her fingers slid slowly up until she had them laced together behind my neck.

Oksana was about to kiss me, but I met her halfway and our lips collided. Her kiss was a fist wrapped in velvet. I kept my defenses down and let her deliver one blow after another. Kiss after soft, gentle kiss, lulling me in. I wouldn't feel the damage until it was too late.

"Thank you," she whispered against my lips. She was thanking me for stopping him.

It jolted me from my stupor, and I shoved her back. "Don't."

She pressed her fingertips to her kiss-swollen mouth, checking to see if my lips were still attached to hers, and when she discovered they weren't, surprise washed over her. "Don't kiss you," she asked, "or don't thank you?"

"Either." Fuck, I needed to get out of this room where I'd lost all control. Put some distance between us and figure out how to get my shit together. My face turned to stone. "Get dressed. I don't care what you wear as long as it's something I bought."

Her shoulders drew back at my abrupt change in attitude, and confusion splashed on her face, but I wasn't going to explain myself.

I turned and high-tailed it out of the room, trying to flee the uncomfortable sensation in my chest I hadn't experienced in years.

It felt a lot like shame.

chapter
THIRTEEN

Oksana

I banded my arms across my stomach as my knees gave out, collapsing me to sit on the bed. There was a tinge of pain, reminding me of the injection site, but I was too mixed up to process it.

I'd kissed Vasilije twice now, and been rejected by him the same number of times.

The lunch I'd eaten churned in my belly. I'd come dangerously close to throwing up when I thought the stranger was going to touch me. I believed Vasilije when he said the man was a doctor, but it was horrifying, regardless.

I shuddered, holding myself together. I didn't have time to sit on the edge of the bed. Aleksandar was likely still in the house, and I had to talk to him. Who knew when I'd get my next chance?

I ripped the tags off a pair of jeans and a black sweater, and yanked the clothes on. Adrenaline was still pumping through my system, along with the terrible throb that could only have come from kissing Vasilije. I hated my stupid body's response to him. How it wanted him no matter what he said or did.

Vasilije and the doctor were in the office with the glass paneled door closed when I came down the stairs, so instantly I began to search for my reluctant partner.

Aleksandar wasn't in the living room or the kitchen. I wandered past the fancy dining room with its gleaming table and ten chairs, and the crystal chandelier glinted in the sunlight coming from the oversized windows. Where the hell was he? Outside?

I went to the hall closet by the garage to get my shoes, and startled as he stepped out of the laundry room. A gasp cut off in my throat when he grabbed my waist and yanked me into the room with him. I spun out of his hold as quickly as possible, wanting his hands gone.

"I told you he'd go for it," Aleksandar said, hushed. He looked upset, which I understood. He'd been heavily coerced into helping me. He was a serial gambler who owed half of Chicago money. Not just the Serbs, but the Italians, the Irish, the Chinese, and us. My father had fronted him the money to consolidate his debts in one place, but it meant we owned Vasilije's right hand man in totality. He'd fought so hard against this plot, claiming he'd be loyal to Vasilije till death. That was easy enough to arrange, my father had told him.

Aleksandar didn't like it, but he had no choice.

"Here," he said, bending beside the washing machine and pulling out a thin black box that was tucked between the wall and the machine, hidden from view. "Everything you need is in there, all right?"

I ignored his agitated tone, took it from him, and opened the box. Encased in foam, the black squares were the same size as a 9V battery. These were the surveillance devices I had agreed to hide in Vasilije's house so my father could know all the moves the Markovics were making as soon as the decisions had been made.

I lifted a corner of the foam and peered at the card with licensing code for hacking Vasilije's mobile. I'd need two minutes with the phone to install the hidden app. A month of training meant I had both the steps and the code memorized, but it was included, just in case.

My pulse picked up. So far my father's plan had aligned with mine, but I was about to veer in my own direction, and everything was going to become riskier. "How long is the battery life on these?"

Aleksandar was a breath away from chewing at his fingernails, he looked that worried. "Up to ten days. Why?"

"Ten days?" I faked outrage. "After everything I'm doing, that's not long enough. We talked about using the thirty day ones."

Anger swirled in his beady eyes. "Hey, that's on you guys. I held up my end of the deal. You plant those tonight, I get you out of here tomorrow while he's at work, and then we go our separate ways."

I shook my head. "Tell Petrov I need the long-lasting ones. We've only got one shot at this. I'm not wasting it on a device where the battery runs out in a week."

He stared at me. "Are you fucking crazy? You don't get it, girl. Every day you're here, it's another day he might figure out you're setting him up. You know what'll happen then?"

"Vasilije will kill me." My voice was flat.

"Yeah, and if I don't get you out of here alive, your people will kill *me*. Assuming Vasilije doesn't do it first."

I tried to feel bad for him, but couldn't. Aleksandar worked for the Markovics. He had more blood on his hands than I did, and he reluctantly agreed to turn against his own people. Aleksandar was also stupid if he thought he could tell me what to do. My position with Vasilije meant I got to call the shots. If I demanded different devices, my father would make it happen. He couldn't trust Aleksandar to plant the devices himself, and wouldn't waste the opportunity I was giving him.

"So," I said, "I'd suggest getting me those devices as quickly as possible."

Aleksandar made a sound of frustration, ripped his phone from his pocket, and made a call. I listened to the terse conversation and tried not to give anything away. The more upset Aleksandar sounded, the better it was for me.

He hung up and shoved the phone in his jeans. "It's Thanksgiving this week. Earliest the Russians can get their hands on them is Monday."

He looked furious, but I shrugged. I'd just bought myself

another week with Vasilije. I had to ignore the competing feelings I had about it.

"Let me talk to Vasilije," he said abruptly. "Maybe he'll let you come home with me. The less you're around him, the better for both of us."

I must have overestimated Aleksandar's intelligence. I barely knew Vasilije, but I could tell he wouldn't give me up. He was a cat and I was his captured mouse. He was enjoying playing with me, not ready yet to move in for the kill.

"No, don't say a word. All it'll do is make him suspicious." *You know what else would make him suspicious? If he finds you whispering to Aleksandar in the laundry room.* "I'll see you in a week," I said, leaving him standing there as I went toward the kitchen.

What was my father thinking about my request right now? I was a stupid girl. He didn't care. Either I got him full access to Vasilije's life, or I'd be killed trying. It was a win-win for the man who'd never see me as a legitimate daughter, no matter how many paternity test results proved I was.

I went hunting for a glass, and found one beside the refrigerator. I filled it with ice and water as movement to my right caught my eye. Aleksandar had followed me. Why didn't he go wait for Vasilije outside the office door? I couldn't have him hanging around me.

"Oksana." Aleksandar's hushed voice was urgent. "Vasilije will hurt you. He likes making people suffer."

It was true, wasn't it? He'd tried to humiliate and degrade me. He'd pinched me so hard in the dressing room, it had ached for a long time afterward. But he'd also stopped the doctor upstairs. Was he a sadist? Did he like inflicting pain as long as it was physical, and not emotional?

Aleksandar put a hand on my arm. Maybe his touch wasn't sexual and he was only trying to offer me comfort. Perhaps it was supposed to be a friendly gesture, or he'd done it to try to get through my stubbornness. It didn't matter. I jerked back. "Don't touch me."

If it was any other attack, I could fend it off, but all my strength abandoned me when a man moved on me like this.

"Alek."

Vasilije's voice was a gunshot, tearing through my core. Aleksandar backed off instantly, putting several feet of space between us.

The devil stood in the center of the kitchen, his eyes burning red. He had to be considering murdering Aleksandar right that moment. Judging by the expression on his face, there could be no other thought in his mind. His right hand twitched, and then curled into a fist. He wanted to reach for his gun, and maybe thought better of it.

"Fucking put a hand on her again," Vasilije said, "and you'll spend the rest of your short life wishing you hadn't."

It was shocking how territorial he was.

"It was nothing, Vasilije. I swear," Aleksandar said in a rush. "We were just talking."

Vasilije's dark gaze slid to me. "About what?"

Jealousy flamed in his eyes. I'd have to be very careful. I kept my face benign. "The American holiday this week. He was explaining it to me." I took a sip of my water and pretended not to be affected by the tension radiating from the men. "Do you celebrate it?"

"No." He said it like a gut reaction, and then scowled as he considered it further. "What's the point? It's just me here." He turned his attention back to Aleksandar. "Amit and I are finished. Take him wherever he wants to go."

Aleksandar hurried out of the kitchen, visibly grateful for the excuse to leave.

Vasilije captured me with an intense stare. We stood as mannequins, our gazes trapping each other, listening to the sounds as Aleksandar and Amit went out the front door. The security system panel chirped and brought Vasilije back to life.

"I don't believe that bullshit was about Thanksgiving."

I licked my lips, because my mouth felt dry. "He was worried."

"About?" When Vasilije rested his hands on his hips, it pushed back the sides of his suitcoat and gave me a hint of the strap of his holster, reminding me of his gun.

"What you might do to me."

"He was warning you?"

I nodded.

God, his black eyes were magnetic, and he blinked them slowly. "He needs to mind his own fucking business." He sighed and shook his head. Then, he turned on his heel and headed for the stairs. Was I supposed to follow him?

"Where are you going?" I asked lightly.

"To work out." His tone was gruff, telling me he wanted to be left alone.

I glanced at the piano. "Do you mind if I play for a while?"

He climbed the stairs as he took off his suit jacket. "Do whatever the fuck you want." He made it two more steps before he hesitated. "Oksana."

I lifted my gaze to him. He was near the top of the stairs. He had a hand on the railing, his suitcoat folded over his other arm. The black gun and straps of his holster contrasted against the white dress shirt, and his burgundy tie was the same shade of a dried bloodstain.

"He won't touch you again," he said.

My breath stuck painfully in my lungs. Vasilije wasn't the first to make that empty promise.

His expression was resolute. "From now on, no one touches you but me."

chapter
FOURTEEN

I PLAYED UNTIL THE SUN SET, turned on the living room overhead lights, and tried to compose for two more hours. The most frustrating two hours of my life seated in front of a piano. I hated everything I put down. It wasn't bright enough. It had no lift. The music felt . . . *manufactured.*

The song I wanted to write was going to be sweeping and moving, but darkness kept creeping in. It threatened every measure. It tainted each chord. I blamed the untuned piano and the boy who seemed to be hiding from me upstairs. How could I write anything in this space that wasn't ominous? Or sexual?

I fought myself on every note.

Loud rap music had thumped for more than an hour from the room that contained a treadmill, a weight machine, and a rack of free weights. After it cut off, I heard Vasilije go into his bedroom. He'd been in there for a while. Hours. Was he was avoiding me?

I couldn't turn off my thoughts about him. Should I go up there? I was wasting time sitting at this piano when I should be trying to gain his trust. I needed a partner when the time came to take down my father.

Instead, I stalled and told myself when I finished the song I'd seek him out.

I scribbled another measure in my notebook, slammed down my pencil, and let out a sigh of frustration.

"Having fun?"

I jumped at Vasilije's voice, making the piano bench squeal across the hardwood floor. I found him standing on the stairs, his gaze cast down on me and his expression unreadable. He wore jeans and a t-shirt, and no holster. No gun, unless it was tucked in the back of his jeans. He looked relaxed, casual, and almost . . . normal. Like any other regular guy.

As he moved down the stairs, I stood from the piano and closed my book. "Sometimes," I said quietly, "it's hard to write."

His eyes were as black as the piano keys. "Has to be, especially when you don't have any *feelings*."

Like I'd done from the beginning with him, when I didn't know what to say, I said nothing. His feet were bare as he padded across the floor, silently approaching. It was cold in the huge room, or at least it was by the windows. Most of the back of the house was glass. Wasn't he freezing? Goosebumps lifted on my skin.

"I ordered dinner," he announced. "Make yourself useful and set the kitchen table."

Confusion slammed into me. "For you?"

He glared like I was being stupid. "For us."

Us. The word was unsettling and interesting. I shivered and refused to examine whether it was from a chill, or anticipation. I went hunting in the kitchen for plates and silverware, ignoring the flutter in my stomach. Dinner at the table meant conversation, and I was eager to glean more information from him.

I'd also confessed my darkest secret to him during our last real conversation, and the way he'd looked at me after . . . Like he was proud. It was so wrong, yet it filled me with warmth. We were strangers, but there was a connection too powerful to suppress. We felt less like strangers now.

When I'd found everything I thought we'd need, I sat at the kitchen table, listening to him answer the door and pay the delivery person. Vasilije appeared, set the white plastic bag on the table, and dropped into the seat across from me.

He helped himself to the Chinese takeout, then stared at me

expectantly.

    I grabbed one of the open cartons and dumped some food on my plate. I wasn't hungry, but I ate anyway. It gave me something to do while I worked up the nerve to start a conversation. Vasilije didn't seem like he was going to. He ate quickly and barely looked at me. The screen of his phone was far more interesting than the Russian girl across from him.

    "May I ask you something?" I said.

    He set the phone down, and his shuttered gaze focused on me. He gave no other indication, but I felt like that was enough for me to proceed.

    "How did your parents die?" I knew the answer, but I hoped by asking, it might cause him to open up.

    "My mother was killed in a car accident when I was five." His voice was empty. "My father was like yours. Gunshot. Last April."

    "I'm sorry," I said automatically. "Did they catch the guy?"

    They had.

    Ivan worked with the Serbs for years before we turned him to our side. He'd seen how powerful the Russians were becoming, and he'd felt disrespected by Vasilije's father, Dimitrije. Ivan had been happy to carry out my father's horrific plan and launch the first strike in the war.

    The moment I'd overheard what had been done, how Ivan had burned a house down with a family trapped inside . . . it still haunted me, a year and a half later. I was glad the Markovics had caught him and made that piece of garbage pay with his life. The man who'd killed Ivan was sitting across from me, staring at me with chaos swirling in his eyes.

    The rumor was both Vasilije and Luka had been there to witness their father's death at Ivan's hands, and the younger, more ruthless Markovic son didn't hesitate. Luka Markovic didn't have the stomach to avenge his father's death, and had fled to the east coast.

Vasilije had killed Ivan and ascended into the position of next in line to run the Markovic business behind Goran.

Vasilije considered my question for a long time. *Too* long, and an odd sensation prickled over my skin. Ivan had killed Dimitrije. My father had heard it straight from Goran when they'd negotiated the unstable and short-lived truce last year.

"There was a shit-stain named Ivan who died here, down in the basement. A baseball bat, a whole bunch of times, right here." The devil tapped two fingers to his temple. "That shit was messy. It took forever to clean up." A slow smile worked its way across his lips, flashing his dimples. "But it was worth it."

I wasn't fast enough to hide the tiny burst of satisfaction from my face. I was glad Ivan hadn't gotten a quick death. A little bit of justice for that poor family he'd murdered.

Vasilije blinked back surprise. "I tell you this guy got brained with a bat, and you don't look sick. You're not disgusted. You kinda seem interested." His expression shifted toward excitement. "Goddamn, Oksana. You want me to tell you all the details? How his blood and brains went everywhere? What his skull looked like, caved in like a rotted pumpkin?"

I shrugged. "If he killed your father—"

A dark, serious expression overtook him. "Ivan murdered a family. Normal, nice fucking people who didn't have shit to do with anything, all because their daughter was dating my brother." His eyes hardened. "Your people did that."

My heart tripped over itself. I was outraged by what my father had ordered, too, and I didn't want Vasilije to see me as an enemy. "The same ones who'd drug me and put me to work in a brothel? Does that sound like they're *my* people?"

Yes. It sounded exactly like my family's business . . . because it was.

Vasilije took a bite of his food and stared vacantly over my shoulder. I felt him slipping away, and scrambled to find anything to keep the conversation going.

"Was it satisfying? Killing the man who murdered your father?"

He gave a humorless laugh. "I didn't kill him."

"I thought you said . . ." I was so confused. What did he mean he hadn't done it? "You didn't kill Ivan?"

Vasilije leaned forward, resting his elbows on the table. "Was it satisfying killing the guy who'd touched you?"

"No." I frowned, not liking the topic change or the focus being placed on me. I closed my eyes, unable to look at him as I said it out loud. "And yes."

A pleased chuckle came from him. "Tell me about it."

"I don't want to."

His eyebrow arched up. "I don't fucking care."

I swallowed a breath. I was willing to do a lot to make this work. Sacrifice my body, and do things I wasn't proud of, but talking about Ilia was a hard line to cross. I grabbed my plate, stood from the table, and marched to the sink.

"Get back here," he ordered.

The silverware rattled on the plate as I set it down and turned on the water. His chair moved noisily and his angry footsteps pounded toward me, launching my heart into my throat. It was the first time I'd disobeyed him, and I gripped the edge of the sink, preparing myself for his reaction.

A hand latched onto my waist and he reached around me with the other, slapping at the handle to turn the water off. His fingers bit into my flesh, but I stayed quiet.

"What the hell," he snarled, "makes you think you get to say no to me?"

He spun me around and pressed his hips into mine, pinning me against the counter. He leaned over, forcing me to bend back awkwardly as his cold body loomed above.

"I shot him and he died," I said in a rush. "There's nothing to tell."

"*There's nothing to tell?*" He mocked my nervous voice and tangled a hand in my hair, yanking me back further. "Bullshit. Where'd you shoot him? How many times did you pull the trigger? What kind of gun was it?" His intensity built with each question. "What happened after, Oksana?"

"Please," I whimpered. "You're hurting me."

"Talk, and I'll stop."

My throat closed up. I couldn't force my lips to move or my vocal cords to produce sound, and I watched the rage gather in his furious eyes.

It was so scary, it stole my breath.

Abruptly, his grip in my hair was gone and he stepped back. I nearly fell forward into him—and then I was falling as he bent, wrapped his arms around my thighs, and threw me over his shoulder. As he stood, it squeezed a grunt from me. His bony shoulder dug into my stomach, and it was disorienting being upside-down, hanging in the air.

"Vasilije!"

He trudged toward the living room, making me bounce painfully on him. His voice was so deep and dark, I felt it vibrating up his back.

"I warned you," he said. "I always get what I want."

chapter FIFTEEN

Vasilije

Even though Oksana didn't weigh a lot, she shifted around and was a bitch to carry. I'd done more of a leg day today than upper body, and thank fuck for that. I stormed toward the sectional leather couch and hurled her on it, watching her head bounce as she flopped down on the cushions.

Her blonde hair splashed around her, and she gazed up at me with wild eyes. Did I look deranged? She pissed me off. One minute I'd thought we'd had something, like . . . an understanding. Her faint smile when I'd told her the gritty shit about Ivan's death had lit me up.

But why wasn't she willing to return the favor, and tell me the details when she'd taken someone else's life? If she wanted to be unfair, I'd show her just how unfair I could be.

She tried to scramble backward, but I put a knee on the couch cushion, seized the belt loops of her jeans, and jerked her back to me. I jammed the top of my thigh between her legs and watched discomfort twist her face. "What?" I growled. "You don't like it now? You fucking loved it last night."

I undid the snap at the top of her jeans before she realized what I was doing. She tried to push my hands away, but I was stronger and faster, and dropped her zipper. I dug my fingers around the waistband and jerked her pants down, even as she twisted and struggled to make me stop.

"Fuck me, you're not wearing anything under these?" I grinned, as the virgin scowled. She hadn't wanted to put the panties back on after her shower, but what about the bra? I shoved a hand under the hem of her black sweater and flipped it up, getting a flash of the white, see-through bra.

"You listened when I told you to get dressed in the shit I bought you." I shifted so I was standing beside the couch and put one hand on the back of it. "Why'd you decide now to stop being a good girl?"

She was distracted trying to put her sweater back in place, so I used the opportunity to pull her pants the rest of the way down to her knees. I loved the look of her. The pale, smooth skin covering her thighs and the darkened triangle just above her pussy. I wanted to bury my face in it. Lick her from front to back until she was begging or screaming, or both. But I wasn't about to reward her. She needed to get her ass back in line, and realize who she belonged to.

And speaking of ass . . .

When a panicked Oksana sat up and reached to pull her pants back in place, I grabbed her arms and shoved her over the back of the couch so her ass was up in the air. It looked heart-shaped like this, her pretty pussy peeking out at the bottom. I put one hand on the small of her back, pushing her down when she tried to move. Then, I slapped my other palm against her skin, and the loud crack echoed under the vaulted ceilings.

"*Ahuyet!*" she gasped.

I spanked her again, and it had to hurt because my palm stung. "Speak English," I ordered. "What'd you just say?"

Her breath came and went in heavy heaves. "It doesn't make sense in English."

I slapped her on the other cheek and watched it pink up. My handprint was already visible on her skin, and I curled my mouth into a half-smile. She looked good like that. Branded as mine, even if she wasn't wearing anything I'd bought her there. "Try me."

Her voice was tight. "It's like a . . . more vulgar way to say, 'oh my fucking God.'"

More vulgar. "I like your obscene mouth, especially when it's blowing me." As I smacked her ass, the impact rippled over her skin. It was so incredibly hot. As she whimpered, my cock twitched. "But right now, I want you to tell me every goddamn detail, you little murderer."

She jolted as I slapped her bright red ass, and this time I left my palm against her burning skin. I moved my fingertips over the curve of her cheek, sliding them down until they grazed her pussy. Her skin was damp and slick, and I rubbed a tight circle over her clit.

Jesus fuck, her strangled moan had me rock hard in a half-second.

"*Vasilije . . .*" She was pleading, but for what? For me to fuck her? To leave her alone? Maybe I was playing this all wrong. What if the best way to punish her wasn't with pain, but with pleasure? To turn her body against herself?

I grabbed the ankles of her wadded jeans and tugged until her legs were free, leaving her naked from the waist down. "Get that goddamn sweater off now."

Her arms shook as she pulled the knitted fabric over her head and let it drop over the back of the couch. I sat down and pulled her on top of me so she was sitting in my lap facing away from me, wearing only the flimsy bra. I fisted the band behind her back and pressed down on her hip, making her grind against my aching cock.

"Nothing to say?" I demanded, tugging on the elastic band. I wanted to undo my jeans and shove my cock so deep inside her she'd bleed all over me, but I was too focused right now. This was a battle of wills, and I was going to fucking win. No one was more stubborn than I was.

"Awesome," I said. "We get to do this the fun way. Get your knees under you." She turned and peered at me over her shoulder, looking as if she were both nervous and confused. I pushed and pulled at her until I had her positioned as I wanted—her straddling my lap away from me and shins against the couch cushions. I opened my legs to make room.

She cried out as I shoved her forward, and she flung her hands out onto the rug, stopping herself from tumbling face-first off my lap and onto the floor. The submissive position couldn't be that comfortable for her. Her head was down and her ass up, but it was fucking perfect. I was comfortable and had all the access I wanted, her pussy right in front of me. She'd stare at my feet and her hands that were on the expensive Persian rug as I played. I'd tease and torture until she gave me everything.

"You stay like this until I say otherwise, you understand?" I spanked her, but this one was nothing. All it did was get her attention.

"Yes," she breathed. Her body was quaking, and I skimmed my fingertips over the ridges of her spine. Power flooded through me.

"Did you plan it?" I asked. "Did you have murderous thoughts in that little head of yours leading up to it?" Her pink pussy was so lush and soft. I ran a finger through her wetness, swirling it over her clit.

"It was . . . defensive."

Ah, so the girl was willing to talk after all. But . . . "That's only half an answer." I pressed two fingers to her and slid them back and forth, manipulating the bud of flesh that made her squirm.

She got her words out through pants of breath. "It was impulsive. But I thought about . . . killing him before."

"Why?" I tensed. "He touched you more than once?"

It took her a goddamn lifetime to answer. "Whenever my father wasn't around, he'd find a way to get me alone."

Rage fired along my muscles. Not anger at her, but at the asshole she'd killed. "Why didn't you tell anyone?"

"I *did*."

Shit. I didn't blame her for sounding defensive. I smoothed my hands over her ass. She must have removed the Band-Aid at some point, and I couldn't see where the needle had gone in. Had the spankings hurt more against the sore muscle? She'd barely made a sound. How high was her tolerance for pain?

"Who'd you tell?" I asked.

"My father. He didn't believe me. He said he talked to the guy and he... wouldn't touch me again." Her words were full of significance. "But nothing changed. If anything, it got worse."

I'd made her the same promise, but the difference was I'd absolutely keep mine. "When I said no one else would touch you, I fucking meant it. I don't like people touching my shit." I skated my fingers through her crevice. "And this? This is all mine. You're my property."

Shivers rolled up her legs. Goosebumps pebbled on her skin. Once she got over her initial reaction, she was so responsive to my touch, and that wasn't lost on me. She was wet. Turned on, not disgusted.

"Sounds to me," I said, "like your dad was a piece of shit." I rested my left hand on her ass and swirled the pad of my right thumb over her clit, making her shudder again. I lined up my index finger and slowly began to press it inside her, just up to the first knuckle. "Tell me what happened."

Her whole body tensed at the intrusion, and the words spilled from her. "The man cornered me in my father's office. I fought back, and—oh!"

I eased a little further, and one of her hands wrapped around my ankle, squeezing. I paused, letting her get used to the sensation. She was tight. Her pussy gripped my finger. "Keep talking."

"I knew where the gun was stashed in the room. I thought I'd just threaten him with it, but then it was in my hand, and he was... he was *smiling* at me..."

I'd seen that same smile and knew what it meant. "He didn't believe you'd use it."

She said it like a joke, but her voice was shallow. "I showed him."

NIKKI SLOANE

Yeah, she certainly did, and I grinned darkly. She *was* like me after all, and I had no fucking idea why I liked it so much. I sank my finger deeper inside and moved my other hand down so I could rub and finger fuck her at the same time.

My dick pressed against my fly and throbbed, and it got worse when she moaned softly. I wanted to make her come, but I wanted to finish the conversation, and that desire won out. "Where'd you get him?"

"The chest. My hand was shaking too much to aim for his head." She gulped down a breath. "Oh my God. I can't talk like this."

I pulsed my finger in and out of her slowly, watching it disappear inside and come back out glistening from how wet I was making her. My tone was evil. "But you're doing great." Her grip on my ankle tightened and her hips moved. They shifted subtly, but I caught the action. Oh, it was feeling good for her now. "What'd you do with the body?"

"He was still alive when my father came in, but he died on the way to the doctor. I don't know where they dumped him."

"How'd you feel right after you did it?"

She didn't answer.

"Tell me the truth, and don't feed me that line of bullshit again about how you don't have feelings." I fucked her faster and increased the pressure with my fingertips. She didn't respond, and it annoyed me to no end. This question was really the heart of what I wanted to know. To see how deep our similarities ran. "Oksana. Answer me, goddamnit."

"I felt empty," she admitted, her voice breaking. "I was supposed to feel bad, but . . . I couldn't. I stared at him bleeding out, and I was so fucking glad I'd pulled the trigger. That's all I felt."

Her words poured pleasure on me, and I froze. I had to hold perfectly still as the effect washed through me.

My lack of movement sent the wrong signal, because she tried to pull away. Like she thought I was judging her. I had to stop and lock my hands on her waist to hold her in place. "Of all the girls that night, how the fuck did I pick one who's just like me?"

She gasped. "I'm *nothing* like you," she fired back. "And you didn't pick me."

"Wrong, and wrong." The moment I'd seen her, I'd known she was... different. "I would have grabbed you if Alek hadn't."

Since I couldn't see her face, I pictured her floundering. It sounded like she was trying to convince herself more than me. "We're not alike."

"*Wrong.*" Her ass was right there, all bare and waiting. I spanked it and reveled in her grunt of discomfort.

"You're a virgin, too?" she asked, faking shock.

I laughed, not just because she was ridiculous, but at how she'd suddenly decided to grow a pair. Didn't she realize when she shoved me, I'd shove back, harder, and enjoy doing it? She was making it worse for herself. "I lost my virginity almost a decade ago."

"Okay. Are you secretly Russian?"

When I gave her a matching set of red handprints on her lily-white ass, she yelped.

"Don't let that mouth of yours get your ass into something it can't handle." Color burst on her skin, and it was fucking beautiful. "Unless you want to get in trouble? Maybe you like pain." I caressed her warm flesh. "Maybe you'll get off on it when I pop your cherry."

"Sure, whenever *that's* going to happen." Her patronizing tone burrowed under my skin.

When the fuck did she get so mouthy? "Is that what you want, baby?" I mocked. "Are you just dying for my cock to fill you up and make you a woman?"

Enough of this game. She was reckless to even attempt playing against me. I put a hand on each cheek and peeled her apart, and then I spit on her, right on her asshole. Her body turned to stone, but I wasn't done yet. I moved my thumb to where my spit dribbled down, and put pressure on the puckered ring of muscle.

Her fingernails dug in so hard on my ankle, I could feel them through the denim of my jeans. Whatever confidence she'd had drained away with her loud exhale of breath.

"Maybe I'll only fuck you here," I said. "Would you like that? If I fucked your dirty hole and you stayed a virgin forever?"

"Ahuyet," she whispered.

This time I recognized the appropriate, vulgar word.

chapter SIXTEEN

Panic burst from Oksana's lips. "Vasilije, no!"

Because I was a sick fuck, I faked confusion. "You don't want me to leave you a virgin?"

"Stop. *Please*."

She was asking me to stop touching her, and a dull alarm went off in the back of my mind. I was a monster, but I wasn't going to force myself on her. The plan was to twist her around so many times on the inside, she'd do it herself. I'd already convinced her body, but I'd make her believe she wanted me.

I skated my palms up her back and leaned forward so I could grab her biceps and yank her upright, crushing her back against my chest. Her hair smacked in my face and strands caught on my whiskers, and I brushed them away.

The curve of her neck was fucking sexy, and I moved without thought, wedging my head beside hers, edging her to bend her neck and allow me access. My mouth was on her, licking and sucking the spot below her ear. My hands roamed over her body. I'd touch her everywhere else until she asked me to stop there, too.

She rasped for air and shook. I liked the position, but hated I couldn't see her, and took one hand off to fumble around for the TV remote nearby on the couch. It took the system ten long seconds to boot up, so I bit down on her earlobe and breathed in her ear. It was seduction, which I didn't need to do with her, but for the first time ever, I enjoyed it. Her soft sigh was loud in the quiet room.

A few buttons were all I needed to press before the camera to my PlayStation leapt to life, and the image of us filled the giant screen across the room. We both froze as our gaze locked onto the television.

"God. Fucking. Damn," I said.

Her face was flushed, maybe from being half upside-down, or maybe from shock when I'd threatened to fuck her ass. All she had on was the see-through bra, which just made her amazing tits look even better. I couldn't keep my hands off her. I shoved my fingertips beneath the cup of the bra, and let my other hand glide down over her smooth stomach toward her pussy.

"Put your hands on top of mine," I ordered. She needed to feel me touching her in every fucking way. "Move them how you want me to touch you."

She did it so slowly, it was painful and amazing. My dick was in agony locked in my jeans as her hands closed on top of mine. I shifted to one side so I could see better around her body, and watched both lust and nerves battle on her face. But my hands began to move under her suggestions, which were too timid to call commands.

Down our fingers went. Over the hollow of her bellybutton. Into the stubble above her pussy. And finally, the sweet spot that made her melt and her eyes hood. Her fingers pressed mine, urging me to grind against her soaking pussy. I straightened and set my lips on her shoulder while I began to stir.

Her moan was better than any porn star, not just because it was real, but because I was causing her the pleasure.

"Yeah?" It was so low from me, it was barely loud enough to call a whisper. "Right there, baby?" I stirred faster, and her breathing hurried to match my tempo. "Are you watching?"

I knew she was, because, fucking hell, how could she not? The girl writhing in my lap was too hot to ignore.

The lighting in here was shit. There were shadows, and her hand covered mine so it was difficult to see everything onscreen, but my strong forearm moved with a steady rhythm. The tendons flexed beneath my skin as I massaged. There was no doubt what I was doing to her, and her throaty moan announced how much she liked it, even if her face said she didn't want to.

I gripped one of her tits, and she hung onto my hand, not to pull it away, but to encourage. I sank my teeth into the side of her neck, wanting to give her both pleasure and a hint of pain at the same time. She rose up on her knees an inch and swiveled her hips, fucking my hand.

Jesus, she was so sexy, it fired through me like an electric current.

"That's it, get what you need," I said. She made a tight sound, a desperate whine. I could hear her ache. "You're so fucking wet, it's running down my fingers."

I picked up speed, going as fast as I could, rubbing her clit back and forth, and made it hard for her to breathe. Hopefully, hard for her to think. She gasped and bucked, like her body was beyond her control and she wasn't sure what she was supposed to do. I was as urgent and desperate for her release as she was. Maybe more.

"Oh my God," she cried, the words streaming together. "Ohmigod, *ohmigod*—"

"Shut up and come. Now, Oksana." Through the bra, I pinched her nipple as hard as I had earlier in the dressing room, and it catapulted her over the edge.

She screamed, and her quivering body sagged against mine, heavy as the orgasm surged. Her struggle to find air competed with the cries of pleasure that ripped from her throat, and I damn near came in my jeans listening to it.

Knowing I was the only man who'd made her come? It unleashed something territorial and primal. I wrapped my possessive arms around her shuddering body, holding her as she slowly came down from her climax. Her head lolled back, resting on my shoulder, and with her eyes closed, she looked blissed out. Like the feeling I got when I'd bought exceptionally good weed.

I was anxious to feel that kind of pleasure. Her breathing hadn't even slowed to a regular pace before I made my demand. "Get on your knees. Suck me off."

I shoved her off my lap to help her along, dumping her to the floor. Like last night, she gaped at me, and this time I wasn't going to waste her mouth's invitation. I undid my zipper and got my cock ready. Not that it needed any help. I was hard as steel.

I snaked a hand behind her head and dragged her into my lap, pushing her mouth down around me. Searing heat enveloped my tip and descended as she took me between her lips. Had she taken notes last night? It was only her second-ever blowjob, but you'd never know it. Fuck, her mouth. *Her tongue.* Hot as hell and better than heaven.

The leather of the couch squealed as I slumped down and spread my knees wider. I gathered her hair up in my hands, holding it back and using it to guide her pace. "Slow," I murmured. "Good."

So fucking good.

My gaze bounced between her and the mirror image of us on-screen. She was kneeling between my legs, and her toes peeked out from beneath her ass, which was barely pink anymore. The back of her head bobbed at a deliberate crawl, just as I'd dictated.

I focused back on the live image. My thick cock disappeared between her lush, pink lips. Her eyes were pinched closed and her brow furrowed in concentration as she sucked. She looked amazing like that, but I needed all of her.

"Eyes on me." Did she notice the stumble in my voice? It was getting harder to pretend she had no effect on me. Her intense eyes fluttered open and settled on mine. "You look at me when my cock's in you."

Her blue irises seemed to deepen in color, but it had to be a trick of the lighting.

The idle tempo teetered on the edge of torture, and I pushed on her head, showing her I needed it faster now. And it was like she knew what I wanted next. Her hand gripped me at the base, and she slid it along my shaft like I'd done last night.

"Tighter," I said. I dropped my grip on her hair with one hand, tipped my head back on the couch, and put the hand on my forehead. My heart thundered in my chest. Did she have a direct link to my lungs? As her grip tightened on my dick, my body constricted from the pleasure.

The soft sucking sounds graduated into loud, sloppy noises as wet skin moved through wet skin. I bucked my hips, sliding my dick in and out of her mouth, faster with each thrust. The sensations built, rolling like a stone down a hill, picking up speed. "I wanna fuck all the Russian from your mouth."

If she didn't like hearing that, I couldn't tell. She matched my tempo, keeping up with me as I pumped my hips, fucking her face. Need screwed me tighter until I was so tense I couldn't speak. I jerked her roughly by the hair, back and forth, up and down. I needed it deeper. I needed it faster. I needed...

She gagged, but it fed into my enjoyment. "Oh, fuck, I'm gonna come." I exhaled loudly, and a tremble crawled up my spine. "I'm gonna... Shit. Oh, *shit*, I'm coming."

Pleasure ripped from my center and tore through me. It was a white-hot flash of euphoria that fucked with my breathing and my heartbeat. It felt like I was so high, I was never going to come down.

As I pulsed and filled her mouth, pleasure zipped along my cock from base to tip, and then repeated. Each wave was less powerful than the last, and left me weak. When I came, that was the closest I got to being powerless.

I sucked in a deep breath and began to even myself out.

Oksana had frozen with her lips still wrapped around me, and it took me a second to realize what she was doing.

"Swallow," I said. When she did, it gave me an aftershock of pleasure and I jerked, half-laughing at the crazy sensation. It was thrilling she'd waited for my command, and she might have just given me the best BJ of my life. I mean, how the fuck was that possible? I had to be a phenomenal teacher.

She retreated off me, but I still had hold of her hair, and wasn't done looking at her like this, her kneeling between my legs. Under my direction, she tilted her head and laid her cheek against my thigh, her big, doe eyes staring up at me. Her parted lips were damp and swollen, and she took in deep breaths as if I'd worn her out.

Or maybe looking at me was doing that to her, making her out of breath. I liked that idea.

One push of the power button on the remote shut the entire system down, and the TV screen went dark. I kept hold of her hair, dropped the remote, and cupped her face with my free hand, brushing my thumb over her lips. She blinked lazily as I pressed it inside her mouth, and she did what she was supposed to. Her lips closed around it and sucked. I'd just come, so my cock was out of commission, but my orgasm had done fuck all to take away the lust.

"Tomorrow," I said, "when I get home from work, you'll wear that 'wedding night' shit I bought you, and my robe. Be sitting on my bed at six o'clock, ready for me."

I withdrew my thumb and smeared the wetness over her lips as I watched anxiety and excitement flash through her eyes. *Yes,* I answered her unasked question. *Tomorrow I claim what's mine.*

The rush of my orgasm left me both lax and awake, and apparently goddamn chatty, because the words spilled out. "You asked if it was satisfying killing the guy who shot my father. Thing is ... Ivan didn't do it."

Her posture straightened. The question was on her face, but before she could ask, she seemed to suspect the answer. Her shoulders tensed.

"Yeah." My lips curled in a lifeless smile. "My dad was a piece of shit, too, and it was satisfying as hell to put a bullet through his head."

chapter
SEVENTEEN

OKSANA

EVERY ALARM WENT OFF IN MY BODY. Warning sirens screamed danger. It wasn't news Vasilije was a killer, but to murder his own family? Any kill was hard, but my brother said the personal ones were the worst. They fucked you up, sometimes permanently. The alarms wailed louder that I wasn't disguising my thoughts from my face. I was only supposed to know what Vasilije told me.

Dimitrije Markovic had been almost as powerful as his older brother Goran. How the hell was Vasilije still alive? It had to be because Goran didn't know. Holy shit. Did *anyone* know? And . . . why had Vasilije told me?

Because you're a stupid toy for him to play with. I was his pet, and nothing more. I needed to remember that, but I couldn't help how my voice was tight, choked with eagerness. "Tell me every detail."

His wide grin reached all the way to his glittering eyes and he looked like he wanted to swallow me whole. "Yeah?"

He sat up and seized my head in his hands, tilting me up to meet his harsh kiss. His mouth was rough and dominating. Was this kiss he was delivering now the closest Vasilije got to passion? His tongue tangled with mine as we battled for control over my mouth. I lost, of course. He was the devil and tasted like sin. Dark, delicious evil.

"You tell me again," he muttered against my mouth, "how we're not like each other."

An icy chill clung to my skin, but I didn't mind it. I was cold, like he always was. And if anyone would understand him, it was me.

Vasilije had done what I was trying to do.

My father deserved to die. If I couldn't do it, I'd ask Vasilije to volunteer.

He reached behind my back and undid the hooks of my bra then pulled it away from my body. It dropped silently to the thick rug, and I set my palms on his knees, smoothing my hands up his denim covered thighs. But his kiss ended and his expression turned smug.

"Go clean up the dishes from dinner, and then maybe I'll tell you."

I filled my lungs with a deep breath as he tucked himself back in his underwear and did up his jeans. He was completely dressed and I was stark naked, and as he pulled us both to our feet, I knew what was going to happen. I'd have to clean and put everything away while he watched me.

Following his order wasn't too bad when I focused on the tasks and not his gaze lingering on my body. A weird part of me kind of liked it. I closed the cartons and put the leftovers in the fridge. I carried his plate to the sink and rinsed it, then racked it and my own in the dishwasher. He said nothing, but I felt his presence on every fucking inch of my skin, and when I spied his lust-filled expression, I nearly burst into flames.

His desire for me was sexual, but I was beginning to wonder if I'd scratched the surface of more with him. He said we were alike, and he fucking loved himself, so it stood to reason he might someday feel something for me besides mere tolerance. Never love—because, like me, he didn't have the weakness of a heart—but maybe we'd come to have mutual respect. Even loyalty.

I was losing my mind. Loyalty with a Serb? With a Markovic? They weren't capable. If they had any loyalty, their family wouldn't be this broken.

When I'd finished my 'chore,' Vasilije turned off the kitchen light and padded into the living room. I followed, stood beside the couch, and waited for his next command. He collected my clothes in his arms, dumped them in a pile at the foot of the stairs, and motioned up. At the top of the landing, his cold fingers curled around my wrist and tugged me toward the door to his bedroom.

He didn't turn on the light, and I stared at the bed, lit only by moonlight from the window.

Had it only been last night since I'd stood in this room? It felt like both a lifetime ago and like no time had passed at all. I was gripped by the same nerves, and they worsened as he skimmed his fingertips over my collarbone. They skated between my breasts, drew an S on my belly, and journeyed onto my back as he rounded me.

Was he trying to get me used to his touch? Impossible. His touch wasn't bad, it was just . . . different. Unlike anything else. I was sure he could touch me a million times and it'd always feel this way. Dangerous and a little exciting. His palm closed on my shoulder and urged me down. Without a word, his command was clear. I sat naked on the carpet in the center of the room as he tugged off his t-shirt and tossed it aside.

His body was like his personality. Hard and cold, yet appealing. He undid his jeans and stepped out of them, casting the heavy fabric away with a thud. I sat perfectly still, my legs gathered to one side of my body as he went to a dresser and fished out a metal lunchbox.

I'd thought I'd smelled pot last night, but I'd been a bit of a wreck when I'd come out of the bathroom wearing nothing but his robe. He cracked a window, pulled out a rolled joint, and flicked on a lighter, making the end of the joint glow briefly as he sucked down air. The lighter was thrown down on the dresser in a noisy tumble.

Vasilije grabbed a bowl and sat on the edge of the bed, smoking the entire joint without saying anything, but his gaze never wavered from me. What was he thinking about? His eyes went narrow at one point and he had to be evaluating me critically. It should have made me feel small, but I wasn't going to let it.

I sprawled out on the floor, propping my elbow on the carpet and resting my head in my hand, giving him the most confident look I could muster, even though I was more vulnerable than I'd ever been. It was pointless. It seemed like Vasilije Markovic could see right through me, and I probably looked like an idiot lounging on the floor.

Yet all he did was smoke his goddamn joint and stare with his black eyes.

It was freezing with the window open, and I tried not to shiver. He wasn't. Shouldn't he be cold? It was supposed to be fiery in hell, after all. The only thing warm in this room was the joint and the white line of smoke he blew from his lungs. Eventually he stubbed out the tiny remainder in the bowl, put it on the dresser, and slammed the window shut with a loud bang.

"I barely remember my mom," he said abruptly.

My breath caught in my throat.

"I can't even tell if my memories of her are real, or just pictures I've seen so many times I've turned them into memories." He leaned against the dresser and focused on me, crossing his powerful and threatening arms over his chest. "But she loved me and my brother. I know that. And she loved my dad for some stupid fucking reason."

I pushed up to sit and pressed my hands together in my lap, hoping he'd keep talking.

"He fucked around. I guess he always had women on the side, but when my mom came home one night and found him balls-deep in some nineteen-year-old whore, that was it. She'd been disrespected too many times, and tried to leave him. In fact, she fucking told him she was going straight to the police to rat him and my uncle out."

I swallowed thickly. Nineteen. A year younger than me. My pulse banged along and threatened to shake me apart. "What happened?"

His eyes had so much gravity, I couldn't look anywhere else.

His expression hardened. "My father called my uncle and had her killed before she could do it." He stood from the dresser and stalked toward me. "For more than fifteen years, I thought she died in a car accident, but he'd been lying through his goddamn teeth the whole time."

Vasilije dropped to his knees before me, bringing our gazes level. His pupils were dilated, announcing the drug was starting to hit him.

"He fucking took her from me," he continued, "so I took his life from him." He leaned forward, putting his lips against my jawline and kissed a sloppy line down my neck. "Now I'm an orphan, just like you. Alone in this big, stupid house."

I held perfectly still as his mouth waged its assault against my skin. One attack after another, chiseling away at my ability to stay strong. If he kissed me on the lips, I kissed him back, but I'd promised myself I wasn't going to initiate again.

"What happened to your brother?" I asked. "There are pictures of him in the house."

He considered my statement. "Luka isn't like us. He knew what our father did, but couldn't pull the trigger. And now he's so pussy-whipped, he goes wherever his girlfriend does, and she went off to med school in Baltimore."

I had to tread carefully. Trying to get close to him too fast could make him push me away. I forced a casual tone. "Do you two talk much?"

"Not really. He's older." A faint scowl threatened his expression. "He's smart, and loves to make sure people knows just how much smarter he is than them."

Arrogance must be part of the Markovic genetic code. "Does he know you killed your father?"

"Yeah, he was there when I did it. He'd confronted our dad about the night our mom died, and when the truth came out, I couldn't even look at either of them. My dad kept talking, saying some more bullshit lies, but I was fucking done. I pulled my gun and shot out the back of his head."

His eyes drilled into me, and it felt like he was silently demanding I ask him. My voice fell an octave. "How did you feel after you did it?"

"Empty," he said. "I felt nothing. Luka told me I was in shock, but fuck that." He sat back, propping his elbow up on his bent knee. Stripped bare of all his clothes except for a pair of underwear, and in this comfortable, casual position, he still looked threatening, the same way a sleeping lion did. "Sometimes I wish my father was still alive, only so I could kill him again."

He'd closed the window, but the temperature continued to drop, and I shivered. I'd had the same thought about Ilia more than once, and Vasilije stared back at me like he knew. Presented with all this evidence, I still refused to accept we were alike. I was a different kind of animal than he was.

Wasn't I?

"Tell me about your mother," he demanded.

What? "You want to know about my mother?"

He shrugged. "You don't like talking about yourself, so I'm going to make you do it." When I made a face, his eyebrow arrowed upward. "You want me to bend you over my lap? I bet your ass still hurts from the last time I had to persuade you."

He was right, but I wouldn't give him the satisfaction. "I told you, she was an opera singer." His glare was razor sharp, and I sighed. "She had a beautiful voice. Such gorgeous tone and vibrato, which I wish I'd gotten."

"You can't sing?"

I skewed my lips to one side. "I can carry a tune, but my singing voice is average. My musical instrument is my mind, not my vocals."

"How come your parents didn't get married when she got

knocked up with you?"

There were plenty of reasons to choose from. Because my father was already married with a kid. Because he lived in America. Because he was a fucking son-of-a-bitch. "My mother didn't talk much about him, and what she had to say . . . wasn't very nice. They were only together that one time."

"One night stand?"

It wasn't something I'd shared with anyone else. "I don't think she was . . . willing."

It was bad enough being a bastard, but to be a product of something unwanted? At least my mother had never looked at me with resentment. She'd loved me with all of her big heart, which, like her voice, I had not inherited. No, the cold dead spot in my body that beat as a machine must have come from *him*.

The boy staring at me suddenly looked cold. Mortal after all. Chaos churned in his eyes. What was he thinking about? That he was putting me in the same place as my mother? Forcing himself on me? I had to make it clear that wasn't the situation. I'd chosen this path.

I . . . wanted it, just a little.

His gaze swung away. "I'm tired. Go sleep in your room."

I disobeyed him for the second time tonight, and as I crawled over to him, his eyes narrowed with suspicion. I put my hands on his shoulders and straddled his lap, all while distrust slid down his face. I'd never practiced seduction before, but I prayed it came as naturally to me as tempo.

It came out breathlessly when I tried to control it. "You're not alone in this big, stupid house anymore."

He peered up into my eyes as his hands settled on my waist, but his expression was impossible to read. "And if you want to stay here in the big, stupid house with me," he leaned forward and brushed his lips over the pulse thrumming in my neck, "you'll do what I tell you to."

He shoved me hard, tossing me off his lap.

"I sleep alone." His harsh tone made me feel like a fool. "Get the fuck out, Oksana."

chapter
EIGHTEEN

I SAT ON THE END OF VASILIJE'S BED, wearing the white lingerie he'd bought me and covered with his black robe while my insides rattled. I'd washed the lingerie last night before going to sleep, and my hands shook when I put it on this afternoon.

It was necessary and just sex, right? People did it all the time. I'd done harder things. Worse things. Fucking Vasilije shouldn't be a big deal. All I had to do was lie there and let it happen. But I wasn't an idiot. Nothing was simple or easy with him, and no amount of psyching myself up could mentally prepare me for the moment. He enjoyed my confusion. He liked my discomfort.

Six o'clock came and went.

The bedroom was a tomb, and the quiet ate at me.

I made the bed. That was the only thing I did to ready the room. If I lit candles, he'd never let me hear the end of it, and it wasn't my style anyway. I didn't do romance, and was sure he didn't, either. I just wanted to get this over with.

Time dragged, and I stared out the window with nothing to do but think about him. I could have been downstairs, seated at the piano and working. Even though the thing wasn't tuned, I'd never gotten so much undisturbed time to write, and it made me greedy for more. Was this calculated? Was Vasilije making some sort of statement by having me wait for him?

Because it was late November, the sun had set almost two hours ago, and I stared at my reflection in the glass. My blonde hair fell loose around my shoulders, and I looked pale wrapped in the black robe. If I'd had makeup, I'd have done something to cover the dark circles under my eyes, but there was nothing in this house for me to use. I'd slept a full eight hours last night, but I didn't feel rested. It was like all that had happened was the passage of time.

I looked... plain. Unremarkable.

At six thirty, my anxiety morphed into anger. I'd been on pins and needles all day, so dragging this out was cruel, which led me to believe it was intentional. I stewed in my frustration. I couldn't exactly leave, and I'd gone too far to give up my goal.

I heard the garage door on the far side of the house at six forty, and blew out a breath. All this waiting, and instantly I wished I had a few more minutes. His loud, rapid footsteps pounded out downstairs, and then he was coming up the steps... two at a time? Was he hurrying?

The door burst open, and he looked as startled to see me as I was him. He was carrying a red plastic bag and flung it down on top of his dresser, while his hand went to the knot of his tie. "Fuck, that took a lot longer than I thought it would."

His tone was strange. Almost apologetic. He stared at me on the bed. "Have you been waiting for me this whole time?"

Was he serious? "You told me to."

He unthreaded the tie from his collar, moving slowly as if distracted. "I did. I'm kinda surprised you didn't give up."

It wasn't in my nature to give up. Like Vasilije, I usually got what I wanted, but I actually had to work for it. I was banking hard on the enemy of my enemy becoming my friend, but as I evaluated the guy in a suit across the room from me, I wondered if I was a fool. He didn't look at me like he wanted to be my friend.

He looked like a guy who wanted to fuck me and throw me away, just like my father had done to my mother. The difference was I knew who I was dealing with. I might not outsmart the devil, but I was willing to deal with him.

He pulled off his shoes and socks.

I sat straight on the edge of the bed, my legs crossed and the sides of the robe stacked over my knees to cover me. My pulse ticked upward as he stalked forward and undid the top two buttons of his dress shirt, raw lust dripping from his expression. He was so fucking attractive. Vasilije was a beautiful, poisonous flower, luring me to come closer. I'd be so distracted I'd never notice his trap, or how he started to devour me until it was too late.

He gripped my chin and tilted my head back, forcing my gaze on his. The smile smeared across his lips was lewd. "Have you been thinking about fucking me all day today?"

"Yes." It was the truth.

"Me, too." Satisfaction gleamed in his eyes. He bent down, bringing his lips almost to mine, and my eyes closed as I prepared for his kiss. Just as I felt his warm breath on my skin, he pushed my chin away and drew back, teasing me. Denying what he'd been promising a split-second ago.

Fuck him. Did he think I cared about whether he kissed me? I didn't, I told myself. I absolutely did not care if he wanted to cover my mouth with his or slide his soft tongue past my lips and taste me.

His focus and hands went to the knot at my waist, and he ripped it free, flinging the robe open. His gaze scraped down me from head to toe, inspecting the white mesh and lace decorating my body. "You're such a good girl." He scrubbed a hand over his face, and the gesture made it seem like he could barely contain his excitement. "Too bad I'm going to ruin you."

"Please," I said, holding back the eye roll. "How good can I be? Are you forgetting I killed someone?"

He chuckled darkly. "Fuck, no, that makes you hotter." He shoved a hand into my hair and gripped the strands at the base of my skull, yanking me to my feet. "I meant I'm gonna ruin your virgin pussy."

Well, get on with it, then. I'd waited long enough, had endured his threats. It was time for him to show me they weren't empty.

It was cold as he peeled down a side of the robe, letting it hang on one shoulder. My chest rose and fell with my rapid, shallow breaths, which drew his attention to my bra. I watched his tongue as he licked his lips, and it made my stomach clench.

Cool fingertips skimmed over my hips and around my back, drawing me into his arms, and then Vasilije's warm mouth was on my collarbone. It carved a path downward, leaving a trail of damp skin behind and causing goosebumps to break out on my flesh. Like every molecule of my skin was rising up to get close to him.

The tip of his tongue drew a line between my breasts, and when he reached the small band at the center of the bra, he changed course. His lips followed the curve of my breast, sucking and nipping at me through the lace.

I took in air in controlled sips. What he was doing felt shockingly good, and the sight of it was even better. His open mouth soaked the bra cup, and his tongue stroked my hard nipple through the damp fabric. When I issued a soft sigh, the fingertips on the small of my back urged me forward. They urged me to arch my back and push my breast deeper into his mouth.

Not only did I comply, I threaded a hand through his hair and held his head. His noise of approval sent a rush of desire through me. How long would he tease me like this before taking the bra off? How long until the virginal white panties were wadded on the floor?

"You like this?" he said, and ensnared my nipple between his teeth, pulling it away from my body. It hurt, but in a good, pleasurable way, and it was so sexy how his dark eyes looked up at me.

"Yes," I whispered.

His sexual expression was going to melt me. I was overheated and wanted the robe gone, but I held still and let him continue to lick and torment me with his sinister mouth. The ache between my legs intensified as he tugged the strap down over my shoulder and pushed the bra cup out of his way.

"Oh," I moaned. His rough bite on my sensitive, bare skin was almost too much. That edge of pain faded into overwhelming heat and my knees softened.

My moan pulled a trigger on Vasilije. He wrenched the robe off me and flung it on the bed. Rough, urgent hands spun me around to face it. The bra was unhooked and yanked from me, the straps tangling in my arms for a moment before he hurled it to the floor.

I yelped when his hand cracked against my ass, and he left his palm there, using it to push me forward. "Up. On your hands and knees."

The bed rocked as I climbed on and crawled to the center, hovering over the robe. I stared at the gray stone wall and let my gaze trace the patterns while he grabbed the back of my panties and jerked them down, tugging until they were halfway down my thighs. It left me on full display for him. Any second I expected a painful blow. The staccato slap of his hand against my exposed, waiting skin. God, what was wrong with me? I almost looked forward to it.

But it didn't come.

He wasn't even touching me. My lust-filled mind was distracted, and I hadn't been listening to what he was doing. The mattress shifted as he climbed on behind me. There was rustling. Then, he set a cold hand on the flat of my back, causing me to flinch.

A panicked noise of surprise burst from me when something velvety-soft and round stroked me. I'd expected foreplay, or spankings, or . . . *something* first. After all his mocking, he was just going to get right to it and fuck me? My body locked up, beyond nervous. I thought I was ready, but I felt so off balance.

The tip of his hard cock glided over my damp pussy, running the length along me, and I shuddered with pleasure as it made contact with my swollen clit. It felt physically good, but my brain went haywire over how close we were to having actual sex. He rocked back and forth, drenching his dick in my arousal and teasing what was going to happen.

"Goddamn, Oksana." His voice was breathless, and pride surged through me. I was the one who'd made it hard for him to catch his breath. "I'm gonna slide my cock so deep inside you. All the way in. I'm going to fuck this pussy raw."

A shuddering breath fell out of me. I'd envisioned how I thought this was going to play out tonight, but I'd been wrong. I was supposed to be on my back, staring up at him as he took me, after hours of torturous foreplay. Not on my hands and knees, with my underwear still on and my pussy untouched.

He was still dressed, which wasn't surprising. It was a power thing, I assumed. But there was more rustling. A thud as the gun and holster came off and were set on the floor. I saw a flash of white in my peripheral vision. He'd pulled his dress shirt off. The bed rocked slightly as he pushed his pants and underwear to his knees on the mattress.

The head of his cock brushed over my clit faster, and the sensation was amazing.

His low voice rang out from behind me. "You want it in your tight, pretty little hole?"

I bit down on my lip, silencing the gasp that would give too much away. Because . . . I did. Heat was building from between my legs where he was simulating sex, and the tension from waiting all day had me so tight, I threatened to snap.

"Yes," I said.

"Tell me," he demanded. When I didn't right away, I got what I'd been expecting. His punishing spanking stung and burned across my backside. He growled it out. "Tell me."

"I want it," I gasped. "I want it in my tight, pretty little hole."

The word was loaded with sin. "Yeah?"

He was gliding so fast through my slickness I could hear it, and

I knew what game we were playing. He wanted me to beg, so I would. It wasn't a stretch of the truth. My hand curled around a fistful of the robe beneath me. "Oh, God. I want it, Vasilije."

"So eager." He mocked me with a dark tone. "Not yet."

chapter
NINETEEN

THE CONTACT OF VASILIJE'S DICK WAS GONE.

He delivered another brutal spanking, and I fell forward onto my stomach on the bed, running from the pain. The panties were jerked the rest of the way down, and then he dug a hand under my arm, flinging me over onto my back. He moved me like I was a ragdoll, and I gawked up at him, wide-eyed.

Looking at him was the same as staring at the sun. He was scorching. Beautiful. Fascinating, but I couldn't do it for too long or I'd risk permanent damage. He catapulted forward over me, bracing himself with his hands by my shoulders, and as he lifted up, he kicked off the pants wadded around his ankles. His thick erection swayed and bobbed as he moved, and nerves clamped my stomach. All of that was about to go inside me.

When he was as naked as I was, he lowered and set his cock in the cradle between my thighs. I shuddered with pleasure and anticipation, and my lungs refused to work. All he had to do was slide back a few inches and then he could charge forward. Is that how he'd do it? Take my virginity in one quick thrust? If that was the most painful way to do it, it was likely the choice he'd make.

He reared back, but instead of positioning himself at my entrance, Vasilije continued to move down my body, until his mouth was on my breasts and his stomach was pressed against my pussy.

"Oh, fuck," I groaned. It was a mixture of pain and pleasure as he chewed on my nipple. I peered down at him and watched his cheeks hollow as he sucked so hard on my flesh, it ached. I writhed and squirmed beneath him, but never asked him to stop.

Only because I wanted to please him. I mean, I didn't like this . . . right? His cruel mouth was leaving red marks on my white skin, and it was going to look a hell of a lot worse tomorrow. I kneaded and clawed at his shoulders. I arched my back, shifting away from his sharp teeth, but all that did was roll him from one breast to the other, and I couldn't help but think I'd done it subconsciously.

Oh my God. I wanted the marks on me to be even.

I whimpered and whined. I rubbed my wet clit against the notches of his abdominals, desperate for his punishing mouth to let up, and needing relief from the ache in my core. He had me pinned to the mattress, holding me captive with his lips and the promise he was going to fuck me.

There was a loud pop as my nipple broke free from his mouth, and he shifted once more, moving further down the length of my body. So, I hadn't been wrong after all. It was going to be hours of torturous foreplay. The skin he'd abused was warm and tender, but the burn was sexy. I felt thoroughly used.

"Get these fucking legs open wider," he snarled, and he slapped his fingers on the insides of my thighs. I yelped with pain and immediately obeyed, yanking my legs wide open. The gasp that poured from my mouth was so loud, I should have been embarrassed, but when his tongue swiped through my pussy, all I could think was I needed him to do it again.

My thighs were on fire from the painful slaps he'd inflicted, but I held perfectly still, and moaned as he feasted on me. His tongue wandered over my flesh, toying with my clit, flicking back and forth until everything from my waist down was shaking. His eyes were closed, and his eyebrows tugged together, separated by a crease. He was concentrating so hard.

Working to bring me pleasure.

It was dirty, and erotic, and my mouth fell open watching. The sensation of his wet, soft tongue was like nothing else. A dark, primal need took control. It demanded satisfaction, and made me a slave to this man. I'd do anything to keep him going.

"Oh my God, Vasilije," I cried.

"You like how I'm eating you out?"

"Yes," I whispered. It was vulgar, but I didn't fucking care. Once again, I was so far removed from what was normal for me, I felt overwhelming freedom. I could say or do anything dirty and nasty and wrong, without shame. I put my hands on my knees, pressing them further open, widening to the point of discomfort. I didn't want him to have any excuse to stop, but once I started touching myself, my hands had a mind of their own.

They roamed over my legs. Up my thighs, my stomach, all the way until I filled them with my breasts and relished the lingering pain from his vicious mouth. It felt so bad, it was good. *No, better.* It was perfect.

"You're going to make me . . ." My lips trembled as the words failed me. He'd taken a flamethrower to my body and torched me. The heat from his mouth had burned me beyond recognition and I was a completely different person.

"Come on, now. Get there." His voice was urgent and excited, encouraging my orgasm. "You like that?"

I fisted a handful of his hair, locking him in place. I was wild and out of control. Completely out of my mind. "I do," I moaned. "I do, I do, *I do* . . ."

The tremors started in my hips and rolled toward my knees. Pleasure erupted from my center and flooded outward, sweeping heat across my skin, followed by numb bliss. My mind went blank. White with pleasure as the orgasm exploded in a rush. Its catastrophic fire consumed me, and left me shaking as it burned through, gone as quickly as it arrived.

My moans had swelled and ebbed, leaving no doubt what had happened, but when I'd gotten lost in the ecstasy, I'd closed my legs, clamping my thighs down around his ears. I forced my legs apart, but it was too late. Vasilije rose onto his knees, his mouth wet and glistening with my desire, and his eyes burned with a dark lust. Shit, he looked powerful and terrifying.

I flinched and cried out as he struck the inside of my thighs a second time, first one side and then the other, punishing me for disobeying him. His worst spankings on my bottom weren't that bad, but these? They *hurt*. They throbbed afterward, matching the need beating in my foundation for him.

"Fuck me." I blurted it out, unable to get a handle on the throbbing.

"You want it? How bad do you need it, good girl?"

"Please," I said, reaching for him. I grasped a hand on his hard dick, but he swatted it away, twisting my hand until our fingers were twined together. He leaned over me, pressing the back of my palm to the mattress above my head.

Time slowed until it seemed to suspend.

Vasilije rubbed his erection over my pussy, rocking his hips as our flesh glided against each other, leaving us both breathless. At some point, he grabbed my other hand and laced our fingers together there, pinning that hand beside the other. I was at his mercy. The gorgeous devil hovered over me, threatening a kiss with his lush, full lips just a breath away, but he never gave it to me. Like he was waiting for something.

I don't know how long I endured it.

It felt like eons. His hard body thrust against mine, giving flashes of pleasure and causing me to buck, but his grip on my hands was firm. He handcuffed me with his hold and his piercing black eyes, which seemed to watch each breath I swallowed.

He must have wanted me to vibrate apart. I shook so hard, the headboard of the bed tapped quietly against the wall, but perhaps his movements were causing that. He teased, swiveling his hips, but never sank into me. I grew so frantic, I tried anything I could to make him do it. I lifted my hips, but he pushed away and gave me a malicious smile. Like he enjoyed it.

So, I did the only thing I had left. I surged forward and planted my lips on his.

When I connected us in this way, he chose to connect us in the other. The hard tip of his dick lined up and began to creep inside.

Oh, shit.

It was too much. I turned my head away from his kiss, but he released my hands and slammed both of his palms on my jaw, framing my head in place. Making it so I couldn't run from him. His tongue dipped into my mouth as he advanced inside me, and a moan gurgled in my throat.

It didn't exactly hurt. It was more uncomfortable. A stretch past the point of what I liked, and while I wanted him to back off, he just kept pushing deeper. I managed to get my lips free of his, but only enough so he could speak.

"That's it. Take it."

I couldn't find any air to breathe. His mouth was right beside mine and his hot breath filled my lungs as his cock filled me. The ache grew into a stabbing pain, and I whimpered.

It wasn't shocking that it hurt. I knew it was likely to the first time I had sex. What was surprising was how beneath the pain, I still enjoyed it. The swollen fullness of it all. Another person was inside me, and judging by the emotion ringing Vasilije's eyes, he loved it. Inch by inch, he took me, and pleasure choked his expression.

I undulated beneath him. My trembling legs gripped his hips and tried to stop his descent into me, but it was futile. When I closed my eyes, he jolted my head in his hands, startling them back open.

His tone was severe. "Eyes on me."

Didn't he know how hard that was? His dark eyes lured me in, and I worried I'd lose myself in them completely. A soft whine fell from my lips as he pressed all the way inside and his body was fitted against mine. The ache throbbed everywhere and I stopped moving, forcing myself to breathe through the uncomfortable situation.

I wasn't a virgin anymore.

Vasilije Markovic was my first, and if things went terribly wrong, he'd be my last, too.

He only gave me ten seconds of stillness before he began to move. His hips drew back and I scrunched my face in displeasure. His expression was unchanged. It was just as intense as it'd been throughout this whole thing. He studied me like a teacher watching a piano student's fingers, ready at any moment to correct a mistake.

A deep thrust rocked my body, and my mouth rounded into a silent scream as his hard chest pressed against mine. I wanted to sink into the soft fabric of the robe beneath me, melt away from the pain his thrust delivered.

His next one was worse, and I couldn't stay quiet. I whimpered and slapped my hands on his broad shoulders, pushing at him. His eyes tightened on mine, and he paused. "Slower?" His uneven question threw me even more off balance. So far, he'd given me nothing but orders. He didn't take requests or ask for permission.

I swallowed thickly and nodded.

His eyes flooded with heat as he retreated and advanced on me, moving at a fraction of his previous speed and with less aggression. He was probably making his best attempt at being gentle. His shallow thrusts came at an adagio tempo I could handle, and then his lips were on mine, muting the discomfort. His skin and heart were cold, but his mouth was fire. It was addicting. I was thirsty for his heat.

He maintained the slow rhythm while his lips were sealed over mine, and I focused on that. I enjoyed his kiss. He hadn't rejected me this time when I'd instigated it. His open mouth moved against mine, letting our tongues meet and stroke, and I moaned with satisfaction.

It was another pull of a trigger.

That was when Vasilije really began to fuck me.

chapter
TWENTY

Vasilije

Oksana's pussy squeezed me like a fist, and I clenched my jaw against the pleasure. Something strange was happening to me, though. Whenever I fucked, I didn't care much about the girl attached to the pussy I was balls-deep in. I wanted them to come, but not because I wanted them to have pleasure, but because it made me feel powerful. And listening to a girl scream was sexy, and there was nothing better than feeling them coming on my cock.

Right up until the moment I slid inside her virgin pussy, I'd . . . *fuck me.* I liked giving her a dose of pain to go along with the pleasure. A few girls had tolerated me when I'd gone rough, but it was amateur hour in comparison to what I'd done to Oksana. The Russian had taken whatever I dished out and barely said a goddamn thing.

The sick fucker inside me whispered she liked it rough. She got off on the pain I inflicted. My blood rushed loudly in my ears, whooshing along with excitement. But then I'd shoved my cock inside her, and saw agony in her eyes, and I went cold. It was only fun when she liked it.

The slow pace I fucked her at was a nightmare of pleasure. She was wet but tight, and her muscles were tense, which probably made it hurt more. I distracted us both by kissing her. Got her to loosen up, and when she moaned, it broke the wall holding back the asshole I was.

I lifted onto my hands, gazed down at her pussy, and my cock pumping in and out of her. The thick muscle glistened with her juices, and there was the trophy I'd wanted. A smear of blood. Fucked up satisfaction overtook me. I'd been first to plant my flag. Oksana was all mine.

"It's so hot," I said between two tight breaths, "watching my cock fuck you." And it felt even better.

She said nothing. Her face was blank, and I didn't like it. She'd come alive when I'd had my tongue all up in her pussy, and I was greedy. I wanted more of that. "Does it still hurt?"

Oksana's lips pressed together. She didn't use words, but it was enough of an answer.

"How bad? Does it just hurt, or does it hurt but feel good, too?"

"It feels good, too," she whispered.

A current jolted through me and my cock flexed, liking the sound of that. I dialed back the urge to drive into her. We weren't there yet. I kept at the same pace, easing my dick in and out of her soaking body, watching the glide and how I disappeared inside her.

I thought of all the ways I was going to fuck her. Doggie style. Reverse cowgirl. Maybe bent over the back of the couch downstairs where I could watch us onscreen again. Definitely on the piano bench. We'd be on fire.

Oksana's tense body beneath me began to relax one muscle at a time. Her clipped pants for air were interrupted by moans, and these were sounds of pleasure. The soft, sexy cries shot straight to my dick. I slammed my mouth over hers, giving her a kiss that was how I liked to fuck. Hard. Rough. Dirty.

She wasn't going to come from sex her first time. She'd probably already made up her mind about it and nothing I'd do was going to change that. But I was glad she didn't seem to be hating it. A few more times and I'd have her coming all over me.

I'd get her addicted to my cock, so when I came home from the dealership or some stressful bullshit, she'd be waiting by the door, salivating for me. No more empty house, or logging hours at some bar while I had to convince some lame girl to let me get my dick wet. None of the girls I'd found compared to the one I was currently inside. And she was *mine*.

Mine alone.

I jammed my hands under Oksana, between her back and the mattress, and railed into her tight pussy. I couldn't wait to come inside her. Would my cum scald her raw insides? Was she already sore from taking all of me? It made my dick insanely hard.

The plan was to take my time, but I couldn't hold it back. My hips moved faster than I wanted them to, responding to the driving need in my balls. I'd swear I'd been waiting a lifetime to fuck her, and now my body demanded satisfaction. It wouldn't settle for anything less, and no more delaying the inevitable.

"Aw, fuck," I groaned, crossing a point I couldn't return from. This shit was about to happen, and once the decision was made, I went at her full force. I pistoned in and out of her, slamming our bodies together in a series of loud slaps. She gasped with each one. Her nails dug into my ass, holding on.

The orgasm erupted, spewing my pleasure deep inside her as I slowed to a jerky stop. My arms shook as I cased her body, trying not to smother Oksana with all of my weight. The orgasm hit me in waves, rocking back and forth like a seesaw of hot and cold bliss, slowing down on every turn until I could breathe again and hear over the blood roaring in my ears.

Her rapid breathing decelerated, and I buried my nose in the side of her neck, letting her hair tickle my face. She smelled good. Her skin was warm and soft, and it was crazy how comfortable I was right this very second. My cock was still lodged inside her. My sweaty chest stuck to hers.

I was tempted to stay here. I'd get hard again and maybe this time I'd make her ride me. Would she like feeling like she was in control, even if it was an illusion? But we couldn't stay like this. I hadn't eaten since lunch and was starving.

When I moved off her, I rolled onto my side, lying next to her on the spread-out robe. I'd thrown it down on the bed so we wouldn't make a mess, but she'd barely bled. Her gaze was locked on the ceiling, so I grabbed her chin and pulled her head toward me.

Her face was blank. Not traumatized, or nervous, or even bored. Just . . . empty. Unease tightened uncomfortably in my chest. I shouldn't care, but for some reason, I did. "You okay?"

"I'm fine," she said. "Now that it's over, I wish I hadn't made such a big deal about it in my head."

Did this chick just tell me that sleeping with me wasn't a big deal? Anger flexed its muscles, stretching out as it prepared to take up residence. I was awesome at sex. A *fantastic* fuck. "You want me to make it a big deal? Next time, I will," I threatened.

Her eyes went wide. "I didn't mean it like that." She rolled onto her side, facing me. "When are we . . . going to do that again?"

Anger disappeared faster than a snap of fingers. I had her flat on her back and was over her, my mouth attacking hers. I kissed her harder than I'd ever kissed another girl before. Usually I used it as a tool. A weapon to get what I wanted, but with Oksana . . . I didn't.

I kissed her just for the hell of it.

Because you like her.

She was gorgeous, and talented, and I found her fascinating. She looked so pure and good on the outside, but inside she was dark like me. An evil creature dressed up in pretty packaging.

We made out, which was weird as fuck because usually the kissing came before the sex, but whatever. Maybe I hadn't liked kissing before. It was a chore to get to the good part, except with her . . . it was a good part.

My stomach growled and finally I climbed off her. "Stay there."

I went to the bathroom and cleaned myself off, and when I came back, I leaned against the door frame, crossing my arms. She'd followed my order, but had also pulled the robe on, covering herself.

"I like you better when you're naked."

"I was cold."

Maybe it was the truth. I'd seen her naked plenty of times, she should be used to it by now. I went to the dresser and grabbed the red plastic bag, then tossed it down on the bed beside her. "This is for you."

She stared at it like she expected the bag to explode. "What is it?"

She sat up, tucked a lock of hair behind her ear, and reached hesitantly for her present. The bag crinkled as she pulled out the book, and she seemed to recognize what it was instantly. Her gaze flew to me, and the question was loud in her eyes, "*What's this?*"

"You have your theme song," I said, watching her page through the empty composer notebook. "Now you'll write mine."

What was the emotion that flicked through her eyes? Interest? She stared at the paper. "I'm not sure I could fit all of you into one song."

I grinned. "Then write a goddamn symphony."

The emotion *was* interest. She liked this idea, but then she sobered. "That might take a while."

"You've got something better to do?"

I watched as she curled her arms around the notebook and held it to her chest. She clutched it like I'd take back the book and the idea at any second. Not possible. I'd had her haunting song stuck in my head most of the morning, and decided I needed my own.

"It better not be like most of the garbage you wrote," I said. "I want it like yours. Got it?"

She peered at me like I was an imposter, but nodded slowly, too stunned to speak.

"Good. The piano tuner comes tomorrow at noon." I'd scheduled it around my lunch break so I could keep an eye on both Oksana and whoever the music studio sent over. "Get cleaned up. We're going downstairs for dinner."

She crawled off the bed, moving gingerly. Was her body reminding her she wasn't a virgin anymore? I fucking loved it. I wanted her thinking about me every time she had an ache or saw the marks I'd put on her skin.

"What if I can't do it?" she asked.

"What the fuck are you talking about?"

She took a deep breath. "What if you don't like what I compose?"

I shrugged. "Then I guess I'll have to motivate your ass to try harder."

chapter
TWENTY-ONE

OKSANA

THE WOMAN WHO CAME TO TUNE THE PIANO reminded me of the first teacher I'd had, an older woman who spent more time in front of the piano than anywhere else, including a mirror. Her frizzy hair, streaked with gray, was stacked on top of her head in a messy bun, and her clothes looked well worn.

Vasilije watched her every move, and I could tell it wasn't with fascination. He was making sure she did nothing other than put the tuning hammer on the pins and go painstakingly key by key.

She was good. I'd watched my old teacher tune the piano at the opera house, and the woman today followed the same technique, working from the center keys outward. Although she was tuning quickly, it wasn't fast enough for Vasilije. He glared at her and often glanced at his phone to check the time, sighing with impatience.

"How much longer?" he demanded.

The woman turned the lever a miniscule amount and hit the key again. "At least another hour." She seemed just as put out by him as he was by her. "I'm sorry," her tone was pointed, "when did you say this was last tuned?" Her passive-aggressive comment had thoughts of murder flashing in his eyes, and she wasn't done. "Pianos are extremely sensitive to temperature changes. It shouldn't be near these windows."

"Great. Finish up and I'll move it."

"No!" the woman and I said at the same time.

The tuner answered before I could. "You move this, and I have to start all over."

"For fuck's sake," he muttered under his breath and his hard gaze traveled to mine. He could blame me all he wanted, but I needed this.

"It'll be worth it," I said as my throat tightened.

"It better be. It's costing me a hundred and fifty dollars an hour."

Whatever I composed, if he didn't like it, I'd pay with my body, and I was all right with it. He wanted a song, and although he wasn't compensating me in money, it didn't make a huge difference. He'd keep me around until it was done.

It also meant he was the first person who'd ever commissioned a piece by me.

I'd spent the morning eager to get to work, but decided to refrain until the piano was ready to go. I already heard a few strains of a melody I wanted to try. It'd start out sickly sweet, take a dark turn in the middle, then rise into an anthem that sounded as powerful as it was terrifying.

He got on his phone at one point, telling someone he wasn't going to be back for another hour, so I assumed it was the dealership. With his attention off me, I felt lighter, but I weirdly didn't like the feeling.

My body was sore and bruised from last night. Red-purple hickeys dotted my chest, and I'd stood in front of the bathroom mirror this morning, stunned at how beautiful the color was. What would he think of them when he saw me tonight? Surely we were going to have sex again. We hadn't after dinner last night. He'd gotten a call from his uncle, disappeared into his room, and never came out.

Vasilije pocketed his phone in the suit jacket and cast a dark look at the woman before his gaze finally drifted to me. He looked good in his black suit, gray checkered tie, and a sneer on his lips. I wondered how his employees liked working for him now that he'd taken his father's place. He'd usurped Dimitrije. Did the people at the dealership hate taking orders from a twenty-four-year-old punk?

Or was he charming as I'd heard he was, but never seen for myself?

"We're going out tonight," he said abruptly. "My cousin is coming over at five to help you. You'll wear the dress I bought."

He said it like it was no big deal, but my stomach lurched. He wanted me to wear the dress he'd described as what I'd wear when I'd meet his family. "Help me with what?"

"She's a makeup artist," he said.

"Oh." It was all I could think to say. How was I supposed to take that? Did he think makeup was needed with me, or was he simply wanting me to look my best and make a good impression?

"We have reservations downtown at seven." His gaze was piercing. "It's an important dinner."

He communicated everything he wasn't saying out loud with a single look. Did my life hinge on the outcome of this dinner? If it was with Goran, it seemed likely. Vasilije had told me his uncle wanted me gone.

"I understand," I said, although I really didn't.

We never spoke the rest of the time the piano tuner worked. The only sound was her tuning forks and the repeated tapping of keys to compare frequencies. We watched her work, and I'd swear I could feel every turn of the hammer tightening inside my body. But I worried it was the same for Vasilije, and if she pulled him taut enough, he'd snap and lash out at her worse than a broken piano wire.

Thankfully, it didn't happen.

She fixed the sticky key I pointed out, and as she packed up her kit, Vasilije looked beyond relieved the ordeal was over. He ushered her to the entryway and paid her in cash. She took it hesitantly, probably surprised, and scurried out the door a moment later. My guess was she was as happy to be gone as he was to be rid of her.

I sat at the piano, anxious to get started, but his heavy footfalls carried him toward me. "I have to get back to work." He grabbed a fistful of hair at the base of my skull and jerked me back with a gasp.

His expression was restrained, but his eyes were wild. "I wanted to fuck you when she was done, but that took too fucking long."

His mouth crushed against mine and his tongue shot past my lips. It was like he was fucking my mouth, and a whimper slipped from me. It shouldn't have turned me on the way he manhandled me, but... it did. Oh God, it did. His unapologetic domination was insane. How the hell could I capture it in a song?

He ended the kiss as brutally as he'd started it, shoving me away from him, and my hands flew out, bracing myself against the keyboard in a sound of panicked discord.

"I'll see you tonight. Be nice to Jennifer, or I won't be nice to you later."

Had he been *nice* to me before? I kept the comment to myself, because maybe I didn't want a nice Vasilije. My new muse was complex enough. He didn't say a real goodbye and left out the garage. The house felt cavernous when he was gone, but it made it easier to breathe.

I lost all track of time as I sat at the piano composing.

It was only when the sunlight faded enough that I realized how late it was. Was I supposed to be dressed when his cousin arrived? I dashed up the stairs, darting into the green-stripe wallpapered room, and dressed quickly in the black patterned dress. I'd just finished zipping it up when I heard movement downstairs.

"Hello?" a female voice called.

I went to the landing at the top of the stairs and looked down at the first floor. "Hello," I said.

She was petite. Blonde like me, but hers was a golden honey. The woman was early thirties and dressed stylishly in boots, jeans, a slim-fitting sweater, and a colorful scarf looped around her neck. Her hair was done in perfect soft curls and her skin looked flawless. In a single look, I could tell appearance meant everything to her.

"I'm Jennifer," she said, grabbing the handle of a large rolling tote and heading for the stairs.

"Nice to meet you." I slapped on a pleasant smile. "I'm Oksana."

Jennifer lugged her tote up the stairs and was disinterested in my greeting. When she reached me on the landing, she evaluated me critically and her tone was matter-of-fact. "He wasn't wrong when he said you were beautiful."

The offhanded comment nearly knocked me from my feet. Up until now, I'd only attracted unwanted attention from Ilia, so it was thrilling to have it reciprocated for once. Even if it was Vasilije Markovic.

"Thank you," I said.

Jennifer stared plainly at me. "Which room is yours?"

While she got organized and set up in the bathroom, I brought in a desk chair from one of the other bedrooms at her request. I sat in the center of the bathroom, facing the mirror, and held still as she began to work.

It was surreal as she draped a towel over my shoulders to prevent any makeup from getting on my dress. She slathered on moisturizer, followed by primer, then foundation. I kept waiting for her to start a conversation, but it didn't happen. I'd have to fire the first shot.

"You're Vasilije's cousin?" I asked lightly. I didn't know everyone in the Markovic family tree, just the major players, and she wasn't one of them.

"By marriage, yeah." She swept powder over the bridge of my nose.

I thought I'd kicked the conversation off, but it died instantly, and I scrambled for something else. "How long have you been a makeup artist?"

It did the trick. Useless info poured from the woman, telling me about how she'd done a wedding last week where the bride had a bad reaction to a facial peel, but Jennifer had been able to work a miracle. She loosened up as she moved on to doing my eyes, chatting about celebrities and their Instagram accounts like I had a clue, but I nodded back enthusiastically. Could I get her relaxed enough to tell me something useful?

The answer was no.

I tried everything to steer the conversation toward the Markovics, but she shut me down every time. When I had exhausted all my options and she'd finished, she pulled out a mammoth bottle of hair spray and a tray full of bobby pins, sectioned by color. A large-barreled curling iron was plugged in and flicked on.

"You're doing my hair, too?"

"Yeah." She wasn't gentle, either, but I stayed silent as she tugged my hair up into a ponytail and began curling and pinning. When she was done, my hair looked sophisticated, matching both the dress and the understated makeup.

If my half-sister Tatiana could see me now, her jaw would hit the floor and then she'd be pushing me out of the chair, demanding Jennifer do her next.

"Thank you," I said genuinely. "You're very good." I didn't have many emotions, but knowing I looked nice was an advantage.

She smiled warmly at my compliment. "Goran's going to do a double-take when he sees you."

I watched in the mirror as the smile froze on my face. That confirmed it; dinner was with Vasilije's uncle tonight. If I was being sent to my doom, at least I'd leave this world with a pretty face. I pretended to be confused, disguising my dread. "Who?"

Jennifer sucked in a breath. Clearly it had been a slip. She wouldn't look at me as she hurried to pack up her supplies. She put samples and a business card in a zip-top plastic bag and set it on the counter. "I can order more of whatever you like."

I almost laughed. She was trying to sell makeup to a girl who could be dead tomorrow.

She dragged her tote bag down the stairs and rolled it through the entryway, tossing a perfunctory goodbye over her shoulder as she left. I went upstairs, collected the black heels, and carried them back down to the piano, figuring I'd play until Vasilije arrived—

The garage door squealed and clanked as it rolled up.

I jammed my feet into the shoes and did the tiny buckle around the ankles, using the action to focus myself and tamp down my nerves. Vasilije didn't want me dead. He'd paid thousands of dollars in clothes. He'd had the piano tuned. He'd commissioned a piece and said it was all right if it took me a while to write. Why do any of that if he was going to hand me over to his uncle or get rid of me himself?

"Jesus."

Vasilije's stunned voice drew my attention up from my shoes and I froze. "What's wrong?"

His expression was shock and it turned my bones to ice. "Nothing," he answered. He stared at me like he wasn't sure I was real. "You look..."

I braced myself. He liked to fuck with me, so I expected almost anything to come out of his mouth.

"Acceptable," he said finally. He pushed back the sides of his suitcoat and set his hands on his hips. "This thing tonight is important. I need you to be quiet and do exactly what I say."

"You want me to be your obedient bitch?"

"That'd be perfect." His eyes were intense, or perhaps it was the grip of his Glock peeking out of his suit. "My driver is here. Let's go."

When I reached for my coat in the closet beside the garage, Vasilije scowled. "No, you'll look stupid. I'm sure the dress cost ten times what the coat did."

"It's freezing outside."

"Good thing we're not eating dinner outside, then." He wrapped his hand around my wrist like a shackle, pulling me through the open door into the garage. His tone was mocking. "Besides, I can keep you warm."

How? He was cold-blooded. It was twenty degrees colder in the garage and I pulled my arms tight against my body, as if it would do anything. The same man from my first night sat behind the wheel of the SUV. John, Vasilije had called him.

Vasilije yanked the backseat door open, I climbed in, and wasn't surprised when he followed. At least the car interior was warm. I buckled my seatbelt and crossed my legs, as I watched him out of the corner of my eye.

He played on his phone while John opened the garage door, backed out, and set off. Vasilije must have told him where we were going already. I wanted to ask, but at the same time, a warning sounded in my mind. Maybe I was safer without his attention on me.

"Are you sore?" he asked, not bothering to look up from his phone, but loud enough I suspected so John would overhear. If it was an attempt to humiliate me, it was wasted. I was a bastard child in the outskirts of Kazan, where the community was tight-knit and religious. I'd lived my whole life with shame and rarely felt it anymore.

"Sore from when we fucked?" I said casually. "Not really."

The phone was no longer the most interesting toy in the car for Vasilije, and his black eyes focused on me. "That's surprising." He threaded his tie through his fingers, smoothing it down. "Because it seemed like it hurt a lot."

John's gaze found mine in the rearview mirror, but I shrugged. "As I told you last night, I'm fine."

"You feel different? Now that you're not a virgin?"

The devil wanted to play, and I rose to meet him. "Not really, but I forgot to thank you."

"For what? Making you a woman?"

I smiled widely. "For finishing so quickly."

When the sound rang out of his seatbelt unbuckling, I readied for retaliation. Just like the last time we'd been in the back together, he flew across the seat and I wore his hands as a cold, unwanted collar. This time there wasn't pressure, though. Only dominance.

"Was that you trying to hurt my feelings?" he snarled in my ear.

"No," I said honestly. "You don't have feelings."

His smile was like mine, devoid of warmth or joy, and failed to reach his eyes. "You're wrong, I can feel plenty of things." He trapped my earlobe between his teeth and drew it away painfully until it snapped free of his hold. "Like what it feels like when your smart mouth is sliding up and down my cock."

His hands were gone and he slid back into his seat, palming himself through his pants. My mouth went dry and my throat closed up in anticipation of his next move. He'd escalate the game as he tried to humiliate me.

His strong hand rubbing on his crotch was distracting, almost mesmerizing.

"You want me to go down on you?" I whispered. "Right now?" I flicked my gaze to the driver who was within arm's reach.

Vasilije oozed confidence. "I told you tonight's an important dinner. Your mouth can take the edge off for me."

He was so smug about it, expecting me to balk, and I savored the moment. "All right," I announced plainly. "Just be careful of my makeup."

chapter
TWENTY-TWO

Vasilije's sexy mouth parted to say something, but he was wordless. I undid my seatbelt, said a silent prayer John would keep his focus on the road and not kill us all while I had my lips wrapped around a Markovic dick, and reached for Vasilije's zipper.

I stared at him as he let me undo his pants and stroke him through the cotton of his designer underwear. He was already erect, filling my hand, and his eyes were terrifyingly gorgeous when they burned with lust.

"Oh, fuck," he uttered. "You get me so goddamn hard." He cupped the back of my neck, staying clear of my styled up-do, and pushed my head down into his crotch right as I tugged the elastic over his erection.

It was dark in the back seat, and since Vasilije was sitting behind the driver, it was unlikely John could see anything. But he could definitely hear the wet sounds as I lowered my mouth over the thick head of Vasilije's cock and sucked it down as far as I could go. And if the driver couldn't hear that, he had to notice the profanity streaming from Vasilije's mouth, some of it in English, and some in Serbian.

I swirled my tongue, tumbling it over his damp, hard skin, as I worked up and down. I slid him between my lips, letting my teeth scrape over the veins pulsing in his firm muscle and he shuddered. The cold hand on the back of my neck tightened in response. I sucked and fucked him exactly as he liked it, but this time, I began to enjoy it, too.

I was in control of his pleasure, which meant I had the power. Every uneven, deep breath he took was like gaining ground in battle.

Each dirty word he groaned was a tiny victory. It might be temporary, but he was currently under my spell and at my mercy.

So, I made the blowjob last. I moved at a languid pace, slow passes with just my tongue like he was candy I couldn't get enough of, followed by deep sucks that hollowed my cheeks and made him sigh with satisfaction.

"That's so fucking good," he said, rasping. His left hand rested on his thigh and it curled into a tense fist. "Such a good girl. So good at sucking my cock."

I moaned.

It just happened, and it turned me on. He sank back into the seat, spreading his legs wider so he could thrust up into my mouth. "You like it?" he whispered. "Oh, fuck, yeah. Me, too. Use your hands."

He was slippery and throbbing as I ringed his shaft and pumped my grip on him, moving faster and gripping tighter as his responses encouraged me. It was *sexy*. So sexy, heat pooled in my body, and I grew damp between my thighs.

I shouldn't like what I was doing.

Vasilije and his family sold drugs, and guns, and worst of all, girls who were forced to do the exact thing I was doing now. Plus, he'd murdered his father. And most of the time he treated me like I was an object and not a person, although the last one wasn't as big of a deal—I rarely felt like a person anymore. I was just an empty husk, fueled by the need for justice. Or revenge. I couldn't see the difference between the two and no longer cared to.

All that mattered was the goal.

Despite everything, in addition to the fact Vasilije and I weren't alone in this vehicle, I couldn't stop my heart from racing, or my nipples from hardening inside my bra. I was turned on so much it was painful. I felt it all over, from my sensitive skin brushing against the expensive lace, to the dull ache where he'd fucked me last night.

His loud, labored breathing was the only thing I could hear, and getting him to the edge was all I could think about. Listening to him come was ... *intense*. Exciting and still so new.

"Fucking get me deeper in your mouth." His demand was strangled with desperate need.

I tried to relax and allowed him to pump upward with force while he held me down with a firm hand on my neck. My eyes watered as he pushed past the point of comfort, but I blinked back the sensation and endured. He quickened his tempo until he was jerking in and out of my mouth, his legs flexing and straining, and ...

He came, hot and hard, blasting his thick liquid into my mouth where it pooled, and I awaited his command, listening to his pants of uneven breath sandwiched between swear words.

"Swallow." His voice was like gravel.

It was strange how this sex act was solely about his pleasure, and yet when I followed his order and he shuddered with an aftershock, I felt it, too. All the way down my spine, to the tips of my toes. I drew back from him when he let me up, and tried to wipe my damp lips, but his hand never came off my neck. He used it to pull me into his savage kiss.

He was ... disorienting.

Everything came to a standstill when his lips pressed to mine. His kiss took from me. My power. My submission. And I gave it all up without a fight.

When the kiss ended, his eyes were closed and our foreheads pressed together. He was still struggling to catch his breath when he spoke. "Don't say anything tonight. Not unless I tell you it's okay to speak. Got it?"

Vasilije's tone was different. Was it the aftereffects of his orgasm? Instead of ordering me around, it seemed like he was concerned. It wasn't possible. The devil didn't care about anyone but himself. The car hit a bump, jostling us, and broke the spell. I was shoved out of his way as he did up his pants, and his eyes turned cold.

"Put your seatbelt back on," he said.

I sat against the leather seat, latched the buckle, and turned away from him to watch the traffic, even as his taste lingered in my mouth

♪

The sign over the door to the restaurant read *Il Piacere*, and pinpricks of awareness tingled in my mind. I'd heard of the place before... but where? What was the significance of this upscale Italian restaurant in the Chicago Loop? John pulled along the curb, and one of the valets opened my door. He eyed my lack of coat with interest, but then Vasilije got out behind me and wrapped an arm around my waist, propelling me under the awning and through the glass doors.

The lobby was travertine tile, exposed brick and textured walls. Soft, warm lighting twinkled from hidden spaces, making the restaurant space feel intimate and inviting. All of the tables were empty except one. That wasn't too strange. It was the night before Thanksgiving, and most people were home cooking, or traveling to be with family.

The large, round table in the back of the room was draped in a white tablecloth, and although it had six men sitting at it, my attention zeroed in on one. Goran Markovic was distinguished looking and handsome. His once-black hair was now mostly gray, but his black eyes were as alert as Vasilije's and twice as scary.

He sat facing the door, giving him the best line of sight of the exit, which was the same thing my father did when he went out. Goran's focus went to Vasilije, and then settled on his hand cupping my arm, just above my elbow. The discerning gaze continued up to meet mine, and I shivered.

It had nothing to do with the cold.

Confusion played on the older Markovic man's face, and his scowl intensified as Vasilije escorted me toward the table.

Nerves bubbled in my bloodstream, but I stayed calm and collected, planting one steady high heel in front of the other as we closed in. There was no need to be intimidated, I told myself. I knew worse men than Goran. In fact, I was the product of one of them.

"Vasilije," Goran said, and although his tone was mildly pleasant on the surface, I could hear the contempt beneath. "I need to remind you this is a business meeting?"

"This girl is part of the business," Vasilije answered.

There were other men sitting at the table, and I jolted to a stop, stumbling on my heels. My blood froze in my veins. My heart refused to keep pumping. All functions ceased.

My father stared at me with stunned eyes that were the same color as razor blades.

What the hell was happening?

I tried to get my mind to work. I must have been made. Maybe Vasilije had brought me here as some sort of bargaining chip to trade. But if so . . . why was he now staring at me with confusion?

The restaurant name clicked into place suddenly. *Il Piacere* was the restaurant where the Serbians had met us to negotiate the truce last year. It was neutral ground, so no matter what was about to go down, in theory, I should be safe here. But what was happening? Were the Russians and Serbians about to negotiate a new truce, and I was part of it?

Vasilije's fingers bit into my arm, wordlessly demanding I keep up, and I did the best I could. "It's the new shoes," I whispered, not sure what else to say. I'd play my part until the bitter end.

Sergey Petrov, the man who'd made me a bastard, was seated to Goran's right, with a bodyguard separating them. My father's straight, graying hair was parted perfectly to one side and as exacting as his personality. I'd been told by my friends that he was attractive as far as older men went, but I didn't see it. His long nose and equally long face seemed to be cast in a permanent look of disdain . . . at least that was how he always looked at me.

He peered at me with barely-hidden contempt, as if I were going to get him killed. Who the fuck was in more danger here?

Vasilije grabbed one of the empty chairs and pulled it out, and the moment hung in suspension. I realized it at the same moment everyone else did. He'd pulled out the chair for *me*. The rest of the men at the table lumbered to their feet, standing until I took my seat.

My half-brother stood beside my father, and Konstantine's expression was pure shock, although I couldn't tell if it was at seeing me, or at what Vasilije had just done. A Markovic pulling out a chair for a Russian, who didn't carry the Petrov name, but was Petrov blood.

This was the most surreal moment of my life.

It was a table full of murderers acting like they were gentlemen, and regarding me as a lady. I sat hesitantly and allowed Vasilije to scoot the chair in, and then everyone else settled down into seats. My gaze flicked to Goran, who was directly across from me. His scrutiny was so sharp, it felt as if he were peeling the skin from my body, one layer at a time.

"It's nice to see you again, Sergey," Vasilije said, and my eyes widened at his friendly, familiar tone. He nodded toward my brother. "Konstantine."

My father's lips pulled back into a thin smile, but his eyes were dead. "You, too, Vasilije." His gaze slid to me, but he asked it casually. "Who's the girl?"

Vasilije grinned. "You don't recognize her?"

chapter
TWENTY-THREE

I TENSED AND AIR STUCK PAINFULLY in my lungs. How the *hell* had Vasilije figured it out? Had Aleksandar outed me? No, that didn't make sense, unless he had a death wish.

Vasilije leaned back in his chair and slung an arm over my shoulders. It was possessive. "I picked this one up from a warehouse over on the south side a few days ago. Saved her from a life of fucking and sucking cock to line your pockets."

Relief swept through me that he didn't know the truth, but also fear at what he'd just said. Why not pull a pin on a grenade and throw it in the center of the table? The tension would be the same.

Goran's face turned to stone, and he said something sharp in Serbian, where the only word I understood was Vasilije's name. All he did was shrug in response. What the hell was Vasilije doing? He stared at my father with a sick smile smeared on his face.

"It's a big loss for you. She's good," Vasilije said. "I had Oksana blow me on the ride over here."

Every pair of eyes turned to me. Konstantine's jaw fell open so hard, it was a miracle it didn't hit the table, and that was the moment Vasilije finally believed he won the game at shaming me. My gaze dropped to the tablecloth.

It didn't matter what my father thought. Whatever evil deed I did was nothing in comparison to him. But my brother...

He'd been the only man to stand up for me. If it wasn't for Konstantine, I'd be dead. If I had killed Ilia without my brother's story to back me up, my father would have murdered me. I knew it down to the marrow of my bones. He'd loved Ilia almost as much as he loved his own son, and certainly much more than me.

I stared at the tabletop, not wanting to see the hurt and concern in my half-brother's pale eyes.

"Wonderful. We didn't arrange this sit-down," my father said, his tone indifferent, "so we could hear about your whore's oral skills."

I snapped my gaze to him and a humorless laugh almost bubbled out, but I caught it in time. I understood why he'd said it. He was playing his role as much as I was, but he was enjoying it. He liked getting to openly treat me the way he secretly wanted to. Like I was nothing.

Goran's commanding voice drew everyone's attention. "What do you want to discuss?"

"I'm going to give you a gift, my friend."

I blinked at my father's warm tone. Sergey Petrov calling Goran Markovic a friend meant the world was upside-down.

"A gift?" Goran asked it with polite surprise, but in his eyes, I saw his thoughts. He was wondering if the gift was the kind that came from the barrel of a gun, or even worse.

My father's voice carried across the table. "And in return, you won't touch another shipment of girls again. We'll run our business, and you're free to run yours with your own women." His steel-colored eyes slanted to Vasilije. "Even though we've established how Russian women are better at fucking and sucking cock."

So, it was negotiations for a truce, at least in one aspect of business. It was the biggest part of my family's empire. Most of my father's money was made off the backs of women he sold into sexual slavery. The whole process of recruiting women and getting them to America was risky, expensive, and time-consuming. He lost tens of thousands of dollars in investment every time the Serbians hit us, not to mention the lost income when my father had no product to sell.

He'd been ready to crush the Serbians, but war couldn't be

waged without casualties, and although we were larger, the Markovics had been in Chicago longer. They had powerful support, including the Italians, and winning the war against them wasn't a sure thing.

My father would try diplomacy first.

Goran looked intrigued, yet suspicious. "That would have to be quite the gift, *my friend*."

"You're under FBI surveillance."

Vasilije snorted. "Tell us something we don't know."

Sergey Petrov didn't like being disrespected, and he glared at Vasilije as if he was a bloodstain on an expensive tie. "The blindfold club your uncle frequents just hired an undercover agent. The next time he goes inside, he'll be arrested."

Blindfold club? What the hell was that?

My father's focus went back to Goran. "I believe you're a smart man like I am, and you've done your best to protect both your family and what you've built. I respect that. I respect how your business survived when they took your son down. But you know as well as I do, no amount of maneuvering will save you once you're in the hands of the FBI. They'll come after every Markovic, and they will be ruthless."

Vasilije's expression didn't change. He looked calm and indifferent, but I knew he was not. His fingers had been brushing over the bare skin of my arm as his hand dangled over my shoulder, and they ceased moving. I felt the temperature of his blood rise.

His tone was dark and skeptical. "If that's fucking true, why tell him? They take us down and that solves all your problems."

Because my father didn't want the Serbians arrested. He wanted to rule them. He needed the Markovics under his control.

My father sneered. "You think if your family disappears, no one else will rise to fill that hole? The need for a steady supply of women is too great. This way is fast and clean. We make this deal today, and that's the end of it." He reached for his glass of red wine and took a sip. "Do what you want with the information, Goran. I'm a man of my word, as I know you are. If you strike me again after I've saved your legacy, I'll bury you, and your friends will help me do it."

Goran considered his options for a long moment, even though he had none. My father was a horrible excuse for a man, but he didn't tell lies. There was no upside. No other option but to take this deal. If the Markovics struck a shipment again after my father offered an olive branch, the Italians might turn on the Serbs.

It was better when everyone played nicely. There was plenty of crime to go around in Cook County.

"How do you know about the undercover agent?" Goran said, his discerning gaze focused on my father.

"I have a person on the inside."

Goran Markovic's face twisted with disappointment, unhappy to give up whatever the club was.

My father drummed his fingers on the table, starting with his index and rolling through to the pinkie finger, then repeated the action over and over. Each series of thumps seemed to make Vasilije tenser.

Impatience got the best of my father. "Do we have a deal?"

"Yes," Goran snapped. "My people won't go near your girls from now on." He took in a deep breath and rolled his shoulders back, assuming a more confident posture. "Other aspects of our businesses overlap, as you push further into areas you shouldn't. I worry you're stretching yourself too much, my friend."

Was he talking about drugs, or guns? My father's greed and ambition was insatiable. He'd been undercutting the Serbians every chance he got, and pushed further in on their territory each year. The brief truce had lulled my father into a false sense of security, and it'd come back to bite him by way of a bullet to the shoulder.

"I understand your concern, Goran."

That was all my father would say on the matter.

If the evening wasn't surreal enough, the men proceeded to order dinner, and then chat as if they were ... coworkers. Savage men pretending to be civilized. I was introduced to everyone at the table even though I already knew their names.

I could barely tolerate it when Vasilije struck up a conversation with Konstantine. It looked like my brother felt the same way, but he politely participated while stealing glances at me. He wanted to know if I was all right.

"Is there some reason you're eye-fucking my girl?" Vasilije said abruptly, and the table went silent mid-conversation.

"No," my brother answered, looking embarrassed. "I wasn't."

Vasilije's deep eyes were acute. "Yeah, you were. I get that she's gorgeous, but she's fucking *mine*."

I dry swallowed so hard, it was shocking it wasn't audible. Wasn't it obvious to Vasilije that Konstantine wasn't looking at me with anything other than concern? Or was he too possessive to notice the difference? And ... he'd just announced to the table he thought I was gorgeous.

"Relax, Vasilije," my father said. "He's not interested in your whore. He's a Petrov. I bet this girl," his icy gray eyes locked with mine, "is only worth what's between her legs."

Bile rose in the back of my throat and I had a vision of spitting in his face. I'd watch the glob of it drip down his cheekbone as rich satisfaction overwhelmed me, but I didn't get the chance. Vasilije straightened in his seat and his expression turned to steel.

"You've no idea what you're talking about."

Sergey Petrov pressed his lips into a thin line, visibly irritated. People didn't speak to him like that. "I don't?" he charged back, patronizing.

"First off, she can't be a whore since she was a virgin until yesterday."

My face flushed with heat. I wanted to melt down my chair and disappear beneath the tablecloth.

Only, Vasilije wasn't done. "And second, you should hear her play the piano. The songs she writes? They're amazing, and that's coming from me, who could give a fuck when it comes to music."

I couldn't breathe.

Vasilije Markovic was defending me against my own father, and his words burrowed into my cold heart when I didn't want them to. Foreign emotion fluttered in my center, and the friction heated me from the inside out.

My father's attention snapped to me and his eyes churned like a violent sea. He'd paid for me to go to college, after my stepmother forced him to, and when I'd changed my major to music, he'd been furious. He pulled me out of school and told me I would clean houses with the Russian women he could no longer turn a profit with at the whorehouse. That 'career' would make more money, he'd said, than my music.

So, I'd presented the deal to my father. I plant the surveillance devices in a Markovic home, and in return, I could re-enroll next semester at Randhurst University, continuing to pursue my music degree. I was willing to make sacrifices to get what I wanted, and life was too short not to go after my dream. You never knew when it would end. Tomorrow you could perish in a house fire on my father's orders, or your plane could fall from the sky.

My father let out a joyless laugh. "You fucked her one time, and it sounds like she already has you by the short hairs. Be careful, Vasilije." He held his glass of wine by the bell and swirled the liquid inside. "Russian women are dangerous."

Vasilije had been right. My father had no idea what he was talking about.

♪

TORRID

As I scrubbed my hands under the faucet in the restaurant's bathroom, I stared at myself in the mirror. It was like looking at an actress in stage makeup playing the role of Oksana Kuznetsov. She looked and sounded like me, but wasn't.

I pulled to a stop when I exited the restroom. My father lurked, waiting for me in the dark back hallway.

"I'm impressed," he said in Russian. "I didn't think you had it in you."

We were out of view of the table, but I kept my voice low. "We shouldn't speak to each other. If anyone sees—"

"I want the devices in Goran's house."

My blood slowed. "What?"

"Vasilije isn't involved enough."

"No. That wasn't our deal, and how the hell would I do that?"

He looked at me like I was stupid. "You seduce him. Look at how fast you turned Vasilije. The boy is in love with you."

I wanted to laugh. It had only been four days, and Vasilije didn't do love. But I didn't have time to explain any of this. "How am I supposed to seduce Goran? I've never met him until tonight, and Vasilije will kill me if I try."

Not to mention, I didn't want to seduce Goran. He was the same age as my father. Both the Markovic men scared the hell out of me, but Vasilije . . . the fear I felt around him was different. Tolerable. The unsettling connection between us grew stronger the longer he kept me around.

"It'll be easy." My father's expression was cold and deadly. "Now that Vasilije's staked his claim, Goran's going to try to take you away from him."

My heartbeat sped up. "What makes you say that?"

"It's what I'd do. Vasilije is all talk. He needs to learn his place in the family."

My father didn't know what I did, and I choked back the desire to warn him not to underestimate Vasilije. It was much better for me if he continued on, blindly unaware of the dangerous people circling around him.

"Our deal was for Vasilije, and you told the table full of men in there that you're a man of your word."

His jaw set. "You changed the deal first. Don't be surprised if Goran makes a play for you before then." He pushed past me, flinging a hand on the door to the men's room, but paused. "Good luck, Oksana. You'll need it, now that you've become a pawn in their game."

He disappeared inside, and didn't see the dead smile that widened on my lips. He was forgetting how a pawn who survived crossing the board could be promoted to a queen.

I could go from the weakest player to the strongest one in a single move.

chapter
TWENTY-FOUR

Vasilije

Oksana was quiet on the drive back to the house. A lot of shit had been said at the table, and it'd been shocking she kept her mouth shut through it. All because I'd told her to. Fuck, the way she obeyed me made my blood run south, straight beneath my zipper.

Taking her to dinner tonight had been a calculated risk. It hadn't irritated Sergey or the other Russians, but it had definitely gotten under my uncle's skin, so I would call it a win. I liked poking the bear and was curious what kind of response it'd provoke out of Goran.

Oksana sat in the back seat with her legs crossed, so prim and fucking proper. My gaze started at her ankles and traveled upward, coasting over her long, pale legs. I couldn't wait to have them wrapped around me. I needed to reward her for being such a good girl, and goddamn . . . when I'd come home to her in the dress and the heels, with her hair up and makeup done, it'd been a punch of lust right in the dick.

I'd considered blowing the meeting off.

That was how good she looked. Sergey hadn't been wrong when he'd said Russian women were dangerous. This one might be lethal.

"Are you pissed about dinner?" I asked, breaking the silence.

Her head swung slowly toward me. "Why would I be?"

"Because of all the shit that was said." I hadn't exactly been nice, and Sergey Petrov was a fucking dickhole.

"Are you asking if my feelings were hurt? I told you, I don't have any." Her tone was casual. Hollow. I didn't like it. She was the most exciting when she was alive, and that seemed to happen whenever I had power over her.

"You're so full of shit, Oksana." I'd been able to embarrass her tonight and prove my point, but . . . winning the game hadn't been as much fun as I'd thought it'd be. When I'd told everyone about the blowjob and she'd stared at her lap, I'd felt like a piece of shit. It was why I'd run my mouth later when Sergey had said she was nothing more than a piece of ass.

My hand had twitched, wanting to reach for my Glock. She was more than a piece of ass.

John pulled into the garage, and as I dismissed him, she got out of the car and hurried inside the house, out of the cold. I was right behind her. I'd taken care of business with some Russians tonight, but was most looking forward to the one who waited for me in the hall.

I peeled off my outer jacket and dropped it on the tile floor. Her eyes widened and she backpedaled. As I moved deeper into the house, chasing her, I shed my suit coat, dropping it on the hardwood. There was enough distance between us that she could hold my gaze and still see the gun in her peripheral vision.

Off the holster came, and it thudded to the countertop in the kitchen.

"I'm gonna fuck you under that dress. Now."

Oksana's chest rose with a deep breath, but she'd stopped moving when we reached the kitchen and held her ground as I came at her. I seized her face in my hands and slapped my lips down on hers. I gave her the same violent kiss I'd delivered this afternoon, only this time she was giving it right back to me.

Her soft mouth moving against mine slowed my reaction time like getting wasted on expensive vodka. I both did and didn't want her to stop. It made it harder to dominate her like this, when her intensity matched mine.

Like a partner.

I broke the kiss and squeezed her cheeks with one hand as I pushed her, stumbling along. There was a large, open arch separating the kitchen from the living area, and I walked her toward it until her back was against the square column base. A gasp burst from her as she collided with it, but it didn't disrupt her. It didn't even slow her down.

Her fingers dug at my tie, tearing at the knot with both hands as I stared down into her eyes. Everything else about her was composed and elegant, but her fucking eyes were wild. She got the tie undone in record time, and moved to the buttons.

I slapped her hands away. "Stop."

This was supposed to be my show, not hers, and definitely not *ours*. I moved in, shoving myself against her and pinning her to the narrow column. Her hair smelled good. Her eyes looked even better when her lashes were thick and dark. Whatever makeup Jennifer had used had done the trick. I couldn't stop looking at her.

I ground my lower body against hers, and the nearly silent moan Oksana gave was sexier than if she'd screamed it. I sucked on her neck and wasn't careful about it, either. I ran the sharp edge of my teeth along the curve of her flesh, and bit down. Hard, and then harder, going until she whimpered.

"Fuck," I spat out, swiveling my hips away from her. She'd reached down and stroked me over my pants. "Do that again and I'll tie you to this column."

Goddamnit. As soon as the warning was out of my mouth, I wanted to do it. If I bound her arms behind her back, securing her to the column, it'd look amazing. But tying her up hadn't been in my plans for this evening, and I'd have to save it for another time.

Surprise blanketed her face. "You don't want me to touch you?"

Of course I did, but she was getting ahead of herself. "Only when I tell you to. Pull your dress up."

She moved immediately, and it gave me a rush as I watched her place her palms on the fabric and start dragging it up.

"Faster," I barked. Fire raged in my veins, and I cupped her tits through the dress, squeezing them together. Every inch she exposed of her milky white thighs made me burn hotter. She got the skirt of the dress all the way around her hips, revealing unsexy cotton underwear.

"Where's what I bought you?" I demanded.

Her eyes widened. "I'm not a virgin anymore."

She had a point. I'd have to do some online shopping tonight and fix that. I'd buy her the sluttiest stuff I could find and make her wear it underneath the classy, expensive clothes I'd bought her. It could be another secret only we shared.

"Tonight, I won't be holding back," I said.

Her throat bobbed with a hard swallow. "Good."

She hooked her thumbs under the waist of her panties and shoved them off. They glided down her legs and fell around her heels, where she stepped out of them. Oksana looked at me with an anxious expression. Nervous, maybe, but not fearful. Like she believed she could handle whatever I'd throw at her.

I was beginning to believe it, too.

Since she was up against the column, it held the dress around her hips. She closed a warm hand around mine and pressed our fingers between her legs. Her pussy was hot as lava, and wet. I clenched my teeth, sucking back a groan. It turned me on, but why was she being so aggressive?

"I guess I need to show you who's in charge tonight." I ripped my hand away, and slapped the inside of her thigh. She cried out from the first strike right as I launched the second and smacked her other thigh.

Her pale skin turned a beautiful shade of pink, bright against her lily-white flesh. I loved how I could see the instant proof of my touch. I wanted to paint more of her red. Lay claim over her skin.

"What—"

It was all she got out as I yanked her away from the column and pushed her into the living room. I threw her against the back of couch, and she made a startled noise, but she didn't cry out. I was rough, but not *too rough*. Just enough so we'd both like it.

I shoved her over the couch so her cute, tight ass was in the air, and I spanked her with my open palm. I gave her short, stinging swats. Her head was down, and her hands gripped at the couch cushions, and even though she jolted and flinched, the girl said nothing. She gasped for breath, sure. Sometimes she inhaled so sharply, it sounded like a hiss.

But Oksana never said no.

"You tell me to stop, and I'll stop," I said over the sound of my fingers slapping against her bare skin.

Tension filled her shoulders, like she was bracing herself. She took it as a challenge, and I grinned darkly. She wasn't going to give in that easily. This girl wanted to be unbreakable, and I was thrilled to help her test her limits.

I undid the buttons and stripped off my dress shirt. It was good not to have it in the way. I rested my left hand in the small of her back, pushing her hips against the top of the couch, and then I really let her have it.

Slap. She jumped and I watched the reverberation ripple subtly on her skin.

Slap. Oksana's heart-shaped ass was blotchy. Some of her was pink, while other spots that I'd hit multiple times were fire engine red. It was gorgeous. I dug my phone out of my pocket and took a picture. She flinched worse from the camera's flash than any time I'd spanked her.

"What was that?" she asked.

"Don't worry about it."

Slap, slap . . . slap. The last one was so hard, it stung my hand, and her foot came up off the floor. Her black heel was up against her ass, as if trying to protect herself. I shoved it out of my way. "Ask me to stop," I ordered.

"No." She was breathless.

"Why not?" I was goading her, but couldn't turn the asshole side of my personality off. My father had activated that part, and then broken the switch so it couldn't be disabled. She groaned as I spanked her viciously. "Because you like this?"

What a surprise. She said nothing.

She yelped with my next one, and tried to squirm away from both the pain and my hand holding her down on the couch.

I raised my voice, letting it fill the room. "Either tell me to stop . . . or tell me you *like* it."

"Vasilije," she whined.

Her soft-spoken word was more powerful than the demand I'd yelled at her, and suddenly I was on my knees behind her, my mouth latched onto her pussy. Her moan was as much surprise as it was bliss. I stuck my tongue inside and fucked her as her legs quivered. She reached a hand back and ran her nails through my hair, scraping at my scalp and holding me to her.

"I like it," she gasped. "Oh, God, I like it."

A half of a chuckle came out of me. Of course she did now, but the good news was . . . "Me, too."

I put my hands on her abused ass and lifted, pulling her cheeks away so I had more room. I fluttered and sucked at her clit while I squeezed so hard on her ass, the skin dented around my fingertips. But the moans that rolled out of her were pure pleasure.

I paused so I could speak. "Reach back and put your hands like mine."

She did, and I grabbed her wrists, pulling them so she'd hold herself open for me. Then, I shifted on my knees and got more comfortable. I settled in to reward her, and got rewarded myself as she murmured something in Russian. No idea what she said, but it sounded dirty.

Since I had my hands free, I put my thumb on the hood of her clit and pulled it back, and spun the tip of my tongue over the sensitive spot. Her shudders were fucking sexy. She writhed against both the couch and my mouth, like the pleasure I gave her was almost too intense to take. She could, though, and she *would*. Her heels tapped quietly on the wood floor as she shook uncontrollably.

"*Nyet*," she cried when I licked a straight line up, right between her cheeks.

My cock jerked in my pants. Her hurried 'no' hadn't sounded like an order to stop, it'd been gasped in shock. And I'd told her I'd stop if she asked me to, but I hadn't said shit about doing it if she said it in Russian.

chapter
TWENTY-FIVE

I STARTED AT THE BASE OF OKSANA'S PUSSY and ran my tongue up again, all the way over her asshole. She whined in her native language on a stuttering breath. Was my dirty action so shocking she'd forgotten English?

Her hands came off her ass, but I was ready for that. I pulled her apart and swirled my tongue where she was still a virgin, and her choked moan got my heart banging in my chest. It sent my head buzzing with lust, and her body betrayed her. "You like it," I said, half teasing, half serious. She liked it even if she didn't want to.

Did she feel the same way about me?

The unexpected thought shot through my brain. Why did I care if she liked me? She wasn't, and never would be, a friend. This was about sex, and once I got bored, I'd send her away.

How'd that plan work out for Luka?

Shit. I climbed to my feet and stared down at the girl bent over the couch, letting my gaze trace the zipper on her dress that mimicked her spine. She remained in that awkward position, not moving other than her exaggerated breathing. She didn't complain that I'd stopped before I'd made her come. She waited patiently for my next command.

My voice was rough as gravel. "Get on the couch, on your hands and knees."

She straightened and the dress dropped down in place, hiding her pink-stained ass. Her heels clip-clopped hurriedly, and the leather squealed when she placed her knees on the cushions. She moved gracefully, planting her hands on the seat of the couch so she was on all fours, and tipped her head up to me, watching for my approval.

I dug my cock out of my pants so fast, I almost broke the zipper. Two pumps and I was as rigid as the column I'd pressed her up against. I grabbed the back of the dress and jerked it up to hang off her hips. "I want to look at that cherry red ass you've got as you suck me off."

I stood at the side of the couch and held my dick steady for her. She didn't need a fucking invitation, she knew what to do. Her warm, wet mouth closed around me and heat seared up my back. Her glossy pink lips moved along my length, and I let her take over, pushing my pants and underwear down until they fell in a heap at my ankles.

Her mouth was like fucking a volcano, and I thrust at her, wanting more. In retaliation, she brought her hand up and wrapped her fist around me. It blocked me from going too deep. She thought she was in control, huh? I pulled her hand away, gripping her wrist, and placed my palm on the back of her head. I thrust my hips into her mouth as I pushed her head toward my body, and it made Oksana gag. She coughed and sputtered as I retreated.

I'd already gotten head from her once today, and it was fucking spectacular, but . . . enough. I wanted her cunt. I shuffled backward. I toed off my shoes, kicked off my pants, and tugged off my socks, leaving me naked. If she stood right now, she'd be dressed. I didn't give a fuck for once, probably because I was too focused on my destination.

I put my hands flat on her back and shoved, getting her to collapse forward on her belly, and she let out a burst of air as she hit the leather.

"Hands behind your back." I straddled the back of her thighs and dropped my hard cock right on her ass. It looked good up against her pink skin. She did as told and crossed her wrists. Her head turned so she had one cheek flat against the cushion, and she watched me out of the corner of her eye.

I spit loudly in my palm and used it to lube my dick up. It was probably overkill since her pussy was drenched when I went down on her, but better safe than sorry. I wanted to slide deep inside. I'd promised her I wasn't going to hold back, and last night was as close to gentle fucking as I got. She'd get a good look at the real me now.

She tensed as I stroked the tip of my cock up and down between her legs, and it swam in her wetness. Did she have any idea how excited and crazy she made me? No other girl put up with my rough shit, let alone enjoyed it. I couldn't wait another goddamn second. I clenched a hand around her wrists, lined myself up, and drove so deep into her pussy, she cried out.

Waves of warmth hugged me. Her tight body gripped at my dick, maybe trying to force me back out, but forget it. Jesus Christ, it felt so good, maybe I'd never leave. Not unless she asked me to, which she still hadn't done. She didn't say no, or *nyet*, or demand I stop. I curled my free hand on her shoulder and delivered my first thrust.

She exhaled loudly, and her hands tightened into fists.

My second thrust was harder and deeper, and she groaned. The low, guttural sound was fucking hot. My third thrust made her bounce on the cushions, and I held her steady with my grip on her shoulder, making it so her body wouldn't recoil off me.

As I began to pound into her, the grunts shifted to moans, and it was the signal I needed to go all-out. I let go of her shoulder and dug my fingers into her hair, grabbing strands and pins, and jerked her back toward me. Her back arched. It had to hurt, but she'd never say it.

"You're so good to me, baby. You let me fuck you exactly how I want to." I slammed my body into hers, so deep it crushed my balls against her clit. Wait, shit. I struggled to put distance between what I'd just said, and my tone went brutal. "I own you, Oksana. You're my motherfucking property. You got that?"

She panted, either through the pain or the pleasure. Couldn't tell, but it was getting hard to focus. Thoughts broke down in my brain. All I wanted to do was fuck like a savage and come. I'd make it so any man who came after me wouldn't be inside her the same way. No one else would compare.

"Say it," I ordered.

She parroted it back without hesitation. "I'm your motherfucking property."

Pleasure coursed through me, filling the room until I was panting right along with her. I was getting sweaty from the exertion, but mostly from the dark creature writhing beneath my hands. She moved with the rhythm of my body, so as I plunged into her, she was there to meet me. Fucking hell. It was insane, and once again, I wasn't going to last long. I'd wanted her too much all day.

At least tomorrow was Thanksgiving and I didn't have to work. I planned to fuck her until my cock gave out.

She moaned, and it sounded faintly like pleasure. It felt good for her, and I . . . liked that. I slid as far in as I could go, until I was pressed all against her, and ground my body, rubbing her clit.

"Oh." Her word was surprised.

It gave me a white-hot flash of satisfaction. Not just with how good it physically felt, but knowing it was pleasurable for her. "That's my dick that's making you moan." I'd do everything I could tonight so my cock made her come.

I released my grip, both her hands and hair, and she flopped forward. She clutched at the couch as I rammed into her, and the impact made her slide away. Her hands flew out to brace herself on the armrest, so I could keep fucking her deep.

I grabbed onto her ass, squeezing as I watched my cock disappear inside her. It was slick. Once it started feeling good for her, Oksana got wetter. I peeled her ass cheeks apart so I could see better, and I did it so hard, she probably felt like I was going to rip her in two. She whimpered. Pain mingled with pleasure.

Fuck her until she comes.

The muscles in my thighs were warm and tight. Any position during sex eventually got exhausting if you did it too long. I wouldn't be able to maintain this one forever, even though it was sexy as fuck and felt amazing.

"You come, and then I come," I said in a rush. "Okay? You come, then me."

Her pussy clenched tight around me. Her gasps for breath increased in intensity. *Yes.* She was getting close. I picked up my tempo, leaning back so more of my body would strike her clit with my thrusts.

I tried to soften my voice and pull it from her. "Tell me. Are you going to come? Are you gonna come for me?"

She moaned something I couldn't make it out, but it sounded positive. Her cries swelled. Her body locked up. Fuck me, she was about to go off. I gripped her ass like it was the only thing keeping me attached to the world as I fucked her, slamming into her over and over again.

"Are you coming?" I asked, even though I knew the answer. I could feel the pleasure detonate inside her. "Oh, fuck, that's a good girl. Fuck, it feels so good." I pumped all through it, watching her writhe and squirm as she shattered. She rode it out, moans pouring from her slack mouth, and I felt more powerful than I ever had. Even as she began to recover, I kept my punishing tempo, hanging right at the edge myself. "Whose turn is it now?" I asked between ragged breaths. "Tell me. Whose turn is it?"

"Oh, God, it's yours."

Fuck right, it was. I came, surging into her with heat and ecstasy so great, my mind went blank. It unloaded into me like automatic fire, each bullet striking me with stinging pleasure until the magazine was spent and I collapsed on top of her.

"Goddamn fucking shit," I groaned into the nape of her neck, and then kissed her there. My offline mind couldn't process what was happening as my lips moved over her ear, and her cheekbone, seeking her mouth. When I found it, everything in me that wouldn't like this went dark and shut down. My tongue stroked against hers, our lips moved together, and as our heavy breathing began to fall, we both murmured with contentment.

Sergey said Oksana had me by the short hairs, and it was probably a little true, but in this quiet, slow moment, I didn't fucking care. It didn't matter who actually owned who between us.

My phone rang, jarring me.

It rang again. Who the fuck was disturbing me with a call and not a text?

I lifted my head and glared at my wadded pants on the floor. Uncle Goran, probably. He preferred speaking instead of sending texts, which left a word-for-word record. And if it was my uncle, I had to answer it. I groaned, climbed off Oksana, and snatched up my pants.

It wasn't my uncle. It was the private investigator I'd hired two months ago, and I hit the 'accept' button as quickly as I could.

"What do you have?" I said as a greeting.

"An address."

A thrill cracked through me. "Yeah?"

"Yeah," my PI said. "And it's in the northwest suburbs. If you're going to move on this, you'll need to do it sooner rather than later. He's moving to Florida for the winter."

Soon wasn't going to be a problem. I'd been waiting more than a year for this. Every day since the morning in the basement where I'd taken my father's life. "Where is he?"

chapter
TWENTY-SIX

OKSANA

EVERYTHING HURT AND BURNED, but it also felt . . . weird. Not unpleasant. My head was a mess.

Vasilije pulled on his pants while he continued his phone call and rose from the couch, striding quickly toward the office and abandoning me. The quiet, tender kiss we'd just shared was clearly forgotten.

His voice was hushed in the other room. I could hear he was speaking, but not make out the words. Was I supposed to stay like this, lying face-down on the couch? He'd climaxed inside of me and I could feel it dripping out, so I needed to get up, but I also ached from how rough he'd been.

I moved slowly, grimacing as I got off the couch, and an angry voice boomed in my head. *Why did you let him treat you like that?* I wanted to ignore it, not because I didn't have an answer, but because the truth was terrifying.

I could say I was just doing my job.

Or I could argue since I'd taken a life, and I planned to take another, I deserved whatever Vasilije gave me. But the reality was so much worse. I enjoyed what was supposed to be punishment. His dominance was scary and too much, but it made me feel alive. His control was . . . freedom.

I cleaned up in the half-bath and pulled the pins out of my hair, raking my fingers through the curly mess to get it to lay so it didn't look quite so ridiculous. When I came out, I glanced down the long hallway and sucked in a breath.

He was off the phone. He stood shirtless in the darkened office, his hands resting on his hips and his head tipped down, looking like he was deep in thought. Light from the arched window nearby played over his lean, sculpted form. He was violently beautiful.

Had he sensed my eyes on him? His head lifted and our gazes met. I couldn't interpret his expression. The closest word I could use to describe it was 'conflicted.' His focus swept down my body, and then back up again, moving more deliberate this time.

"Come here," he said.

The world tilted on an angle at his quiet request, and it made it difficult to walk down the hallway on heels to meet him at the base of the stairs.

"Are you all right?" I whispered.

He blinked. "I'm fine." His eyebrows pulled together. "Are you? I was . . ." His tone was uneven and he held up a hand like he might pull the word he was looking for out of thin air. Instead, his hand dropped abruptly. "Rough."

I licked my lips, trying to keep my mouth from going dry. Maybe I'd been wrong about him. Perhaps the devil did have feelings, because this reaction seemed like concern. He was thinking about someone other than himself. He was worried about *me*. My knees softened and my lackluster heart tripped over itself. "You didn't do anything I couldn't handle."

I was pulled into his embrace, and my body sang a beautiful melody of ache. I hadn't realized how badly I needed this until his strong arms were circled around me.

"You didn't answer my question," he said, his strict tone forced. Like he was using it to disguise his worry. "Are you all right?"

"Yes," I lied. It'd been true until this moment, and now I was falling apart, not understanding the cause.

"You're shaking."

I was. A tremor rocked my foundation. "I don't know why."

His black eyes grew deeper. "Sit down."

He urged me onto the steps, and as I leaned back, I cupped his cheek and pulled him with me. Did he think I was crazy for wanting him close, especially after what he'd just done, and how I was acting like I was terrified? I was seated with my back against the stair treads, and Vasilije knelt between my parted legs. He supported himself on his fists, hovering over me.

He was too far away. I snaked my arms around his back and dragged him the rest of the way down, clinging to him as our bodies flattened together. I'd never felt so fucking needy in my life. I gripped him tighter and tighter, until I was sure there was no more space between us.

His head was buried in the side of my neck, and as he tolerated my ferocious hold, his breathing went shallow. I expected him to push off me at any moment, or for him to make a shitty comment, but he didn't. Vasilije crouched over me on the steps and allowed my embrace. He wedged his arm beneath my back and between two steps, holding me as much as I was him.

We stayed like that for a long time.

All the way until the tremble faded from my body, and my arms softened around his shoulders. I felt less shattered, and more like myself as the strange, unwanted emotions drained away.

"Who were you talking to?" It came out soft, but I was stunned at how steady my voice was.

There was a long pause before his lips moved against the side of my throat. "Someone I hired to track down a guy."

"What guy?"

Vasilije lifted his head, just enough so I could get a look at his intense expression. "A man I need to kill."

My mouth rounded into a wordless "oh," as if that were enough information.

"The night my mom died..." He sighed. "My dad believed my mom was cheating on him. It's why she came home to find him with his dick inside another woman. He wanted to get caught. It was revenge." Vasilije's expression clouded like an approaching storm. "Except the whole story about her cheating was made up by my uncle's bodyguard."

It took me a moment to process. "Why would he—"

"Uncle Goran didn't like my mother, and he trusted her even less. He planned the thing to drive my parents apart, and it worked like a fucking charm. My dad didn't know the truth until right before I killed him."

I swallowed a breath. Goran had orchestrated the death of Vasilije's mother?

Vasilije shifted over me, moving until he was more comfortable and I was better trapped beneath him. "Goran told my father he'd had the bodyguard killed, but instead my uncle offered him a deal. Tell the lie about fucking around with my mother, and he'd get two hundred grand to start over somewhere else."

Which the man had obviously taken. Vasilije leaned forward and the tip of his tongue traced the edge of my ear, causing me to shiver. "You found him."

"He moved back here to be by his family once he heard my father was gone."

Goosebumps broke out on my legs. Vasilije had probably started planning this bodyguard's death the moment he went looking for him. "How will you do it?"

"Kill him?" His hot breath rolled down my neck. "My gun. It needs to look like someone broke in."

"When?" I asked. I should have felt alarm at the ease we were discussing his plot for murder. His tone was casual and distracted, and he sucked on my neck as if he liked the flavor of my skin.

"Tomorrow night."

I closed my eyes, enjoying the sensation, but I tried to focus my thoughts. I was already in deep with Vasilije. I felt like I knew more about him than anyone else. Could I build the bond between us so strong that when he learned the truth, he'd let me live? Strong enough he'd stay by my side?

Nerves raced in my bloodstream. "Let me come with you."

His body solidified and the lips on my neck ceased. "You want to, what? *Help* me?" His tone was so dubious, it bordered on anger.

"No." I had zero desire to take part, and it wasn't my place. "What you're talking about doing is personal."

"Then, what the fuck are you talking about?"

"I can stay in the car."

He pulled back and suspicion cast a dark shadow on his face. "Why?"

"So you can tell me every detail when you're done. I don't want to wait until you get home later. I want to see you right after."

His smile was a mouthful of fangs. He acted like what I'd said was easily the best thing he'd ever heard. "You say shit like that and it makes me want to fuck you again." In a heartbeat, he had his hand under my dress and his fingers stirred between my legs.

I choked on air. I was so sore, just the idea of his fingers sliding inside me made me ache. I glanced away and put my hand on his wrist. He'd said if I told him to stop, he would, but I was nervous he wouldn't hold to his word.

"No," I whispered.

His eyes burned with wicked amusement. "Okay." His cold hand slithered away. "You can tag along. But be prepared. Your evil little mind turns me on. I might not take off my bloodstained clothes to fuck you on the drive home tomorrow. You'd probably get off on that, wouldn't you?"

I had absolutely no answer.

♪

Thanksgiving morning, Vasilije slept in. I'd eaten breakfast and was seated at the piano composing when he came downstairs, shirtless and his hair askew. I jotted a few chords down in the notebook and played them, but wondered if I had the right key for the whole piece. My gaze drifted from the paper to watch the boy in the kitchen.

My muse.

I smirked at the thought. Wouldn't he just love it if I called him that?

Items were pulled from the fridge and stacked noisily on the counter. Bell peppers. Mushrooms. Green onions. Cheese. A carton of eggs. He went to a cupboard, retrieved a bowl, and then drew a large knife from the butcher's block, the sharp edge gleaming.

I watched as he chopped the vegetables and tossed them in the bowl. He moved efficiently and with precision. I didn't expect him to be good with a knife. It was an intimate weapon—one you had to be close to use.

I also didn't expect Vasilije to know how to cook, but he clearly did.

A skillet was put on the stove, the gas turned on, and he dropped a pat of butter into the pan before cracking eggs into another bowl. He didn't look up as he whisked them. "Are you going to fucking stare at me while I eat, too?"

"You can cook?" I asked.

He cast an annoyed look at me over the top of the piano. "I can do a lot of things, Oksana. You want an omelet?"

I was glad I was sitting down because shock overwhelmed me. "You're making me breakfast?"

"I've already got everything out."

"You don't seem like a guy who cooks for a girl after he fucks her."

He sneered. "You're right. I don't." Had I just... offended him? He closed the carton of eggs and put it back in the fridge.

I didn't know what to say. "I don't like mushrooms."

"Yeah? Well, you're fucking weird." He poured the eggs into the heated pan.

I'd already eaten, but watching him cook made me hungry. I rose from the piano and drifted closer, my gaze fixated on the guy who seemed to command the kitchen as well as he did my body. He lifted the skillet off the heat and flipped the omelet over in the pan with a clean jerk.

My mouth hung open, and Vasilije's eyebrow arrowed up. "Whitney taught me how to cook," he explained.

Anger sliced down through my chest. Who was that? An ex-girlfriend?

I didn't understand my instant reaction. I couldn't be jealous. It wasn't even possible. My tone had a too-bright edge as I overcompensated. "Who's Whitney?"

"My chef. She does all the shopping for the week. If you want something, you can tell her tomorrow when she's here."

"Oh." That couldn't be relief in my system, because I wasn't jealous. My gaze fell to his hands, and I watched him slide the omelet onto a plate, folding the egg perfectly onto itself. "That looks good."

He set his hands on the counter. "If I made you one without mushrooms, will you pick at it like a fucking bird, or will you actually eat?"

I turned, opened the fridge, and pulled the carton of eggs out. "I'll do my best."

He didn't smile, but I could see he was pleased. I watched him craft my omelet with the same technique, and eagerly took the plate when it was passed to me. It tasted great.

We stood at the counter and ate, all while morning sunlight glowed from the windows. It was too bright and warm in the house to talk about what was going to happen tonight, so we stayed silent. In addition to cooking like a man who'd been trained by a chef, he cleaned like one, too. I put the produce away while he handled the dishes, and when it was done, he set his hands on the low-hanging waistband of his sweatpants.

"Upstairs," he said, flicking his gaze upward. "You can show me how thankful you are for breakfast while we're in my shower."

I nodded slowly, accepting whatever he wanted. Part of me didn't mind. There might have been a sliver of me that was looking forward to it. We took pleasure from each other.

I climbed the steps, went down the hall, and into his bedroom, listening to his footsteps as he followed me. The bed was unmade and the lumpy comforter was pushed to one side. I'd lost my virginity in that bed, but it looked . . . like any other bed.

His bathroom sink was messy, dotted with whiskers from where he'd trimmed and maintained his scruff. I didn't wait for his order to do so, and began to tug off my clothes as he started the water running. It was still awkward being naked around him, but I was smart enough to know it gave me an advantage.

Vasilije froze with the shower door halfway open and gaped at me.

"What's wrong?" I asked.

His eyes weren't on mine, and I followed his gaze down to the red-purple blotches on my chest. He stared at the marks with fascination. *His* marks. I quirked an eyebrow. *You think that's something? Wait until you see this.*

I tugged off the jeans and underwear, and turned around to show him his handiwork.

"*Puši kurac,*" he said under his breath.

When I'd gotten dressed this morning, I'd stared in the mirror at the beautiful variety of marks covering my ass. A perfect handprint in purply-blue could be made out on one side.

"Does it hurt?" he asked. His voice was unsteady.

I shrugged. "Sometimes. Mostly when I'm sitting on the bench." Because the piano seat was lacquered wood with no cushion. Since I was stark naked, I turned back around to face him, and Vasilije slowly came back to life. He undid the string holding his pants up and they flooded to the floor, making him as naked as I was. His eyes heated as they noted every mark he'd given me.

"When we're done here," he said, ushering me toward the shower, "you'll play me what you have."

I locked up halfway across the door frame. "What? No, it's not ready."

When it was clear I wasn't going to move, he shoved me inside the tiled area that was almost large enough to call a room. I breathed in the heavy, thick steam and stepped out of the way of the falling water.

"I don't care," he said flatly, coming in behind me.

"I told you it might take a while for me to—"

He pressed his palm into the center of my chest, right between my breasts, and walked me backward until the cold, wet tile was against my back. His eyes were unforgiving. "I didn't say it has to be done, but you'll play it for me. I get to hear it today, got it?"

I felt sick to my stomach. I liked what I had so far, but it wasn't much. It barely scratched the surface of the man looming over me. When I didn't answer, he took it as confirmation. He stepped back into the water, letting it pour down his bulky frame, and he pushed the wet hair out of his eyes.

"Good," he said. "Get on your knees."

chapter
TWENTY-SEVEN

Vasilije

David Garvin's house shared a driveway with two other homes, but not any walls, thank fuck. According to the real estate listing last year, it had a finished basement. That was where I'd need to pull the trigger to keep this shit quiet.

Oksana and I sat in the back seat of the Lexus, with John behind the wheel, and all our gazes went beyond the windshield to the top of the hill, where the back of David's house was visible through the trees. The lights had gone off over an hour ago, but I was cautious. It'd be easier to persuade with my gun if he was asleep and unarmed when I got to him.

She'd been jittery on the car ride over, and now drummed her fingers on the leather.

"Stop," I said, covering her hand with mine. "I don't like useless noise."

The hand was just like the woman it was attached to. Soft, delicate, and warm.

I'd come in her mouth in the shower this morning, while the water poured down on us and her wet hair was coiled around my fists. I figured she needed a break from the fucking. Didn't want to wear out my new favorite toy so soon.

After she'd swallowed, she'd gasped as I'd shoved her back to sit on the ledge in the shower, and the sound echoed off the glass. I'd crouched down, put one knee near the drain, and slung her legs over my shoulders. Listening to her compose a symphony of sex as

I worked her over with my tongue sounded amazing. Her cries of need, and those moans of pleasure? I could listen to that shit all day.

Oksana exploded with a loud cry, shuddering while my tongue was massaging her and her fingers scratched at the tile. The wet ends of her hair dripped onto her heaving chest and gorgeous tits. I'd almost told her she'd be showering with me from now on, but realized I'd never fucking get anything done. The girl and her delicious pussy were distracting.

"I'm going," I announced to everyone in the car, including myself. I wasn't scared, but not super comfortable either. I'd done as much research and planning as possible, but there were a lot of unknowns in the house on the hill.

Her hand shifted, turning until she could wrap her fingers around mine and squeeze. Her blue eyes looked nervous. Who would have thought this Russian girl would be worried about me? And that I'd like it?

"Good luck," she whispered.

It was weird as hell, the need to kiss her, but I gave in to it. If I was about to walk into that house and not walk out, who fucking cared if I kissed her? I planted my lips on hers and slipped my tongue deep in her mouth, kissing her in a way she'd never forget me.

She swayed at the end of it, disoriented.

I turned to John. "If I'm not out in an hour, text Aleksandar and tell him where I am. You take Oksana back to my house and call Luka."

John nodded.

"Don't take an hour." Her voice was tight as she tried for a stern tone. "I don't want to wait that long to hear about it."

I flashed her a full grin. Bringing her along instead of Alek wasn't too smart, but it was way more fun. I pushed open the car door and got out.

There was no ID on me, other than my phone, which would be

tough to unlock. My clothes were dark and utilitarian. I only carried two tools, a lock pick and my Glock. No under-arm holster tonight. I needed concealment and went for a rear waistband one, hidden beneath my black shirt. It'd be slower to draw, but hopefully I wouldn't need to pull in a hurry.

Dry leaves crunched under my boots as I hustled up the hill, sticking close to the trees and ducking under branches. It was overcast tonight, making it unlikely anyone would see me. My lungs were tight in the cold air and I wanted to cough, but I held it in until the sensation passed. I made it to the back patio door and listened for any sounds from beyond the glass.

There was a sign in the front yard announcing the home was protected by a security system, only my PI said it was bullshit. The house might have been wired at one time, but the company didn't have an account for this address on file. I put my gloved hand on the sliding door, curious. Might as well see if he'd been dumb enough to leave it unlocked, and save myself the trip to the front door and the time it'd take to pick.

The door slid open and I shook my head in disbelief.

It was noisy as hell, and I opened it just enough so I could slither through. The kitchen was dark. No dogs came rushing at me. No men waited with guns in their hands. I dragged the door closed and surveyed the room. Dirty dishes with half-eaten dinners were stacked on the counter beside empty beer bottles.

I unholstered the Glock and set off in search of David.

The depressing house wasn't large, so it didn't take long. He was asleep in the bedroom to the left of the kitchen, snoring away with his mouth hanging open. I stepped around the piles of clothes and carefully searched for his piece. David might not have security monitoring his home, but he'd been my uncle's bodyguard for years. His security would be a gun or two within reach of the bed.

There was one hidden under the metal frame. I slipped it quietly out of the holster and jammed it in the back of my jeans. I didn't find a gun under the pillow on the far side of the bed, which meant he might have the second one beneath his fat head. If he did, I'd shoot him before he could go for it.

He was in his mid-fifties, and it looked like he'd let himself go over the last twenty years. Fuck, he was a hairy bastard. Maybe after I woke him up, I'd make him put on a shirt. I didn't like looking at the forest of curls that covered most of him.

I set the barrel of my gun an inch from his forehead. "Hey, fuckface. Wake up."

David jerked awake. His sleepy eyes focused on the gun and immediately went alert.

"Hands where I can see them," I said. "Right, fucking, now."

He probably thought about going for the gun beneath the mattress, but his split-second calculation was run and he figured it wasn't going to work out in his favor. He cautiously raised his hands.

"Sit up. Slowly," I ordered.

His anxious eyes didn't stray from mine. "I don't keep money in the house. You picked a bad guy to rob, kid."

My finger ached to pull the trigger, but the rest of me was strong. *Get him downstairs first.* He didn't recognize me, and why would he? I'd been five years old the last time I'd seen him. "If I was going to rob you, why the fuck would I wake you up?"

He drew in a deep breath. Yeah, it was sinking in now.

When his eyes shifted away, I chuckled. "Thinking about going for the gun under the bed? Because, surprise. I found it." I enjoyed the grimace that rolled through David's expression. "On your feet. Let's take a walk."

He was wearing a pair of blue boxers, and thank God for that. I didn't need to see any more of him. "Where are we going?" he asked as he came to his feet.

"Downstairs."

His shoulders pulled back. "Why?"

"Because I love the smell of mold. Fucking move."

I'd explored the whole place as a precaution, and had made sure the only thing that could kill me in the basement—outside of David—was the musty rot in the walls. He went down the steps at a snail's pace, probably stalling for time, or hoping I'd slip up and get too close so he could take a gun off me.

My impulse control had improved over the last year. I understood when to be patient.

"What's this about?" he asked when he reached the bottom of the steps. "Who do you work for?"

It was both the truth and a lie. "Goran Markovic."

He hadn't been afraid when he'd woken with a gun in his face, but he was scared shitless now.

"What the fuck?" His face turned an ugly shade of purple. "I did what he told me and kept my mouth shut."

I flicked the tip of my gun toward the center of the room, then aimed it back at him. I'd prefer not to get anything on myself when I pulled the trigger.

David's agitation ramped up. "Why'd he send you? There's no mess to clean up here. Dimitrije died last—"

"No *mess*?" Anger was a thick knot in my throat, choking me. "What you did ruined people's lives."

He looked guilty, but visibly swallowed it back. "If I hadn't done it, Goran would have killed me and found someone else."

I knew it was true, but it didn't matter. "You think that excuse is going to save you?"

He began to shake. Not so much a tremble in fear, but with frustration. Like he knew this day was coming. "Look, kid, I didn't want to do it, just like I'm sure you don't want to do this."

He was even dumber than he looked, and I sneered. "You don't know shit." Actually, not true. He knew one vital piece of information

I wanted. I had my suspicions, but needed him to confirm it. "Am I supposed to feel sorry for you, you pathetic piece of shit? You murdered an innocent woman, after smearing her name. She had two fucking kids."

David's body quaked violently. He didn't argue the statement, so this was pure guilt.

There was plenty of blame to share between my father and uncle for my mother's death, but David's reaction meant I was now staring at the man who'd physically killed her. The gun burned in my hand, all the way through my gloves.

"I know she did." His voice was tiny. "I think about them a lot, actually."

My mind went white-hot with rage. I wasn't going to stand for bullshit. "You do, huh?" My eyebrow tugged upward so hard, it hurt. "How old do you think they might be these days? The younger one would be, what? Twenty-four?"

He jolted. His mouth fell open, and his eyes went so wide they were nearly all white. I watched with rich, evil satisfaction as the realization dawned on him. He was totally and completely fucked.

"Vasilije?" he whispered.

The smallest amount of pressure on the trigger was all it took, and the gun went off.

Even though I hit him with my first shot, I gave him several more slugs to the chest. I stopped as his body began to fall and before I used the entire magazine, though. That was proof how much I'd improved my impulse control.

Once David collapsed into a heap, and his brains and blood were soaking into the carpet, I dug my pair of wireless headphones out of a pocket and hooked one onto each ear. I pulled out my phone, unlocked it, and scrolled to the app I was looking for.

After the shower this morning, Oksana had asked for more time before playing me what she was working on. She was close to being done with the first song, she'd said, so I'd given her until after dinner. The music would be better when it wasn't so bright in the house anyway, I'd convinced myself. I was impatient, though. I really fucking wanted to hear it.

She'd mentioned the bruises I'd put on her ass hurt, and when she sat down at the piano to play for me, she winced. Her body was tight with apprehension, and she hesitantly set her fingers on the keys. But once she started to play, she dove headfirst into the music. Her long fingers attacked the keys, striking them at times in a similar way that I struck her.

Calculating. With purpose.

When she'd played the final note, she took in a deep breath and turned to me, desperate for feedback.

"It's good," I said simply.

Her lips parted, and shock overtook her. She'd expected me to hate it, or at least have more to say, but I just shrugged and got out my phone.

"Play it again," I demanded, setting my finger over the button onscreen to start recording.

I'd been lying through my teeth to her. The song wasn't good; it was *magnificent*. I couldn't tell her that, though. Didn't need her getting a big head and then deciding one song was enough. I wanted more from her.

As I stood over David's body, the gun still warm from firing, I pressed 'play' and the opening song of my symphony began. Fuck, Oksana had composed it perfectly. From now on, every time I listened to it, I'd remember this moment. Her music had captured my satisfaction so I could enjoy it again and again. Endlessly.

I couldn't wait to tell her about it.

chapter
TWENTY-EIGHT

Oksana

Movement among the bushes caught John's attention, and I followed his gaze out the window. The tight feeling around my racing heart evaporated as Vasilije burst from beneath a tree and barreled for the Lexus. I didn't get a good look because of how fast he was moving, but he seemed okay. The engine purred to life while he yanked open the door and ducked inside, and the second it thudded closed, John put the car in gear.

Off came Vasilije's gloves. A thin sheen of sweat clung to his face, even though it was freezing outside. What had happened? Had David put up a fight? I scoured the boy sitting beside me, looking for signs of injury, but if he were bleeding, I couldn't tell with his dark clothes. Vasilije didn't have any holes in him, which was good. And he hadn't come to the car limping or clutching a part of his body—

"What?" he asked, looking down at himself. "Did I get some on me?"

I almost laughed, but was too distracted by my relief. "No. I was just curious if you were okay."

A slow smile crept across his lips as he unclipped the holster from his back and dropped it to the floorboard with a thump. "Worried about me, baby?" He stabbed a finger on my seatbelt, releasing it, and tugged me into his lap so I was straddling him. His eyes were wild with adrenaline. "Don't be. I'm fine."

"That's great." I made half an attempt to get out of his lap. I wasn't as motivated to put space between us as I should have been.

"Are you going to tell me what happened?"

Lights from the highway streaked across his handsome face as he kept me from scrambling away. "Jesus. Let a guy catch his breath first."

The breath he wanted to catch must have been my own, because his icy hands inched beneath my sweater and grazed my belly. I flinched at the contact, but mostly from the cold, rather than his touch. His glittering eyes connected with mine in the darkened back seat, and the air thickened.

As his palms burrowed up my sweater, the story spilled from him.

There'd been no hesitation pulling the trigger, even though the kill was personal. It gave me hope that when the time came to end my father's life, I'd be able to do it. If not, perhaps the man whose hands closed around my breasts could. But I still had a long way to go before I could tell Vasilije the truth.

He trailed his fingertips over my bra as he talked about ransacking the house afterward, which explained why he was sweaty and short of breath when he'd reappeared. I wasn't prepared for the bombshell he dropped, though. I had to say it again.

"You listened to the song I wrote?" My brain wouldn't function. "Why?"

"Because it's mine?" He said it like I'd asked a stupid question. "The music was fucking perfect, Oksana."

Holy shit. My spine went weak. He'd been impossible to read before, only offering me the infuriating comment that the song was good. Was he fucking with me? I repeated it in disbelief. "Perfect?"

His expression was serious. "Yeah. Now stop squirming or you're going to get me hard and I'm gonna make you blow me again."

I swallowed a breath. "John didn't seem to mind last time."

"You want it, huh?" He pinched my nipple through the bra, twisting until I whimpered, and his eyes flooded with heat. "You're so turned on, you'll take my dick in any hole you can get, won't you?"

It wasn't the murder that had worked me up, but Vasilije, who was riding the high of invincibility right now. His power leeched off onto me, and I grew hot and damp between my thighs. Having him call my composition *perfect* had taken me right to the edge. I was desperate. Needy to connect with him in any way possible.

"Go on," he said, leaning back against the seat, oozing confidence and sex. "My pants aren't going to undo themselves."

♪

Vasilije had to work on Black Friday. He'd explained the shopping holiday to me last night and I'd nodded, pretending to be clueless. He was up and gone before I was awake, so I went to the piano, eager to compose a second song.

He'd killed someone last night, and all I could think about was music. How fucked up was I?

Whitney, his personal chef, appeared at eleven a.m. I'd been too engrossed in my playing to hear her at first. She'd brought in several plastic bags, set them on the counter, and lingered in the kitchen, listening to the song.

As soon as I finished, she strode toward me. She was younger than I expected, appearing as if she wasn't even forty. Her brown hair was cut short and stylish, and as she smiled widely, it showed off her perfectly straight, white teeth.

"Oksana," she said warmly. "I'm Whitney. You play beautifully."

I rose to stand and took her offered handshake. "Thank you. It's nice to meet you."

Her grip was ferocious and she shook my hand a fraction too long, as if distracted. "First Luka, and now this."

"I'm sorry?"

"The way these Markovic boys are when they find a girl they like. They just go all in, don't they?" She gave a light laugh. "I didn't even know he was serious with anyone." She sobered a little, contemplating her own statement. "But then again, we don't talk like we used to. He's been . . . different since his father passed."

Her expression was surprising. She was sad, as if she missed her friend.

I took in a deep breath. I'd been told Vasilije was charming and the life of the party, but hadn't seen it for myself. Learning the truth about his mother's death and killing Dimitrije had changed him.

Whitney pushed her thoughts away and brightened. "Anyway, I'm excited you're here. Cooking for two is easier than one." Her eyes gleamed with amusement. "I've been told you eat like a bird, and Vasilije wants me to introduce you to American cuisine."

"I think he wants to fatten me up," I said dryly.

She just laughed. We chatted for a while about meal ideas. Usually Whitney prepared the upcoming week's menu and left instructions for Vasilije to execute. He ate well. Not just large meals, but healthy ones. Should I have been surprised? He liked staying in shape, and his diet played a big role.

"Will it bother you if I play while you're cooking?"

She grinned like I was being silly. "Um, no. I think it would be amazing."

Back I went to the piano, leaving Whitney to her meal prep while I worked on my symphony. I heard the song in my head as a full orchestra, and the strings would feature a haunting melody. It flowed from me so fast, I struggled to keep up with my pencil on the paper. I worked feverishly, trying not to lose the inspiration as it struck—

A hand closed on my shoulder, and I startled. My body went on red alert. This hand was male, but it did not belong to Vasilije. It was too large and warm. I jerked away and whirled to face the owner.

I sucked in a breath so fast, it was painful.

Goran Markovic.

What the hell was he doing here? I stared up at him, unable to find words. He wore a suit. Black, but not as dark as his eyes. Nothing seemed to be as pitch black as those. Cold washed over me at his intense expression.

"I didn't mean to startle you," he said. "I've been standing here a while. You didn't hear me come in?"

My vocal cords refused to work. I shook my head as I subtly slid away from him on the bench. My gaze went to the front door, glaring at it for letting him in.

He must have figured out what I was wondering. "I have a code," he said. "No one answered the door when I rang."

Whitney's strained voice came from the kitchen. "I'm sorry, sir. I must not have heard it either."

The way she said it made me wonder if he'd used the doorbell at all, or had he planned to sneak up on me. I stood from the bench and smoothed my clammy palms down my thighs. I wasn't mentally prepared to face Goran, especially without Vasilije around. My father's warning echoed in my head. What reason did Goran have for showing up unannounced?

"My nephew was right," he said. His eyes drilled into me, and I'd rather do scales for hours than endure his scrutiny another second. "You're talented." His voice dropped low. "I wonder how talented you are at *other* things."

I couldn't breathe.

My father wanted me to seduce this man, and here he was, giving me the perfect opening. Goran was the head of the Serbian mafia, but I wasn't a fool. I saw right through to the motivations beneath. This was a power struggle between the family. Whether Goran was interested in me was irrelevant. His goal was to weaken Vasilije.

And since it seemed like the younger Markovic man was infatuated with me, the older one would use me to make his first strike. My throat closed up as my pulse skyrocketed. The look in Goran's eyes was sexual and dominating. I'd come to enjoy that same look from Vasilije, but on this man? It was revolting.

In the kitchen, Whitney dropped a pan and it clattered loudly in the sink. I flinched at the sound, and his irritated gaze flicked to her before returning to me. "I need to speak with you in private," he said. "Come on."

The head of the Serbian crime family didn't make requests. I would have to do as he said. While he strode toward the office, I glanced at Whitney like she could save me. She looked back with concern. The thought that struck me right then was shocking. I didn't want to be alone with any man—

Any man except for Vasilije.

I had a terrible suspicion of what was about to happen in the office. Like a sick déjà vu, I started thinking about scenarios. If Goran tried to force himself on me, could I get to the gun in the desk drawer in time?

Stay calm. Maybe all he wants to do is talk. I marched to the office, sure I was heading toward ruin.

It was noticeably colder in here. The room was all dark, elegant wood, and a tufted leather couch sat opposite the desk in the center. On the other side of the huge arched front window was a built-in bookcase and fireplace, and I stared at one of the pictures on a shelf. A beautiful dark haired woman stood beside the piano, holding a baby in her arms while a young boy clung to her leg.

Vasilije's mother.

I faced the man in the room, who was responsible for that woman's death.

"Close the door," Goran ordered. He knelt at the fireplace and turned the key beside it, making orange-yellow flames burst to life over the ceramic logs. "The insulation has always been terrible in here. The window lets out all the heat."

He straightened and his gaze evaluated me surgically.

"You're a skittish little thing." His tone was amused. He'd noticed how I was trembling, and seemed to enjoy my apprehension.

"Do you speak, girl?"

I forced it out. "Yes. What did you want to talk about?"

If he advanced on me, I'd step to the side rather than backward, and move toward the ornate desk with the gun in the bottom drawer.

"Vasilije shouldn't have brought you to dinner the other night."

No, he shouldn't have, but like I had a choice in going? I bit back the response and chose to stare at the flickering flames rather than the imposing man in front of me. We stood several feet apart, and yet he was much too close.

"You overheard us talking about things I would have preferred you didn't."

Had Goran only come here to tell me to keep my mouth shut? I straightened, feeling the first tug of relief. "I don't repeat things that aren't my business."

Usually a smile was meant to put a person at ease, but I was learning a Markovic grin signaled danger.

"You do seem like the quiet type." He took his first step in my direction, and I knew it was just the beginning. I shifted subtly toward the desk as he kept talking. "I'm partial to women who can be quiet."

It was so heavy with meaning, it was crushing, and he took another step. I adjusted, keeping the distance between us.

"The club the Russian man mentioned at dinner," he said, "has women like you. They're young, and beautiful, and they don't speak unless told. In fact, they'll be absolutely silent if I tell them to." Goran's stride was larger than mine and he was gaining ground. "It doesn't matter what I'm doing. Fucking them, getting rough, however I want. They are paid to obey, and I enjoyed going to that club very much."

The side of the desk dug into my thigh. Even with heat pouring from the fireplace, it was arctic in the office. Goran casually rested a hand on his belt, but this movement had a threatening purpose. Like Vasilije, his uncle preferred an under-the-arm holster, and the grip of his black gun appeared beneath the side of his suitcoat.

"Since I can't go there anymore," he said, "you will be an adequate replacement."

chapter
TWENTY-NINE

I BIT DOWN ON THE SIDE OF MY CHEEK once more and tried not to react. The words tasted strange coming out of my mouth, but not unpleasant. "I'm with Vasilije."

Goran shot me a look of disdain. "Then, be with Vasilije. I don't care." His heavy voice was absolute. "But when I'm here, you'll do what I want."

Fear was a hard lump in my throat I couldn't swallow down. Vasilije wouldn't share. "He won't allow that."

"He won't like it, but perhaps now he'll think twice about challenging my orders."

"If I touch anyone else, he'll kill me."

Goran's shoulders lifted in an indifferent shrug. "You can come with me. My house is even larger than this one. I'll figure out somewhere to put you."

That wasn't an option. Vasilije wouldn't care if I was forced or not. Leaving him for his uncle would be the ultimate betrayal. Goran had taken Vasilije's mother and destroyed their entire family in the process. He was possessive of me like a child with his favorite toy. Vasilije didn't love, but he cared about me in his own way.

And . . . I felt it, too. I hoped to turn him into a partner, and the connection to him wasn't like anything else I'd had.

The man peering at me with desire dripping off his expression would *never* see me as a partner. He'd fuck me to screw over Vasilije, and once I'd served my purpose, I'd be taken care of with a bullet, or something slower and more painful.

"I'm not going anywhere," I said.

Goran blinked and delivered an evil smile. "All right." He glanced at the couch. "Have a seat."

My knees nearly gave out.

If I called to Whitney for help, he might lose his patience with me, or do something to her. I was on my own, and I had to make my decision right now. Either I went for the gun, or I abandoned that plan and followed his order. I might not get another chance, unless I was able to wrestle his gun away from him, but that seemed impossible. He was much bigger and stronger.

But if I killed his uncle, Vasilije was going to be pissed. Mostly, because he wanted to do it himself.

Could I make it to the drawer in time? I'd have to fire as soon as I had the gun, before Goran could pull his own. *Don't forget to check the safety.* If it was still on when I tried to shoot, I'd lose valuable time. Thank God Konstantine had agreed to take me to the firing range when I'd asked years ago.

"Did you hear me?" His voice was annoyed because I'd stood stock-still, trying to figure out what to do.

I wasn't ready to make the decision where either option could end my life. "I don't feel like sitting."

"I don't remember asking." Irritation flared in his cruel eyes and burned greater than the fire.

When it was clear I wasn't going to move from my spot beside the desk, his expression hardened, and every molecule of air evaporated from the room as he charged forward.

"Please, don't touch me," I gasped, hating how weak I sounded, but my request did nothing to stop him. He dug a hand under my arm, squeezing the pressure point right above my elbow, and I wilted. His grip was intense, and nothing like Vasilije's. The pain was flat, aching misery.

I was so stupid, and my inaction was going to get me killed. Why hadn't I moved faster? Now that he had ahold of me, my opportunity was slipping away. I wasn't going to waste one more second, or let another man put his hands on me when I didn't want him to. As Goran began to tug me toward the couch, I struggled to break loose and latched my free hand on the edge of the solid desk.

"No!" I cried loudly. "Stop!"

I gripped so hard on the wood, my hand ached, and his squeeze on my arm tightened until it took every ounce of strength to keep from screaming. Footsteps pounded on the hardwood and approached rapidly. Whitney, coming to save me. If I could reach the gun, she'd witness the whole fucking thing.

The door swung open and—

Blyad!

Vasilije—not Whitney—rushed in. His gun was in hand and hung ready at his side, and his face was a mask of aggression. Goran and I froze at the same moment, and I watched as the younger Markovic took in the scene. He noted his uncle's hand on my arm, switched the gun to his left, and then swung his right fist into the side of Goran's head with a loud crack of flesh hitting flesh.

The impact knocked me free and I slammed both hands on the desk, stabilizing to stay on my feet. Goran said something in Serbian, which had to be a swear or two, as he stumbled to the side.

"What the fuck are you doing?" Vasilije demanded.

Goran cradled his head in his hand. The blow had shaken him, and done the same to me. Watching Vasilije punch his uncle had rocked my foundation. As he recovered, Goran reached for his gun.

"Before you do that," Vasilije said, putting his own back in his dominant hand, "maybe consider how Luka's gonna react."

Whatever that meant, it did the trick, and Goran abandoned the idea of going for his weapon. But he was still full of rage. "You think you can put your hands on me, you little shit?"

"Well, you put your hands on my property first."

His uncle's eyes went so narrow they were mere slits. "Your

property has no loyalty. The girl came on to me. She was all over my stick from the moment I got here."

I choked at hearing the lie. "I didn't!"

Vasilije didn't look at me and he didn't hesitate. "Not a chance."

"You're going to believe your Russian whore over me?"

Vasilije's dark eyes sharpened. "When you're lying? Yeah." He squared his shoulders and widened his stance, preparing for a punch to be headed his direction. Yet, none came. "What the fuck are you doing in my house? Did you forget the system tells me when someone keys in?"

I suspected Goran hadn't forgotten. He wanted Vasilije to come home and either find me gone, or catch me with his uncle. Goran took a long moment to respond. "I was curious how serious you are about her, or if Wednesday night was just an act for the Russians."

"Are you fucking kidding? You could've just asked."

"And I told you to get rid of her."

Vasilije sighed. "Yeah, you did, but I don't want to. I'm having fun, so she stays." His voice was pointed. "I've always done what you wanted, and I deserve this. You owe me." Unexpected amusement flickered over his face. "Come on, look at her. She's *harmless*."

I was so tense, I was fighting to keep my lunch down and couldn't acknowledge his hidden meaning.

Goran's expression was rigid. "I don't owe you anything after that punch. You're lucky I'm willing to let it go, but you need to stop thinking with your dick, and start using that brain your father gave you."

Vasilije had some choice words simmering under the surface, but he reined them in and stayed quiet.

Goran let out a noise of deep frustration. "I allow this and you fucking fall in line. You have a place in this family, and it's beneath me." He rubbed the tender spot where he'd been hit. "Beneath me, or *nowhere at all*."

"I get it," Vasilije spat out.

His uncle's calculating gaze swung to me like I was garbage, and back to his nephew. "A Russian girl. I'm embarrassed for you."

"Do your eyes not work? Why would I be embarrassed?"

Goran smiled, and alarm spiraled once more through my system. "All right," he said. "Since you're so proud of her, I expect you'll be bringing her to Christmas Eve?"

Vasilije hesitated. Only long enough for us to see his reluctance. Then, an easy smile snapped into place, complete with his dimple. "Of course."

"Wonderful." His tone was full of sarcasm. He cast a final hard look at me, said something else in Serbian, and left. I remained in place, my hands supporting myself on the desk, and stared at Vasilije while we listened to the front door open and slam shut.

He jammed his gun back in the holster, but didn't move otherwise. His posture was tense. "Are you okay?"

"I'm fine." Except my voice was shaky, and I worried if I took my hands off the desk, I'd collapse. My heart was still pounding like a war drum. It'd been life and death in this room a few minutes ago, and I hadn't recovered.

A concerned female voice rang out from beyond the office doorway. "Vasilije?"

"Everything's all right," he answered to Whitney. He took a cautious step, and somehow didn't seem threatening for once. He asked it quietly. "What happened?"

"He said he needed to talk to me in private, and told me I had to do . . ." the words lodged in my throat, "whatever he wanted." My gaze dropped down to my splayed hands. "There's a gun in the bottom drawer. I thought I might have to kill him."

Vasilije took a long moment to contemplate my statement, and . . .

He *laughed*.

"Fuck, you and me both. Good thing you didn't. I'd have been pissed." He delivered his perfect smile, flashing the dimples, but it was menacing. "I'm the one who gets to kill him."

Should it have bothered me that he was the most attractive when he looked evil? A rush flooded through me. "That was the same thought I had when I went for the gun."

"Goddamn, Oksana." He swept toward me and dug a hand in the back of my hair, gently tugging me up to meet his gaze and caused me to peel my hands from the desk. My hair was the only place he physically had a hold of me, but his intense eyes kept me upright. He was touching me, but not really.

Almost . . . as if he were waiting for a signal it was okay to put his hands anywhere else on my body.

"You can touch me," I said.

His eyes flared with hunger, and something that looked like desperation. "Like I need fucking permission."

His mouth announced one thing, but his actions said the opposite. As soon as I'd given him approval, his lips sealed over mine and his hands seized my waist. I was fitted to him, pressed against his hardened frame until I could barely breathe.

Everything was spinning out of control.

The burn of his hands on my body was pleasurable and erotic. A strange sensation I enjoyed, and the discomfort made me feel alive. I shouldn't want his touch, but I was already beginning to crave it.

"He comes near you again," he said between his rough kisses, "and fuck my plan. I'll murder him."

I believed it.

I could have used the opportunity today to get close to Goran and follow my father's order, but I'd made my choice. I was all in. With Vasilije, we could both get what we wanted. My father underestimated me, just as Vasilije's uncle underestimated him, and hopefully it would be both their downfalls.

♪

Saturday evening after dinner, Aleksandar showed up at the house. Vasilije had taken me on a second shopping trip during the day, buying me more clothes, some makeup, and—in a shocking move—a cell phone. The only two numbers programmed were John's and his. Was it to keep tabs on me, or a way to call for help if his uncle came around again?

I was ushered into the back seat of the Lexus with Vasilije, John behind the wheel, and Aleksandar in the front seat like last time.

"Where are we going?" I asked, forcing casualness.

"Out," Vasilije said.

He didn't elaborate, withholding the information simply because I wanted it. He loved to keep me off balance.

After I'd calmed down from Goran's visit yesterday, Vasilije and I had eaten lunch cooked by Whitney, and he'd had to return to the dealership to finish out the day. I'd tried to write, but spent most of the afternoon staring at the keys and trying to forget everything but the way Vasilije's mouth moved against mine. It'd kept my anxiety away, but wasn't enough to get the notes flowing again.

He'd taken me to his bedroom after dinner last night and fucked me until I'd shaken with an orgasm so violent, it forced tears in my eyes. He'd groaned out his release and I heard music again, and twenty minutes after he fell asleep, I'd been back at the piano.

During the drive, Aleksandar talked with Vasilije about things I had no interest in. Video games. Sports. Who had the best pair of tits among celebrities. When we arrived at the bar, the bouncer didn't check any of us for ID. The oversized man at the door gave Vasilije a smile and gestured for us to bypass the line of people waiting.

I wasn't sure what was more stunning. The fact that Vasilije took me out to meet his friends, or the effortless way he interacted with them. He was so easy to smile, or tell a joke. He listened to conversations without dominating them. We sat in the VIP section, and all the drinks were put on the Markovic tab. His friends, mostly guys but a few of their girlfriends, were his age, and had been his frat brothers in college.

They *adored* Vasilije.

The guy who had fucked me bent over his bed last night was gone. Seeing him now was like watching a stranger.

I barely spoke the entire night. I drank the drinks he ordered, sat beside him on the couch, and smiled vacantly like a good little whore until I was buzzed enough I didn't care. It made it possible to ignore Aleksandar's glares when Vasilije wasn't looking.

I didn't like the reminder how I was running out of time. It was possible I could stall Aleksandar a few more days once the new devices arrived, but eventually he'd realize I was double-crossing my own people, and he'd out me in a heartbeat.

"I'm drunk," I announced to Vasilije, loud enough for his friends to hear. "I want to go home and fuck."

A few of them snickered, and some looked at him with envious eyes. I wasn't drunk. I'd said it because I wanted to be alone with him, and sex was the fastest way to connect.

Vasilije smirked. "Then let's get the fuck out of here."

John delivered us back to the house, and Aleksandar left without saying a word, and when I finished hanging up my coat, I discovered Vasilije in the kitchen, a box in his hands.

"This is for you." He flashed his dangerous smile.

I swallowed hard, took the small, unwrapped box from him, and opened the flaps. Inside was black lingerie, the opposite of the virginal stuff he'd bought me before.

His eyes were electrified with desire. "Time to go upstairs and see how it fits."

chapter
THIRTY

VASILIJE SAT ON THE BED and played on his phone while I carried the box into his bathroom and changed. It wasn't just a black bra and panties, it was also thigh-high stockings and a garter belt. I was as careful as possible while sliding the silky stockings on, determined not to get a run in them. Would he punish me if I did? I put on the garter belt next, and hooked the straps to the lacy band near the top of each thigh.

The underwear and bra were similar to the white ones I had. The sheer mesh and lace obscured just enough, only teasing nudity. When I was finally dressed, I gazed at my reflection and watched a flush color my face.

It was amazing what a few scraps of lace could do. I was confident when I walked out into the bedroom, Vasilije was going to like what he saw. I grabbed a tube of the new bright red lipstick he'd bought me and smeared it on. The blue undertone of my pale skin made the color even more dramatic. I combed my fingers through my blonde hair, fluffing it out, and sauntered into the bedroom.

"*Puši kurac,*" he said.

His heavy gaze etched over the skimpy bits of fabric covering me, and I half expected drool to leak out of one side of his mouth. He stood and ran a hand over his crotch, massaging himself through his jeans. "Stay here."

He left, only to return moments later with my black heels, which he thrust at me.

"What does that mean? The Serbian you said?" I asked as I stepped into the shoes, completing the look.

He smirked. "Suck my dick."

I blinked.

Slowly, I knelt, folding one knee and then the other as I reached for the button of his jeans, but he swung his hips away.

"It's an expression, not an order." He scooped a hand under my arm and tugged me to my feet. "We'll get to that, don't worry, but I want to take pictures first."

"Do you have any space left on your phone?" He'd taken a lot of pictures last night.

He rewarded me with a swat on my ass, and I was sure it left a perfect red impression of his hand. I bit my bottom lip. Wearing the lingerie turned me on, and his aggressive touch was the foreplay I desired.

His photoshoot didn't last long. He was having a hard time keeping his hands to himself, and when he kissed me, his erection dug low against my belly.

"Pull your panties to the side," he commanded, stepping back and pointing the phone at me. I darted my fingers to the crotch of my underwear and tugged it aside, and when he made a noise of approval, it sent a current of desire thrumming through me.

"I want you to fuck me," I said. It wasn't an act. The raw need in my voice was real.

"Do you?" he mocked. "Just a second and I will." He looked down at the phone in his hand, scrolling through the screens. "I want to make sure Petrov gets this first."

His words cast me into a pool of ice, and I strangled it out. "What?"

Vasilije's expression was devious. "I'm in a giving mood."

"You're sending those pictures to Sergey Petrov?" I didn't feel shame about most things, but even this was beyond my limit. The man was my father.

"No." He said it like I was ridiculous. "They're going to the other Petrov, Konstantine. The shithead who was staring at you, remember?"

"*Ahuyet!*" I reached for the phone to stop him. "You can't."

Vasilije drew back with surprise. "What do you care? You'll never see him again."

Panic was whirring so loud in my mind, it was deafening. "You can't know that."

When I scrambled for his phone a second time, he stepped away and distrust clouded in his eyes. "I do, because he'll be dead by the end of the week."

"What?"

"The Russians pushed my uncle too far. He gave the order last night. The Russians want to control us, but instead? They're getting war." Vasilije acted like he was talking about a simple thing. "I'll give him a few dirty pics and send him out with a bang."

I latched my hands onto his forearm, half needing him for support. I was shaking with fear for my brother as my mind raced. "No. Vasilije, no. Please."

"What the hell?" Confusion ate at his expression.

I closed my eyes and dry swallowed, unable to see any other way out of my situation. "You have to stop this. You can't kill Konstantine."

"Why the fuck not? The Russians are—"

"He's my brother."

The statement hung, suspended in time while Vasilije processed it.

I felt a connection to him, stronger and more real than I thought possible. Did he feel any of it, or would he kill me now that I'd shattered the trust?

Finally, he gave me a dubious look. "I've seen Konstantine's sister, and you aren't her."

I knew my next statement could be the nail in my coffin, but said it anyway. "Tatiana is my half-sister. Konstantine is my half-brother."

Doubt washed away and left a hard look in its place. I could see him trying to put it together in his head. He was looking for a way to connect me to the family without going through my father, but I needed to get the whole truth out.

"When my mother died, I was sent to Sergey Petrov." My voice cracked with stress. "My father."

Had I broken him? Vasilije simply stared at me. He didn't seem to be breathing.

The room grew colder than Siberian winter.

"I don't believe you," he said, but he was lying. I watched his gaze flit to the dresser drawer where we both knew his gun was stored, and pain stabbed at the hole where my heart was supposed to be. He was considering murdering me. "If Sergey had another daughter," he said, "I'd know."

I shook my head. "No one knows. It'd be an embarrassment to my family, especially my stepmother, if it got out. I'm sorry I lied to you, but—"

He sneered. "*I don't believe you.*"

"—most of what I said is true. I hate my father. I'm not the enemy, Vasilije. I'm your ally."

He moved so fast, it wasn't until the sharp pain of his fingers dug into my waist that it registered he was touching me. He was right in my face. His eyes were dark and furious, and all I could see. They threatened to incinerate me. "I. Don't. *Believe.* You."

I gasped from the pain. Usually I liked it when he was rough, but this was different. It wasn't sexual. He wasn't doing it to bring on pleasure. This was pure, raw anger. Punishment.

"Please, just listen. We can help each other. I want to kill him," I bit out. "But I don't know how to and not end up dead."

He picked me up and flung me down on the bed, so hard my teeth snapped together and I cried out. I scrambled backward on the mattress, and—

Oh, God. He stomped to the dresser, yanked the drawer open so hard it went off the slides, and withdrew his gun. "And what the fuck do you think I'm going to do now that I know you're—" he visibly struggled to get it out, "—a fucking Petrov?"

"I don't know." It was the most honest answer I had. "My father deserves to die, and maybe I do, too, but not Konstantine. My father sent me here to plant listening devices, knowing you'd kill me if I got caught. His own fucking daughter. I'm nothing to him. An expendable pawn, just like those men at the warehouse." I spoke even and measured for emphasis. "Just like Ivan."

At the mention of the man who'd murdered Addison's family, the barrel of the gun came up, and I died a little. He pointed the gun at me like I was a stranger. That wasn't fair. Perhaps he thought everything I'd said was a lie, and now I was a stranger.

"Please, wait a minute," I pleaded. "Konstantine saved my life. He was the one who pulled Ilia Volkov off me."

The name pinged recognition, and it wasn't surprising. Ilia was sure to have been on the Serbians' watch list. "Jesus Christ! *You* killed Volkov? They said it was an accident."

"No, it was me, and I'd do it again. But Konstantine . . . He convinced our father that what I'd done was justified. I'm still alive because of him, so, please." Under the steady aim of the gun, I climbed onto my knees. "*Please.* You can't kill him." I shook so hard, it was a miracle I didn't come apart. "You can kill me instead," I whispered, "as long as you take my father out first."

"I don't give a fuck about what you want."

Like the first night I'd come here, it was too hard to look at him, and I tore my gaze away. I blinked back the burning sensation in my eyes while I stared at the sheets beneath me. The only sound was my labored breathing and the roaring pulse in my ears.

"What do you want?" I asked.

"Some goddamn answers," he barked. "The night at the warehouse... Tell me how you knew I'd pick you."

I swallowed so hard it was audible. I was about to sign someone's death warrant. "If you didn't, Aleksandar would have."

A slew of Serbian came out of his mouth, and without understanding the words, it was so sharp and laced with anger, I felt little barbs cutting my flesh. In my peripheral vision, I sensed the movement. Vasilije had taken a step closer, bringing his gun closer to my head.

"He was in on it?"

"My father used Aleksandar's gambling debt as leverage."

"Motherfucker!" More Serbian rolled from him. More imaginary barbs sliced into my skin, leaving me exposed and raw. All my planning had led up to this moment, and as I felt Vasilije slipping away, I realized how fucking stupid I'd been. I should have just killed my father when I had the chance. I was going to die anyway, but at least that way I would have had my revenge.

"You weren't scared last time I held a gun on you," he snarled.

I closed my eyes. "Because you might actually use it tonight."

"You're goddamn right. Look at me."

I flinched at the cold metal when he pressed it against my temple, and forced myself to drag my gaze up his body. When our eyes met, I couldn't hold back the cry of anguish. I wasn't so much sad for myself as I was for the loss of what we had. It was so fucked up.

His tone mocked me. "Why are you crying when you told me you don't have feelings? Or was it just another lie?"

"Almost everything was real. I am the daughter of an opera singer from Kazan. I killed a man who put his hands on me when I didn't want him to, and after it, I wrote the dark song I've only played for you."

The barrel traced a line down the side of my face, skimming along my neck. My skin felt warm and irritated in its wake.

My voice threatened to fail, but I kept going. "You've done what I want to. My father's evil. When I told him what Ilia was doing to me, he didn't believe me. Or maybe he didn't care to. Either way, his indifference was betrayal. It was *worse* than Ilia's touch. Sergey Petrov could die a hundred times and I'm still not sure it'd be enough."

Vasilije kept his gaze on mine as the gun's path carved lower. It crossed over my collarbone, moving deliberately to the skin covering my heart.

"You're the only person who knows what I want," I said. "Who really knows me."

The barrel pressed uncomfortably against my heavy chest. It forced the words from me.

"You're the only guy I've been with." I gulped down a breath. "The only man I've let inside my body, and inside my head."

His eyes flared with perverse lust, and the tip of the gun shifted course. It followed the edge of the lacy bra, kissing my trembling skin and dipping down between my breasts. The air swirled around us, charged with sex and danger. It flowed like a current, bringing on unwanted waves of tingling across my flesh, and causing me to break out in goosebumps.

My nipples tightened into knots. A muscle clenched low in my belly as he continued to drag the hard steel down the center of my stomach. His pupils dilated and his breathing picked up. Holding this kind of power over me was probably the ultimate turn-on for him, just as it was for the submissive side of me. It was sick, but we were sick together.

"You're the only one," I said, "allowed to touch me."

As if he needed validation, his free hand shot out and snaked behind my neck. He tugged me on my knees closer to the edge of the bed and pressed the gun between my legs. The cold seeped in through the lace, but the contact was both painful and pleasurable on my heated skin.

His gaze went to my mouth and watched as my lips fell open. For a moment, he seemed to consider kissing me, but drew back as he thought better of it. "I'm not going to kiss your lying fucking mouth."

The gun moved, and the slide massaged my swollen clit, drawing a soft moan. His broad shoulders lifted in a deep breath, and he didn't stop me as I laced my fingers together behind his neck and set my forehead against his.

"You want to punish me?" I should have felt weak, but instead I found strength. "Go ahead, Vasilije. I'm yours. I'm your motherfucking property. You can do whatever you want."

chapter
THIRTY-ONE

Vasilije

My head was a fucking disaster. Rage boiled in my veins, and the need to punch something was overwhelming. Alek was working with the Russians, and Oksana had betrayed me. I was almost as mad at myself as I was at her. I should have seen this coming. The more beautiful the woman, the more likely she was to fuck you over.

And wearing that expensive lingerie I'd bought her, and the whore-colored red lipstick, she was the most beautiful thing I'd ever seen. I hated her. Goddamn her for twisting me up like this.

I thrust the gun, grinding the top of it against her pussy, and she shuddered. She wanted me to punish her? I'd do it, all right. She needed to feel the way she made me feel.

I'd lost control once. I'd reacted impulsively and taken a life, and swore I wouldn't again. Death wasn't something to be decided spur of the moment. But it was still touch-and-go for me now on whether Oksana should live. She said she wanted my help taking down Sergey Petrov, but she'd also said he was her father and had sent her here. It reeked of a setup.

My father's words haunted my mind. Was it already too late for me?

Her hands slipped down from my neck and fisted my t-shirt when I stroked the gun between her legs. She moved in time with it, fucking the gun in my hand. I didn't want it to, but it got me hard.

"Whatever I want," I repeated.

She nodded, distracted by the sensation the weapon was giving her, and whimpered when I pulled all the way back, leaving her quivering.

"Downstairs. At the piano. *Now*."

Like the obedient pet she pretended to be, she climbed off the bed and followed my order. When she was gone from the room and her footsteps creaked down the stairs, I raked a hand through my hair, not sure what to do. I felt like I should kill her, but I didn't want to. The knee-jerk reaction went away as quick as I'd had it, and all I was left with was stinging anger.

Even if I wanted to believe her, I sure as shit couldn't trust her anymore.

And I needed to. She knew secrets about me no one else did.

I scanned the room, searching for options, and when my gaze landed on the black plastic bag on my nightstand, I went for it. She claimed loyalty to me, but she was going to have to prove it.

When I reached the top of the stairs, I glanced down and hesitated.

She sat at the piano like a statue, her back stiff and her fingers waiting on the keys. Bright moonlight poured from windows, casting a silver glow. Her white skin against all the black lingerie was fucking gorgeous. Picture perfect, but I was too pissed to get out my phone. The image would probably stick in my memory forever anyway.

As I walked across the hardwood toward her, she swiveled just enough to look at me. She sighed softly when she saw I didn't have my gun anymore, but eyed the bag I held in a fist with a hint of anxiety. *Good.* She should get used to feeling uncomfortable.

I dropped the bag and it thudded loudly on the floor, making her flinch, and I strode into the kitchen. What I needed was in the bottom cabinet, closest to the basement door. The roll of black duct tape was practically new.

Her anxiety ratcheted up, and her eyes went wide with fear when she saw it.

"Whatever I want," I reminded in a hiss. "Stand up."

I ignored how she was trembling, tore a strip off, and plunked the roll down on the piano keys. The noisy, unsettling sound echoed under the ceiling. Her heels clicked frantically and she stumbled when I pulled her around to the other side of the bench. I wanted her behind it, facing the piano, and I put a hand on her back, shoving her forward.

"Down," I growled. "Knees on the floor."

Oksana took in huge gulps of breath, but did as told. She knelt behind the black lacquered bench, and tucked a lock of her hair behind an ear, probably too nervous to know what to do.

"Lean over and grab the legs." I guided her to set her chest against the flat of the wood, and watched her hands curl around the uprights. The piano was my mother's, and I didn't want to damage it, so I knelt beside her and wrapped the strip of tape with the sticky side out around both her wrist and the piano bench leg. I fumbled for the roll of tape and tore off another strip. This one I used to cover the sticky part.

"Vasilije, I—" she whispered as I worked to do her other wrist with the same technique.

"Shut the fuck up." I didn't want to hear a goddamn thing from her right now.

When I finished, I looked at my work and a surge of lust hit me. I was depraved. The Russian girl kneeling over the bench and bound to it was shuddering, and it got worse when I trailed my fingertips over the length of her spine. Her lies had left me feeling weak, but the control I had now settled the emotions churning inside.

It helped me focus on a goal.

Her head hung down and the curtain of her hair draped to the floor. I had total access to her body, and she had to be expecting me to start taking my anger out on her ass any second. But she'd be wrong. I jerked the back of her panties down, exposing her nakedness, and jammed two fingers inside her pussy.

"Oh," she groaned. Didn't sound like she'd enjoyed what I'd done, but I didn't fucking care. I didn't do it for her benefit.

"I want you wet, so I can shove my cock inside you, you lying cunt."

She gasped at my brutal words, but her body tightened on my fingers. I pumped them in and out, watching them grow slicker with each deep thrust. The muscles flexed in her back as she tried to move her arms. Did she hate being tied up? Completely at my mercy? Or did the girl like it?

I did.

I yanked my fingers out of her, undid my jeans, and dug out my nearly hard dick. My brain was still beyond pissed, but I needed my body to get on board. I spat in my hand and stroked myself. Liar or spy, the whore was still my property.

Wasn't she a whore? Fucking me only because she needed something?

I moved behind her and urged her knees apart. They slid easily across the wood because of the sexy thigh-highs I'd bought her. I held my dick steady and ran the tip along her seam, half expecting her to tell me to stop, and not sure I would if she did.

Instead, she sighed.

I gave her all of my dick in one cruel thrust. She gasped and made a choked sound, but said nothing. I delivered another vicious thrust, stabbing into her tight heat, and tried not to lose focus.

For the first time, I was fucking with the goal of *not* getting the girl off. Oksana needed to feel as used as I did, and I established a brutal tempo, driving my body deep inside her. I let the anger at her betrayal fuel me.

She groaned when I clenched a handful of hair at the top of her head and jerked her back so she was staring at the ceiling. I was savage with her. I braced my other hand on her hip while I fucked her, and the slap of my body hitting hers was as loud as it was whenever I spanked her.

She grunted. It sounded like pain mixed with pleasure.

I let go of her hair and tore my shirt up over my head. I was on goddamn fire, consumed with rage. "Tell me to stop," I challenged.

She stayed silent.

I knew a way to get her to back down. I snatched up the plastic bag, stuck a hand inside, and grabbed the bottle of lube. I dumped two pumps'-worth in between her cheeks and, as she tensed, a joyless grin spread across my face.

"Tell me to stop," I goaded.

Her silence was infuriating, but it made me harder. I flexed inside her, strangling back the need to fuck her until my cum dripped out of her pussy. I moved my hand onto a cheek, my thumb seeking the spot between that she'd ruled off limits.

"If you don't say anything, you're gonna get a thumb in your ass."

Her chest was heaving, and her body ricocheted with the impact of my punishing thrusts, but no words came from her. Not in English or Russian. I pushed the pad of my thumb down, burying the finger inside.

"Oh," she cried, and sucked in breath through clenched teeth.

Fuck me, it was hot. It was wrong and dirty, but I couldn't stop. I'd push her until she made me stop. Oksana was stubborn, but so was I, and she'd be the one to break first. "Say you want to stop." My tone dared her to do it. "Say it, or I'll give you another finger."

Her voice was clipped. "Do it."

"Yeah? God, you're filthy. What a filthy, fucking slut you are."

I had no idea if her reaction was to my words, or the way I retracted my thumb and began to work my first two fingers inside her virgin ass. It was so tight, and I could feel the fingers moving against my cock as I fucked her. The sensation was amazing.

"Oh, my God," she whined.

I jerked to a stop, throbbing inside her pussy, and pulled myself together. I'd gotten right to the edge and needed to back off. I pulled out my fingers and slapped her ass, making her yelp. "You better tell me to stop, or I'm going to fuck this ass."

She jerked against the tape, and the bench squealed an inch across the floor. "*Nyet.*"

"*Da.*" I knew the Russian word for 'no,' just as I knew the one for 'yes.' I pulled out of her, sat back on my haunches, and gave her a matching red handprint on her other cheek. "You tell me no in English."

Her legs shook as she knelt over the bench, and her hands squeezed the uprights so tightly, her knuckles were white. Her muscles were tense, and her back rose and fell with hurried, uneven pants. "Do whatever you want," she said. "I'm yours."

"If you say so," I patronized.

chapter
THIRTY-TWO

I silenced the sirens in my head that said I was too fucked up and about to go past the point of no return. I squeezed some more lube in my hand and slicked it over my pulsing dick.

Oksana's skin was soft and warm against my legs as I came back to her. I fisted my cock and used my other hand to hold her open, and lined up where I wanted to go. My gaze darted from her, to my dick, and back again, waiting for her to announce I'd called her bluff.

But she didn't. I pressed against her, and—

"Oh, shit! *Slow!*" she cried. The head of my cock was just seated inside her.

Slow is not the same as stop, my dick relayed to my brain. I spanked her. "Don't fucking tell me what to do."

Her body's grip was so strong, my vision blurred. When she swallowed a huge breath, I pushed deeper.

Inch by slow inch, she took me inside.

The sensation was different. New and dirty. I owned her completely now, and liked that I hadn't shared the experience with anyone else but her. Fuck me, it felt so good. I dragged my hand over her back, caressing her skin as she grew to tolerate where my dick was.

I swore every cuss word I knew in Serbian, and then repeated it in English so she'd understand. I drew my hips back, and slowly pressed forward. She made a noise I hadn't heard before and didn't understand. It could have been pain or pleasure.

"Do you like it?" I asked, expecting her to lie.

Her voice was strained. "No."

"That's too bad. I like it." I eased my hips back and forth, sliding my cock into the tight ring of her asshole. "You don't like being used? Now you know how I feel."

"How have I used you?"

"You want me to kill your father." It was getting hard to hold back. Her grip on me was too tight, too good.

"No. I want... your help. Be someone who'll have my back," she whispered. "My partner."

She wanted someone to cover her ass. Ironic, given I was actually inside it at that very moment. "Why should I believe anything that comes out of your lying mouth?"

She turned her head to the side so I could see her profile and the grimace she made. "I'm not lying."

I spanked her like the strike would punish, but it had no effect. She kept talking.

"We can work together."

"Shut up!"

I slapped a hand on her shoulder and held her firm as I drove into her. My vision narrowed. My heart pumped blood through my system at the speed of light. My knees ached against the hardwood, but I fucked her relentlessly. She didn't like it, but she didn't hate it either. Or at least, she didn't hate it enough to give in.

"You're gonna make me come," I groaned. My body took control. I leaned over her, crushing my chest to her back and shoved a hand down between her legs. I wanted to turn her body against her. I stirred her clit, rubbing my fingers furiously from side to side, and bit down on her shoulder.

"Oh, shit," she whined. "Shit, Vasilije."

"Fuck, yeah." I grunted it between thrusts. "Oh, fuck, yes."

Pleasure shot from me. It ruptured from my core in waves of heat, traveling like flames through gasoline. I came in a torrent, one gush of ecstasy after another, filling her in spurts. She moaned through it, like my enjoyment was hers, and fuck me... was it? Did she get off knowing I had?

As soon as the last pulse thudded through my body, I reached over and grabbed the plastic bag. I'd bought her more than just lingerie to wear, but thought it might be a while before I sprung the small plug on her. It had been more a gift for me than her.

I turned the small velvet drawstring bag over and dumped the silver plug out into my palm, and slowly retracted my dick.

"What—" she started, and the rest of the words died as I slid the metal plug into place.

I yanked her underwear back up. "Maybe I'll fuck you again and pull that plug out so you've got my cum dripping out of both holes."

"Oh my God."

I stood, went to the bathroom, and cleaned up, and when I came back, she was as I'd left her, waiting for me. "You're still here," I said. It would have been easy for her to lift the bench and slide the duct tape handcuffs off.

Her breath came and went rapidly. "If this was an attempt to drive me away . . . it failed."

"You're fucking stupid. Get the fuck out of my house before I change my mind and kill you."

She was bound, yet she stared at me defiantly. "Then do it, because I'm not going anywhere."

Did she have a death wish? No, I thought bitterly. At this point, what did she have to lose?

"Go," I said. "Run back to daddy for protection." Or at least her brother. Konstantine wasn't as powerful as his father, but like me, he was next in line. It was fucking inevitable one day I'd be pitted against him, if he survived to succeed his father.

She shook her head. "I'd rather let you fuck my ass again."

I came to her, kneeling beside the bench and got in her face. "You're seriously starting to piss me off."

"Look at me. Do you think I care anymore?" She spat the words like bullets.

I'd degraded her. Pushed and humiliated her, and yet she stayed. Every second she stayed made me nervous. When was she going to give up? She wasn't loyal to me. She couldn't be. I was eager for her to break.

"You don't get to choose your family," she said quietly, "but you can choose your friends."

Was she fucking nuts? "We'll never be *friends*, Oksana."

She let out a sigh of frustration and squirmed against the tape. "I'm still the same person I was before you knew about my father, and you, Vasilije Markovic, are the *only* person I've shared that with."

Fucking her had been a bad idea. It messed with my hormones and made me weak. If she had told me the night I brought her home she was Sergey Petrov's illegitimate daughter, she would have left in the trunk of my car. It shouldn't be different now, but . . . fucking hell.

Everything was different.

I'd thought we were the same, and I'd liked her so goddamn much. Now, I stared at the woodgrain in the floor, and considered leaving her here while I went upstairs to smoke a joint. It was all too much. I felt heavy.

"Please," she said. "I need you to tell me my brother is going to be okay. If you want to kill a Petrov, you know which one is the bigger threat."

It slipped out before I thought better of it. I was used to saying whatever I wanted around her. "We can't get to him."

"But I can."

Well, shit. At least that was true.

Her voice was firm. "You don't want me anymore, fine. But we can help each other. Think about it. How much better would it be for your family if Sergey was gone? And my father doesn't care about me . . . but Konstantine does. My brother's not going to do something if he thinks it might get me killed."

It all sounded too good to be true.

I found myself on my feet and walking toward the kitchen, and as I came back to her carrying the chef's knife, her panicked look was sharper than the steel blade in my hand.

"I can help with your uncle," she said in a rush. "I could—"

"I don't need your help." My voice was hard and cold. Her eyes doubled in size with every step I took.

"Oh, God, don't," she cried. "Not with a knife."

Her gasp of horror was surgical, cutting deep to my bones, and I fell to my knees. I slipped the tip of the knife between the tape and the bench leg, and jerked upward. She used her newly freed hand to wipe away a loose tear while I cut her other wrist free, and the knife clattered to the floor.

She scrambled into my arms, and I went on autopilot, allowing it for a moment before I realized what she'd done. It was wrong to hold her, but it didn't make it feel any less good, and I hated her for it. I dumped her from my arms.

"If you stay here," I said, "I'll come to my senses and kill you."

She pressed her blood-red lips together, but otherwise didn't move.

"I'll probably fuck you again, and then kill you," I added. Although, I'd thrown everything at her and she was still here, sitting on the floor and looking at me with her big doe eyes like I was her savior and not the devil.

"I'm not leaving." Her tone was firm. "You said you always get what you want, but you also said we're the same. I want your help."

I stood. "I need a shower to wash your fucking stink off me."

I trudged toward the stairs and lumbered up them, ignoring her as she followed. I kicked open the door to my room and stormed through it, walking directly into the shower. I didn't even take my clothes off, and neither did she. Only her shoes were left outside the glass shower door.

I turned the water on. It blasted us, cold at first and then so fucking hot it should have melted our skin off. I wanted it to wash away her lies, but all it did was soak my jeans until they were stiff and heavy.

Water cascaded down her pale skin, drenching the lingerie. I finally gave her my attention, backing her up against the wall and putting my hands on either side of her head, trapping her in. Although I wasn't sure why. She'd had every opportunity to leave and hadn't done it, even after I'd ordered her to.

She reached a hand up and set it on my jaw, but I pushed it away and slapped my palm against the tile right by her head, making her flinch. "You don't get to touch me unless I say so."

I moved, gliding my hand down her body, following the flow of the water, making my point without words. I didn't need permission to touch what was mine.

"If Konstantine dies," she said, "my father won't stop until every Markovic is in the ground. But if you kill him, and your uncle . . . Vasilije, you'll run this town."

If I put the personal shit to the side, deep down I knew she was right. I couldn't trust her, but the opportunity was hard to ignore. Killing my uncle was my priority, but inheriting the family empire afterward was a nice perk, and the idea of her keeping the Russians at bay was tempting.

I'd stay on my toes and could always kill her if I sensed her loyalty was fake. Which gave me an idea. "If I stop the order on Konstantine, I'm going to need something from you."

She looked eager. "Anything."

"You need to kill Alek."

Oksana barely blinked. "Fine. How do you want me to do it?"

chapter
THIRTY-THREE

OKSANA

AFTER THE SHOWER, I went to my room and dressed in the outfit I'd been wearing the first night I'd come to the house. Vasilije had instructed me to. He wanted to burn my clothes after I took care of Aleksandar.

It was him or Konstantine, I reminded myself repeatedly. If it would save my brother's life, I would have to pull the trigger. I might be a panicked mess while I did it, but it would happen. Killing Ilia hadn't been premeditated. It had felt right, and I had no regrets.

However, this murder felt... muddy.

Vasilije sat on the couch in the living room, and looked up at me when I entered. His gaze was cold and impersonal, and it stung. I'd shown him the side of myself no one had seen, and I believed he'd done the same.

I'd been so wrong.

"Alek's on his way," he said, setting his phone down on the coffee table. "There's the gun in the office. You know how to use it?"

"Yes."

"Go get it."

It felt like a test. I strode into the darkened office, yanked open the bottom drawer, and scooped up the gun. When I came back into the living room, he eyed the weapon in my hand. I'd had plenty of opportunities to kill him, and hadn't. Wasn't this proof I wanted to work with him?

I sat on the oversized chair opposite him and tucked the gun under my leg, hiding it from view. Vasilije's gaze was crushing, and the silence stretching between us was painful. My anxiety about what was going to happen made me honest.

"The only thing I lied about was my father."

His expression was fixed. "Yeah? Well, it was a big fucking lie."

"I'm sorry I had to tell it." I borrowed a tactic from my stepmother, and went the passive-aggressive route. "I didn't want to hurt you."

"You didn't hurt me," he snapped, but his quick answer was too revealing. The Serbian boy had feelings after all.

"Then working together shouldn't be a problem."

He seethed as he searched for the perfect comeback, and then he stood abruptly, as if he'd found it. "I don't know how I didn't see it before. You're a lot like him."

My blood slowed to a stop. "Like who?"

"Your father."

The terrifying statement landed, and I launched to my feet as if I could get away from it. "I'm nothing like him."

"You're getting awfully worked up for a girl who said she doesn't have feelings."

I took in a deep breath. "Maybe I only have feelings around you."

He jerked back. His surprise lasted only a moment, and then evaporated into suspicion.

"It's not a lie," I said softly. "God, Vasilije. I wish it was."

His mouth dropped open to say something, but he was cut off when the security system chirped and the front door swung open. My heart climbed into my throat as Aleksandar stepped inside and dusted the snow off his jacket. He hesitated when he saw me.

"What's up?" His guarded gaze went to Vasilije.

I sat down on the chair, concealing the gun. It was a hard, uncomfortable lump beneath me. I wasn't supposed to use it right away. Vasilije wanted to confront him first, although I was sure he was drawing this out to torture me. The anticipation was its own kind of murder.

"I need your piece," Vasilije said.

The statement put Aleksandar on high alert. He stiffened, his hands balled into fists, and his angry gaze snapped to me.

"Don't look at her," Vasilije ordered. "I'm handling it, and she's not the one you stabbed in the back."

Fear mixed with regret, contorting Aleksandar's face into an ugly mess. "They got to me, Vasilije. I'm sorry—"

"I need to know how," he said flatly. "I was good to you. I deserve a goddamn answer on what they had that got you to turn on me."

Aleksandar's shoulders slumped and his voice went small. "I needed money."

That seemed to piss Vasilije off. "I've got lots of fucking money."

Aleksandar shifted his weight, uneasy. "I was in deep, with a lot of different families. Some of them, you'd told me to stay away from."

"So, that's it? A shitload of money was all it took for you to sell me out?"

"They'll kill me if I don't do what they want, and besides the money . . ." His gaze flashed to me. "When it was done, Sergey told me I could have her."

My pulse climbed as Vasilije's voice did. "What the fuck does that mean? Have her?"

"After she did what she needed to, she'd be mine. I could fuck her, or marry her, or . . . whatever. He promised her to me."

There wasn't anything left of me to crush. I'd never intended to hold up my end of the deal with my father, and obviously, he hadn't either.

But Vasilije didn't like this at all. "She'd never be yours. Oksana's been mine from the first moment I saw her." Even without looking my direction, I knew he was addressing me. "Did you know about that deal?"

"No, but after burning down a house with an innocent family

locked inside, nothing Sergey does surprises me anymore. I told you, he's evil."

"And that's who you work for now," Vasilije said to Aleksandar.

The guy's face twisted with remorse. "I don't!"

"Then give me your fucking gun, Alek."

For a long moment, he considered not doing it, but must have realized there was no upside. Even if he outdrew and killed Vasilije, he'd have both the Russians and the Serbians after him, and they'd tear through his family until they got what they wanted.

He moved cautiously, pulling the gun from behind his back and reluctantly handing it to Vasilije. "She's the one who works for Sergey," he muttered.

Vasilije's head swung toward me, and his smile was so wide and sinister, my heart stopped. "Go ahead, Oksana."

I jammed my hand beneath my thigh and closed a fist around the 9mm. As I stood from the chair on shaky legs, I raised the gun, and Aleksandar's beady eyes flooded with horror.

"Does she look like she works for Sergey?" Vasilije snarled.

The gun weighed a million pounds in my hand, but I kept my aim fixed, waiting for Vasilije's final command. I was stunned he wanted me to do it right here in the entryway. It'd take hours to clean, but then again, I'd gotten lots of practice over the years, cleaning up after my father's downsizing meetings.

"If I tell you to pull the trigger," Vasilije said, "will you?"

My voice was so much stronger than I felt. "Yes."

He looked pleased. "You can put that down. I've seen what I need to."

My gasp of relief was internal, but Aleksandar's was loud, and he was so overwhelmed, he nearly collapsed. I lowered the gun, grateful to have the strain gone.

Vasilije's focus turned to Aleksandar. "Don't look so fucking relieved. The only reason you're still alive is because I don't want your blood ruining my floors."

Aleksandar froze. "What?"

Vasilije strode to the front door and yanked it open, revealing the man lurking on the front steps. Filip's gun was out—not up—but it didn't make him any less dangerous. His critical eyes surveyed the room. When his gaze caught mine, they widened a degree. He was probably thinking about the last time he'd seen me, when I'd been crouched down on the dirty warehouse floor, pretending to be cowering in fear. I'd watched Goran's top enforcer kill one of my father's men with surgical precision that night. His expression had been cold and joyless.

"Don't make it quick," Vasilije said. "I wouldn't if I was doing it."

Aleksandar stumbled backward, maybe thinking about running, but where would he go? He was the only one not armed. "Vasilije, just wait a minute."

But he was ignored, and Vasilije kept talking directly to Filip. "When you're done, make sure he's somewhere the Russians will find him. It needs to send a message. I already talked with my uncle. We'll hold off on Konstantine, and see how they react."

Filip stepped through the door, and his swift approach seemed to paralyze Aleksandar. He peered up at the man with the shaved head like he was God himself, and didn't move as Filip grabbed his arm.

"I have to ask a favor, though," Vasilije said abruptly. "He's going to say some shit about Oksana, and I need you to keep it from my uncle. Not forever. Just until I've got it handled, which, trust me—I will." If Goran believed I was a spy for the Russians, my fate would be worse than Aleksandar's, yet Vasilije's tone was casual. "Do you mind?"

Filip considered the statement as he began to drag a blubbering Aleksandar toward the door. "How long?"

"A few weeks. If you want to tell him before then, I respect that. All I ask is a heads-up."

"Vasilije!" Aleksandar sniffled, sucking back tears. "Please, I'm sorry. Don't do this!"

"I'm not doing shit," he fired back. "You tried to set me up. You made this choice for me."

Filip put both hands on Aleksandar and wrenched him from the doorframe he'd latched onto. "If it's only a few weeks," Filip said, "I can sit on the info."

"Thanks." Vasilije smiled. "Get him out of here and . . . have fun." He shut the door on Aleksandar's cries for help, and they grew quieter after a thud, making me think Filip had thrown a punch to shut him up.

Vasilije's dark eyes focused on me and the gun still clutched in my hand.

"Put that back where it was. I'm going to bed," he announced. "If I decide not to kill you, I'll see you in the morning."

♪

I poured everything I felt into my music. When Vasilije came downstairs and saw me at the piano, he said nothing. He ignored me for a good portion of the day. After dinner, he demanded a blowjob, which I gave him, and then I went back to not existing for him.

The first week was hard, but every day I stayed chipped away at his anger. I had years of practice living with my father's cold indifference, so this was almost easy. If Vasilije thought I'd give up, he was so very wrong. I'd work on his symphony until it was done, and if he didn't let me back in by then, I'd just start on another until he did.

I'd destroyed any warmth Vasilije had toward me by revealing who I was, but it crept back in, ever so slowly, on the nights we were together. He didn't want to like me. Sometimes he'd let his guard down too much, and then overcompensate by threatening to kill me. I didn't believe it. I knew him too well.

The second week, I'd laughed when he said it, which pissed him off and earned me a set of beautiful red handprints across my skin, but every strike he gave me was the same as a wrecking ball against the wall he'd put between us.

Things weren't the same, but they improved dramatically when I explained how I envisioned us killing my father. Together. The graphic detail I gave him . . . even the logistics of it . . . it turned the devil on.

Our conversations about murder became foreplay.

I hadn't finished the final movement of his symphony before he revealed the first step in his plan for his uncle, and I was impressed. "You've been planning this a long time."

A slow smile worked across his lips. "Don't you know? Planning's half the fun."

chapter THIRTY-FOUR

Vasilije

I jolted awake.

The sheets were tangled around my legs, I was cold with sweat, and the bed beside me was empty. Shouldn't have been a surprise. It'd been four weeks since I'd 'rescued' Oksana from the warehouse, and she hadn't slept a full night in my bed once. Every once in a while one of us would fall asleep after we'd fucked, and it'd be late before she snuck off to play the piano or go to her own room down the hall, but we didn't cuddle after.

I always woke up on my own. I'd told her that was how I wanted it because I didn't trust her, but as the weeks went by, my stance began to shift. I wasn't going to kill her, and she wasn't going to kill me. Maybe I wouldn't mind if she stayed in my bed.

I glanced at the clock on my nightstand and scrubbed a hand over my face, trying to organize my thoughts. The weed I'd smoked last night had made me paranoid. That had to be what this feeling was. Everything was fine.

But there wasn't piano music wafting up the stairs.

I was out of bed and moving swiftly down the hall to the bedroom on the other side of the house, nervous. What if she wasn't in there? I threw open the door to her bedroom, and when I saw the splash of blonde hair on the pillow, the tightness in my throat eased.

Fuck me, she was beautiful, and she was still here. Still loyal.

Still mine.

"Oksana."

She stirred. Her head lifted and she peered at me with bleary, disoriented eyes, then her gaze went to the clock. She launched upright in the bed, her posture stiff because it was three in the morning. "What's wrong?"

"Nothing." And everything. "Come on. You're sleeping in my room tonight."

She stared at me like I'd just burst into song. "What? Why?"

My eyebrow shot up. "Because I had a dream you left, and it's stupid I had to come all the way over here to figure out if it was real or not." In the nightmare, I'd spanked her so hard, she'd screamed and run from me, and I remembered it in vivid detail. When I got up and she hadn't been at the piano, I was half convinced her room would be empty and all her shit gone.

"Get up," I ordered. This wasn't a discussion.

Her mouth dropped open, but no words came out. Why wasn't she moving? Couldn't she see how worked up I was? Finally, she swung her legs out of the bed and stood. She had on an old Randhurst t-shirt from some rush event my sophomore year, back when I still gave a fuck about going to school, and it was so large on her, it was like a dress.

She looked sexy as fuck in it, even with her hair a mess and indentations from the wrinkles of the pillowcase pressed against her face. We'd been together a month. A whole freaking *month*. If she was conning me, she was playing the long game, but I felt in my gut she wasn't.

She hadn't told me a lie since, and got more interesting the deeper I dug.

Oksana padded over in her bare feet, and when she tried to get past me in the doorway, I snared her in my hands. "After you told me about your father, I told you to get the fuck out of my house."

Her eyes filled with confusion.

I wanted to stop talking, but my mouth kept going. "I changed my mind. If you leave me, we're going to have a problem."

It was a threat, but she didn't treat it like one. She placed her soft hand on the side of my face. "I told you. I'm not going anywhere, Vasilije."

I was done with this shit. She was right, after all. She couldn't change who her father was, but she planned to do something about him, and I enjoyed how she wanted me to be a part of it. Besides our plan, I liked coming home to her. I cooked dinner for us while she played her songs on my mother's piano, and after we'd eaten, we'd watch movies and talk, or I'd smoke weed and fuck her until she nearly passed out from an orgasm. Being with her was... easy. I tried not to feel anything, but it was getting harder every day.

She didn't make a sound as I picked her up. Her arms banded around my shoulders and her legs wrapped around my waist, holding on as I carried her down the hall and into my bedroom. We fell in a heap onto my bed, our mouths slamming together.

I knew all her noises now.

When I scraped my fingernails over her tits, clawing at her nipples through the thin t-shirt, the whine she made was need. As I sank one finger into her damp body, her cry was desperation. And when I withdrew, she delivered a sound of pure frustration.

I shoved the waistband down on my underwear, gripped my cock, and buried myself as deep inside her pussy as I could get. Her gasp of satisfaction was better than any music she composed. More real and perfect, and I could listen to it forever.

She raked her fingers down my back, scoring my flesh, but I ignored the sting and pounded into her. I mumbled Serbian against her collarbone, and she murmured back to me in Russian. We didn't understand the words, but knew exactly what the other was saying.

The fuck was rough, and fast, and so amazing, I lost control way too soon. After I came, I pulled out and slid my middle two fingers inside her. I fucked her like that, my fingers sticky wet with my own cum, until her pussy clamped down in rhythmic pulses and she flung her head back in orgasm.

"Christ," I groaned, "there's nothing sexier than watching you come." I collapsed beside her, my arm thrown over her chest, and tugged her tight against me. It felt so fucking nice, I made the decision instantly. "You sleep here from now on."

She inhaled sharply, and her word was barely audible, but I heard it anyway.

"Okay."

♪

It'd been a shit day at the dealership. Some fuckhead crashed a BMW during his test drive and totaled the thing, and I wanted to shove my Glock up his ass and pull the trigger until the magazine was empty. On top of that, one of our coke dealers had gotten busted for, of all things, solicitation. Like he hadn't a clue we could get him any kind of ass he wanted, and ass that wasn't secretly attached to a cop.

I came in from the garage, tired from the day. I yanked off my coat, tossed it in the closet, and headed for the living room—

Why did it smell like a goddamn pine forest in the house?

I skidded to a stop in the kitchen, noticing the new addition in the living room. "What the hell is that?"

"I chopped down an evergreen on the golf course," Oksana said from behind the piano.

My pulse jumped. "Tell me you're fucking joking." Because if she wasn't and someone found out, the association would bill me thousands of dollars.

A faint smile twitched on her lips. "They were selling trees on the lot outside the grocery store. John helped me set it up." Whatever song she was playing stopped, and the opening bars of *O Holy*

Night came from the piano.

I glared at the undecorated tree. Christmas was only a few days away, and I'd dragged my feet long enough I thought I could avoid the whole fucking thing.

The song cut off and she stood from the bench, her expression filled with concern. "You don't like it? I got it half-price—"

"It's fine," I ground out.

I didn't convince either of us, and Oksana took a hesitant step toward me. "What is it?"

"You bought a Christmas tree, which you're probably going to want to decorate." The knot of my tie gave me trouble and I yanked it off in frustration, tossing it on the kitchen counter. I set my hands on the cold granite and leaned on it.

"I don't understand why that's . . . upsetting," she said quietly.

"All my Christmas shit's in the basement." I said it like she should get it, even though she wouldn't. I sighed. "I haven't been down there since I killed my father."

Her lips parted with surprise, but it was forever before she spoke. "I'll have John get rid of it in the morning."

"No." I pushed off the counter and straightened. I was being a coward about this. My father had deserved to die for what he'd done, so why did I care so much about going down in the basement? Luka and Addison had helped me clean it up. There was nothing down there but memories, and wasn't I stronger than some stupid fucking ghost?

"Come on," I said, forcing my tone to be indifferent. "Help me carry the boxes so I don't have to make as many trips."

"I can go get them—"

I cut her off by marching to the basement door and gripping the knob. When I'd been a kid, the unfinished basement had scared me. It was dark. Full of shadows, spider webs, and strange noises, and as I got older, I learned all the secrets that lurked down there.

It was easy to wash blood off the floor because it sloped toward the drain in the center of the room. There was a well-window beside the side door to the garage. It meant nothing had to go through the main house if you didn't want it to.

The stairs creaked as I went down, and I could hear her following me. Even when I flipped the switch at the base of the steps and the bare bulb flicked on, the place felt like a cave. Cold, dark, and damp. I stared at the pockmark on the far wall. My bullet had gone clean through my father's head, and Luka had been forced to dig the slug out of the concrete.

I'd lost control in this room.

I swore to myself I wouldn't do it ever again, and so far, I hadn't.

The sound of cardboard sliding against stone grabbed my attention. Oksana had found the boxes labeled 'Christmas' in a pile behind the stairs, and as she lifted one of them in her arms, she gazed at me. "You okay?"

I glanced back at the chip in the cement . . . and a slow smile worked across my face. I'd been such a pussy about the basement, and it was stupid. What had I expected? That all the guilt I should have felt about killing my father was lying down here, waiting for me? It wasn't, because it didn't exist. Bad people got what they deserved.

No point thinking about it. Someday my number would be up, too.

chapter
THIRTY-FIVE

Oksana

I WAS SITTING AT THE COMPUTER IN THE OFFICE, working on Vasilije's Christmas present, when the alarm system chirped and the front door groaned open. My heart stopped. Only a few people had codes, and Whitney and Vasilije always came in through the garage.

My hand shook as I jerked open the bottom drawer and palmed the 9mm. If it was Goran who'd just entered the house, Vasilije would never make it home from the dealership in time. Hadn't he revoked his uncle's code?

The man who walked past the office doorway stopped and backtracked, swinging his gaze into the room to focus on me. I slowly lowered the gun back into the drawer and pushed it closed.

"Who the hell are you?" he demanded.

Luka Markovic looked like a serious, formal version of his younger brother.

"Oksana," I said, standing from my chair.

His eyes scrutinized and judged every inch of me, and his eyebrow crept up with displeasure. "I don't think my brother's going to be happy to hear his staff was using his computer while he's not here."

His . . . what? I stumbled over the words. "I'm not staff. I'm his . . ." Partner? "Girlfriend."

Luka didn't blink. He just stared.

A female voice came from beyond the doorway. "Oh my God, Vasilije put up a Christmas tree?" The owner of the voice stepped into view. She looked similar in age to Vasilije. Her brown hair was swept back in a ponytail and her cheeks were rosy from the cold outside, and as she unbuttoned her wool coat, her hands slowed. She looked at me, curious.

Luka's hard expression made him seem even older than the twenty-eight years I knew he was. Vasilije didn't talk about his brother much. He was an accountant who preferred numbers to people, all except for Addison, the girl who stood beside him.

She was pretty in an effortless way, but I could barely look at her. I'd had nothing to do with her family's murder, but I felt crushing guilt by proxy. My father had done that. He'd ordered the horrific death of her parents and brother. If I'd known before it happened, would I have been able to do anything to stop it? Would her family still be alive?

"Vasilije didn't mention a girlfriend." Luka's tone was an accusation.

"Well, *Luka*," I said pointedly, "he didn't mention you would be coming by either."

Did a smile just flit across Addison's lips? It vanished instantly. His eyes squeezed down into slits, and just as he opened his mouth to say something, my phone on the desktop rang, silencing him. I didn't have to look at the screen to know who it was. Vasilije was the only person who called.

I picked it up and tapped the screen. "Hello?"

"I just got an alert," he said in a blur. "Someone used my brother's code to get in the house." There was noise in the background like a car door slamming and an engine starting. Was he rushing to try to get to the house? "Get a gun, go upstairs, and lock yourself in my closet. The door's reinforced and—"

"Vasilije, it's okay. Your brother was the one who used the code."

"What the fuck? Luka's *there?*" He made a sound of exasperation. "Put him on the phone."

I extended it out to the man staring at me. "Vasilije wants to talk to you."

He crossed the room, took the phone from me, and held it to his ear. "There's a Russian girl in the office, claiming to be your girlfriend." Whatever Vasilije said in response made Luka soften. He was still stiff and on edge, but seemed less adversarial toward me. "Addison's on break," he continued, "and I got time off. So, surprise. We caught a flight this morning, and we're here for Christmas." He looked uncomfortable. "Yeah, we're going. He didn't leave me much choice."

Was Luka talking about Goran's party?

As the phone conversation continued between brothers, I sensed Addison's gaze on me, but I stared at the pattern in the rug. Would Vasilije tell his brother the truth about who I was? Would he tell *her*?

I'd been with him for five weeks. The wound I'd put in our trust had scabbed over and was healing, faster each day. I looked forward to his days off from work, when we could spend more time together. I enjoyed it when he took me along on nights he carried out his uncle's orders. On paper, I'd thought he was a thug who spent all his time trying to convince others he was a badass . . . but I was wrong.

Vasilije didn't put any effort into who he was. It came as naturally as breathing.

I couldn't wait to help him carry out his plan for Goran, and hoped when the time came, he'd be there for me.

The conversation ended and the phone was handed back to me.

"We're starving," Luka announced. "We'll have lunch and get to know each other better." Like Vasilije, his tone made it clear this wasn't a request.

♪

Even though I'd cleared my stuff out of the green striped

bedroom, Addison and Luka took the smaller guest bedroom beside it, which didn't have an attached bathroom. He was obviously the one in charge of their relationship, but when he'd picked up their luggage and she'd whispered, "not the green room," he'd nodded instantly.

We went out to dinner with them. I sat beside Vasilije at the table, his hand resting on my leg beneath the tablecloth, and did my best to act natural. I was the only one in the group who hadn't been in the basement when he'd killed Dimitrije. The sickest part of me hated that I wasn't bound to Vasilije like they were by the event.

If everything went right, soon I would be.

Luka and Addison went to bed early, and as Vasilije and I sat in the living room, watching a movie, a soft, feminine cry rang out from their room. Was that . . . pleasure? I turned to him with wide eyes and he shrugged.

"When they lived here, it was like that all the time. I found a bunch of shit when they moved out. I guess my brother's a kinky fucker."

I blinked and flattened my voice with sarcasm. "But you're so normal."

He grinned. "I'm not normal, but neither are you, Oksana. You've got my bite marks to prove it."

I shivered with satisfaction, and watched his eyes pool with heat. He liked giving me pain and pleasure, almost as much as I liked receiving it. We didn't make it to the end of the movie. He shut it off, dragged me upstairs, and gave me a blistering session. He encouraged me to be loud, probably wanting to one-up his brother, and I was happy to help.

Christmas Eve came too quickly. After lunch, which I ate hardly any of, I put on the silver cocktail dress Vasilije had bought me and got ready for the party. Nerves rattled in my stomach. On top of what I was going to do, I was about to be surrounded by Markovics.

I hadn't seen Goran since the day Vasilije had punched him.

I was putting on a second coat of mascara, swiping the brush over my lashes as Vasilije appeared in the bathroom mirror. He wore his dark gray suit and a bright red tie, and my knees went weak. He looked so good like that. Deceptively dangerous. His smile was disarming, and if you didn't know him, you wouldn't believe there was a gun tucked inside his suit.

"You look fucking hot." His gaze lingered over my bare legs, then worked up my body. The dress was decorated in faceted clear beads, making me shimmer and sparkle. It dipped low in the front. Although I didn't have much cleavage, it was flattering.

"Thank you," I said, capping the mascara and straightening. "So do you."

He waved my comment off like I was being silly. "Maybe we'll sneak off after dinner and I'll fuck you in my uncle's bed."

Vasilije wasn't joking. It was absolutely his style.

"I'd like to stay far away from his bed, thank you." I faced him and smoothed my hands down my skirt, which was a few inches shorter than I would have liked. He'd said it was necessary.

A sly smile warmed his lips. "By the way, I've never brought a girl to meet the family. Be prepared. My aunt is nosy. People are going to be all up in our business."

I deflated a little. I didn't want any attention on us, but then again, Vasilije had dressed me like a fucking disco ball.

He insisted on driving so John could have the holiday off. We piled into a silver Mercedes-Benz, and the air in the car was tense as we got on the expressway. Luka and Addison didn't like Goran much either, and the mood was somber as we headed to the 'party.'

Vasilije's home was a mansion, but Goran's was a palace. The estate was a sprawling compound tucked behind a formidable gate. We pulled up in the circle drive, got out of the car, and a valet darted behind the wheel.

I was so far removed from the poor Christmases my mother and I had celebrated, it was disorienting. The interior of the house was lavish. An enormous tree, decorated in so much gold it was more ornaments than pine, was centered on the back wall of the spacious living area. Someone took my coat, and when Vasilije's arm draped around my waist, I shrank into him.

"We're going to want to leave as soon as possible," Luka muttered to his brother under his breath.

"Fine by me," Vasilije said, moving us deeper into the house and toward the herd of people near the tree.

There were servers floating around the party, dressed in black and white uniforms, and carrying trays of hors d'oeuvres. On Christmas Eve. It had to cost a fortune for this extravagant event. As I'd assumed, most of his family frowned at me as soon as Vasilije uttered my name. I sensed them whispering behind our backs, and although I didn't feel shame, I was annoyed.

I cared about Vasilije.

I didn't want them looking down on him because of me.

We mingled for a long while, and I started to grow nervous. We hadn't seen Goran all night. I leaned into Vasilije and asked it as casually as I could. "Where's your uncle?"

Vasilije gestured to the kitchen.

At just that moment, the crowd of people parted and I got a peek at the current king of the Markovic empire. He must have sensed my gaze, because he zeroed in on me and delivered the same look he'd given me last time.

Lust mixed with violence.

"Fuck," Vasilije said under his breath. "Let's get this over with."

chapter
THIRTY-SIX

Goran seemed to abruptly end his conversation with the man he was talking to, and my heart clogged as he made his way over. His dark, terrifying eyes trapped mine.

"Nice to see you again, Natasha," he said.

"Oksana," Vasilije corrected.

"Oh. Yes." Although I suspected Goran remembered my name and this was an intentional slight to show us both how little he cared.

I said nothing, choosing to deliver a tight, polite smile.

Goran wore a suit with ease like he didn't own any other type of attire, and he held a glass half full of ice and an amber colored drink. His gaze flitted to the crowd, and he surveyed them like they were his subjects. His attention slowly worked its way back to us.

"It's good to have Luka back here." His tone was deceptively casual. "Maybe you can convince your brother this is his home, and get him to stay."

Vasilije glanced over to Luka, and Addison at his side. "He'll never leave her."

"Get her on board, too. She'll be useful."

I felt tension roll through Vasilije's body, and his face soured. "Addison's been used enough, don't you think? Luka doesn't want her near any part of what we do."

"Fucking Russians," Goran muttered under his breath before taking a sip of his drink. "How much longer do you want to wait on Konstantine?"

"A few more days."

Goran's black eyes slid to me, like he somehow knew, even

though he didn't. "I'll admit," he said, "I'm surprised you're still around. At first I thought my nephew was trying to piss me off, but he must be really taken with you."

I hadn't eaten much today due to my nerves, and had downed a drink for courage. The alcohol warmed my veins and made me indifferent. "Vasilije and I have a lot in common."

Vasilije chuckled, enjoying my admission, but Goran's eyebrow lifted. "Such as?"

Oh, shit. I couldn't exactly say we both wished he was dead, or how we had murdered people who'd wronged us.

Vasilije had me covered. "I love sticking my dick in her, and she loves when I do it."

His uncle lifted his gaze to the ceiling, visibly annoyed. "Charming." When Filip materialized at his boss's side, Goran motioned to me. "Filip, this is Vasilije's whore, Natasha."

"*Oksana*," Vasilije hissed. "Is your memory going, old man?"

There was a silent battle over which Markovic could lift their eyebrow higher in displeasure, and Vasilije seemed to win. Or maybe I just wanted him to.

"Hello, Oksana," Filip said automatically, before turning to his boss. "The caterer is asking for access to the wine cellar. We're almost out of white."

Goran waved a hand. "That's fine, but go with her."

"I'll come with you," Vasilije said. "Filip and I've got shit to talk about."

The younger Markovic cast a look to me, heavy with meaning and wordlessly wishing me luck. My blood pressure spiked as I watched the men go, leaving me alone with Goran. With Vasilije gone, his uncle did nothing to disguise the desire from his face, raping me with his eyes. "That's some dress you're wearing."

"Thank you. Your house is nice." I shuffled forward on my heels, closing the distance between us, and dropped my voice low. "Maybe you could give me a tour and . . . show me what I turned down."

Suspicion clouded his eyes. "It doesn't sound like you're having regrets, given how much you 'like him sticking his dick in you.'"

I sighed. "It's the same every time with him. Vasilije's boring," I lied. "He's a boring . . . *boy*."

As I hoped, implying Goran was a superior man caught his interest. "Is that so?"

It was easy to stay silent. I didn't have a clue what to say, and he'd told me he liked quiet women.

He searched the crowd and his expression turned down in disappointment. "I don't have time to give you a proper *tour* right now." He made the simple word sound dirty. "I can't leave my guests."

"Maybe some other time," I forced out. Hopefully my tight voice came off to him as eager, rather than anxious.

He blinked his dark eyes slowly. "Tomorrow."

I hesitated. "Christmas day? I'm not sure I can—"

"I'll send Filip over to pick you up after dinner." His grin was terrifying. "If Vasilije has an issue with it, I'll explain it to him." He probably viewed this as the ultimate power trip, taking Vasilije's favorite toy away on Christmas. "I have a big house," he continued. "It may take a while, but I think you'll . . . enjoy it."

I bit down on the inside of my cheek to distract myself from throwing up in my mouth. His gaze moved over my head, and he motioned to someone behind me, and then his attention returned, settling on my blood red lipstick.

"I'm sorry, I need to talk to someone, if you'll excuse me." As he stepped to the side, he set his hand on my arm, and I tried not to bolt from his touch. "But I'm looking forward to tomorrow, Natasha."

"Oksana," I whispered back, but he was already moving through the crowd and out of earshot.

We had to stay through dinner, and as I sat at one of the long tables and listened to Goran give his speech about family and loyalty, my insides churned. Not because my family had been enemies with the Markovics for years, but the hypocrisy of Goran's words. Luka's face was a cool, emotionless mask, but in his eyes I could see him struggle to contain his anger.

Vasilije was the opposite. He smiled at all the right parts, flashing his dimples and laughing at jokes, putting everyone at ease. It seemed like he was in a great mood. And maybe he was. Now he had a firm date of when he was going to take his uncle down.

♪

Christmas morning was . . . weirdly wonderful.

We slept in, and when we went downstairs in our pajamas, we discovered Luka and Addison hovering around the coffee pot, not dressed for the day either. Vasilije cooked breakfast for everyone. We ate and had conversation like we were two normal couples celebrating Christmas together. The strangest part was how it didn't feel strange.

After breakfast, we gathered around the tree Vasilije and I had decorated a few days ago with ornaments from the basement he'd been reluctant to go in. He'd admitted to me later that night, after having smoked some weed, he was glad I'd gotten the tree. Some of the ornaments were from his childhood and it was good to see them again.

It made him feel less like an orphan.

There were only a handful of presents between the four of us, and since I had more than one, Vasilije demanded I go first. I tore the fancy silver and gold paper, recognizing the Faire Avenue branding, and laughed as I opened the box and peered inside.

"What is it?" Addison asked.

I held up the red, gauzy lingerie for her to see.

"Oh," she said, like the word had been punched from her lungs.

Her cheeks tinted, but I smiled. She thought I should be embarrassed, but I didn't feel shame, and she must not have realized how Vasilije and I had heard them having sex the other night.

This lingerie set was elegant and sophisticated. "Did Daphne help you?"

"She did." His dark eyes were full of lust and a promise I couldn't wait for him to fulfill. "Open the other one."

He sounded impatient as he tossed the small, letter-sized box at me. This one looked like it'd been wrapped by a man and not a clerk at a department store. I peeled back the paper and lifted the lid.

Now it was my turn to gasp. I had to read the tickets to the Chicago Lyric Opera more than once. "*Salome?*" I whispered. "You got me tickets to see *Salome?*"

"I got us tickets, yeah." He tried to play it cool. "They should be good seats, because they were fucking expensive."

"What is that?" Luka asked.

"An opera," I said, pulling out the two sheets of folded paper and handling them like they were printed on gold. Vasilije had gotten us box seats, and the idea of sitting beside him while we watched one of Strauss's masterpieces made my insides flutter.

I hadn't been to the opera since my mother died.

Luka stared at Vasilije like he had two heads. "Jesus. You bought opera tickets?"

Vasilije cocked his eyebrow. "Fuck you. I heard the girl gets naked on stage."

"I heard that happens at strip clubs, too."

I choked back a giggle. Vasilije was right. As Salome performed the "Dance of the Seven Veils," she removed each one until she was naked. Like most operas, the story was one fucked up piece of work. Salome demanded the head of her lover on a silver platter, and once she had it, she kissed it until her father Herod had her crushed to death.

"It doesn't open for two more weeks," Vasilije said.

I grinned. "It's perfect. Thank you."

It really was. The opera was twisted, and erotic, and dark, just like we were. I scrambled for his present and shoved it at him with nervous hands. He looked down with surprise. I hadn't asked him for money, and was used to not having any, so my gift was something that couldn't be bought.

He ripped at the paper and threw open the lid to the box.

His long fingers dipped inside and pulled out the stack of paper, bound with red ribbon. His eyes scanned the pages as he flipped through them, his fingers trailing over the printed sheet music. And then he noticed the other item in the box. He lifted the flash drive out and looked at me with confusion.

"It's finished," I breathed. "Your symphony." Last week I'd asked if he would buy me composing software, and he'd done it. "The program you bought can play back the composition as a full orchestra." It wasn't anywhere near as good as a true, live performance, but the recording had depth and layers my performance on the piano couldn't capture. "I hope you like it."

Vasilije's pleased smile was a slow burn and warmed me to my core.

After we'd come home from the party last night, he'd fixed me a glass of vodka with a splash of cranberry juice, taken me to our bedroom, and we discussed everything we had planned. It led to him fucking me until I was beautifully sore all over. I'd lounged in the bed, recovering and sipping my drink, while he went to the drawer and got out his metal lunch box.

The smell of his burning joint turned me on, even though he'd left me satisfied. Usually he smoked before the sex, and I had a Pavlovian response to it.

"You want some?" he asked, blowing a puff of smoke out the window and into the freezing night air. "Could be our last night together." He extended the joint out to me, but I shook my head. I'd never smoked before, other than one tiny puff on a cigarette when I was fifteen, and it had sent me into a coughing fit.

"No, thanks." I took the final sip of the glass and set it on the nightstand. "I'm already drunk."

He finished, stubbed it out, and shut the window before crawling into bed beside me. The cold skin of his chest pressed against mine as he kissed me. He'd given me rough tonight, and now seemed to want to give me the other side. He gently brushed his lips over mine, slow but needy.

We made out for a while. Long enough for the alcohol to make me sluggish and warm, and long enough for him to reach the peak of his 'high.' His mouth was everywhere. It roamed from my lips, over my cheekbone, and onto the shell of my ear.

"It's a good thing," he murmured, "I don't have a fucking heart."

"Mmm?" I had my eyes closed, enjoying the sensation of his warm breath filling my ear.

The cadence of his voice was slow and hushed. "If I did, I might love you."

I drew in a deep breath, letting it fill my body and using it to try to push away the warnings flaring up. This was the weed talking, I was sure. But . . . could it be true, just a little?

"Lucky for you," I said on a shaky breath, "I don't have one either. Because if I did, I . . . might feel the same."

"Good," he whispered. Then, his mouth sealed over mine and there was no more conversation.

chapter
THIRTY-SEVEN

AFTER LUNCH, I sat on the edge of the leather sofa in the office, wanting to chew at my nails as Vasilije listened to my music pour from the computer speakers. *Our* music, really.

I felt like I'd swallowed a bag of nails, and with every expression that crossed his face, the nails scratched at my insides. I'd listened to the movements so many times, I could no longer tell if they were good or not, and I wasn't going to throw around the word *masterpiece*, but I was proud of the work.

He listened to the entire thing without saying a word, his gaze out the window, watching the wind kick up snowdrifts in the front yard. A line creased between his eyebrows when he took in the third song, the scherzo. It was the frantic one I'd written in triple time, and was about how I viewed holding back my secret from him. But the crease went away and his lips hinted a smile when he listened to the final piece, which tied the movements together and built to a bombastic finish.

Vasilije went through a series of clicks with the mouse, then picked up his cell when it chimed. He'd transferred the file to his phone.

I couldn't wait any longer. "Any notes?"

He sat back in the chair and tented his fingers, savoring my uncomfortable state. "I don't know about that one in the middle."

I let out a slow breath, trying to be patient. Like any artist, receiving a few words of feedback could be uplifting, or crushing.

"Otherwise," he added, "it's really fucking good. I like it."

I collapsed back against the couch, letting relief swell

through me.

Before I could say anything in response, Luka stepped into the office. "I'm going to borrow a car. I'm taking Addison to her aunt's house in Joliet for a Christmas dinner thing."

Vasilije stood and pocketed his phone. "Keys are in the drawer like usual."

"Thanks." Luka paused, hovering awkwardly. "What you asked me to do . . . it's done now. I had him sign the final paperwork last night."

Vasilije's smile was wider than I'd ever seen, and I understood. I felt the same rush of excitement he did. Luka's role in all of this made it so much sweeter.

"Awesome," Vasilije said. "You think he has any idea?"

"Not a fucking clue."

Luka didn't have a smile like his younger brother's. There were no dimples, and when his lips pulled back, it wasn't as infectious. Instead, it gave me the same sense of impending danger as Goran's smile did, only the danger wasn't directed at me.

Luka sobered into his serious expression. "Be careful."

"Yeah, I will be." Vasilije glanced at me, and his face gave nothing away. He didn't look nervous at all, and I wished I had his same sense of confidence.

Luka and Addison left soon after, and as the clock ticked closer to dinnertime, my stomach bottomed out. I didn't eat anything, but Vasilije stayed quiet about that. He gazed at me across the kitchen table, his plate empty and mine untouched.

"You want me to go down on you?" he asked casually, between two sips of his beer.

I couldn't process his question. "What?"

"You're so tense."

Of course I was tense. "Everything we've been planning is happening tonight."

"Don't worry, baby." He faked bravado. "I'm going to make all our dreams come true."

I was so high-strung, the ridiculous laugh tumbled from my mouth. "Except our dreams are other people's nightmares."

He grinned ear to ear.

♪

Rock salt crunched under my shoes as I climbed the front steps of Goran's house. It seemed so different than it had yesterday. The large portico awning with columns was like a mouth stretching open, waiting to devour me.

Filip looked at me as if needing my approval, and when I nodded, he opened the door and ushered me inside.

The only light in the main room came from the gaudy, gold Christmas tree, and a fire that crackled in the fireplace. It took me a moment to adjust my eyesight to the dim lighting, and I didn't notice Goran until he got up off the couch.

"Oksana," he said. "Please, come in. Let Filip take your coat."

I hated him for a lot of reasons, but in this moment, I hated how he'd made my name a weapon, picking and choosing when to use it. He sauntered toward me, wearing a button-down shirt with the sleeves rolled back and a pair of dress slacks, and I wondered if this was as casual as he got. Like last night, he had a glass in hand. Bourbon? Scotch? It'd be some adult-tasting liquor I'd hate.

As I slid off my coat and passed it to Filip, I kept my eyes glued on Goran. "Merry Christmas."

Something like victory flared in his eyes. "Did Vasilije give you any trouble?"

I shook my head slowly. I didn't want to speak unless I absolutely had to, worried my nerves would seep into my voice.

"Good. Do you mind holding out your arms for me?"

My breath caught. "What?"

He set his drink down on a side table. "It's just a precaution."

"I already searched her," Filip said.

It drew an annoyed look from his boss. "No harm in being thorough," Goran said. He just wanted an excuse to put his hands on me, and as he waited impatiently for me to move, my stomach flipped upside-down. I wasn't going to be able to avoid it.

I trembled as I lifted my arms and shut my eyes, but otherwise I stood as still as possible. I didn't even breathe.

I wore a long-sleeved wraparound dress made of wool, and thin leggings beneath, so nearly every inch of my body was covered, but it didn't matter. Goran's hands started at my shoulders, and I could feel them through the fabric as if his palms were made of sandpaper. They dragged and scraped over my body, lingering in all the same places Ilia's had, and I was only a hair's breadth from a nervous breakdown.

It's almost over. Just hang on.

I stepped back at the same moment he seemed to finish, and air poured back into my lungs. Goran looked at me with curiosity, not sure what to make of me.

"I'm sorry," I said between hurried breaths. "Strangers make me nervous. Could we . . . be alone?"

He acted like it was the greatest idea ever. "Have a good night, Filip."

"Should I tell Clive he can go, too?" Filip asked. "It's Christmas."

Once more, he earned a dirty look from his boss. Goran didn't want me knowing there was someone else in the house. But he gave me a discerning pass, and must have decided he was safe with me. He withdrew his phone from his back pocket, and thumbed out a message. "I've let him know."

I didn't wait for Filip to leave before I blurted it out. "Vasilije said your library has a map painted on the ceiling. Can we start there?"

Goran's black eyes lit with amusement, like I was a silly girl he'd humor. "Why not? It's this way."

I varied the length of my stride as we went like I'd done years ago, making it difficult for the predator beside me to get too close. I knew from experience that if he caught me, we might not make it to the library. Goran didn't seem to be in a rush to move on me, though. He likely thought he'd have all night to fuck me.

Too bad, I was about to fuck him.

He pushed open a door and flipped on the light. Bookcases lined the walls and were full of picture-perfect books, spines in a variety of colors and heights. The room was classic, like a library set from a movie. My gaze went up to the large antique map on the ceiling, painted in earthy gold colors. It was beautiful, and my eyes flitted over Russia, finding the place where I'd grown up, before I knew anything about Sergey Petrov or the Markovics.

While I found the room comforting, Goran did not. He pulled up short as he discovered a young man half-sitting, half-leaning against the desk, a gun in hand and an eyebrow arched upward into a sharp point.

chapter
THIRTY-EIGHT

Vasilije

I'd worn my favorite black suit for the occasion, but my uncle didn't seem to notice. His gaze was locked onto my gun.

"Sit," I said, flicking the barrel to the brown leather wingback chair.

He didn't move. "Be careful, Vasilije. I can take everything away from you. She isn't worth this."

The dumb fuck thought I was throwing a tantrum about her being stolen from me. He was wrong on so many levels. I stood and my expression hardened. "Sit. The. Fuck. Down."

He rolled his eyes, and lowered into the chair like he was humoring me.

I motioned to the gold colored couch for Oksana to sit, and I plopped my ass down beside her. I wanted her close. If things went sideways, I could protect her better this way.

The lighting in the room was soft and everything was designed to make you feel comfortable. It was a space where you wouldn't mind to stay and read. But the air in the library was warm. Too warm for me. It pressed down on my skin, making me feel sluggish when I wanted to be on my motherfucking toes.

"When we're done here," he said, "I'm going to kill your whore. Or maybe I'll just cut up that pretty face she has."

"You aren't going to do shit, and don't call her that again. This isn't about her."

"Oh? Then why's she here?"

"Because we don't keep secrets from each other." He looked at me critically, but I didn't let him get in a word. It was my show now. "Not like the way you and I work. Lots of skeletons in both our closets."

"*Fuck*," he said in Serbian. "*Stop being so dramatic.*"

I stayed in English. "You used to have a bodyguard named David. What happened to him?"

He stiffened. Then he had the balls to act resigned. "I don't know if your father told you boys the story. He always tried to protect you from the negative stuff, especially when it came to your mother."

Was he fucking joking? My dad had done nothing to hide his shit.

"When I found out your mother was fucking David on the side, I had him killed."

The grin began slowly, and then raced across my face. He was a good liar, I had to give him that. "Wow. That's a really great *story*."

He didn't like what I'd implied, and beneath his fake outrage, I could see the flicker of worry. "What the hell's that supposed to mean?"

"It means cut the fucking bullshit. All of it. The stuff about family, and loyalty, and anything else you pretend to care about, but don't. You didn't have David killed, because I went to his shitty condo a few weeks ago," I grew louder and more bitter with each word, "and I fucking *did it myself*."

He cracked, just a little. Wrinkles puckered around his eyes and made him look old and weak. "Then . . . I guess you're not a pussy like your brother."

I balled my free hand into a fist, fighting the urge to pull the trigger. *Not yet. Be patient.* "You had David lie. Tear my mother's name down. And when that was done, you sent him to kill her."

"She couldn't be trusted." He leaned forward and rubbed the crease on his forehead. "When you run the family, safety is everything, and sometimes you have to . . . make hard choices."

I choked out a hollow laugh. "Yeah, well, I guess I'll find out about that soon enough."

The phone in his pocket chirped. As I pushed up off the couch and came to my feet, rather than look threatened, my uncle was amused. "Am I going somewhere?"

"First your memory fails you, and now it's your eyesight, old man. I've got my Glock pointed right at you."

"You're a stupid, impulsive little boy, Vasilije. I sent an alert to Filip before I sat down, and all this time you've been going on, it's given him time to get back to the house." He raised his voice. "You can come in."

Filip's shadow darkened the doorway, and then he stepped into the room. His gun was in his holster, not drawn. My uncle stared at him, concerned at the lack of defense. "What the hell are you doing?"

"Oh," I said, "he doesn't work for you anymore." Who was impulsive now? "It's because you're fucking broke."

Goran jerked back in his seat. "What the fuck are you talking about? I've got more money than God."

"Oh, yeah?" My cheeks hurt from how hard I smiled. "Who helps you manage it?"

The frozen expression on his face was fucking *priceless*.

"Luka told me," I continued, "you don't always need a gun to destroy a man. Sometimes all you need is an idiot who doesn't read the shit he signs, and patience." It'd been fourteen months since Luka had started transferring investments and titles, burying the language in refinancing papers or opening new bank accounts so our uncle could 'avoid taxes.'

His face flushed and his breathing picked up. Worry had been far away seconds ago, but now it was right on top, crushing him. As Oksana had distracted him last night, I'd taken the risk of reaching out to Filip. He hadn't told my uncle any of the shit Aleksandar had said about Oksana.

I could trust Filip, and showed him he could trust me when I'd laid out all our plans. It hadn't taken him long to agree. He wanted to be on the winning side of this evening, and thank fuck. Having Filip meant I also had his men, and that'd make the transition easier when I was the most vulnerable.

I aimed for my uncle's heart as I spoke to Filip. "Is he armed? Any weapons nearby he can get to?"

"Nope."

Perfect. I stared into Goran's black eyes and savored the moment. He'd stolen my mother away from me, and I loved watching it dawn on him that everything was being taken away from him. His money. His men. His throne.

"Oksana," I said.

She'd sat so still and silent, my uncle's gaze went to her with surprise, like he'd forgotten she was there. She pulled out her phone and tapped the screen until music played from it. The overture of my symphony. I was being dramatic again, but didn't care what anyone thought about it.

"Sergey will eat you alive," Goran snarled. "Everything I've built, he'll destroy. You won't last six months."

The music was just like me. Seemingly pleasant, but evil beneath. "Sergey won't be a problem. Konstantine will take the truce I give him."

"You're fucking nuts. The Russians won't deal with you."

I took a step back, realizing I was too close. I didn't want to get blood on the suit. "They will, because the girl sitting on your couch? She's Sergey Petrov's *other* daughter."

The music swelled, revealing the dark nature. Real panic overwhelmed my uncle and transformed his face. Jesus Christ, he looked pathetic. "Vasilije, put it down. I'm family. I'm your blood." He lifted his hands, half in surrender. "You can't do this."

"You're going to play the family card? Didn't stop you from killing my mother, and it didn't stop me, either."

His fear was halted by confusion, and I laughed.

"Oh, shit, I forgot. You still think it was Ivan who killed my father."

His mouth fell open.

I gave him just enough time for it to soak in, then I pulled the trigger before he said another goddamn thing.

Three shots popped off, peppering his chest. Even though I wanted to go for his head and wipe his face clean from the goddamn earth, I couldn't. There was satisfaction in killing him like this, anyway. It probably wasn't my first bullet that ended him, and maybe not the second one either. It took a full three seconds for him to die. Three seconds of agony before his piss-poor heart stopped pumping.

As the music raged on, his body slumped in the chair, his face frozen in a horrified expression.

Unlike with my father, premeditating the death made the moment more fulfilling. I jammed my gun back in the holster, riding an adrenaline high, and admired the picture before me. The front of his shirt was dark and wet with blood. Did he realize how perfect the chair was he'd sat in? It was as close to a modern-day throne as you could get.

My kingdom now, motherfucker.

The song rolled to a close, and I turned to Oksana. She sat with her usual perfect posture, staring up at me as she turned off the music. She hadn't shied away from what I'd done. A smile teased her lips, and her eyes swam with admiration. If I was the king, she was definitely my queen.

Filip cleared his throat, returning me to the present. There was a lot of shit that needed to be taken care of, and he seemed anxious to get started.

"My uncle was feeling lonely. There's enough money left in his accounts to buy a plane ticket somewhere. A last-minute getaway for Christmas, or whatever the fuck. He's going somewhere international. After you buy the ticket, pack a bag and his passport." I dug my phone out of my pocket. "Oksana and I will clean him up and get him in the back seat. I'll text you the address of where I want you to drive the car. The guy knows someone's coming and he'll take care of it."

He nodded and headed for the door, but I stopped him.

"Call me when you're done and I'll pick you up. We've got another stop to make tonight. Oksana wants to wish her father a merry Christmas."

"All right." If he was nervous about that, it didn't show. He disappeared through the doorway.

I went to Oksana, pulling her up onto her feet. She put her arms around my shoulders. "How do you feel?"

Not empty.

I felt justice, and it was sweet. "So fucking good."

She smiled knowingly. "Like all your dreams came true?"

"One down," I said. "One to go."

chapter
THIRTY-NINE

Oksana

A NORMAL PERSON WOULD HAVE BEEN HORRIFIED watching Vasilije sink three bullets into his uncle, but I wasn't normal. All I felt was satisfaction, and envy.

Vasilije and I sat in the back, and Filip in the front beside John, and we sped through the snowy night toward the south suburbs.

At the front gate outside my father's house, I rolled down the car window and blinked against the flurries. I gave the security guard a too-bright smile, but he recognized me anyway.

"Merry Christmas," he said, trying to peer through the tinted windows. "Who've you got with you?"

"Vasilije Markovic," I said. "He'd like to speak with Mr. Petrov."

The guard went ashen and disappeared into his glassed-in hut, pulling the phone from his belt. After a brief discussion, we were waved through.

It was the house I'd lived in for the last four years, but it wasn't home.

After the flight from Kazan, my father had ordered another paternity test, and when he couldn't argue the results, Konstantine and Tatiana had welcomed me as their secret sister. My father's wife had been warm, too, but she was a deceitful, calculating bitch. She claimed moral high ground when Sergey tried to get rid of me, and installed me in the house as staff.

Punishing him and me.

Keeping me close meant she could remind me every day what a

fucking saint she was for supporting the bastard of her husband's infidelity. I had clothes, food, a house, and even an education. She was never outright mean to me, but sometimes I wondered if it would have been better if she had been. Her fake smiles turned my stomach, and every biting comment she needled into me was impossible to defend against.

The exterior house lights were on, but the windows were dark. Two figures stood at the front steps, waiting in the falling snow. Fat snowflakes collected on the shoulders of my father's two bodyguards.

John pulled the Lexus to a stop, and I took a breath to fortify myself.

As we got out, my father's men didn't pay attention to me. They watched Vasilije and Filip intently, ready for anything.

"I need a word with Sergey," Vasilije said. "It's urgent." He opened his outer coat and pushed his jacket to the side, showing them his holstered gun. Then he buttoned the coat closed, signaling he didn't intend to use it. "I'm only here to talk."

"Leave your gun," one of the men said, "and you can come inside."

Vasilije gave them a dubious look. "I'm not going in unarmed. He can come out here and freeze his balls off like the rest of us."

Negotiations ensued, and after we'd been searched, we were brought inside. Vasilije and Filip were allowed to carry their guns since security knew where they were, and could watch for them.

The entryway of the house was grand. My first time here, I'd gotten angry as I looked at the inlaid medallion on the hardwood and the space large enough it had a couch in it. As if someone would need to rest the moment they walked in here. The room was nearly as large as my mother's apartment in Russia. The massive staircase curved upward, and beneath it, the arched doorway led into the rest of the house.

Sergey Petrov stood at the top of the stairs, inspecting us like we were fleas. He had on a black and blue striped robe, one hand on the belt and the other in a pocket, no doubt holding a gun inside. Was he wondering about me? Did he think I'd been forced to bring Vasilije here?

"Vasilije Markovic," I said, my vocal cords strung so tight it barely sounded like my voice, "would like to speak to you."

We'd caught him off guard, but he had to see this meeting as advantageous. This wasn't public, so no one would know what happened, and it was in his home, where he was comfortable and could control nearly everything.

"Merry Christmas," Vasilije announced. "Sorry we're showing up late and without calling, but it's important." He used the same friendly tone he'd had at dinner last month, and it set me more on edge. I only had a fingertip's grip on it.

"Let me get dressed." Sergey's distrust was so huge, it flowed down the steps and nearly knocked me backward.

"You don't need to do that," Vasilije said. "This won't take long."

My father was irritated, but controlled. "Fine. I'll come down and we can discuss in my office. I don't want to wake my wife."

Only I was sure she was wide awake and hiding around the corner, just out of sight from where my father stood. She'd have a gun in her hands, ready if my father needed her.

He took his time coming down the stairs, cautious as a cat. His gaze landed on Filip.

"I'll speak to you, Vasilije, or Goran without my security if that goes for both of us. Your uncle's man will have to wait outside." My father knew what Filip was capable of.

"Your men go, too, then I'm fine with it."

Sergey gave a look of disdain. "I'd also feel more comfortable if you're not armed."

Vasilije unholstered. "Same. Also, Filip is my man now. My uncle's dead."

Sergey's movements slowed as he considered the news. He

glanced at Filip, who gave a single nod in confirmation. My father produced the gun from his pocket and set it down on a side table with a quiet thud. The wheels were turning in his head. He believed Vasilije would be easier to control than Goran, but he was dead wrong. My father gave a perfunctory smile. "I'm sorry for your loss."

"Feels more like my gain," Vasilije said flatly. "I'm the one who killed him."

He plodded to the side table, set his gun beside my father's, and told Filip to wait outside with the other security guards.

My father had no response to Vasilije's statement. Instead, he turned and paced toward the office.

I'd only followed the men a few steps when his sharp voice made me flinch. "No. This conversation won't include you."

"Except she's the whole reason I'm here," Vasilije said.

He looked so confident and carefree walking into my father's office, when he should have been studying every inch of space. I'd drawn him diagrams. I'd explained the layout in the best detail I could, but it wouldn't compare to the real thing. I'd told him the couch was only a few feet from the bookcase, but I'd underestimated.

I needed to know Vasilije would succeed if I failed. He promised if anything happened to me, he'd finish what I started, and he told me he'd do it with pleasure.

It still smelled like darkness and death in the office. I'd killed a man in this room, but Ilia was just one of many to die here. It was my father's preferred spot to end business deals. He moved toward the desk, but Vasilije was smart enough to stop him before the gun taped beneath the center drawer was within reach.

"You tried to get a spy into my house, and failed."

"Did I?" Sergey's half-smile chilled me to my center. "She got into your bed fairly quickly."

"I'm not going to complain about that, but I wanted to make sure you got that you failed. Not just with Aleksandar, either. You played this all wrong."

"How's that?"

Vasilije smiled. It was all dimples and teeth, and I wanted to possess the same grin. Did it trigger danger alarms in my father's head?

As Vasilije wandered further into the room, I followed his lead, and let my gaze linger on the books on the bottom shelf where the 9mm was stored. He did better than I did. His focus didn't hover over the hiding spots I'd told him about.

"You sent her to plant a few bugs, when you should have had her kill me. A woman who looks like she does, and doesn't mind getting her hands dirty? Oksana could have been your greatest asset. And loyalty wouldn't have been an issue. I mean, she's your fucking daughter, but then you go and treat her like shit. She probably could have turned me—"

Sergey's hand came up, silencing him. His jaw set. "What makes you think she didn't? You killed Goran, and came straight here, didn't you?"

My eyes widened.

My father's lie was simplistic but perfect and believable. After coming clean to Vasilije, I'd shattered the trust. I believed we'd built it back up, but what we had was fragile. When a broken bone heals and is hit in the same spot, it's likely to fracture the same way. Would this lie do the same damage?

If he fell for it and left me, I was as good as dead. Not just because of what my father would do, either. How would I survive without this man, who'd seen the real me and might love me anyway?

"Nice try, but I know Oksana a hell of a lot better than you do."

"What do you want?" Sergey asked. "An apology for attempting to get surveillance in your home? For turning one of your men?" His condescending tone was like being lectured. "If you think Goran hasn't tried worse with me, you're naïve. That's the price you pay when you're the head of the family business. Which I'm sure you—"

Vasilije shrugged. "An apology would be great, but it needs to be to her."

It was like he'd been slapped. My father's incredulous gaze swung to me. "For what?"

It'd all been building up to this moment, and the blood roared in my body so loud, I couldn't hear my own thoughts. Every cell in me screamed. I'd been silent the whole time in this office.

God, other than my music, I'd been silent practically every second I'd been in America.

And I was fucking done with it.

I spoke in Russian, the language of my mother. *"You can apologize for murdering an innocent family. You can apologize for treating me like I was less than garbage just for being born. And most of all, for how you're a spineless fucking cunt."*

There was no tremor in my hands as I went for the gun. I bent, yanking at the books and flinging them away, and—

The shelf was empty.

No. *No!*

My hands moved on their own, or maybe they were connected directly to a part of my brain functioning on a higher level, existing above the thick fog of my panic. The gun was still here somewhere. My father was too cautious to remove it altogether.

I tore at the books and the decorative clutter, hurling everything on the shelves I touched toward the floor in a thunderous crash. I knocked over a silver bowl, sending the polished stones inside raining down on my feet, where they bounced and clattered on the wood.

There!

The 9mm dumped out the side of the bowl, hidden beneath the stones.

The metal was cold and sure in my grip, and everything felt so incredibly... *right.* I swung around and took aim, and the air buzzed and swirled. Sergey was racing to get around the desk, but he'd never make it in time.

I pulled the trigger with no hesitation.

God knew I'd waited long enough.

The gunshot was as loud as a cannon firing, and the recoil on the gun caught me by surprise, but I struck him in the back. The black and blue fabric of his robe exploded and Sergey grunted in pain, his knees going weak. He stumbled into the side of the desk, his hands splaying on the desktop, but got back on his unsteady feet.

I fired again, hitting him in the shoulder this time. The impact spun him halfway to face me, and as he went down, his expression was comical. He was so surprised, which was stupid. I'd killed Ilia only inches from the spot where he stood. He grabbed blindly at anything to keep him upright, and as he fell, he snagged the corner of the desk calendar and pulled most of the contents of the desktop down with him.

I pulled the trigger again—

It wouldn't budge.

I squeezed, but there was no give and no sound from the weapon. I stared at my extended hand, confused. The safety couldn't be off. I'd just fired twice.

Gunfire erupted outside, and movement dueled for attention. Vasilije closed in on me, and my father was getting up off the ground. There was something in his hand. Something metallic, and sharp.

Where the fuck had he gotten a knife?

Vasilije wrenched the gun from my hand. He slammed his palm against the base of the magazine, and racked the slide in a fluid movement, clearing the jam, and although he was fast, by the time he turned and fired, the knife sliced at his neck.

chapter
FORTY

AFTER THE GUNSHOT, something heavy fell to the floor, but I couldn't see anything beyond Vasilije, or the way he brought his hand up to his neck. Dark red blood slipped between his fingers.

"*Nyet!*" I screamed.

Or maybe it had been in English. I couldn't think in a specific language at that point. I threw my hands up around his, squeezing with all the life in my body.

"Calm down," he said, his tone pained. "I'm all right." Only his face said otherwise, and he was bleeding like a sieve. I risked a quick glance away to see my father had a disgusting red hole in the side of his face. His glassy eyes were fixed on the ceiling.

Vasilije said he was okay, but I didn't believe him, and when I took one hand off his, my palm was wet with blood. He slung an arm around my shoulders, keeping us together as I urged us out of the office, grabbed his gun off the table, and hurried toward the front door.

A booming sound came from above, and wood splinted right behind us. I jerked and yanked on Vasilije, pulling him faster than his sluggish legs could keep up. My stepmother was apparently a terrible shot, but we wouldn't be as lucky with the next one.

I threw open the front door and ran straight into Filip's chest. It took him a nanosecond to survey the situation, and Vasilije was pulled from my arms. We moved as a blur through the snow, shuffling to the already-running Lexus. I nearly tripped over the body of one of my father's men. His blood stained the pristine snow in the front yard.

All three of us were squished in the back seat when the SUV

launched forward.

It was chaos in the back seat as the vehicle careened through the icy streets, speeding toward the front gate and barreling through it.

"Keep pressure on it," Filip ordered, although I wasn't sure which one of us he was talking to. I clamped both of my hands down on top of Vasilije's fingers. "Anyone following?"

"No," John answered. The back end fishtailed on the entrance ramp to the expressway and made me queasy.

Filip got out his phone, and when I heard Amit's name, I knew we weren't going to a hospital. "I don't think it's an artery," he said to whoever he was talking to, "but he's losing a lot of blood."

Every mile in the car, Vasilije turned a lighter shade of gray. His hand beneath mine began to go slack and his eyes dulled. I could tell he wasn't all there, and it scared the shit out of me.

His head lolled toward me and I had to shift my grip on him. "Aren't you happy?" he said slowly. "You did it. Why don't you look happy?"

Because I was worried he was dying, and it was so un—fucking—fair, I wanted to scream. I was a bad person, but I'd only killed other bad people, so wasn't I allowed to have this evil boy just a little longer?

He wasn't coldblooded after all. It poured through my fingers, boiling hot. "I will be a lot happier when you're not ruining the really expensive clothes you bought me." I tried to sound strong, but wasn't successful.

His blood was all over the back seat. At one point, John took a turn so hard I had to put a hand on the ceiling to brace myself, leaving a smeary mess. I expected Vasilije to groan about the resale value, but his eyes fluttered closed, and it sent my heartrate into overdrive.

"Vasilije!" I cried. "Don't you dare leave me!"

The car pulled in, the top barely clearing the garage door as it rolled up, and as soon as we jerked to a stop and John disengaged the locks, Luka was there, yanking the back door open.

"How long has he been unconscious?" Addison asked.

"He's been in and out the last few minutes," I rushed out.

I was pushed out of the way as she took over and the men carried Vasilije inside, moving as a team toward the dining room, and he was set down on the long table.

I scanned for space for the short Indian man I needed to save his life. "Where's Amit?"

"Two minutes out," Filip answered.

Addison climbed onto the table, straddled Vasilije, and pressing both hands on his neck. He groaned in agony. "Fuck, Addison."

"What's your blood type?" she demanded. His eyes blinked and rolled, making her turn her gaze toward his brother. "Luka?"

"I . . . don't know."

My heart lurched. "Doesn't matter. I'm O negative."

Her focus flew to me. "You're sure?"

"Yes." My second paternity test in America, when the pathologist had discovered I was O negative, she'd lectured me non-stop about how lucky I was to be a universal donor, and the gift I could give. I'd sat in the chair, feeling anything but lucky that Sergey Petrov was my father.

Headlights flashed through the front window, and Luka sprinted to the door.

Time decelerated.

I stood blood-soaked at the table beside Filip and Luka, watching as Addison and Amit worked to clamp the bleeding and stitch the wound closed. When Amit announced the bleed was stopped, Addison grabbed his medical bag and set her sights on me.

I sank down on the couch in the living room and pushed up my sleeve. She wasn't yet a doctor, but she moved like this was the hundredth time she'd taken blood from me and not the first. After the prep, she slid the needle easily into my vein and set the line over the side of the couch so it could drip into a collection bag.

As she pulled off the rubber gloves, I grabbed her wrist with my free hand. "I need you to tell me he's going to be okay." She looked down at my fingers wrapped around her. My grip was ferocious. "He's my..."

My partner? My muse? My... other half?

I couldn't explain it, and went with something simple. "He's mine."

There was understanding in her expression as she set her hand on top of mine and squeezed gently. "He's going to be a lot better with your help."

"Thank you." My voice was barely a whisper. I released her, and she left me, returning to assist Amit.

Would she ever know that Vasilije's wound came from the same man who'd taken her family?

I sat alone in the living room and heard music in my head. A sweet adagio piece that could only be described as a love theme. If I got a chance, I'd write it and replace the Scherzo. It was a better representation of how I felt about him.

After Amit pulled the line from my arm, Luka appeared with a glass of water, a bag of pretzels he'd pulled from the pantry, and a wet washcloth. I scrubbed Vasilije's blood from my skin as best I could while I told his brother the highlights of the night. I left the big things for Vasilije. I didn't feel like it was my story to tell.

"He's awake," Addison said, appearing at the edge of the living room. "He's asking for her."

I was woozy as I got to my feet, but didn't know if it was the blood loss, or the evening's effect. Everything had changed.

My father was dead.

Goran Markovic was dead.

And if he survived, Vasilije Markovic would rise to power with me at his side.

He was still on the dining room table, but they'd brought in pillows and blankets, propping him up. He was shirtless, but his color was back. A white bandage was wrapped around his neck. Even in this state, he looked intimidating and like himself.

"You look like hell," he said.

I wanted to smile, but couldn't. "So do you."

His voice was commanding. "Come here."

I moved one foot, then the other, until I was beside the edge of the table. I was close enough I could touch him if I wanted to. His head swung away from me so he could gaze at the ladder on the other side of the table. An IV bag hung off the top with barely any of my blood left in it.

Vasilije gave me a fake scowl. "Luka said that's Russian blood going in me."

The tension in my body broke. It shattered into a billion pieces and I laughed, feeling twenty pounds lighter. He was going to be okay. Back to his regular asshole self.

"I like your laugh," he said abruptly. "Maybe you'll do it more often now."

I shrugged. "Maybe I will."

"And maybe I love you."

My breath caught. "If you had a heart."

"I do. It's fucking pumping Russian blood through me right now."

I leaned over the table, set a hand on his cheek, and whispered it just before I kissed him. "And now we're really the same."

chapter FORTY-ONE

Vasilije

Oksana drummed her fingers on the tabletop, and the muscle along my jaw ticked. She knew I hated that shit, but I stayed quiet for once. She was nervous.

And Konstantine Petrov was fucking late.

Renting out *Il Piacere* for the evening wasn't cheap, and this was the second time I'd done it. I looked at the empty tables around us and tried to keep my anger at simmer, rather than rolling boil. This was going to be his second no-show. We'd killed his father. He was allowed to be pissed about that, but it'd been more than a month since they'd put Sergey in the ground.

The side of my neck itched. The stitches had come out two weeks ago, and the scar was a red, angry line. I didn't mind it, and Oksana said it was sexy. A reminder of what we'd been through. Proof I had part of her inside me.

As I expected, no FBI showed up the next day to take us into custody. Sure, the cops would find my DNA all over the place, but what else might they find? Oksana said the office was her father's favorite room to take people out. They might find stuff to close half a dozen missing person cases. It was too risky for Konstantine to get authorities involved, and it'd make him look weak.

Sergey had a heart attack. That was the story they chose to go with. Did anyone wonder why it was a closed casket funeral, or why his two bodyguards weren't at the service? I smiled to myself at the thought.

Filip glared at the server who lingered. "We're not ready to order yet."

Oksana sighed. "Maybe we should. We've been waiting half an hour."

Thirty-three minutes, actually, but who was counting? "If he doesn't show tonight, we'll keep doing this until he—"

Konstantine appeared in the lobby, flanked by two enormous men. Their necks were thicker than their heads. It was overkill, but whatever. As they approached the table, her brother's gaze locked onto me. Konstantine wasn't his father and didn't have as hard of an edge, but the sudden promotion in his family had sharpened him up. Impressive hate burned in his eyes.

That wasn't fair. Sergey had tried to slash my throat. It was a miracle he hadn't hit an artery, or I would have bled out in the Lexus and been dead minutes after leaving the house.

Konstantine wore a gray suit and smoothed a hand down his black tie as he sat, but his posture cried he'd like to be anywhere else but this table. He looked at Filip, then back to me. His blue eyes wouldn't move toward her.

"Thanks for coming," I said.

"Let's get this over with. What the fuck do you want?"

Oksana took a breath. "To tell you why I did it."

He kept his gaze on me. "You said this was business."

"It is business. My uncle was going to have you killed. He wanted all-out war. But me? I don't want that. Do you?"

Konstantine stared at the folded napkin propped up on the plate in front of him. "You came into my family's home and murdered my father. We're already at war."

"Vasilije didn't kill him," Oksana said. "I did."

It was semantics. Her first shot had been lethal. Sergey had been wheezing as his lung collapsed, and only minutes left to live before I'd delivered my head shot and ended him. Her brother's attention slowly, finally shifted to her, and her already stiff posture somehow straightened under his intensity.

"He was our father."

She raised her chin, defiant. "I know you loved him, but you also know he was a monster, and he had it fucking *coming*."

I put my hand over my mouth to hide the smile. God, she was sexy when she was strong. She went with me everywhere now. My silent, lethal queen.

"Business," I reminded. "My uncle wanted you dead, and Oksana saved you. We don't need a war. There's enough business here to go around."

He looked offended. "You want a truce? You think I'm going to—"

"A partnership." I set my hand on top of Oksana's on the tabletop. "Our families can work together."

He acted like I just pulled a gun on him, and jolted back in his seat. "Are you fucking insane?"

I smirked. "Probably."

"No," he said. "Absolutely no."

I clenched my teeth. "Feel free to take some time to think about it." He was too emotional about this. A smart guy would see the deal I was offering was good.

Konstantine's expression hardened as he stared at his sister. "You betrayed the family. You're not a Petrov anymore."

Her tone was incredulous. "I never was."

"You betrayed *me*, Oksana."

The pain in his voice was mirrored in her eyes, and I couldn't stand it. I owed this guy. He'd stopped Ilia from doing more damage than he already had, and protected the girl I'd eventually fall in love with.

"She saved your life," I announced. "We're not at war, unless you come after her." Then, all bets were off. I'd tear Chicago apart to keep her beside me. "It's your move, Konstantine."

He pushed away from the table, stood, and left without a word, the bodyguards trailing behind him.

She was tense, probably unsure what to say or do.

I picked up the menu and scanned the print. "Let's order. I'm fucking starving."

♪

We sat in the back of the dealership's newly acquired Range Rover, heading home, when I unbuckled my seatbelt and slid over to her. She was wearing the same dress she'd worn when we'd gone to see *Salome*. It was the exact shade of red I could turn her skin with the palm of my bare hand, and such a beautiful color on her.

The conversation with her brother had bothered her, and I wanted to distract her from it. He'd come around. In another life, it was possible Konstantine and I could have been friends.

I gently placed my fingers on her neck, and felt her pulse beneath my fingertips quicken. Her throat bobbed with a swallow. Without words, she understood. I always wanted her, but the need was fierce tonight. I stroked my thumb along the curve of her neck and leaned in, making the tip of my tongue follow my thumb's path.

She shuddered with pleasure, and her tone was teasing. "Can you wait until we get home?"

"Please?" came from up front. John sounded half-serious.

"Everybody just relax," I said, annoyed. "I'll keep my hands to myself." I leaned in again, putting my lips beside her ear. "For now."

A slow smile spread over her lips. "Promise?"

I matched her smile. "You know me."

"I do. Better than anyone else."

Fuck, I loved this girl.

THANK YOU

Always to my husband for everything. You gave (and continue to give) endless support, be it a week away from your job to help with mine, letting me bounce story ideas off you, or holding purses for ten friends while we're at the dick show in Vegas. I love you so very much!

To my beta readers Joscelyn Freeman Fussell, Andrea Lefkowitz, Rebecca Nebel, Jennifer Santa Ana, and Nikki Terrill. Thanks for having the courage to tell me the first draft was slow and unbalanced, and Vashole needed to live up to the name. You give me notes where they encourage and motivate no matter how big they are, and I'm so grateful.

To V. Thanks for the daily conversations I couldn't function without. Sorry for all the rambling messages and the meowing cat in the background. That's just her trying to steal your soul if she could get to you.

To my editor Lori. Thank you for your hard work, for making me look good, and for fitting me in when I ask frantically for a second edit. You're the best!

TO THOSE WHO SUPPORTED SORDID

Whether you were a reader, a fellow author, or someone who purchased the book because you wanted to make a statement, thank you from the bottom of my heart. Thank you to those who reached out, either to offer help or share thoughts about my work. Your messages were a bright spot in a stressful time and much needed. Thank you to those who shared the book's status and spread the word about which retailers it was available on.

An extra thank you to the fabulous Mara White. Thank you for your words, your work, and for allowing the situation to reach a broader audience.

An extra, super-duper THANK YOU to my publicist Heather Roberts. This woman, you guys. She was my voice when I didn't know what to do or how to talk to the folks at You-Know-Where. When things got tough, she held me together and told me, "You got this."

And thank you to all the blogs who spread the word about great reads and new authors. I wouldn't be anywhere without you, believe me. I'm in awe of what you do. (The reviews I write take forever and they're, like, a paragraph.) Thank you so much for everything and being awesome!

IF YOU ENJOYED THE BOOK

Thank you so much for taking the time to read Vasilije's story. If you enjoyed it, would you be so kind as to let other readers know via an Amazon review or on Goodreads? Just a few words can help an author tremendously, and are *always* appreciated!

WANT TO TALK WITH OTHER FANS OF NIKKI'S BOOKS?

Join the private Facebook group! This isn't a street team and you won't be asked to do anything. The group is a fun spot to hangout, discuss books (Nikki's or other hot reads), and share pics of man candy. It's called Nikki's Naughty Nymphs.

ABOUT NIKKI

Nikki Sloane fell into graphic design after her careers as a waitress, a screenwriter, and a ballroom dance instructor fell through. For eight years she worked for a design firm in that extremely tall, black, and tiered building in Chicago that went through an unfortunate name change during her time there. She is a two-time Romance Writers of America RITA© Finalist, married with two sons, writes both romantic suspense and dirty books, and couldn't be any happier.

Find her on the web: www.NikkiSloane.com

Contact her on Twitter: @AuthorNSloane

Send her an email: authornikkisloane@gmail.com

FROM NIKKI SLOANE:

the blindfold club series

IT TAKES TWO (PREQUEL)
THREE SIMPLE RULES
THREE HARD LESSONS
ONE MORE RULE (A NOVELLA)
THREE LITTLE MISTAKES
THREE DIRTY SECRETS
THREE SWEET NOTHINGS

also available

SORDID
A DARK EROTIC ROMANCE

Made in the USA
Monee, IL
09 September 2024